Down by Contact

Jami Davenport

Copyright 2013 Pamela D. Bowerman

Down by Contact

After twelve years in the league, all Zach Murphy wants is a Super Bowl ring. He's been about hard hits not smooth manners, about breaking quarterbacks not making small talk at cocktail parties. But now he's shattered something else. After dumping a tray of drinks on the team owner's snooty daughter and accidentally feeling up the Governor's wife, his tenure with his team looks perilously short. And things are getting worse.

Life is looking up for Kelsie Carrington-Richmond. A onetime beauty pageant star and mean girl, she only recently stopped living out of her car. But both those times have passed. Her Finishing School for Real Men has a real shot, and the Seattle Lumberjacks have hired her to polish up their roughest player. Except…it's Zach. Long ago she broke his heart. He's just the beast she remembers—gruff, protective—but she's nothing like the beauty from his past. Yet, getting knocked down happens, and getting back up makes a contender. And they both have the hearts of champions.

Down by Contact

Jami Davenport

www.BOROUGHSPUBLISHINGGROUP.com

DOWN BY CONTACT
Copyright © 2013 Pamela D. Bowerman

Digital edition created by Maureen Cutajar

www.gopublished.com

ISBN 978-1-941260-10-4

To Boroughs and my wonderful editor Jill for helping me make this the best book it can be.

To Laurie Ryan, Adrianne Lee, and Jane Lynn Daniels who've always had my back and don't mind telling me when something isn't working and needs to be changed.

Also to my readers, who've stuck with me through the past two years, waiting patiently for the next book. It's my wish that I'll never disappoint you. I hope you love Zach and Kelsie's story as much as I loved writing it.

Acknowledgments

A very special thanks to my husband, a former linebacker, for his infinite wisdom on how linebackers think and react. When he read one of my locker room scenes and commented that I nailed it, that was just how guys would talk, it was the ultimate compliment.

Contents

CHAPTER 1

Thrown for a Loss

Twelve years and a couple multimillion dollar football contracts changed a lot of things for a kid who grew up poor, but obviously not enough.

Zach Murphy shifted uneasily from one foot to the other. In less time than it took to hike a football, he'd been catapulted from a man who commanded respect and controlled his own destiny to one of inadequacy and uncertainty.

He hated these fancy banquets where everyone pretended to be something they weren't, and the wealthy paid big sums to hang out with professional athletes all in the name of charity. Zach preferred his charitable work to be more low-key and private. Even worse, he hated how these affairs made him feel like an idiot—a guy lacking all social graces. He tried to fit into a crowd like this once, and it'd been a disaster.

The bottom line was he didn't belong here. He'd already managed to insult some millionaire geek's wife by complimenting her on her healthy appetite. Hell, where he came from, a man admired a woman who appreciated good food.

He sucked in social situations, especially highbrow ones like this. His old team never made him attend anything more than a bowling tournament, but the Lumberjacks insisted their defensive captain go to all this shit.

Zach ran his fingers through his unruly hair and almost wished he'd gotten it cut. Too long and curly to be tamed with hair gel and too short for a ponytail, it kept getting in his eyes. He tugged on his bow tie, rebelling against how constricting it was. He'd been here less than thirty minutes, but it felt like a lifetime. These snooty people stared down their noses at him as if they saw right through to his white-trash roots.

Looking for some friendly faces, he walked up to a couple of his defensive guys and joined their conversation. "Hey, guys, did you see our jackass quarterback anywhere? I thought I'd arm wrestle him for a dance with his hot little girlfriend."

They stared at him sort of funny. He wiped his mouth, wondering if he had crumbs on his face or something.

On cue Tyler Harris, the Seattle Lumberjacks' quarterback and Zach's personal enemy number one, sauntered over with his cute, curvy girlfriend, Lavender, beside him. Zach liked Lavender, she was sweet and sassy all rolled into one. Even better, she could put the asshole quarterback in his place with one damning look. Harris might be an uncontrollable bad boy in most circumstances, but Lavender led him around by a ring in his dick, which amused Zach to no end.

Zach grinned at her, and she hugged him then she straightened his bowtie. Harris snaked his arm possessively around her waist and tucked her close to his side. His glare cut right through the bullshit. He hated the linebacker as much as Zach hated him. The jerk's gaze swept downward as if assessing and cataloging Zach's every social blunder. His gaze fixed on Zach's black cowboy boots.

Harris smirked and raised one eyebrow. "Cowboy boots at a black tie affair?"

"Sounds like the words to a country song," Bruiser, their surfer boy running back, quipped, as if he'd ever listened to a country song in his life.

"Hey, I'm from Texas." Zach shoved his hands in his pockets before he did damage to the quarterback's pretty face. He liked his boots. The broken-in Justins hugged his big feet like a comfortable pair of old slippers. Hell, he'd even polished them to a shine for the occasion. Best of all, the extra two inches made him an inch taller than the Jacks' six-foot-four quarterback.

"Yeah, right. But—" Lavender stomped on Harris's foot before he could launch a new insult at the hated defensive player. She cast a sympathetic look in Zach's direction and dragged her stubborn-assed boyfriend to his seat.

Zach barely tolerated quarterbacks as necessary evils, prima donna jerks every one of them, and he had zero fucking tolerance for Harris.

As a middle linebacker, Zach made his living analyzing quarterbacks, studying their body language, watching their eyes then telegraphing his findings to his defensive teammates. Last year when his old team played the Jacks, he'd looked across the line of scrimmage into Harris's eyes and seen—nothing. Nothing but a big fat zero, almost as if the QB had put his body on autopilot and mentally hung out a "closed" sign.

Zach had lived and breathed football from the day he took his first baby step. Football was an all-in game. Either you were all-in or you'd best get the hell all-out. He couldn't fathom a football player who didn't love the game with every cell in his body and leave every ounce of try he had out on the field. But Harris had. Last year. He'd fucking quit on his team, missed practices, put in minimum effort, and only physically shown up for games.

The team had won their second consecutive Super Bowl in spite of Harris. Not that Zach had been in the locker room or on the field. He'd signed with the Seattle Lumberjacks in the off-season a few months after that second Super Bowl. But guys talked, and he'd been in the league long enough to see all the signs, even if he was observing from across the line of scrimmage or via a flat screen TV.

A Super Bowl?

How could a guy not leave his blood and guts out on the field during the game of all games? Harris's don't-give-a-shit attitude baffled Zach and put the two team captains at odds with each other throughout training camp. Zach had no respect for quitters. If he had his way, the Jacks would start a different quarterback on the first day of regular season.

Zach ground his teeth together until his head hurt just thinking about having one Super Bowl ring, let alone a pair. He'd give both his nuts for a ring. Team loyalty had gotten him nowhere. For twelve years, he'd played his heart out on the worst team in the NFL, given them his best and never complained. The team didn't make it past one wild-card win in the first round of the playoffs. During the off-season, his old team dropped him faster than a rabid coyote. Then the Seattle Lumberjacks came calling, needing a guy to bolster their defense and tutor their young players. He'd jumped at the chance.

This year would be different. He'd taken a hefty pay cut to sign a one-year contract with this team just for a chance to win a ring in what might well be his last year. For a linebacker who played as hard as he did, thirty-four bordered on ancient. Or so his body told him.

Reluctantly, Zach took his seat across from Harris. Thank God, Lavender sat to Zach's right because Zach adored her. She shot him a friendly smile. Knowing it would piss Tyler off, he grinned back. "You're as pretty as a dandelion in a weed patch."

Lavender laughed and patted his arm. "You silver-tongued devil. Thank you. You cut a dashing figure yourself." A few of the guys around the table snickered behind their napkins.

"A dandelion is a *weed*." Hoss Price, their three-hundred-pound center, snorted so hard Zach expected his wine to come out his nose. Harris glared at Zach as if he'd called Lavender fat or something equally offensive.

Zach ducked his head. He liked dandelions. They were the only flowers that had grown in his Grandmother Lo-Lo's front yard. He'd screwed up again. He'd meant his statement to be a real compliment, but everyone took it as humorous.

"I didn't know Wal-Mart sold tuxes. Must be a new line or something." John Myers, a prima-donna wide receiver chortled, and his teammates joined in.

"From you, I'll take that as a compliment." Zach looked down at his black tux. He didn't see a thing wrong with it. He'd bought it at a bargain price at a decent menswear store for his cousin's wedding a few years ago. It seemed perfectly functional to him. Sure it was a little small in places, the pants a little short, and it had a few wrinkles, but he didn't see it as a big deal. Off-the-rack clothes never fit him right. He was used to it. He'd be damned if he'd spend five figures on a custom suit with some dumbass designer's name on the label like Harris did just to impress a bunch of people he cared less about.

"Lapels like that went out of style years ago." John couldn't keep his trap quiet.

Zach clamped his mouth shut. Who gave a shit about out-of-style lapels? Not him. He didn't give a hoot about style.

"Zach, you look great—for a hick." Bruiser grinned at him. He liked Bruiser usually, but not so much right now.

"Hey, he's prepared for the rainy season, too. Those pants legs are above the high-water mark." Hoss choked on his wine, spitting some of it across the table. Too bad he missed Harris's face by a mere inch. Hoss didn't have any better social graces than Zach, but his elegant girlfriend dressed him for these occasions. Zach didn't have a woman to make sure he looked put together.

"Zach looks fine." Lavender pinched Bruiser's arm while Tyler yelped. She must have kicked him under the table just for good measure. Zach needed to find a woman like her.

"Zach, you're a handsome devil. These guys are just jealous." Rachel, wife to all-pro wide receiver Derek Ramsey, shot a shut-up-or-die glance around the table, pausing with John. The cocky jerk just grinned.

Being defended by women stung Zach's pride and booted his ego to the basement, but the ladies meant well. He couldn't fault them for that.

Harris narrowed his gaze, seeming to zero in on Zach's blue shirt. Obviously, the quarterback didn't care much for blue. Zach reached across the table for the basket of bread, but John yanked it out of reach before he could grab it. "What the fuck? You got the manners of a stray dog. Didn't your mama teach you any better?"

Zach cringed. He hadn't a clue what he'd done wrong. Besides, his mama didn't teach him a damn thing. She'd been too busy drowning in a bottle or shooting up.

"Hey, why do you think his old team called him *wolf?*" Hoss hooted louder than a train bearing down on a busy intersection.

"Here I thought it had to do with his prowess on the field." Harris started to laugh then flinched. He'd be sporting some nice bruises on those shins of his.

"Hey, being a wolf is a good thing on the football field. Wolves are fierce." Tomcat rose to his defense. He'd known Cat since college. His real name was Thomas but the defensive end stalked unsuspecting quarterbacks like a tomcat on the prowl, hence the nickname. Tomcat had followed him from their old loser team and taken a pay cut just like Zach for one last chance at a ring.

Zach ignored them all. Hell, they were just having fun hazing the new guy on the team, except for Harris. That guy enjoyed every minute of Zach's torture. Eventually the conversation shifted to Sunday's first regular season game.

Heart sinking, Zach stared at the confusing array of eating utensils, plates, and glasses. Nobody needed this much stuff just to eat dinner. Hell, where he came from, he'd been lucky to eat with a fork. This fancy crap reminded him of how much his lowly upbringing still shaped his present.

As the waiter placed the first of many courses in front of Zach, he glanced around to see which fork to use. Harris eyed him like a man probing for an enemy's weaknesses. Pretending to study his oysters, Zach flicked his lowered gaze to Lavender's plate. He picked up the little fork just as she had. Grasping an oyster in his big hand, he tried to dig it out of the shell. The damn thing popped out and flew across the table. It hit Derek's jacket and slid downward, leaving a slimy trail. Harris broke into laughter with the rest of the table following suit. Zach's ears burned, but he held his head high, refusing to let these vultures pick his embarrassed carcass clean.

"Hey, man, no big deal." Derek, who also had the misfortune of being Harris's cousin, smiled sympathetically at Zach, while Rachel wiped off his lapel.

"Why don't you go back to the trailer park where you belong?" John sputtered, laughing too hard to get a breath. Harris just smirked.

Zach ignored them both and pushed the plate away. He'd be damned if he'd try to eat another, never liked the fucking things anyway.

"Hey, man, that isn't funny." Tomcat jumped in.

"It's all in fun. Murphy knows that." John nodded at Zach.

Zach concentrated on a spot across the room, faking interest in the crappy painting hanging on the wall, the one simply titled, *The Cat*. Hell, the kindergarten class from his hometown of Cactus Prairie, Texas, painted better pictures. At least a cat looked like a cat, not an alien space ship spraying people with spaghetti sauce.

Then he saw *her*.

Zach's day went from calamity to catastrophe. He broke into a sweat. Pain shot through him as if he'd dropped a two-hundred-pound barbell on his chest. He couldn't breathe, couldn't muster a coherent thought in his shocked brain, couldn't drag his eyes off her.

The woman of his dreams and his nightmares.

Kelsie Carrington glided across the room straight toward him. His Cactus Prairie High School crush here? In Seattle? What the fuck? Wasn't halfway across the country far enough to escape her and those painful memories? He blinked several times, but there wasn't a damn thing wrong with his vision. His one-date disaster balanced on a pair of heels so high the altitude should require an oxygen mask. Her blond hair shone as brightly as the gold in a coveted Super Bowl ring. Each graceful step of those long legs carried her closer to him.

He held his breath and prayed she didn't recognize him. Just like old times, Kelsie looked right through him, as if he didn't exist. Her patent beauty-queen smile was plastered across her perfectly made-up face. Damn, seeing her transported him back to being an awkward teenage boy who only fit in on the football field. Her fake smile reminded him how stupid he'd been to fall for her particular brand of poison. Her perfect face dredged up a shitload of painful emotions.

Oh, yeah, painful all right. Zach Murphy had fallen in love once and been carried out of the game on a stretcher. He'd stick with football. Football gave him life, while women sucked the life out of him. Football made sense to him. Women didn't.

Especially this woman.

He glanced to either side to see if any of his teammates noticed the fucking bleeding heart dangling on his sleeve. They were too busy staring at Kelsie—she'd always had that effect on men. Well, except for the king of asshole quarterbacks, Tyler Harris. Zach gave Harris a few grudging points for tossing out his womanizer ways and only having eyes for his sassy girlfriend.

Yet something on Zach's face must have clued Harris in. Like a hungry hyena catching the scent of wounded prey, Harris's sharp gaze moved from Zach to Kelsie and back again. The quarterback possessed this uncanny ability to dissect an enemy's weakness—and despite being teammates, they *were* enemies. One corner of the fuckhead's mouth turned up in a knowing smirk. He nodded briefly at Zach and returned to his conversation with his hot little girlfriend, even though Zach knew damn well the jerk kept one eye on him.

Ignoring Harris, Zach scratched his chin and studied Kelsie. What the hell was the cause of his most humiliating moment in a lifetime of humiliating moments doing here a thousand miles from Texas, invading his territory?

He blinked a few times and looked again. Really looked beyond the beauty-queen face and body. Something was very wrong with this picture. A loaded tray of drinks teetered precariously on the palm of Kelsie's raised hand as she moved in and out of the crowd. Rich girl Kel had never worked a real job in her life. Yet, he doubted she was serving drinks just for the unique opportunity to slum with the common folk.

Damn, maybe his life wasn't the only thing that'd changed.

Kelsie scanned the room then did a double take. Their eyes met and crashed with the intensity of a wrong-way collision on I-5. The fake smile faltered. The gliding stopped. She looked around the room as if planning an escape route. Then she straightened her shoulders and turned on the charm, gracing him with her halogen smile—perfect white teeth and hot red lips. Really hot. As if she were happy to see him.

Bullshit.

Zach scowled his best don't-fuck-with-me scowl.

Kelsie faltered. Her stride went from graceful to jerky. The smile slipped off her face, replaced by what appeared to be panic. She pivoted on her impossibly high heels and fired up the afterburners.

Oh, no, she wasn't getting away this easily. Zach jumped to his feet and gave chase, single-mindedly focused on confronting her, something he'd been dying to do since his senior year of high school. Yeah, stupid idea, but he'd never been one for thinking before reacting, a trait which worked well in football, not so well in real life.

She glanced over her shoulder, her blue eyes filled with what looked like fear, as if she expected him to do physical damage to her or some stupid-assed thing like that.

Zach cornered her near the head table. Kelsie changed directions and charged past him. He spun around to follow, refusing to let her off that easily. He clipped her full tray drinks with his elbow. She lurched with the tray, but it was too late. Helpless, Zach watched the disaster happen in slow motion.

The tray teetered back and forth, as Kelsie desperately fought to gain control. The tray won. Glasses of wine sprayed red, white, and pink across the tablecloth, looking like a tie-dye session gone mad. Goblets shattered. Women screamed as wine drenched expensive evening gowns. The team owner leapt to his feet, his sputtering laced with profanity as red wine coated his custom-tux and white shirt. His spoiled daughter, Veronica, didn't hold anything back either, loudly insulting the size of Zach's brain and his dick. Closest to the debacle, the governor's wife leapt to her feet, her low-cut sequined evening gown hung on her like a limp rag. Red wine and mimosas dribbled down her neck and chest and disappeared in her cleavage. Zach grabbed a napkin and desperately blotted at the wine. In his panic, he swiped the napkin across the plump mounds of her breasts. She screamed as if he'd purposely groped her. HughJack, the team's head coach, grabbed him and pulled him away.

"I'm sorry. Oh, fucking hell. I'm so sorry." Zach wanted to crawl under the nearest boulder.

"What did you think you were doing?" Coach spoke in that deadly calm, quiet voice that struck fear in the meanest of linemen. Zach preferred HughJack's ranting and notorious clipboard throwing to *that* voice.

"I—I don't know. I'm sorry."

Veronica, still sputtering and looking for blood, turned on Kelsie. "You! How could you be so stupid?"

"I—I—" Kelsie shoved her fist in her mouth, obviously horrified at the carnage she'd helped cause. She lifted her gaze to Zach's. Anger blazed in her stormy blue eyes.

Wait one fucking minute. She blamed *him*? He hadn't done one damn thing other than be where he was supposed to be—a charity benefit for a charity whose name he couldn't even remember. She was the one who didn't belong here.

Jerking her gaze away from his, Kelsie dropped to the floor and started wiping up the mess with any napkin she could confiscate from the nearby tables. Several other staff joined in the fray, wiping tables, cleaning up the mess, and comforting wet, angry guests.

Zach debated on whether or not to fade into the background or make her night that much worse. Once again, she'd made him look like a backwards hick, her special talent.

A fat, sweating chef with chocolate stains on his white apron waddled out of the kitchen and spoke in a harsh whisper to Kelsie. "You idiot. Did you do this?"

Kelsie didn't look up, just worked frantically to clean up the mess. The chef bent down and pointed a pudgy finger in her direction. "You're fired. Get the hell out of here. I'll be contacting you for reimbursement for the damages." He kept his voice low, but Zach heard him.

Zach stepped forward, a knight not exactly comfortable in his dinner-jacket armor. "Apologize to the lady. It was an accident, and your behavior is abusive."

The chef gritted his teeth and spoke loud enough for only Zach to hear. "Who the hell are you? Some dumb jock? You probably beat up your girlfriend on a regular basis. And you accuse me of abuse?"

Zach exploded and charged. Just before he made contact, two defensive linemen, big suckers, yanked him backward and pinned his arms behind his back. Zach lunged at the fat chef again, dragging the linemen with him. More teammates jumped into the fray and held him back. Several others restrained the chef, who hurled accusations at Zach and Kelsie.

"Stop it, you dumb shit." Harris smacked Zach on the arm none too gently. Zach grunted and squinted into the harsh light glaring in his eyes. Someone had a camera trained on him.

Harris stepped in front of Zach, blocked the cameraman, and faced the furious cook. "Let's calm down and be civilized. It was an accident." He spoke in an aside to his teammates. "Let them go." The men did as Harris ordered. The cook made a move toward Zach but Harris countered it, placing his body between the two dueling men. He put his hand on Zach's chest and pushed. Zach staggered back a step, reining in his temper.

He'd done it again. Screwed up in a social situation and dragged the whole team down with him. His new team. The ones who were counting on him to be a leader on and off the field. He'd led them, all right, almost into a brawl.

Zach released his breath in a whoosh, deflating not just his lungs but his ego. He'd made an ass of himself, embarrassed the team, and even worse, exposed a weakness to Tyler Harris in the name of one high-school-crush-on-the-mean-girl Kelsie Carrington.

Zach glanced off to the side where Kelsie stood. She'd shoved her knuckles in her mouth again, a sure sign of her discomfort he remembered from their high school days—not that he'd forgotten a thing about her from back them. Cheerleader. Beauty queen. Rich and spoiled. The meanest of the mean girls. Tell that to a teenage Zach. He'd dragged his sorry ass after her without an ounce of pride, begging for any crumb she'd toss his way. She tossed just enough to keep him on her trail.

Zach scrubbed his hands over his face. Dropping his arms to his sides, he turned to Kelsie.

Her confidence of a few seconds ago shattered like the goblets on the floor. She hunched over and hugged herself in a gesture of self-protection and flicked a glance in his direction. Their eyes met for a split second, just enough time to send his stomach into vigorous calisthenics and reduce his already damaged knees to mush.

Without another word, she fled the room, but not before his foolish heart lunged for her and missed, once again.

* * * * *

Blinded by tears, Kelsie dashed for the ballroom doors. While making a run for it, she bumped into another waiter, sentencing a tray of deserts to another appointment with destiny. Banging into the doors, she pushed them open, and sprinted down the hall for the elevator. She braked to a stop and wrenched her ankle in the process. An ominous snap a split second later confirmed the worst. Her last good pair of Manolo Blahniks succumbed to the stress of her fifty-meter dash for freedom. Lurching into the elevator, she stabbed at the lobby button with a now broken fingernail.

The elevator doors slid shut and wrapped her in a temporary cocoon of safety. She yanked off her heels and clutched them tightly, realizing the broken heel lay somewhere between the ballroom and the elevator.

Her day couldn't get worse. Or her life.

Of all people to witness her humiliation, fate chose Zach Murphy. And the Lumberjacks team owner. And his daughter. And the governor. She'd hit rock bottom, and the one man who hated her guts more than her ex-husband was probably drinking a toast to her downfall.

She hadn't seen him in person since high school graduation. Zach the teenager had been intimidating. Zach the man was formidable. He'd put on muscle on top of muscle, grown a few inches, and definitely fine-tuned his intensity to a laser-sharp edge. Shaggy black hair framed his tanned, rugged face. His tight, full lips announced *don't mess with me if living is important to you* without him opening his mouth.

She'd been such a fool. A stupid fool.

Sure, she'd convinced herself the move to Seattle had to do with finding Zach and atoning for the sins of her past. But who was she kidding? It had nothing to do with Zach, and everything to do with her. Even worse, Zach saw right through her to the selfish, desperate woman underneath. Sweet, kind, bumbling Zach, the only man who'd ever been there for her and never asked a thing in return but friendship. The same man she'd ridiculed and humiliated. And she'd expected a warm, even lukewarm, reception?

One look at Zach's face, and Kelsie knew she'd made a grave error in judgment. Zach's angry frown spoke louder than red paint dripping down a white wall. He would not be her rescuer. He'd resigned from that job years ago and rightfully so. He'd been her last hope for a friendly face in a storm of angry or indifferent ones, and even he didn't want a thing to do with her.

The elevator doors opened with a pleasant *ping* totally in contradiction with her evening. Squaring her shoulders and straightening her spine, Kelsie strode out of the elevator. Alcohol soaked her white shirt and black skirt. Her stocking feet stuck to the cold tile floor of the lobby. She padded out the door into a misty Seattle night and stood on the street, chest heaving and heart racing. At least it was a balmy—for Seattle—seventy degrees, pretty decent weather for early September, so she understood.

She reached for her purse. Her heart dropped to her bare toes. She'd left her purse and cell phone at the banquet. Not that she had any money in it. She'd spent her last forty dollars on the banquet server clothes. Her stomach rumbled like the Sounder train, reminding her the day's meal consisted of a couple crackers. She'd hoped to eat at the banquet after the guests were served.

No Zach.

No money.

No job.

No future.

And reduced to living in her car.

She'd sunk low in the past couple months, lower than she'd ever imagined. Yet, staying in her former situation hadn't been an alternative. She'd rather sleep on a park bench and dumpster dive for dinner.

Which was exactly what she would be doing.

The hotel valet eyed her with suspicion. She glanced at her reflection in the window. Her disheveled hair, bare feet, and stained clothes didn't exactly present a good impression.

The man walked up to her. "Time to move along. We don't allow loitering."

With a sniff and a toss of her head, Kelsie sauntered off, refusing to let him see her lose it. She walked around the corner to find a nice, quiet place to fall apart. She slumped on a bus stop bench and buried her face in her hands.

"You left something behind."

Wiping her face with her sleeve, Kelsie glanced up to see her purse dangling from the large fingers of the Jacks' quarterback, Tyler Harris. Tyler was a sleek, graceful deer buck compared to Zach's more rangy elk. Her Coach purse swayed back and forth in front of her eyes. She snatched it from his hand and cradled it against her chest. This purse would bring her enough from a pawnshop to keep her going for a little while. She'd fled to Seattle to escape her ex's influence and left everything behind, hoping to find Zach. The only person in her life who'd ever truly liked her for her. She'd found him, all right, and after one look into those angry eyes, she knew she'd made a huge mistake. Zach was not a much-needed ally, he was an enemy.

"Thank you." She sniffed and hiccupped a very loud, unladylike hiccup.

Tyler's girlfriend, a redheaded pixie, stepped forward, her eyes full of pity and kindness. "Do you need a ride somewhere?"

Kelsie chewed on her lower lip. Her pride screamed, "No." Her practical side kicked pride out of the way and took over. "My car is parked a ways from here." She choked back another sob. She'd stowed everything she owned in her out-of-gas car parked several blocks away in a defunct business's parking lot. With her luck, it'd been towed by now.

"We'll give you a ride." Tyler didn't wait for an answer but started hauling her along with them, shoes and purse clutched in her free hand. She resisted, irritated and fearful at the same time. They were all alike, guys like him and her ex-husband, thinking they could force their will upon her. She hated it, hated the weakness, swore she'd never be under the influence of a man like that again. She might be broke, hungry, and homeless, but she was independent.

Kelsie folded her long limbs into the miniscule backseat of Tyler's expensive sports car. His girlfriend turned in her seat. "I'm Lavender. You are?"

"I'm Kelsie. I'm new to town."

Tyler glanced at her in the rearview mirror, his expression calculating. "I get the impression you and Murphy have a history."

Kelsie proceeded with caution, unwilling to divulge too much. "Yes, we knew each other in high school."

"Small world, isn't it?" Lavender spoke with sympathy, as she shot her boyfriend a shut-your-mouth glare.

"Too small." Kelsie pointed out her little Chevy Equinox, the lone car in the lot.

Tyler pulled up beside it. She lunged for the door, hoping he'd just drive off. He didn't. He got out and waited at the side of her car. He studied the inside, most likely taking in the boxes and suitcases filling it to bulging and the blanket and pillow, sure indications she slept in the car. Her little dog, Scranton, bounced up and down on the seat and yapped.

"I just moved here from Texas." Kelsie jumped to explain before he asked more questions.

"I see." Tyler nodded slowly and stepped out of her way. His expression indicated he really did see, which wasn't good at all.

"Where are you going now?" Lavender asked.

Nowhere, except to a pawnshop come morning to get rid of the purse. She didn't have more than a few dollars in change to her name. "I was hoping to promote my business tonight. Thought maybe Zach might have a few contacts for me." Squaring her shoulders, she pulled a soggy business card out of her apron pocket and handed it to Tyler.

He took the sticky card with reluctance and read it out loud, *"Finishing School for Real Men, Specializing in Professional Athletes and CEOs, Kelsie Anne Richmond."* Tyler looked up, a slow smile crossing his face. "No kidding? You're Emily Post for Jocks?"

Knowing she may never get another chance like this and eager to promote her fledgling business, Kelsie launched into the spiel she'd practiced before serving at the black-tie party. "Yes, I offer a charm school of sorts for athletes, many of whom came from unfortunate backgrounds and never had exposure to manners and proper social behavior."

Lavender looked pointedly at Tyler. "Several of your teammates who could use that."

"No joke." Tyler studied the card, as if mulling something over in his mind.

"Ty, can't you help her?" Lavender gave Tyler one of those secret looks full of promises that women used on men they loved, and it seemed to work on him.

Tyler scribbled on the back of the card and handed it back to Kelsie. "Drop by headquarters and ask to speak to this woman. She handles player personnel issues. They just made the final cuts down to the regular roster so wait until later in the week, Thursday or Friday. Tell her I recommended you. I'd bet my last touchdown, she'll set you up with a few clients."

"Oh, thank you. Thank you very much." She might be begging, but tough times called for tough measures.

With a non-committal shrug, Tyler turned back to his car.

"Bye, Kelsie, it was nice to meet you. I'll make sure Tyler paves the way with personnel first thing Monday morning." Lavender tucked something in her hand and hurried after Tyler, who was impatiently tapping his foot as he held the passenger door open. As soon as she got in, he slammed her door and jumped in on his side. With a mighty roar of its engine, the car fishtailed around a corner on squealing tires.

Kelsie opened and stared at the hundred-dollar-bill crumpled on her palm, charity from a virtual stranger. She'd never taken charity before, but survival beat out pride. Visions of a warm meal and warmer bed filled her with relief.

For the first time since Kelsie had fled from her controlling ex-husband, a ray of hope warmed her, even though it was tempered by a niggling of dread. She'd call on the Lumberjacks and sell herself and her business. Her most obvious client might be a certain linebacker with the finesse of a stampeding elephant.

How would Zach feel about that?

CHAPTER 2

False Start

Pads smacked against pads, punctuated by grunts and colorful swearing, all music to Zach's ears. He breathed in the unique smells of sweat, liniment, and fresh-cut grass. After laying Harris out on the ground in the afternoon scrimmage, Zach jogged to the sidelines for a breather and downed a couple glasses of water. Resting his hands on his hips, his chest heaved, his muscles burned, and sweat beaded on his brow. All good.

No pain, no gain, and all that crap.

Zach watched his guys take on the first-string offense making Bruiser fight for every miserly inch he got. Tyler Harris, the asshole, stood back in his protected little pocket and watched the results of his handoff. Arrogant and entitled, he represented everything Zach resented in quarterbacks. Harris traveled in circles Zach avoided, blending easily into any situation. Sure, Harris reveled in being an asshole, but he was an asshole by choice. Zach sometimes got branded with that label not by choice, but because he didn't get how to react in social situations.

Fuck, but Zach hated the quarterback like he'd never hated anyone in his life. Harris had disrespected the game last year by resting on his laurels and not giving one-hundred-percent. His teammates picked up the slack and won another championship, no thanks to him.

Sure, they'd won the season opener this year, and Harris looked decent, but Zach needed hell of a lot more proof than one lousy game. As defensive team captain, he spent every waking hour living and breathing football. He expected the same dedication from the team's offensive leader. So far, they left the training facility about the same time every night and were the first to arrive in the morning, but it'd take more than working overtime for Zach to believe in Harris's renewed commitment. Not that the QB gave a shit what Zach believed.

Only on the football field did Zach belong, doing the thing he'd been born to do with guys who thought like he did. Everywhere else he felt out of place and awkward. His thoughts took a side street down memory lane to one such moment. Zach grimaced and stared at the grass. Odd, the most painful memory of his life was a high school dinner date rather than losing a big game or missing a crucial tackle. He still recalled the flash of pity on Kelsie's face as her attorney father raked him over the coals and her snooty mother puckered her lips in disgust at his table manners. He'd been an idiot to think he could fit in with the country club set. His first date with Kelsie quickly became his last. She'd invited him to the country club ball, not because she liked him, but to make her boyfriend jealous and so the rich kids could make fun of him and his backward ways and shabby clothes. She'd betrayed him and thrown him to the wolves—her friends and family. Then she sat back and watched them degrade him, never once coming to his defense, even when the cops cuffed him and hauled him off to jail.

Zach crushed the paper cup into a wad and slammed it into the garbage can.

What was she doing in Seattle of all places? The last he'd heard, she'd married Mark Richmond. Her high school sweetheart and a former high school quarterback who was now a Houston attorney with political aspirations. Kelsie should be living a life of luxury in some glitzy suburb, not serving dinner at a Seattle banquet.

"Daydreaming?" Tyler Harris strutted by and snapped his fingers in Zach's face.

"Fuck you." Zach gave Harris the middle finger.

The jerk laughed. "Hit a sore spot, huh? What woman has you all tied up in knots? And here I thought your brain circuits linked only to pigskin. Maybe it's the gorgeous waitress from the other night?"

"You're full of shit."

"Yeah, really? Looked to me like you had the hots for her. Never seen you drool over a woman like you did over her. Well, guess what, buddy? You owe me one."

"I don't owe you a damn thing. Stay out of my business."

Tyler laughed, the kind of menacing laugh designed to put Zach on high alert. The jerk thought he had one up on Zach and damned if Zach knew what it might be.

"Lazy asses! Quit trading recipes and get your sorry butts out on the field." HughJack glared at them with his trademark take-no-prisoners glare and slammed his clipboard to the ground. Standing not far from HughJack, Veronica shook her head, disapproval etched a deep frown on her beautiful face. Not good.

Zach strapped on his helmet, and sprinted onto the field. One play later, he knocked Harris on his ass.

* * * * *

With a heavy sigh, Kelsie stood on the sidewalk in the September sun and watched the cars drive by on the busy Seattle street. She'd been rejected again, one more rejection out of a thousand job rejections.

She'd hoarded what cash she had left, using it sparingly by sleeping in her car the past several nights, eating fast food, and taking showers at the Y. During the day, she hung out in the library and searched the Internet for any job for which she might be qualified—which wasn't much given her lack of experience.

All the while, she watched her back, never knowing if and when her ex-husband might appear. As if he cared enough to track her to the Pacific coast. After all, she was nobody to him. He'd harassed her while she lived in Houston, but once she'd left, surely he'd forgotten all about her. Except Mark Richmond never forgot, especially considering his political ambitions. He kept his enemies for a lifetime and obsessed over them like a bad drug. She feared she hadn't heard the last of him.

He couldn't believe she'd dared to divorce him, but she'd done just that, selling her Mercedes to pay for the best attorney possible. He fought her every step of the way. Not that he wanted her, but he saw divorce as a failure. He didn't do well with failure. So he cut off her credit cards, spread false stories to families and friends, and ruined her reputation. The court had decreed a small divorce settlement, but it'd come in the form of monthly payments, which meant he'd need her address or bank account information. She'd walked away knowing she'd never see the money, a small price to pay for freedom and peace of mind.

Not that she had peace of mind, even out from under Mark's tyranny. Men watched her hungrily as she stood in line at the soup kitchen, and a small gang of teenage boys taunted her whenever she walked by. Last night they'd followed her, and she'd run to the safety of her car and sped away. She'd spent a restless night in her car clutching her little poodle, Scranton, and praying they didn't find her. This morning she'd been ten minutes late for her interview.

With a tired sigh, Kelsie ducked into a small coffee shop and ordered a small cup of drip coffee, even as her taste buds craved a double mocha with whip. She counted out her change. Unable to afford a tip, she smiled apologetically at the barista. Setting up her computer, she connected to the wireless. Dozens of emails from Mark filled up the screen, each one angrier than the previous one. Mixed in were messages from her mother, father, and brother, all chastising her for leaving Mark for another man and breaking his heart.

If they only knew. She didn't have another man. The last thing she wanted was another man in her life, attempting to control her every move and emotionally breaking her down until she became a shell of her former confident self. Mark had almost destroyed her, turned her into a walking/talking Barbie doll with no mind of her own. In some ways she figured it was her penance for being such a selfish bitch in her teenage years.

She stared out the window as the never-ending rain pelted the glass. Across the street, a tall man huddled under an awning. He wore a dark trench coat and a fedora. The sunglasses on his face drew her attention. No one wore sunglasses on a gloomy day like today. She squinted and pressed her face closer to the window. The man removed the glasses and locked gazes with her. Her heart rate sped up, and the hairs rose on the back of her neck. A smug smile crossing his nondescript face sent her reeling away from the window.

She'd seen the man before.

This morning when she left the Y, he'd been there.

And last night, he'd sat at a table near her in Burger King as she ate dinner.

And now here he was across the street.

Kelsie swiped a hand across her forehead. She hugged herself, suddenly cold even though she was sweating like a jumper on the Brooklyn Bridge.

Had Mark tracked her down, found her haven? But how? She'd run halfway across the country, avoided using anything that would have her name attached to it, gotten a different car, and been virtually homeless.

Unless—

Zach.

It had to be Zach. He'd called someone back home and told them, and the news got back to Mark.

She'd have a word with the Neanderthal. No more cowering and hiding. She'd confront him for what he'd done.

She didn't want to run anymore.

* * * * *

Weary and nursing the mother of all headaches, Zach trudged out of the training facility. Sometimes, well, most times, he didn't think the facility was large enough for both him and Harris. Especially tonight when Harris stayed to watch game film and hogged the remote, refusing to replay or slow-mo when Zach asked. Damn, when the season ended, he'd beat the living crap out of the asshole, teammate or not.

Zach stopped dead in his tracks when someone stepped out of the shadows and blocked his path. As soon as the dark figure moved into the dim light of the street lamp, he recognized the tall, slender body. "Kelsie?" He glanced around, wondering if she waited for someone other than him.

She stalked up to him, fists shoved against her thighs. Her entire body radiated anger. "Did you tell him?"

He blinked several times and tried to make sense of her words. "Tell who?"

"You did, didn't you?"

"Who's him? Tell them what?"

"That you saw me."

"I never told anyone anything."

"You did. You called someone back home and told them."

"I don't have contact with anyone in Texas. Haven't for years." He tiptoed lightly around this female landmine. If the explosion didn't kill him, the shrapnel from her anger sure as hell would.

"Are you sure?" She deflated a little. Her shoulders slumped, and her chin lowered. Her eyes dimmed a little.

"Positive. I might be a lot of things, but I'm not a liar. You should know that."

The remainder of her anger fizzled like the remnants of a sparkler. "But if you didn't tell him then who's following me?"

"Someone's following you?" Despite his vow to remain distant, his stomach knotted at the thought she might possibly be in danger.

Kelsie swallowed and wrung her hands, looking everywhere but at his face. She stared at his midsection so long he clasped his hands to his thighs to stop from fidgeting.

"Kel, is something wrong?"

She raised her head. "Don't they pay you enough money to buy decent clothes?"

He bristled and looked down at his wrinkled pair of sweats and worn cross-trainers. "They're comfortable."

"You're a professional athlete. Get it. *Professional.* You should dress like one, not like a homeless person who's been sleeping under a bridge."

"How I dress is none of your damn business." How the hell did this become about him?

"Thank God for huge favors. I could use a few right now."

"Well, then, I'll do you another favor. I'm outta here."

She grabbed his arm and hung on. "Zach." She searched his eyes. "Did you call someone back home and tell them you saw me? Like my ex-husband?" For a moment, panic crossed her face, and the sheer terror in her eyes stopped him in his tracks.

"That prick? Are you kidding? I didn't tell anyone from *home* anything about you. I try my best to forget about that place." He'd done enough in his life to apologize for without being bitched at for something he didn't do. Then it hit him. "Your ex-husband?"

"Yes. My *ex*-husband." She lifted her chin, her eyes bright with defiance and stood straight and tall, like the Kelsie he remembered.

"I can't blame the guy. You had to be a bitch to live with."

"Whatever." She blasted him with her I'm-better-than-you-and-you-know-it glower. She hadn't changed a bit. Then her lower lip trembled, like a woman about to—

Cry? Oh, crap, not again. He'd fall right into whatever current web her black-widow heart weaved, trapping him like a wayward fly. "You're mistaken about me."

"Am I?" Despite her brave words, her voice quivered slightly.

"Hell, yes. You're mistaken to think you mean enough to me that I even gave you a second thought after a few nights ago."

"Oh." She deflated like a tire with a nail in it.

That pissed him off because he felt guilty for hurting her, like he should give a dang. "I didn't tell a fucking soul."

"You didn't?" Her face paled, visible even in the dim light.

"No, I didn't." He lowered his voice and ran his fingers through his unruly hair, pushing it out of his eyes. "I'd tell you if I did."

"I assumed—"

"You assumed too much. You're still impressed with your own importance, aren't you? Why don't you quit playing your games and go back to your sheltered life?"

Much to his shock, strong-willed Kelsie's face crumpled. Tears flowed down her cheeks like beer from a freshly tapped keg. She pressed her hands against her eyes and sobbed. Her shoulders shook. She hiccupped several times, gulping in huge gasps of air as she sobbed like a toddler who'd just taken a header off her high chair.

Zach's feet took root in the pavement and refused to move. His tongue back-flipped to the roof of his mouth and stuck there, rendering him incapable of speech. His heart reached out to her, even as he fought to shove it back into place. Damn it almighty, he felt sorry for her. She'd manipulated him again, despite all the cruel things she'd done to him over the years. One word from her, and he'd lay his emotions down in front of her and gladly offer himself as her personal doormat.

Only she didn't say the words. She grabbed her car keys and sprinted to her compact car as if the very devil dogged her heels, a compact car that appeared to be piled high with boxes.

Shell-shocked and speechless, Zach stood in the middle of the parking lot and watched her back out of her parking spot. Kelsie, the consummate mean girl in high school, never cried. This vulnerable version of Kelsie threw him off balance, despite her bluster and anger, he sensed a current of fear ran deep in her. Sucker that he was, he felt sorry for her. And something else. Something dormant but never dead. The poor boy still wanted the beautiful, unattainable girl, his private fantasy and his public hell.

Movement in the nearby trees caught his attention. A man in a trench coat pushed branches aside and emerged from his hiding spot. He hurried across the street toward a nondescript sedan.

Oh, crap, Zach did so not want to get involved in whatever the hell was going on, but he didn't have a good feeling about it. Not one bit. Most likely she'd run off from her husband in some kind of snit and the poor guy was looking for her. Regardless, his crappy compulsion to protect her wouldn't let him dismiss she might be in trouble. Even though he hated her guts.

Zach sprinted after the guy and tackled the stranger just as he reached for the car door. All two-hundred-fifty-plus pounds of

Zach landed on the stranger's back and shoved the air out of the asshole's lungs. The guy gasped for breath, but Zach didn't wait for him to recover. Holding the man's hands behind his back, he hauled the dickwad to his feet and shoved him against the front of his car. With one hand anchored on the man's neck, he pushed his face into the cold metal of the car's hood.

"What the fuck were you doing?"

The guy gasped, taking in big gulps of oxygen. "Nothing. Just trying to get an interview with a player or two."

For a minute, Zach's heart dropped to his knees. He hadn't been stupid enough to tackle a member of the press, had he? But common sense caught up reminding him of what he'd seen. "You weren't waiting for a player. You were following that woman. Why?"

"Look, just let me go. I can explain."

"Don't try leaving until I hear your explanation, and it better be a good one." Reluctantly, Zach released the guy, who skittered away from him. "Why were you following her?"

"I thought she was your girlfriend. I'm doing a piece on NFL girlfriends for a major women's magazine. You keep your love life secret. I saw an opportunity." The guy wrung his hands and stared longingly at the driver side door blocked by Zach's body.

Zach relaxed slightly. What the guy said made sense, even though something still seemed off. "She's not my girlfriend."

"Oh, my mistake. It looked like the two of you were familiar, looked like you were having an argument. The best time to get the dirt on a player is from a pissed-off girlfriend."

Zach couldn't argue that logic. "If I see you around here again, you'll be eating your balls for dinner. Understand?"

The guy nodded and slipped into his car. Zach waited until he drove off, relieved to see he turned in the opposite direction that Kelsie had turned. Rubbing his hand across his face, he got into his own car and slumped in the front seat. Adrenaline spent, he stared straight ahead, not seeing a thing.

Even though the *reporter's* story made perfect sense, doubt picked at him like a kid nagging his mother for a new toy. Something wasn't right. Someone wasn't giving him the straight story. Every instinct screaming through him pointed at Kelsie being in some sort of trouble, but Kelsie's trouble wasn't his, and he'd be smart to stay away. Far away.

Zach rammed his fists into the steering wheel, fearing he might just make it his business to find out.

And knowing he'd be the biggest loser of all if he did.

CHAPTER 3

Taking a Time Out

Veronica Simms, the team owner's daughter and assistant director of player personnel, stared at the nitwit standing in her office doorway. "A trench coat and a fedora? Are you serious?"

"Uh, what's wrong with how I'm dressed?"

"You look like a freaking idiot. Just dress like a normal person. *Anyone* who saw you lurking around would be suspicious." She sighed, wishing she'd never called the first investigative agency in the phonebook and done more research.

"You won't think I'm an idiot once you hear what I found out." He pulled a manila folder from his coat with a flourish and laid it on her desk. "You asked me to research that woman's connection to Zach Murphy."

Veronica shuffled through the papers, greedy for any details she could use against the linebacker. A slow smile spread across her face. "They were high school classmates? She's been married to a prominent Texas attorney for ten years, and now she comes looking for Murphy?"

"That's right. There's a story there."

Veronica couldn't agree more. She sat back in her chair and digested the information. Kelsie Carrington-Richmond, former beauty queen, glamour wife, and now Ms. Manners, might be the key to getting Zach off the team once and for all.

Since Veronica had been a little girl, she'd been wrapped up in the team, banning any item from her room that wasn't navy and gold. She fought like a tigress to convince her father to let her work for the Lumberjacks and climbed up the ranks, starting as a part-time receptionist during her college years.

Nothing mattered to Veronica but the team. Nothing. Zach Murphy was a has-been, a mistake. His public dislike of Tyler Harris would fester like an infected sore until it raged out of control and took the entire team down with it. Except her father and HughJack wouldn't listen to her. She'd make them listen and find a way to get rid of Murphy in the process.

Perhaps she'd just been given the ammunition to do that.

"Keep an eye on them." She waved the PI out the door and fingered the business card Tyler Harris left earlier in her office. With a sly smile, she picked up her phone and dialed.

* * * *

Sometimes when life beats you down to nothing, something good happens and hope springs back like a lone flower after a desert rain, at least Kelsie wanted to believe life worked like that.

Summoned to Jacks' headquarters by Veronica Simms, Kelsie pulled into the parking lot a few minutes before seven p.m. Apparently, the woman worked some long hours. Several cars still occupied the far end of the lot near what she suspected was the player entrance. She wondered if Zach's vehicle might be among them.

As she got out of her car, a sedan parked alone on the side street caught her eye. Surely, she was imagining things, but she swore the dark sedan was the same one she'd seen the last couple days. A chill ran down her spine. She resisted the urge to run, tear out of there and never look back, but she couldn't. Opportunity knocked, the needle on her gas gauge flirted shamelessly with empty, and she'd run out of options.

Kelsie might be a lot of things, but she was a fighter despite years of emotional abuse at the hands of her ex and her parents.

They'd rammed home her weaknesses, torn her down, and forced her to become a walking–talking robot programmed to behave perfectly in any social situation.

Over a year ago, she'd walked into her posh home in a trendy neighborhood. Strange noises lured her into the master bedroom. Mark, his mistress, and another couple writhed together on the large king bed, a tangle of arms and legs. When Mark looked up and spotted her, his total disregard drove the final stake in her marriage and her self-esteem. She ran from the house, leaving everything behind except her miniature poodle Scranton. Her parents demanded that she return and behave like the dutiful wife they'd raised her to be. They'd believed Mark's lies about her.

Since then she'd hit rock bottom more than once, but through it all she clung to her dignity and tattered pride, the only thing they hadn't stripped from her, and the only thing she hadn't stripped from Zach all those years ago. Yeah, karma was a bitch.

In high school, rich, spoiled Kelsie had been a mean girl. So strong was her need to belong to the popular girl crowd, she did everything uber-popular Marcela Winsley dared her to do, too afraid to stand up to her and jeopardize her standing with the in-crowd. When Marcela dared her to invite Zach to the country club ball, she'd done it.

Her friends teased Zach about his outdated, poorly fitted suit, scuffed shoes, and clumsy attempts to fit in with their class of people, and Kelsie joined in. At first, he'd taken their abuse with barely a reaction except for a twitch in his jaw and the hurt in his eyes, a hurt which haunted her even sixteen years later. She'd almost broken him that night with her cruelty and betrayal, and she'd never forgiven herself.

She owed him an apology. A big one. She doubted what she was about to do would earn her any points with him, but it might just be for his own good.

With one last glance in the direction of the mysterious sedan, Kelsie walked purposefully across the rain-soaked parking lot to the main double doors. Security let her in and escorted her to a small cramped office upstairs, not quite the space she'd expected for the owner's daughter.

Veronica waved her in, all business, and dressed in a severe black suit with her hair pulled back tightly in a bun. "Have a seat."

Kelsie sat, clutching a folder that outlined her program. "I'm so grateful to have this opportunity." She bit the side of her cheek to staunch the desperation seeping into her voice.

"Cut the crap. We both know why you're here. Two words. Zach Murphy." Veronica leaned back in her chair, arms crossed over her chest and studied Kelsie with a look that dissected her every weakness.

Kelsie gripped the folder tighter and breathed in and out through her nose. *In. Out. In. Out.* She'd known this was coming. Under any other circumstances, she'd refuse the job. Only she couldn't. Truth be told, she'd always harbored a bit of a crush on the rough yet kind boy who'd followed her like a faithful hound all through high school. Not only did she need the money, but she needed to help Zach whether he appreciated it or not.

"Yes, Zach, I'm familiar with him. We attended high school together."

Veronica didn't look the least bit impressed. Kelsie didn't like the woman one bit, yet she recognized the sad truth. Kelsie had been this woman once. Selfish and driven. Wealthy and spoiled. Inconsiderate and cruel. She so did not want to be like her now.

"I believe he could benefit from my Finishing School for Real Men." Kelsie sat up straighter and hid her insecurities behind her beauty-queen smile.

Veronica snorted. "This coming from the woman who dumped a tray of drinks on the state's first lady and me."

"Ms. Simms, that was an accident. I'm gravely sorry." Panic slithered through her. She took another deep breath and called upon all those skills learned through years of beauty pageant interviews. She hadn't been crowned Miss South Texas for nothing.

"Call me Veronica. I'm sure you are sorry. It was obviously that nitwit's fault." Veronica's lip curled in disgust. She really had an issue with Zach.

Kelsie bit back a retort, almost rising to Zach's defense. Only she didn't, and here she'd thought she'd come a long way toward being a better person. God forgive her. She'd make it up to Zach later along with her other transgressions. Veronica would kick her out of this office on her butt if she showed any sympathy toward the team's socially inept linebacker.

Willing her hands not to shake, Kelsie pulled some papers from the folder. "Here's my résumé. As you can see, I'm quite well-versed in etiquette."

"You were runner-up to Miss Texas?"

"Yes. I've been on the beauty pageant circuit since I was a child. I'm an experienced public speaker along with—"

"Why were you working as a banquet server?" Veronica's violet eyes narrowed to glittering slits.

Kelsie cleared her throat and decided the truth was best. "I've just come to town after a divorce, and I'm still trying to establish myself."

Veronica leafed through the remaining papers and tapped a long fingernail on her desk. "It's no secret I want Zach off the team. He's not a good fit for the Lumberjacks. Unfortunately, those decisions aren't made by me so I have to work with what I'm given."

"I'm positive I can help Zach with his social skills." She'd help Zach and help her business out, a perfect way to make amends. Now if only he'd see that angle.

"One thousand now and two thousand more when the task is completed to my satisfaction. If it's not, the up-front money is to be refunded to the Lumberjacks' organization."

"Certainly." Kelsie nodded vigorously, as her stomach growled at the thought of a decent meal. "What exactly is the task?"

She held her breath and waited. Veronica wasted no time telling her.

A few hours later, Kelsie drove to a small community park on Lake Washington within walking distance of Lumberjacks headquarters, and parked in the lot under a streetlight. Tomorrow she'd cash her check, find a cheap room to rent, and eat a big meal.

After a dinner of crackers—her last box—and water from the tap in the women's bathroom, she took one last look around the area. No sedan in sight. Rolling towels up in the side windows, she placed a sun shield on the dash for privacy, as much as you can get in a public parking lot. A few minutes later, she fell into a disturbing sleep filled with shadowy figures and visions of a shaggy-haired football player with sad brown eyes.

* * * *

With more than a little reluctance, Zach walked into Coach Hubert Jackson's office, aka HughJack. HughJack sat behind his desk looking grumpy and out of sorts. The defensive coordinator, a big, burly guy known as Rocky, sat in one of the chairs in front of the head coach's huge desk.

The short but formidable HughJack was one of the few men that struck fear in Zach's heart. But then the guy possessed the power of life and death over Zach's career. Younger guys vied for his spot as starting middle linebacker, and Zach hung on by a shoelace. They breathed down his neck every time he stepped on the field, gobbling up his every word of advice and using it to their advantage to one day win his job.

One more season. Just one more season to earn that elusive ring. That's all Zach needed. He'd do whatever it took, even dealing with the team's asshole quarterback. Well, almost anything. Playing nice with the quarterback might be taking it too far, yet he knew he had to figure out a way to get beyond his animosity toward Harris.

"Coach, you wanted to talk to me?"

"Yeah, sit down." HughJack motioned to the empty chair across from his desk and next to Rocky.

Zach sat down, certain whatever they wanted couldn't be good, and just as certain Harris was behind it. He clenched his hands on his thighs and took a deep breath.

"So Zach, that little performance at the charity ball last week couldn't come at a worse time. We're heading into our second regular season game, and every team in the NFL is gunning for us. We don't need this kind of distraction."

"It's not a distraction. It's long past."

"Maybe for you, but the front office doesn't see it that way." HughJack stood and paced the floor. The guy was a frigging perpetual motion machine, never sat down for more than a few seconds.

"Uh, Zach, you groped the governor's wife." One corner of Rocky's mouth twitched, as if he found it amusing. Zach didn't find humiliation the least bit amusing.

"Veronica wants your hide and Mr. Simms is livid. I convinced him you were salvageable. Veronica's not so convinced, and you know she wields almost as much power as her father does."

Boy, did he know that. Zach kept his distance from the ball-busting witch. "It was an accident."

"Yeah, just like it was an accident that you toweled off the first lady's boobs? And just like when you told the host of the local sports radio show that he was as annoying as a tick and just as smart? And how about last week when you belched on a national TV interview? Hell, you've only been here a few months, and you've already gained a reputation as a backwards redneck with the manners of a gorilla."

"I'm sorry." Zach stared at his hands. He didn't get the social rules and crap like that. He tried, but he just kept screwing up.

"Things have to change, and like it or not we have a solution."

Zach looked up. His throat dried up like grass during a Texas summer. He held his breath, waiting for the barbell to drop and his career with the Lumberjacks to be crushed beneath the weight of his social ineptness.

"You're going to charm school."

"I'm what?"

"Charm school. You're going to learn social graces if it kills you." HughJack grinned, and Rocky snorted, as if this was fucking funny.

"Like hell I am." Zach sat up straight and squared his shoulders.

"You have two choices. Charm school or be traded."

"Then trade me." Zach wouldn't play these stupid-assed games just to make the rich owner and his bitchy daughter happy. It was bullshit. They signed him to play football, not waste his time on some pansy-assed thing like this.

"You might want to reconsider when you find out what team is interested."

"What team?" Dread filled Zach right down to his size-fourteen feet.

"The Marauders." HughJack paused in his pacing and waited.

"No. You've got to be kidding?" The very name Marauders struck fear in any player's heart, especially one possibly playing in his last season.

"There's not a big market for linebackers of your age and salary, Zach." Rocky shot him a sympathetic look, and Zach knew he was hosed. Even Rocky was throwing him under the bus.

"How long is this class?"

"You'll attend private sessions in the small conference room at the training facility twice a week, starting tonight at seven sharp. We'll work around your schedule as far as games. By the way, for your graduation test, you'll host a black-tie affair at your home, a charity gala during our bye week in December. This homeless charity is Veronica's baby so learn your lessons well."

With that last kick to his ass, the men stood, excusing him.

Zach headed for the door, not happy at all. "Fine."

"Don't be late. It's bad manners." HughJack winked at him, and Zach fought to control his middle finger. Gritting his teeth, he walked out of the office and down the hall.

Harris lounged against the wall a few doors down, a shit-eating grin on his face. Zach itched to wipe the floor with the bastard. Instead, he pushed past him and out the front door. Harris's laughter followed him.

Frustrated, Zach slammed his fist into a tree trunk. The impact jarred his arm and hurt like hell. He stared at his skinned and bloody knuckles, not giving a damn.

Like hell did he need to attend charm school. There wasn't a thing wrong with his manners except he didn't have any. He was a football player, damn it, and a helluva good one. A defensive guy known for his toughness and try, not for his use of the right fork. No fucking way would he let some snooty-assed pansy lecture him on the finer points of all that bullshit social crap.

Except—

The Marauders. League doormats. The only team perpetually worse than his old team.

Getting into his truck, Zach rested his forehead against the steering wheel.

He was so totally screwed.

CHAPTER 4

Charmed, I'm Sure

Kelsie stared at the conference room door and waited for her student to arrive. She tapped her fingernails on the thick oak table then stopped herself when she realized what she was doing.

A lady never showed impatience or revealed her weaknesses.

In other words, never let them see you sweat. She distracted herself by studying the pictures on the wall in front of her—several scenes taken of the celebration after the Lumberjacks won their first Super Bowl. She recognized Tyler Harris holding the large trophy over his head, while his cousin, Derek Ramsey, stood nearby, one arm around Rachel, his now wife, while giving the Number One sign with his free hand. She scanned the rest of the pictures, unconsciously looking for Zach. Of course, there were none. He'd signed with the team during the off-season. Maybe at the end of this season, there'd be a new photo of Zach hoisting the coveted Lombardi. She'd like that for him. She'd followed his career over the years, cheered his victories, been saddened by his defeats, because of the guilt she'd felt over her treatment of him, she supposed.

Her stomach churned with more than just nerves but in anticipation of seeing Zach again—as much as she hated to admit it.

She didn't have a clue how he'd take this new twist on his life—or maybe she did have a clue. He wouldn't take it well, not well at all. First of all, he'd resist etiquette training with his typical determined stubbornness. Second, he'd be pretty darned upset to have her as his instructor.

Well, Mr. Murphy, I'm not doing splits and cartwheels over working with you either, but it's for your own good.

Two to three long months with Zach Murphy didn't bode well for Kelsie's sanity or willpower. One look at the man last week, and her body screamed *I want that* like a spoiled kid in a toy store. As long as Zach maintained a distance, she'd be able to keep it strictly business—had to keep it that way—for his future and hers.

She wondered if he had any idea how much Veronica wanted him gone. Kelsie had no doubt if Zach's manners didn't improve, the owner's daughter would try to get him off the team. She could help him stay on the team and ease her guilt at the same time.

The best thing for both of them is to let him believe she was still the same selfish bitch she'd always been. Of course, that would negate one of the reasons she came to Seattle in the first place—to apologize for her cruelty of years ago. Then again, a lady could apologize and still maintain a smart distance from a rough-around-more-than-the-edges sexy guy.

Yes, she could do this, be coldly businesslike and lead him to believe she didn't care a bit about anything but her bottom line. Yet, as far she'd come so far from her mean-girl past, she still owed him an apology. A big one, straight from the heart.

Kelsie looked down at her dog-eared, autographed copy of *Mabel Fay Buchanan's Book of Southern Charm and Etiquette* and smiled to herself. She'd start with Chapter 1, "Must-Have Social Graces."

Call her weird, but she loved this book. Mabel Fay was like an old friend, a purveyor of common courtesy but also practical advice. Kelsie met the woman once at a dinner in Atlanta and thoroughly enjoyed the grand old dame's spunky charm and grace.

She thumbed through the first chapter and wrote down notes, brimming with her old confidence. The book outlined courtesies so basic she found it hard to believe people didn't already understand them, but not everyone had the formal upbringing she'd had, groomed from birth to be a doctor, lawyer, or politician's charming wife. Zach hadn't had that indoctrination into social graces. Once in high school in a rare moment of letting his guard down, he'd confided in her about his alcoholic mother and abusive father. Later she'd used that information to betray and belittle him.

Kelsie sighed, riddled with regrets and determined to help the man. It couldn't be that hard to tutor a football player and transform him from a sow's ear to a Gucci wallet. Not hard at all. Even if he was Zach Murphy. Even if they did have a history.

She patted herself on the back for leveraging one of the few talents she had besides shopping, cheerleading, and competing in beauty pageants. All those manners her mama drilled into her would finally amount to something. Currently, they amounted to a full belly and a warm—though small and shabby—place to sleep.

Just this morning Kelsie cashed her check and rented a small room from an ancient widow who lived in a decrepit mansion not far from Lumberjacks headquarters. She'd left Scranton curled up on the futon that doubled as a bed. The next thing she'd done was eat an early dinner at a trendy restaurant. Maybe she'd spent a little too much, but she'd earn more. Soon. She'd use the Lumberjacks job to get her foot in the door with other sports teams and businesses in the area. But first things first, to get through this initial meeting with Zach.

Kelsie smoothed the wrinkles out of the skirt of her tailored designer suit, the only one she'd brought with her from Texas. She rubbed her palms together and cleared her throat. She could do this. She'd stand on her own two feet, control her own life, and be successful.

Sure, Mark had emotionally beaten her down and destroyed her self-confidence, but she was slowly gaining it back. She'd be successful, and she'd be nice doing it. Never again would she be labeled a mean girl, or a selfish bitch, or even a diva. Nope, from now on, people wouldn't get so much as a glimpse of the old Kelsie. They'd see her as gracious and kind.

Except Zach. Definitely not Zach.

Then the door opened, and her good intentions flew over the goalposts.

* * * * *

Zach stopped in the doorway. His mouth went dry and his body tensed. He clenched his jaw, as conflicting thoughts warred inside his skull. His worst nightmare had come to pass. This could not be happening.

"What the fuck?" He took another step into the room and kicked the door shut behind him.

Kelsie Carrington sat at the conference table, all prim, proper, and fucking-kill-a-man-with-one-pouty-look beautiful. Her sexy red lips pressed into a thin, disapproving line. Her beautiful face with those high cheekbones and striking features sent his heart to his groin alerting the boys down south to prepare for action. Only there wasn't going to be any action. Not now. Not ever. That train fell off the trestle miles ago.

Kelsie sniffed as if she smelled something foul. "Lesson One. Four-letter words are not necessary to get your point across." She stood and smiled at him with her cool, composed smile and held out her hand.

Zach stared at her hand. What the hell did she expect him to do with her hand? Kiss it? Shake it? High-five her? Feeling like the beast to her beauty, he did none of the above. Instead, he leaned against the door, crossed one ankle over the other, and studied her.

She still had it, that composure, that in-born ability to make him feel like a backwards oaf without an ounce of class. She'd broken his heart once and taken away the only thing he had as a poor boy from the wrong side of town, his pride. Well, Zach Murphy didn't forgive or forget. Besides football, the one thing he excelled at was holding a grudge. Ask Harris.

His high school dream girl—architect of the most humiliating memories of his life—wore a form-fitting light blue suit, which hugged her slender body. She hadn't gained a pound in fifteen years. Except her boobs seemed bigger. Maybe she'd gotten a boob job or wore one of those bras that pushed the things upward. Whatever the hell it was, his dick liked what it saw.

She cleared her throat, and Zach looked down at her angelic face. Only he knew she was no angel. She stared back at him, unblinking, but her eyes narrowed. She'd caught him staring at her boobs, like the moron she assumed he still was. Embarrassed, he focused on her hand still held out to him. A forbidden thought crept into his brain. Her long delicate fingers and manicured fingernails would feel good running through his chest hair. One of her nails was chipped, an imperfect touch on a perfect woman and strangely out of character for her. Yet, he liked that touch of imperfection. A lot. Too much, in fact.

"You may kiss my hand. Just a brief touch with the lips. Don't slobber on me like a caveman."

"Not a chance in hell." He'd be damned if he'd kiss her hand or any part of her anatomy, no matter how tempting that anatomy might be and always had been.

Frowning, she lowered her hand and sighed as if he might just be the worst thing that ever happened to her. Well, the feeling was mutual. With an elegant gesture, she pointed toward the chair across the table. "Be seated please."

He lowered his big body onto the small chair and regarded her warily. Harris had set him up. Zach knew he had. The rat bastard would die for this. He'd wring the prick's neck and throw his remains to the dogfish in Puget Sound. But first he had to get through this etiquette lesson.

Sprawling in the chair, hands crossed over his chest, he glared at her. She didn't even blink. Those deep blue eyes of hers drilled into his with a determination he couldn't help but admire. But then, she'd always been strong-willed.

"Sit up straight. A gentleman doesn't slouch."

"Why the hell not?"

"It's bad manners. I realize you wrote the book on reprehensible manners, but let's see if we can remedy that, tough a job as it might be."

"Since when is it bad manners?" He didn't get it. He hated rules for rules' sake, especially when they didn't make a lick of sense.

"It shows disinterest and a lack of respect for the other person in the room."

Zach raised one eyebrow in answer. Her eyes widened and her sigh said it all. Yes, he was an ill-mannered moron. An ill-mannered moron who couldn't take his eyes off her plump lower lip. He swallowed and ran a hand through his hair.

"Zach." Kelsie's mask of confident superiority vanished, replaced by uncertainty and sadness. Clearing her throat, she met his gaze, and he fought to breathe. "Before we get started, I owe you an apology. One long past due."

He didn't say a word and hardened his expression. He wouldn't make this easy for her.

"I was horrible to you in high school. For what it's worth, I didn't enjoy being cruel, but I was swept along by peer pressure, but I'm not that person anymore. I am sorry. Really sorry that I hurt you."

"What makes you think you hurt me?" He glared at her, refusing to let the surprise show in his eyes.

She blinked, once, twice. "Didn't I?"

Zach looked away. Hurt didn't begin to describe what she'd done to him, try ripped him to shreds, shattered his ego, and laid waste to his self-worth for starters. "Apologies are just words. If you want my forgiveness, I'll have to see something concrete."

"In other words, I'll need to prove it to you."

"Yeah."

She looked down at her book. "Fine."

Zach hated it when a woman used the word *fine*. It meant anything but fine. In fact, it usually meant the targeted male had done an unfathomable thing to piss off the female. "Let's get back to the reason I'm forced to be here."

Blowing out an exasperated breath, she picked up the book and turned all business again. "I'm giving you a homework assignment. You're to read Chapter 1 in this book. We'll discuss it when we meet again next Tuesday evening." She pushed the book across the table to him.

"Are you kidding?" He didn't bother to glance at it.

"I take courtesy seriously, unlike another person I won't name." She raised her head and gave him that haughty look he used to hate with a passion.

"Go ahead and name him, won't hurt my feelings."

"The man in question should be quite aware of his shortcomings in this area." She pinched the bridge of her nose as if he was giving her a headache. He added one point to his mental scoreboard.

"The man doesn't give a shit."

Her eyes narrowed. He'd pissed her off. "It's obvious why they hired me. You have the graciousness of a blind rattler."

"Better a blind rattler than a stuffy, spoiled bi—uh, brat." Zach did have a few rules he lived by. He never called a lady a bitch, even if said lady deserved the title.

She shot to her feet, her blue eyes blazing like six-guns in the hands of a Wild West outlaw. "Why, you—you—"

"Now, now, sugar, watch your manners." He shook a finger in her face, but abruptly pulled it back when Kelsie looked ready to gut him and mount his head over her mantle.

Taking a visible, deep breath, she sat back down. She clasped her hands in front of her on the table. "We need to set up an appropriate time for me to peruse your house to see what we'll need to do in preparation for the gala."

He rolled his eyes. "My house looks just fine."

Kelsie looked him up and down and raised one perfectly plucked eyebrow. The eyebrow said it all. With that one eyebrow she'd reduced him to an awkward high school kid without a penny to his name wearing an outdated suit that didn't fit.

"Okay, fine. We can meet on Monday evening at 7:00 p.m." He scribbled his address on the title page in the book, ripped it out, and gave it to her.

Her eyes grew big as she took the page from his hand.

"What's wrong? It's just the title page."

Kelsie shook her head and sighed. He'd screwed up again, but he didn't see what the big deal was. "Fine, I'll get you another book."

"You don't get it, do you? This book is a cherished possession, more than just a book. Regardless of an article's material value, you need to show respect for other people's property."

Zach stared at a point on the wall over her head. He felt like an idiot, but he'd be damned if he'd tell her that. "This isn't going to work out."

A fleeting moment of panic crossed her face before cool, superior Kelsie took over. "It'll work out fine. I love challenges."

Then it hit him harder than a block by a three-hundred-pound tackle. Waitressing at a banquet. The piece of shit car with all the stuff piled in it. The desperation he'd seen in her eyes at the charity ball. This bullshit career of hers. Kelsie was down on her luck. Maybe even flat broke.

She needed this job. Because of that, she needed *him*.

The thought brought a smile to his face. Payback is a bitch. For the first time, he sensed he had the upper hand with her, and he'd use every bit of power he had to make this mean girl do restitution for all the nasty, bitchy things she'd done to him in high school.

She'd work for every penny the Jacks paid her. He didn't want to attend manners class. He didn't give a flying seagull's ass about Veronica Simms's demands. They'd forced him to attend against his will, and he planned on giving Kelsie as much hell as she'd given him as a high school kid with his first crush. Not that he'd be mean about it, not like she had been and most likely still was. Nope, he'd prove he had more class that she ever did, but he wouldn't cooperate with her stupid demands, starting with homework assignments.

Their gazes met and held. His breath caught in his throat. His heart flopped over, despite his brave stance. She still had the power to make him grovel for a smidgeon of her affection, but she'd never know it. Never.

Despite how much she'd done to him, how much she'd hurt him, she still got to him in ways no other woman ever had.

CHAPTER 5

Opponents on the Same Team

The next morning, Coach Jackson summoned Kelsie to the Lumberjacks' headquarters. She sat in the reception area, hands folded in her lap, knees pressed together, and wearing that one good suit. Eventually, she'd need to get it dry-cleaned, but for now she'd make do. At least, she had a closet to hang it in.

Kelsie had confined her blond hair to a sleek ponytail and added a small amount of makeup to her face, conserving the expensive cosmetics the best she could. Despite her attempts at frugality—a skill she'd never needed in the past—her money was depleting at an alarming rate.

Kelsie sat board straight, a habit honed from years of pageant training courtesy of her impossible-to-please mother. Once, as a seven-year-old, she'd been exhausted after hours of being "on" at a child beauty pageant. Her face ached from smiling. Her feet screamed to be released from their too small patent-leather shoes—ladies didn't have big feet—and her heavy makeup itched. She stood in line while the judges interviewed five finalists. When they finished with her and moved onto her rival Candace Johnson, Kelsie released a breath and every muscle in her body went limp. Her shoulders slumped, and she cocked one hip. Afterward her mother was so furious, she blamed Kelsie's loss to Candace on Kelsie's sloppy stance. When they got home, Carmen Carrington had forced her daughter to stand at attention in a corner for an hour without dinner. Kelsie never forgot that lesson.

Tyler Harris sauntered by and did a double take. Turning back, he dropped into the chair next to her and stretched his long legs out in front of him. His trademark killer grin softened the hard lines of his handsome face. "How's it going with our wolf-boy?"

"Pardon?" Even as she played dumb, the hackles rose on the back of her neck like a lioness defending her cub, not that Zach looked like a cub, more like a lion, all deceptively laid-back until he struck with lightning fast speed and intensity.

"Murphy. How's he doing? Are you making any progress with the social moron?"

"I don't discuss my clients." Her cold glare usually set most men back on their heels but not the brash, over-confident quarterback. Nothing seemed to faze him.

"That bad?" Tyler sat back and propped his feet on the coffee table.

"No, that good." She looked straight ahead.

He chuckled and smiled, a genuine smile, which momentarily allowed the nice guy buried deep under all the egotistical posturing to emerge. "You're one gutsy lady to take him on."

"Who's gutsy?" Zach stalked over to where they sat, dressed in a ratty pair of workout sweats, a towel draped around his neck. His wrinkled clothes, stubbled face, and shaggy hair presented a stark contrast to Tyler's expensive sweats and cleanly shaven face.

Tyler Harris might be a gorgeous specimen, but Zach was oh-so-hot, so male, so sexy. The testosterone poured off him in waves and alerted every female cell in Kelsie's body to his presence, as if her eyes alone hadn't already done the job. She fanned her face. Too young for hot flashes, it didn't take a Rhodes scholar to figure out what started the wildfire burning across her cheeks.

"Kelsie's gutsy for taking on a jerk like you, Murphy."

"Better than a prick like you." Zach dropped into the chair next to Kelsie and ran a hand through his unruly hair, as if a finger combing could tame that rat's nest. Kelsie made a mental note to find him a decent stylist.

Tyler stood, typical alpha male using his height to intimidate. Zach didn't blink. Instead he held a hand up to his mouth and yawned.

Kelsie leaned close to whisper in Zach's ear. His clean male scent seduced her with a naked Zach fantasy. For a moment she forgot what she was going to say. The odd look on Tyler's face snapped her out of it. "Zach, now's a good time to practice what you've learned in class on Mr. Harris." She stabbed him with her best don't-screw-this-up glare.

Zach stared straight ahead, his chin jutting out in stubborn defiance.

"Zach." Kelsie threatened a warning in her tone. The two *men*—and she used the term lightly—squared off like bullies on a playfield.

Zach glowered at her for a short moment. He stood up to face Harris and visibly composed himself. "Mr. Harris, so nice to see you today. I'm looking forward to our first home game on Sunday. I believe we'll have a stupendous time kicking some major ass."

Tyler threw back his head and laughed so hard the sound rang off the walls and tears filled his eyes.

Zach shrugged, seemingly unaffected by Tyler's laughter. He walked across the seating area to one of two championship trophies on display and touched the glass encasing the gleaming silver football like a worshipper touching the face of his idol.

Wiping at his eyes, Tyler shook his head at Kelsie. "Sure you don't want to cut and run now while you can?"

"No, we're making progress quite nicely." Like hell they were. She'd have better luck with a child raised in the wilderness from birth. At least he'd be a blank slate.

"Well, good luck, honey, you're going to need it." Tyler sauntered off, still chuckling.

Zach swung back around, apparently not as unaffected as he'd first appeared. He stared after Tyler, murder in his eyes. "That fu— frigging asshole. I'm going to—"

"Kelsie, Coach will see you now." A short, stocky man interrupted, much to Kelsie's relief. Sucking in a calming breath and letting it out, she stood and left Zach without another word.

Kelsie entered the coach's office and sat. Tastefully framed pictures of players adorned the walls along with some Coach of the Year awards. Autographed game balls sat on the cherry bookcase. The huge desk and leather furniture spoke of a man's domain, a man accustomed to wielding a certain amount of power in his world.

Kelsie approved of the effect and mentally applauded the coach's interior designer.

Coach Jackson stood and shook her hand. "Kelsie, I only have a few minutes, got to get to practice. So, what's your initial assessment of our boy?"

The coach didn't sit down, so Kelsie remained standing. The man picked up a paperweight and tossed it back and forth in his hands. He radiated nervous energy like a pacing tiger in a cage. "Mr. Murphy is a trial, but I'm up to the task."

The coach stood still for a split second. "I hope you are. Ownership is adamant about this. In fact, if he doesn't cooperate, they want him benched or traded."

Kelsie nodded. "There's no need for such drastic measures. We're making progress." Holding her hand behind her back, she crossed her fingers.

"I sure hope so. Do I need to give him a little nudge or is he cooperating?"

"He's cooperating." She slipped her other hand behind her back and crossed those fingers, too.

"I sure hope so. For your sake and his. The gala was Veronica's idea. Hell, I'd be happy if the guy ate with utensils and didn't belch during interviews."

"I'll take care of both." Oh, Lord please help her. Zach didn't exactly cooperate, and she doubted he'd do his homework either.

"Okay, let me know if he needs any added incentive." Coach Jackson glanced at his watch. "Time for practice. I'll be in touch." He zipped out of the room, paperweight still in hand, leaving Kelsie standing in the eye of the passing tornado and wondering what just hit her.

* * * * *

The team won its first home game, making their record two and zero, the best start Zach had ever had as a professional. Afterward, he showered in the locker room and wrapped a towel around his naked lower body. He'd played almost every down on defense in the Jacks' first home game of the regular season. The crowd had been electric, rocking the stadium like he'd never experienced in his life.

His body hurt like hell, but he refused to admit he might be getting too old for this. The whirlpool beckoned, and afterward he might get cozy with a couple painkillers. As a matter of course, he avoided taking pills, but he'd make an exception tonight. It'd been a tough, hard-fought game right down to the wire.

Harris's laughter dragged his attention to his left. Putting Zach's locker next to his had to be coach's idea of a sick joke.

A large group of media guys surrounded the cocky quarterback, salivating at his every word. The asshole charmed his prey like a snake seducing a rat then swallowed them whole. Grudgingly, Zach admired Harris's ability to say the right thing at the right time, tossing out quotes to be used for headlines tomorrow. Whenever Zach opened his mouth to the media, he either inadvertently insulted someone or created a media hoo-ha over some stupid-assed thing. Yeah, like the time he'd called an opposing team's quarterback an over-hyped coward who couldn't knit his way out of the backfield. The next day the guy threw for 350-yards against Zach's old team and booted their asses out of a playoff spot.

Shoving his wet hair off his forehead, Zach ground his teeth together in frustration. The quarterback played an okay game, but the local sportscasters treated him like old ladies treated the only old man on pinochle night at the senior center.

Their worship stuck in Zach's craw. His defense had kept them in the game. They should be fawning over Bryson who recovered a crucial fumble or LeDaniel who intercepted a sure touchdown. Harris had played it safe. He didn't lose the game for them, but he didn't win it either. Zach's defense won it in the trenches.

"We won no thanks to you." Zach grumbled once the press had left.

Harris's hand snaked out and collared Zach around the neck, catching him off guard. He slammed Zach against the locker room wall with a violent force more representative of a defensive player instead of a pussy-assed quarterback.

"What the fuck is stuck up your butt, asshole?" With legs splayed apart, Harris's fingers closed around Zach's neck, not enough to choke, but enough to show he meant business.

Flakes of sheetrock fluttered past Zach's eyes, just as a poster listing the ten steps to winning fell off the wall. Seasoned veterans busied themselves in their lockers, while rookies scattered like seagulls on the beach. They glanced back over their shoulders as they high-tailed it out of the locker room and away from their battling team captains.

Zach blinked a few times, jolted by how strong the quarterback actually was. He only allowed himself a split second of shock before he shook it off and shoved the heels of his hands into Harris's chest. Harris didn't budge despite his sharp exhalation of breath as Zach's full strength compressed his rib cage.

"You're up my ass, and I'm fucking tired of it." Zach tore Harris's hand from his neck.

Harris smirked. "Well, at least I'm warm." He stood toe-to-toe with Zach, who out-benched him by a considerable amount. Zach gave the quarterback a point for his guts, or foolhardiness, depending on how he looked at it.

Harris had a couple inches on Zach, and he wielded his height advantage like the warrior with the sharper sword. His chin jutted out, and he stared down at Zach as if he were a lowly slug on a wet Seattle sidewalk. Neither of them moved—two alpha males refusing to give ground.

Zach leaned into Harris's space. "I don't like you."

"No shit. What the fuck is it with you? I'm working my ass off, just like you are."

Years of frustration bubbled to the surface, years of being stuck on a mediocre team with worthless management and shitty decisions from the front office to the coaching. All those years, he'd watched Super Bowl after Super Bowl with one goal in mind—to one day be the guy standing on the podium hoisting the Lombardi trophy over his head. Despite a sure hall-of-fame career, all his achievements would mean nothing without that championship ring. Yet, Harris had two and didn't seem to appreciate how lucky he was.

Obviously sensing a change in Zach's attitude, Tyler frowned and backed up a few steps. Plastering an I-don't-give-a-shit expression on his face, he crossed his arms over his chest and leaned against his locker.

"I want a ring." Zach spoke with more emotion than was wise.

"Yeah, tell me something I don't know. You'd sacrifice your last friend on earth for a ring, that's assuming you had any friends."

"*You* stand between me and a ring."

"Hey, asshole, get a clue. In case you haven't noticed, we're on the same team." Harris rolled his eyes.

"Seems like we're on opposing teams if you ask me."

"That might be the way you see it. The way I see it you're destroying our chances. You're splitting the team in half, forcing the defense to side with you and leaving the offense no choice but to side with me."

"I don't like what you stand for."

"And what exactly is that?"

"Everything I hate about quarterbacks."

Harris raised one dark eyebrow. "And that is?"

"You think the world revolves around you."

"Damn right, because it does, dumb shit."

"You quit on the team last year."

Harris's eyes turned dark like a cloud blotting out the sun, and he didn't deny Zach's accusation. "I'm not the same guy I was last year. I was going through some—personal issues. I'm fine now. I'm all in."

"Prove it."

Harris closed his eyes for a brief moment and sighed, almost as if he'd grown weary of their constant squabbling. "I have been. Open your fucking eyes and get on board before it's too late."

"I am on board, but I'm not convinced you are."

"Fuck you. *You* are the problem, not the solution." Grabbing his gym bag, Harris stalked out the door and slammed it behind him.

Zach turned to glare at the lone stragglers in the room, a couple of his defensive guys and a few of the offensive linemen, also Harris's cousin, Derek, a straight-up guy, even though he had the misfortune of being related to Harris.

His teammates turned back to their lockers and pretended to be busy with whatever the hell they were doing, except Ramsey. He edged over to Zach's locker and sat down on the closest bench.

"We won, you know. You might want to lighten up a little around him." Derek's expression remained open and friendly.

"Why? Is he gonna kick my ass?" Zach sneered, but his surliness didn't faze Derek in the least. Hell, the guy had spent years with Tyler.

Derek shrugged one shoulder. "Hard to say. He's got a temper, and he can be a scrapper. Used to get in a lot of bar fights in college."

Zach snorted. "I find it hard to believe he'd bruise that pretty face of his."

"Don't underestimate my cousin. Last year was an anomaly. He went through some tough times, but he's back on track. He's not a quitter. He's competitive and tough. He's played hurt, with the flu, and everything in between. You'd be smart to remember that instead of focusing on one off year out of a dozen exceptional years."

"You're taking his side."

"I'm not taking anyone's side, but your bickering is crippling the team. This locker room division needs to stop. I think you're man enough to check your pride at the door and find some common ground. You both want the same thing—a championship. Work together instead of at odds with each other."

"So I'm supposed to cave to his demands, like everyone else in this locker room? How's that gonna look to my guys? I'm the captain of the defense. Do I just lay down and let Harris stomp all over me then thank him for it?"

Derek rubbed the back of his neck and sighed. "If you want a ring as badly as you claim, you'll do what it takes."

Like he wasn't already? Shit. He was busting his balls on the field, while condemned to a hell known as etiquette classes taught by the one woman he could never resist, not years ago and not now. He'd been her doormat once, and if his body's current reactions were any judge, he'd gladly lay down across a mud puddle so she wouldn't get her dainty feet muddy.

Yet he knew Derek was right. They shouldn't be airing their dislike of each other in front of the team. Zach might have the best of intentions but his mouth got in the way of his brain, and dumb stuff came tumbling out. The few times he'd tried to compliment the surly quarterback, the jerk took it as an insult. Now they were at odds to the point where they couldn't say a civil word to each other if their life depended on it.

Zach knew his grudge was stupid, and Harris knew it was stupid, but they were stubborn alpha males who refused to show weakness and be the first to back down. He hated to admit it, but maybe he could use a little training in tact and manners.

Off to his side he heard Derek sigh, and a second later he walked out of the room.

Frustrated by the doubts filling his head, Zach pounded his fist into his locker. But even the dent he left didn't make him feel better.

CHAPTER 6

One Yard and a Cloud of Dust

Kelsie consulted the handwritten directions Zach had scrawled on a piece of paper. She couldn't afford a data plan on her phone so goodbye GPS, hello old-fashioned navigation by paper.

She turned on Sparkling Bay Drive and drove down a street lined with stately maples and historic Seattle mansions, scanning for the correct address. From a block away, she spotted the likely culprit. Not that it was a bad house. In fact, just the opposite, the old Victorian mansion stood tall and proud, defying time and looking down her classical nose at modern development.

No, it wasn't the house that concerned her. If Zach paid a gardener, he'd better fire the guy.

She was speechless.

As she drove next to the house, Kelsie slowed her car to a crawl and craned her neck. A post with a house number partially obscured by overgrown rhododendrons confirmed her worst suspicions.

Zach Murphy, former poor boy turned NFL defensive star, lived at this address. She turned up the once elegant driveway. A forest of overhanging branches scraped along the roof of her car as she drove past a flock of faded, pink plastic flamingoes, one missing a beak, another missing a leg.

Oh, yes, she'd come to the right place.

Unfortunately.

She stopped her car, gripped the steering wheel, and stared. And stared. And stared again. She blinked. Closed her eyes. Counted to ten. Peeked once. Twice. Three times. Nothing changed the landscaping disaster obscuring most of the house from view.

Oh, good heavens.

If a child ventured into Zach's yard, the two-foot tall grass would surely gobble him up and he'd never be seen again, if the tangle of feral shrubbery didn't attack him first. She stared through the car window, expecting to catch a glimpse of the random lion, tiger, or bear that might have taken up residence, also never to be seen again.

Did she dare get out? Especially in her new thrift-store heels? The very heels she would have turned her nose up at in her former life.

Half hidden under an undomesticated wisteria arbor, Kelsie spied the front walkway cleverly disguised as an Amazon rain forest. She gingerly stepped out of her car, hoping she could find it again when it came time to leave.

Picking her way across a concrete driveway pitted with potholes and clumps of grass growing up through the cracks, she approached the clandestine walkway. An errant blackberry vine wrapped itself around her leg despite her best attempts to step over it. Greedy thorns snatched at her legs, as if she were their next meal. She stepped on the vine with her other foot and pulled it off her, but not before it tattooed her ankle with scratches.

Hearing a chuckle, she looked up. Zach stood on a wide porch, which appeared to wrap around the entire house. A smile tickled his mouth. While not prone to violence, one well-placed slap to his amused face would do wonders for her mood.

"Welcome to Branson Manor." His voice sounded strangled, as if he fought to hold back out-and-out laughter.

Kelsie didn't see one funny thing about this situation. "That's what you call it?" Avoiding another blackberry vine, she mounted the front steps, which creaked under her weight. A tattered, blue suede recliner with duct tape on one arm crouched in a corner of the porch, a stack of beer bottles next it, and not good beer, but the cheap stuff.

"Well, it's on the historic register. That's what *they* call it. I guess Branson was a Seattle big-wig a century ago."

"You guess?" She sighed. The poor house had withstood the test of time, but could it withstand a redneck football player with zero taste, a non-existent groundskeeper, and an affinity for tacky?

He shrugged and stuck his hands in his pockets. "Uh, don't really pay much attention to stuff like that."

"I can imagine." She peered through the dense foliage to the barely visible street beyond. "I bet you don't get many visitors here or at least none that you've found." Only the bravest and tasteless of souls would venture forth into this bastion of zero class and redneck adornments.

Zach's dark brows drew together as if he didn't get her humor or her implications. "I'm not much for company."

Again, no surprise there.

"Let me show you the place." His usual distaste of her gave way to pride and excitement. She almost hated to burst his bubble, but the place needed a major overhaul before the gala, and she'd only seen a small portion of it.

Bracing herself, she followed him inside. He walked ahead, leaving the door wide open. With a sigh, Kelsie shut the heavy, old oak door with the oval, etched glass window. It stuck halfway. She leaned into it with all her weight and shoved it shut. Zach watched from a few feet away. "A gentleman holds the door for a lady and closes it after her."

He frowned, looking perturbed and embarrassed at the same time.

The inside of the house shocked her almost as much as the outside, only for a different reason. She fully expected the place to be in a state of disrepair. Looking past junk piled on antique furniture, a Harley parked in the parlor, and the house's basic unkempt condition, the grand old lady's bones bordered on incredible. Beautifully finished woodwork shone from years of loving care. A curved oak banister rose to a balcony on the second floor. An antique Tiffany chandelier hung in the middle of the two-story entry. The hardwood floors gleamed under a layer of dust.

"This way. I call this the man cave." He didn't wait, just headed for a set of oak double doors. Kelsie hurried after him as fast as her heels would allow. She stopped dead in her tracks. Every bit as lovingly restored as the entryway, the library should've impressed, instead she drew back and stared. A scruffy deer head hung over the mantle. A mish-mash of new, poor quality furniture, mostly recliners, were scattered randomly around the room. A big-screen TV took up one entire wall and blocked an old, beautiful built-in bookcase. The bare walls were devoid of artwork, which perhaps wasn't such a bad thing given Zach's taste.

Zach grinned at her. "So? What do you think?"

"The house is beautiful."

"I did the decorating myself."

"I can see that."

"This way." He led her to a designer kitchen with very undesigner-like adornments such as tacky refrigerator magnets taped to the professional grade stainless-steel refrigerator, red rooster canisters, and an array of plastic utensils in a mason jar. Zach watched her, as if waiting for her approval. "What do you think?"

"Needs a little tidying."

"Yeah, my housekeeper quit."

"We'll get another one."

"We?" He grunted as if that'd be a cold day in hell.

He gestured for her to follow him out a set of French doors. Turning around slowly on the sagging back porch, Kelsie surveyed the property, looking past the overgrown landscape. The old mansion perched on a hill high above Seattle like a dowager queen on her throne. Below her, the city and Elliot Bay sparkled in the waning daylight. The sun setting over the distant Olympic Mountains cast ethereal rays of red, purple, and gold across Puget Sound.

Incredible. The view made up for everything else.

Thank God almighty she had almost three months to prepare for this party.

"Seen enough?"

She choked back a very unladylike snort. "Yes, let's talk."

A few minutes later, Kelsie sat in a folding chair at the plastic patio table. Zach sank his big body into the only wooden dining chair in the large formal dining room. Frameless posters depicting various football stars were tacked drunkenly on the walls, not a straight one in the bunch. A life-sized depiction of Tyler Harris hung on another wall, darts stuck in his heart and crotch areas.

"A little hostile, aren't we?"

Zach's eyes followed her gaze, his face colored redder than his neck. "I, uh. Yeah, maybe." He held his hands out with palms up and shrugged. "I keep my grudges close."

"And your enemies closer. Don't I know that." Kelsie opened her laptop, all business. "Let's discuss the changes that need to be made before the gala. We have a few months. What's your budget for improvements?"

"I don't need improvements. I like this place as it is."

"For starters, the jungle outside could conceal a small elephant."

"My lawnmower's busted."

"Fix it."

"I will, just haven't had time."

"Pay someone."

"To do something I can do? No way in frigging hell." His chin jutted out and he crossed his muscular arms over his chest, drawing Kelsie's eyes to his bulging biceps and the dusting of hair on his forearms. She licked her lips. He cleared his throat.

Kelsie's head shot up. She'd been caught gawking. "Your shrubbery is taking your house by siege."

"My trimmers need sharpening."

"Let me guess—and you haven't gotten around to it."

"Nope." He scratched his ample chest and leaned back in his chair, regarding her with hooded eyes, very sexy, hooded eyes, the kind a girl would expect to see in a bedroom. The stubborn set of his chin warned of more trouble to come.

"The boxes in the hallway?"

"Haven't gotten around to unpacking."

"The Harley in the parlor?"

"Need to rebuild the engine and—"

"You haven't gotten around to it." Kelsie buried her fingers in her hair and glared at him in frustration. Death by slow poisoning sounded good about now. His death, not hers. Hmmm. Then again.

"This is the perfect house for an intimate black-tie affair, after some cosmetic changes."

"Intimate, huh?" His mouth turned up at the corners, a wolfish grin, which made her the lamb. "As in you and me?"

"And two hundred other people."

"If that's what you're into, honey, I'm game."

"Cut the sexual innuendos." The man's suggestions were making her wet in all the wrong places. "We need to hire a lawn and garden service, refurnish the rooms, and get a large dumpster delivered."

"*We* aren't doing a damn thing. I'm not holding a black-tie affair, a white-tie affair, or even a T-shirt affair. Understood? You want it cleaned up and all that other fancy crap, you take care of it. I'm not shelling out a penny for this bullshit. It's bad enough I have to attend manners classes, and you're damn lucky I agreed to do that." Zach laid it on thick, projecting complete indifference.

"I wasn't aware you had any options."

He shrugged. "I'm not holding a party."

"Yes, you are." She stared at her notes as if they mattered. He'd just hacked her future to pieces in a few sentences. No black-tie charity gala, no money for Kelsie, no business referrals, no nothing. She'd be back to living in her car.

She met his eyes. His hard exterior softened a bit. "Hey, look, I know you think I'm being an ass, but I feel strongly about this. I'm not gonna compromise my principles to satisfy the owner's spoiled brat daughter. This is who I am, if they don't like it, tough."

Easy for him to say. The roof over his head and food in his mouth didn't depend on this gala. "I wasn't aware you had a vote in this if you want to stay in Seattle. You'd prefer to be tossed off the team and traded to that loser team?"

"How do you know about that?"

"I make it my business to know about my clients."

"I never said I'd spend my own hard-earned cash on this gala."

She squared her shoulders and sat up straighter. Zach wasn't making this easy. "Running a charity event of this caliber costs money."

He dug in, his stubborn jaw jutted out even more. "I'm not spending money on the yard. It'll be dark. They won't see it anyway."

Exasperated, Kelsie considered wrapping her fingers around his thick neck and squeezing. "Fine, I'll do the work myself."

"You? Are you effing kidding me? You wouldn't know how to mow a lawn if it was artificial turf."

"I'm quite handy I'll have you know." Kelsie stood and gathered her stuff, vindicated by the incredulous expression on his masculine face. "I'll be back in the morning, and you will have the lawnmower fixed."

She hurried out the door before she came to her senses and begged for his help.

Or even worse, begged for his body.

* * * * *

Zach knelt in front of the lawnmower he'd dug out from under a pile of boxes in his garage. He didn't enjoy doing stuff like this, but he'd be damned if he'd spend his hard-earned money on something he could do himself. Call him a tightwad, and he'd gladly answer that call. Except when it came to this house. He'd paid a small fortune for this place.

From the time Zach was old enough to know other people didn't live like he did, he swore if he ever got rich, he'd never be one of those pompous assholes with fancy furniture in a house a guy couldn't get comfortable in. Money would never change him. And this beauty queen with a stick up her butt wouldn't change him either—even if she did live in his fantasies all night long and invaded his thoughts at the worst of times.

Zach loved his house. He'd promised his brother—his dead baby brother—that someday they'd have a house like this, put down roots, and never move again. This was his forever home. He had it all planned out, and Zach didn't like it when anyone messed with his carefully laid out steps. One: Win the Super Bowl and get a ring. Two: Retire. Three: Get hired for that UW coaching vacancy coming up next summer. Four: Get married and raise a family and grow old all in the same house.

The minute the real estate agent showed him the old Victorian, he knew it was *the* house, the one he'd imagined when he escaped to that safe place in his head whenever his father beat the crap out of him.

When Kelsie and her friends humiliated him, he swore he'd show them all one day. They'd kicked him when he was as far down as a man could get. He hadn't even been a man, he'd been a seventeen-year-old kid with a murdered brother and mother and an abusive father in prison. Memories of their cruelty twisted his insides into a mass of pain.

Zach gave the wrench one final vicious twist, wiped his greasy hands on a towel and stood up. Righting the lawnmower, he added gas and checked the oil. Kelsie would need more than a regular lawn mower to tackle this lawn, but a vengeful part of him would enjoy watching her try.

A twinge of guilt tweaked at his conscience. Revenge wasn't nearly as fun as he thought it'd be. He didn't like the idea of kicking Kelsie while she was down, even though she'd shown him no mercy in the past.

Okay, buddy, you're getting soft. Mean girls like her don't stay down for long. She'll use and abuse the next poor sucker, and that poor sucker is probably you. She sees dollar signs when she looks at you. Big, fat green ones.

And what did Zach see when he looked at her?

God help him, he wanted to see a mean bitch who no longer held the power to reduce his knees to mush or the beauty to turn every male head in any room, especially his.

No such luck—on both counts.

Zach yanked the starter cord. The damn thing broke and catapulted him several feet, sliding on his ass across the yard and into a thorny bush. Muttering several curses, he clambered to his feet.

Damn it. He glanced at his watch. She'd be here any minute. As much as he'd like to witness her struggles, his practical side warned him to stay clear of the woman. He'd planned on being gone before she showed up for a multitude of reasons, most of which he chose not to explore. He fought his way through the dense weeds and overgrown bushes to the side of the house to the open garage door. Somewhere in this mess he might find an extra lawnmower cord. Zach dug through box after box, throwing the contents onto the already littered concrete floor.

Then he caught the whiff of magnolias on a summer breeze followed by soft footsteps. His entire body snapped to attention and his dick saluted.

Zach clutched the spare lawnmower cord in his hand, took a deep breath, and turned around. Kelsie stood a few feet away, gaping at the carnage in the garage. Her smooth brow furrowed as she clutched a tiny dog close to her chest. Zach wanted to be that dog.

She pursed her lips and pinched her nose as if something smelled bad. Probably him. Old feelings of inadequacy and doubt threaded through him.

"Obviously you don't park cars in here."

"Obviously." He hated how she looked down her nose at him, just like the old days, like she considered him a stupid hick, inadequate and ignorant. He so did not want to be that guy in her eyes. The little dog bared its teeth at him and growled.

Kelsie tapped its nose and uttered, "Shush." The animal focused on him with suspicion, watching his every move with its beady little black eyes.

"What the hell is that?"

"This is Scranton. He's a toy poodle, comes from a long line of champions. Very well bred."

And Zach wasn't. Yeah, he got the message. The dog had better bloodlines than Zach. By far. "I prefer real dogs. Big dogs. Dogs who can chase balls, retrieve ducks, or ride in the back of a pickup."

"I'm not surprised." The smile in her voice burrowed right into his heart. Their eyes met. Hers were teasing and amused, and her nose had come down from its lofty perch. He liked her like this. Like a real person. A nice approachable person. He took a step closer, drawn to her by an invisible magnet of mutual attraction. Scranton snarled and ruined the mood. He didn't know whether to thank or strangle the poodle.

Zach turned away. "I'll have the mower fixed and be out of your way in a jiff." He looked her up and down. "You're doing lawn work in that?" Not that she didn't look damn fine in those form-fitting clothes, but they'd be more appropriate in a Calvin Klein ad than in his overgrown backyard. His heart thumped madly, and try as he might, he couldn't convince any part of his body how wrong this woman would be for him.

Kelsie looked down at her skinny jeans, leather flats, and cotton shirt. "What's wrong with my clothes?"

"You've seen my yard."

"I'll be fine."

"Suit yourself, ma'am." He touched the brim of an imaginary hat and grinned at his good manners, mentally patting himself on the back.

"Well, what do you know? You can teach an old linebacker new plays." Kelsie rewarded him with one heck of a dazzling smile, like lightning hitting a tin roof. He puffed up like a bandy rooster, quite pleased with himself for earning a rare compliment. He wanted to duplicate that smile, to see it light up her face again and again. Hell, more than that, he wanted to touch those full red lips. Just a touch to see if they were as soft as he'd dreamed. He stepped forward, raised his hand—

Kelsie didn't blink, didn't move, except for a fleeting wrinkle of her brow in confusion, as if uncertain about his intentions. Zach ducked his head, as the heat rose right up the tips of his ears. He headed back to the lawnmower, and she tagged along. He wished she'd stay away, let him get this chore done, so he could get the hell out of there with what little pride he still possessed.

"You need to let things go."

He turned to face her. "Such as?"

"Me."

"Would you trust you if you were me?"

She tapped her index finger against her plump lower lip. His throat went dry. "I suppose not, but people change."

"Not in my experience." He'd revealed his deepest, darkest secrets to her in a night of stupidity. She'd led him on, probed for information, and gotten plenty. Then she'd spilled the dirt to her friends, including his father being in prison for beating Zach's brother until he suffered severe brain damage. On the very night his brother finally succumbed to his injuries, she and her friends used his family tragedy as fodder to ridicule him. He'd been hurting and looking for a friend. He'd thought she'd been that friend.

If she had it tough now, well, karma was a bitch.

"So? You haven't changed either." She leveled an accusing gaze at him.

"Money will never change me, make me someone I'm not."

"Everyone has room for improvement."

"Even you?"

She dipped her head then looked at him through lowered lashes. "Especially me. I know you have good reason not to trust me or even like me, but maybe if we work together, we can achieve our mutual goals in the most painless and expedient way possible."

Zach regarded her for a moment. His heart beat a little faster at her admission. Part of him wanted desperately to believe her, to fall at her feet and worship the princess from his dreams. Only she wasn't a fairy princess, she was an evil witch disguised as a princess.

"Zach, I'm so sorry about high school. So very sorry. I didn't understand how cruel I was because I was too selfish to see how much I hurt you. You seemed so big, so strong, so invincible, while I was a screwed-up, insecure mess, needing my friends' approval." She clutched the dog closer, as if it were her protection. Her deep blue eyes shone with sincerity, but she'd always been an excellent actress.

Forgiveness balanced on the end of his tongue, ready to take the plunge and believe her words, but he beat it back. He'd fallen for her beautiful face and cajoling voice before. He couldn't do it again. He'd loved her, and she'd thrown it in his face, used him and abused in a way as painful as the burns and beatings he'd suffered at the hands of his father.

"You need to forgive and move on because you're hurting yourself more than you're hurting anyone else." She reached out to touch his arm.

He jerked away, desperate to put some distance between them and build the walls higher. Very few people in his life had ever hurt him as much as she had. He wouldn't go down that road again. The brief flash of regret in her eyes almost undid him, but he barricaded his heart against her. "Look, I'll read your book and learn your lessons, but I draw the line there. I'm not going to change who I am and what my place looks like for a bunch of rich people who show up and drink my alcohol and eat my food for free."

"It's for charity."

"What charity?"

"The homeless, including veterans, families, the mentally ill. She calls it Hearts for Homeless. It's Veronica's pet charity. She sponsors this gala every year."

Homeless families? Indecision paralyzed him. He almost caved, said fine, he'd cooperate. Instead Zach stood, pulled the cord on the lawnmower several times until it started with a huge belch of black smoke and a racket loud enough to wake the dead. Kelsie jumped back, and Scranton yelped.

With a grimace, Zach bowed. "Your chariot awaits, madam."

Then he got the hell out of there.

* * * * *

An hour later, Kelsie pulled the cord on the lawnmower, just like she'd seen Zach do. Once. Twice. Three times. Her shoulder ached and a cramp started in one butt cheek and traveled down her thigh right to her big toe. After several more body-wrenching attempts, the smoking beast roared to life. She lined it up with the sidewalk, the least overgrown area, and pushed, putting her whole body into it. The mower lurched forward. It bogged down in the first five feet and shuddered to a pitiful, grinding halt.

Sweat ran between her shoulder blades and down her spine. Her hair fell out of its once tidy ponytail. After almost throwing out her back, she managed to get the sorry thing started again. In another two feet, she hit something. Something big. A metallic bang and earsplitting screech sounded the mower's final cry as it died a slow death after a few backfires and more ominous black smoke. Grabbing the cord Kelsie yanked hard and almost dislocated her shoulder as the cord froze in mid-pull.

The beast had mowed its final blade of grass. She didn't blame the poor mower. The task was daunting to woman and machine. She moved it aside and kicked at the grass with her feet, looking for what she'd hit. Several rusty pieces of metal lurked in the knee-high jungle.

With a defeated sigh, Kelsie plopped down on the creaky front steps, put her hands over her eyes and cried. Flat-out broke down and cried. Scranton slipped off his comfy seat on the porch swing and crawled onto her lap. His wet tongue licked the hands covering her eyes. Kelsie only cried harder, deriving little comfort from her faithful companion of ten years.

She'd broken every fingernail, put a hole in the knee of her expensive jeans, and lost the battle—and probably the war—with the blackberries laying claim to the property. The danged thorny devils wrapped around her legs like Boa constrictors, dug in their thorns and refused to let go, branding her with nasty scratches on just about every part of her anatomy.

Kelsie wiped her eyes and sniffled. She looked up and surveyed the progress she hadn't made. She wasn't cut out for this, didn't know the first thing about yard work or the various equipment and tools. The emotional deluge started again. Her shoulders slumped, and her eyes burned from the tears and smoke. She heard Scranton growl and glanced up.

"Hey, are you all right?"

Kelsie rubbed her eyes and looked up at Zach. His hands were jammed in his pockets, and he looked ready to flee from a sniffling female first chance he got. His handsome face screwed into a puzzled frown—that same face she'd depended on in her first few years of high school when he'd been one of her most loyal friends. Until she'd sold her soul for the conditional friendship of the most popular girl in school, and the meanest, Marcela—never to be called Marcie. Marcela's boyfriend, the team's star wide receiver, hated Zach, along with Mark, the quarterback and the man Kelsie eventually married. Why they chose Zach as the target of their bullying, Kelsie never knew. Looking back, she guessed they didn't need a reason, just hated Zach on principle, rich boy versus poor boy. She'd tried to walk down the middle, but eventually they'd forced her to choose. She'd been so awful to Zach. So very awful.

"Hey, are you okay?" He repeated the question, looked back toward his pickup, then yanked his hands out of his pockets and crouched on his haunches next to her.

"I'm okay." She didn't sound okay, even to her own ears. She sounded shaky and defeated.

"You didn't get very far."

"It was a homicide." She hiccupped and stared down at her scratched and damaged hands.

"Excuse me?"

"The lawnmower. I murdered it." She gazed at him through bleary eyes, certain her mascara had run. He managed a tentative smile then reached out toward her, as if to pull her into his arms. If only he'd wrap his big strong arms around her and pull her against the safety of his muscular body. He'd protect her, and she'd never worry about a thing again. Except this little fantasy happened to be just that—the fantasy of a delusional woman who wanted to believe this man who held his grudges near and dear to his heart would actually forgive her. As if reading her thoughts, he pulled his hands back and shoved them in his pockets. He stared at the grass-stained lawnmower covered with soot. "Well, it was old anyway."

Kelsie glanced up, sniffling, knowing her eyes had to be red and puffy. She summoned the same inner strength, which brought her to Seattle in the first place. "I am doing this for you. I could use a little help."

His face hardened, erasing all signs of sympathy for her plight. "Are you certain? Or are you doing it for *you*, just like always. I got roped into the class, but this stupid gale wasn't my idea."

"Gala." She couldn't help the dig. He was being a stubborn jackass.

"Whatever. Same difference in my book. I don't want to do it."

So maybe he might be a little right. Maybe she was doing it for herself. The gala would showcase her talents, build her clientele. Zach didn't have one good reason to help her, except— "The proceeds go to homeless families. Don't you care about that?"

"I care about my privacy and keeping my house the way I like it."

"You're a stubborn, insufferable man."

"Thanks. I resemble that remark." For a minute, Zach wavered, uncertainty on his face. "I'll go to someone else's gala as my graduation test."

Most likely the coach would agree to Zach's suggestion, but the house and grounds would be an outstanding location for the type of intimate event she had in mind.

Fortifying her resolve, Kelsie lifted her head. Out of the ashes arose the fire. Instead of giving up, she'd beat this damn yard into submission, one way or another. Or die trying. Shooing Scranton off her lap, she rose to her feet, and he followed suit. "I'm going to do it, and you, Zach Murphy, are going to help me." She jabbed a finger in his chest.

A grudging respect shone in his eyes, along with something much more dangerous to both of them. "Fine. Hire someone. I'll split the costs with you."

Split the costs? Hardly. She didn't have the money for next week's rent. "You said you never hire someone to do something you can do."

"Yeah, but it'd take the entire football team to get this yard in shape."

"That's a perfect idea."

"Don't even think about it."

"Please." She grasped his arm. Big mistake. The hard-corded muscles flexed under her fingers. His expression changed, went blank for a second. He blinked and stared at her.

Suddenly self-conscious, Kelsie pushed her hair out of her eyes and wiped her dirty face with an equally dirty sleeve. "I must look awful."

"I don't think so." He spoke so quietly, she swore she'd misunderstood him.

"Pardon?" Her heart thumped in her chest, pounding on its cell walls and begging to be released.

"I like this Kelsie, all messy and sweaty, not so untouchable, a woman a man could get, uh, comfortable with."

"If the man was prone to mud-wrestling." She snorted, attempting to lighten the weight of sexual attraction smothering both of them.

"Don't tempt me." His mouth quirked up in a smile that crinkled the corners of his eyes and made him so irresistibly attractive to her.

"You don't like me." Her gaze flicked to a large mud puddle several feet away.

One dark brow crept up his forehead. "You're right. But you're still a hot female with a great body. It's just a physical thing."

"It's always a physical thing with you."

"Not always, but now it is. That's all that's left."

The mood shattered, Kelsie looked away from those piercing eyes that saw too much. "Are you ever going to forgive me?"

He frowned and stared at his hands. "Not sure. I'm struggling with it."

"You don't forgive easily."

"I haven't met anyone who's truly earned my forgiveness. The few times I've forgiven they've proven they don't deserve it."

"You must live a tragic, lonely life, Zach Murphy."

"Yeah, maybe." The sadness in his eyes undid her.

The urge to take away his pain whipped through her, wrapping her in the eye of a tornado and pummeling her good sense. She touched his cheek, mesmerized by his dark eyes, drawn in by animal magnetism. She leaned forward. He leaned forward. The scent of pure male, clean and masculine filled her nostrils. Her hand dropped to her side. She stared at his mouth and moved closer, just an inch or two separated them. His hot breath tickled her nose. She closed the final distance, unable to resist.

His lips tasted just as she imagined, like spearmint gum and all-alpha male. He didn't move as she sampled them, letting her take the initiative. Kelsie ran her tongue over his lower lip and circled to his upper lip. Once she completed the circuit, her mouth followed her tongue. His lips were strong, uncompromising, sensually powerful, everything she knew they'd be.

With a tortured groan, Zach buried his long fingers into her hair and pulled her closer, deepening the kiss, sucking her tongue into his warm mouth. Kelsie wrapped her arms around his neck and held on tight. Her wayward body pressed against his without her permission.

She didn't give a damn. She wanted him with a feral need she'd never felt with another man. Maybe it was a payback thing, a way to give him a part of her and ease her guilt. Right now the reasons didn't matter. Their mouths mated wildly, like animals, freed of all the restrictions placed on them by society.

Society.

Oh, crap.

Her job.

Calling on a reserve of strength she kept for tough times, Kelsie pushed him away. She was here to teach him social graces not to engage in a tongue tango.

Zach backed up a few steps, shaking his head, almost pawing the ground like a bull in the ring. "If you think that's going to make me change my mind, you can forget it."

"That was so not a good idea on many levels." She panted and fanned her face.

"Tell me about it." He leaned back against the steps with a sigh and glanced around. "I'll pay someone to clean up this place." As if what happened was all about the yard and not about this mutual attraction arcing between them.

Kelsie opened her mouth to thank him and get herself out of the garden reclamation business. Then she stopped dead in her beat-up shoes. All her life people bailed her out of her problems then perched her on a pedestal and admired her but never expected anything of substance and sacrifice from her. Sure, she'd sacrificed herself for ten years with a controlling husband, but not that type of sacrifice.

"No." She couldn't believe that word came out her mouth even as a plan formed in her mind. Zach considered her a selfish woman who'd never change. She had changed, and she'd act accordingly.

"No?" He stared at her, his mouth hanging open.

"No. I'll get volunteers to do it, and we'll do it for free. You can donate the money you'll save to a charity."

"What kind of charity?"

"One for battered women."

"Battered women, huh? What do you know about battered women?"

Too much when it came to being emotionally battered, but she'd be damned if she'd solicit his sympathy. "One of the many charities I organized when I was married to Mark." She tossed her ponytail as if the actual charity was of no consequence to her. He might as well continue to think the worst of her to keep him at arm's length.

He nodded and held out his hand. "Deal."

"Deal."

Now for the hard part. How to swing the deal she just made with him and with herself. Not just the gardening part but the hands-off the student part.

CHAPTER 7

A New Game Plan

Finished with her weekly meeting, Kelsie limped out of the coach's office, discouraged and beaten. HughJack spent the entire meeting staring at his computer, while Veronica stared down her nose. Neither was impressed by Kelsie's report, despite her attempts at sugar-coating and spin-doctoring.

She sat down in an empty reception area around the corner from the main doors to the practice facility, pulled off a shoe, and rubbed her throbbing foot. In the past week she'd gained a new respect for people who did physical labor for a living. She'd never see a gardener or repairman in the same way. There wasn't a muscle in her body that didn't ache, or a square inch of skin that wasn't red and chapped.

For the better part of the past week, Kelsie attempted to tackle Zach's yard, but instead it tackled her. She couldn't give up. Not now. Not when her goal hovered on the horizon. A stubborn linebacker and a jungle yard wouldn't deter her. Even if said yard harbored all sorts of nasty, greasy surprises, such as old car parts and garbage and disgusting creatures in the form of slugs big enough to cart off the house on their slimy backs.

Loneliness and longing were almost as bad as her physical pain, lonely for a friendly face and longing for a man who'd never forgive her. Men complicated everything, and she preferred things to stay as simple as possible until she rebounded from her current sorry state.

But she'd kissed him. Not just a nice sweet kiss, but an all-out assault in which she'd attempted to burrow under his skin or at least his clothes. This obsessing over him had to stop. She'd tasted that forbidden fruit for the last time. No more. She was a professional doing a professional job, and she would not *do* her client.

Mercy, but Kelsie needed someone to spill her woes to other than Scranton. Someone who'd be an ally in a harsh world. She craved true girlfriends, the type everyone else had, not the superficial ones she'd had all her life. Of course, you have to be a friend to have true friends. Kelsie was ready to be that type of friend if only someone would give her chance.

Someone like—

She heard a familiar voice and stilled, listening, certain her addled brain must have dredged up an answer to her prayers.

"I'm on my way, Vinnie. Where are we meeting?" Rachel Ramsey's voice drifted to where Kelsie sat. She held her breath, hoping she'd hear the location before Rachel exited out the door.

"Beachfront Pub? Got it. See you there in ten."

Talk about right-place, right-time. Kelsie had better start going to church because someone up their just might be playing on her team.

Slipping her shoe back on her foot, she ignored her protesting toes and stood. She walked up to the old security guy at the front desk and gave him her pageant-winning smile. "Where's the Beachfront Pub?"

He grinned as if she'd just gifted him a winning lotto ticket. A few minutes later, she hurried out of the building as fast as her bruised and blistered feet would carry her.

Kelsie drove ten minutes to the Kirkland waterfront area and parked in the restaurant lot. She glanced in the rear-view mirror, still feeling as if her face betrayed the effects of Zach's kiss last week. She touched her lips. Perhaps the physical evidence disappeared but in her mind those hungry lips of his still roamed across her mouth and face, wreaking havoc with her brain.

No more men. Not a one. Especially not an unsociable loner with the manners of a caveman and a chip on his shoulder larger than most continents.

No. No. No.

Just keep saying the words, Kel, some day you might really believe them.

Taking a deep breath to clear her mind and shore up her courage, she walked into the Beachfront Pub and paused in the doorway, scanning the tables. With the regal bearing of the beauty queen she once was, she wove between the tables to one near the window. Several men gazed appreciatively at her as she strolled by. She ignored them. They weren't part of her plan, now or ever. Two heads bent close together, one blonde, one brunette, gossiped away, totally unaware of her determined approach.

"Imagine meeting you here." Kelsie gushed, using her best girlfriend-to-girlfriend voice.

Both women glanced up at the same time. She caught the quick look between them, almost as if they were on to her but too polite to call her out on her deception.

"I thought I'd drop by for a quick bite."

Again that silent look between friends. A hesitation. Kelsie held her breath, praying they were as nice as she guessed they were.

Rachel smiled up at her, a friendly, open smile. "Please join us."

Lavender nodded her agreement as she sipped on a yummy looking foo-foo drink.

"I'd love to."

Rachel moved her purse out of the way, and Kelsie slid into the booth seat next to her. "I was in the area meeting with Coach

Jackson and Ms. Simms to discuss my progress on a special project."

"Zach's manners class? Tyler told me all about it." Lavender made a face, as if she didn't quite agree with Tyler spreading dirt about Zach.

"Tyler talks too much, and he holds his grudges near and dear to his heart." Rachel sighed.

"So does Zach." Kelsie knew that better than anyone. No sense denying the obvious.

"Tyler says you have Zach all tied up in knots. Mr. Invincible might not be so different from the rest of us." Lavender winked at her.

Kelsie shook her head, hoping to chop that rumor down. "Not those types of knots. He has good reason to dislike me, and he wallows in his grudges."

"Zach won't let it go with Tyler either. Their childish war is dividing the team. I don't understand why the coach allows it to happen."

Kelsie resisted the urge to defend Zach for the second time in a week. No reason to get her panties in a bunch over the truth. Zach did hold onto things long past their usefulness. "Zach's a bit of a stubborn, proud man."

"You knew him from high school?" Rachel signaled the waiter and a moment later one of the incredible drinks showed up in front of Kelsie.

"What is it?"

"Root beer float, only with alcohol instead of ice cream. It's our lunch tradition."

Kelsie sipped the drink and licked her lips. "Heavenly." She held her hands to her heart and looked upward. Rachel and Lavender laughed.

"Hey, sister, you're not distracting us that easily. Spill. You and Zach have a history," Lavender prompted.

Kelsie hesitated, not willing to tell all and paint herself in such an unfavorable light. "He hasn't changed much, except he has more money. In high school, he stayed to himself, looks like he still does." Thanks to her. She'd taught him a valuable lesson when it came to trusting people, and she felt like crap about it.

They ordered lunch, sipped their drinks, and made small talk. Kelsie had so missed female interaction. Her ex all but cut off her friends over the past ten years. He'd embraced her family because both her parents worshipped him as if he walked on water. She could do nothing right in their eyes and his.

A lull in the conversation gave Kelsie the in she needed. "Have you ever done something so stupid you can't figure out how to rectify it?"

"Of course." Lavender paused in mid-chew and studied her.

Rachel laughed. "All the time. I can't even walk on a flat surface without stumbling."

"I could help you with that."

The both stared at her, mouths open.

"You learn how to walk correctly in beauty queen school."

"Beauty queen school?" They said in unison.

Kelsie waved them off. "It's a long, boring story and not important to my problem."

"And that is?"

"When I accepted the job working with Zach, I wanted to sweeten the pot, go above and beyond, give the Jacks more than their money's worth."

"And you did what?"

"I agreed to help Zach host a black-tie fundraiser at his home on Queen Ann Hill with proceeds going to Veronica's favorite charity."

"You took on Veronica's Hearts for Homeless campaign? You're a brave woman. Isn't she, Rae?"

"You'll never do it well enough to please her."

"It's even worse than that. Have you seen Zach's home?" Kelsie picked up a breadstick and gnawed on it.

"Zach is a loner. No one's been invited to his place."

"Good thing. If they wandered off the front porch they'd never be heard from again."

"That bad?"

"You two know Zach. He's not into appearances. He's also a procrastinator. If it's not football, he puts it on a back burner."

Both women met each other's gazes and said in unison. "It is that bad."

"Is he hiring someone to clean it up?" Rachel ordered another round of drinks.

"No, I'm cleaning it up. I got Zach into this mess, and I feel responsible for taking on some of the chores, but I don't really have the cash to hire anyone."

"Girl, you are in deep doggie doo." Lavender grabbed her second drink and took a long suck on her straw.

"I know. Just shoot me. I was hoping we might put our heads together for the greater good. I'm desperate."

"You came to the right place." Lavender's smirk danced across her face. "Tyler might help."

"He hates Zach."

"Exactly. Which is why he'll help. When he finds out Zach isn't cleaning up the place, Ty will grab the offensive guys and jump right in. The place will be ready in no time."

Kelsie thought about it. "That might work, but what's the incentive besides making Zach look like an ass?"

"For Ty, that's enough. Besides I know how his mind works. He'll make it into a competition. Offense versus defense. Zach won't be able to resist the chance to best him. You wait and see."

"And poor Derek will be there to make sure they don't kill each other," Rachel sighed and checked her text messages.

"Do you think it'll work?" Kelsie looked at each of them. Both women's eyes gleamed with mischief.

"Oh, it'll work."

Right up to the point that Zach murdered her with his bare hands.

Kelsie drank up. She might as well enjoy life while she could.

* * * * *

Zach must have fallen asleep and been slammed awake in the middle of a war zone. He pulled the pillow over his head to drown out the sounds outside. Half-asleep, a weird dream swirled in his head—lots of noise, Harris barking orders, guys jaw-jacking with each other. Metal clanking against metal. Loud bangs, noises suspiciously sounding like small engines, pressure washers, brush cutters and the like roared in his head. A diesel truck idled near his window.

The bottom fell out of that space between asleep and awake and plunged him headfirst into reality. Zach shot up in bed, looking every which way in the large tower suite.

What the hell? More banging, more roaring, more guys shouting over the noise.

Not a dream. Not one fucking bit. Leaping out of bed, Zach yanked on a pair of sweats and a T-shirt and stomped through his house toward the location of the majority of the racket. He swung open his door with such force it slammed into the side of the house and shuddered as if it'd drawn its last breath. Hands on hips, Zach surveyed the organized chaos.

"What the hell is this?"

The closest guys averted their eyes and refused to answer. Zach stepped to the nearest machine and cut it off. It died with a sputtering choke, which was exactly what he planned to do to a certain someone or multiple some ones.

Harris stepped forward, a smirk as wide as the Columbia River on his face. "We're cleaning up this hell hole and helping out the pretty lady here. My guys and I are suckers for a damsel in distress."

The entire offensive team down to the lowliest rookie stopped what they were doing, shut off machines and stared. Silence replaced the earlier din as Zach squared off with Tyler. He opened his mouth to kick the quarterback off the property when he caught Kelsie out of the corner of his eye. She stood off to one side, dressed in ratty blue jeans, which looked incredible on her, a dirty white T-shirt, and scuffed tennis shoes. In her hands she held a small towel. Right now she was wringing the daylights out of the defenseless piece of cotton. Their eyes met, and he read her silent plea to play nice.

Fuck. This was Kelsie's stunt.

He glared at her, knowing she'd called his bluff big time. He might not like her. He might figure he owed her a whole lot of pain. Staring at those damn sky-blue eyes of hers, though, Zach couldn't be the heartless bastard he wanted to be.

Turning away from her before he fell to her feet and did her bidding, he narrowed his eyes and snarled at Harris. "Fine, I'll bring some real muscle, and we'll get some actual work done."

In response Harris turned on the pressure washer and cupped his hand to his ear. "What? I can't hear you. Did you say you'd call in more help?" He aimed the nozzle at Zach's feet, and Zach jumped back a few feet.

With a curt nod, he tromped back into the house, threw on some old jeans and started making calls. Five minutes later, he stepped out into the fall sun, shovel in one hand, loppers in another and went to work without a word. He'd be damned if Harris and his prima-donna offense would show up the real workhorses on the team.

Within five minutes fantasies of killing Tyler Harris started to override his good deed. The jerk barked orders as if he'd been named union boss on a road construction crew. Flipping Harris off, Zach stomped to the opposite side of the house and away from the QB. Several minutes later, his defensive players started showed up in several big-ass trucks and armed with lawn tools. They gathered round, waiting for instructions from their captain.

"We'll start on this side, they're starting on that side."

"Yeah, and we'll meet in the middle." Harris popped out from behind an overgrown Arborvitae like a fucking fairy in a Disney movie.

"Middle? Hell, we'll be three-quarters of the way down the back of the house before you ever turn the corner."

"Is that a bet?" Harris cocked his head and grinned.

"Yeah it is."

"All right, I'll bet we reach the back French doors before your guys."

"What does the winner get?"

"The loser buys beers for the other squad."

"And steak," LeDaniel, the rookie defensive end, ate as much as the entire defensive line.

"You're on." Harris slapped LeDaniel on the back. "Hope you're not too hungry, buddy."

"What if one side cheats and doesn't do a good enough job?" Brett, the goody-two-shoes backup QB, always thought about shit like that. Obviously, his mama never told him that life wasn't always fair.

Kelsie stepped forward. A strand of blond hair stuck to her flushed cheeks. "I'll be the judge of that. Everything needs to pass my inspection."

Zach groaned but Harris grunted his consent, then turned to his guys. "Hey, dipshits, quit gawking. Let's get to work." He stalked off with his posse.

Glancing at Kelsie, Zach stifled the odd urge to wrap his arms around her and kiss the hell out of her. He loved her messed up like that. He itched to pluck the hair off her cheek and wrap it around his finger. Beads of sweat moistened her forehead and made him fantasize about better ways to get her sweaty. Much more pleasant ways.

Kelsie leaned toward him. The scent of magnolias and grass clippings drifted to his nostrils. "Good luck, Zach." She spoke quietly so only he could hear, her words letting her allegiance be known.

"You want me to win?" A warm, content feeling curled up in his core like an old hound in front of a fire.

"It's your place, after all." Her gaze met his, suddenly all cool and distant, as if she needed to push him away before he got too close.

"Yeah." He stared down at his feet, pushing a rock around with his shoe. "I should've taken better care of it." He was the worst kind of fool. Of course, she wanted him to come out on top, it would be to her advantage.

"Well, you will from now on. At least until the gala. I'll see to it."

Why did her statement strike equal parts of hope and fear in his heart? Because she'd be underfoot or because he wanted her underfoot? "I'm sure you will."

"We'll start on the inside once we finish the outside."

Zach balked. Invading his privacy outside his house was one thing, but tramping into his house and seeing how he lived happened to be another. He didn't want Harris knowing anything about his personal life. It'd give the ass an opportunity to mine for weaknesses. "I'll take care of the inside."

Kelsie raised one eyebrow. "You will?"

He thought about that one. "You can help me."

"It'll take more than you and me to get this place cleaned up and in shape and keep it that way."

"Then get some friends to help, but not the entire team. No way in hell. And not Harris."

"Fine. I'll see what I can do." Kelsie strode off, as if he'd hit a nerve or something. *Women.*

Zach sighed and raked his fingers through his tangled hair. He hated dealing with stuff like haircuts, but he hated his hair long, too. He'd just as soon shave his head if it weren't so time-consuming. The last time he'd tried it, he'd just about bled out from several nicks on his head. Not a pretty sight unless it was Halloween.

"You got it bad, buddy."

Zach jumped as Tomcat snuck up beside him. "Dammit, quit surprising me like that."

"If she didn't have you all tied up in knots, you'd have heard me."

"She doesn't have me tied up in anything."

Tomcat barked out a loud snort. "Hey, it's me. I know you, bro. You've met your match with the pretty lady. She'll be leading you around by your dick in no time."

"Just cuz you like to be pussy whipped, doesn't mean I do." Tomcat married last fall to a fireball of a woman who put him in his place and loved him dearly. Zach served as best man. Actually, he adored LaShonna. It took a strong woman to tame a man like Tomcat. LaShonna was a strong woman, very strong.

"Yeah, well, stallions get corralled every day."

"And they get castrated every day. Not this stud."

"Suit yourself." Tomcat watched appreciatively as Kelsie moved from place to place, making suggestions on hedge trimming and directing a couple rookies with pieces of a broken concrete fountain to a nearby dumpster—a dumpster which hadn't been there a few hours ago. The rookies fell all over themselves to impress her.

Zach narrowed his eyes, not liking how his friend was looking at Kelsie. "You're married." He growled out a reminder.

"Hell, I know, but a man can look. She's a fine one. You should avail yourself of her charms, my man."

"I'm not availing myself of anything when it comes to that woman. We have a history. I might be dense, but I'm not a total idiot."

"A man-eater, huh?"

"Well, look at her. What do you think?"

"I think she looks mighty fine. If I were you, she could eat my manhood anytime she pleased." Tomcat elbowed him.

Zach sighed and turned his attention to the crow bitching at them from a bow of the nearby red cedar tree. "You know crows are actually good-looking birds, but they're scavengers eating off the misfortunes of others."

"Can't judge a bird by its feathers."

"Nope, you can't. The ugliest birds turn out to be the most useful, eating their weight in bugs and mosquitoes rather than eating garbage and bitching to the high heavens."

Tomcat raised one black eyebrow. Chuckling, he turned away and went back to work.

With a frustrated groan, Zach hacked at the overgrown rhododendron blocking the front windows of his house.

"Cut it down to a few feet off the ground. Open up the house to the sunlight." He didn't need to look to know Kelsie stood beside him. His body told him about two seconds before she opened those ruby red lips of hers.

"What sunlight? This is Seattle."

She laughed, a wonderful, heart-enslaving sound. Zach attacked the tree with the frustration of man who saw paradise and knew he couldn't have it because it was an illusion painted by a deceptive beauty with all the charm of a southern belle and the deviousness of a scam artist.

* * * * *

Later that evening Zach stood on his porch with his hands propped on his hips and surveyed his small kingdom in wonder. His yard bore no resemblance to the overgrown jungle it'd been just this morning. One-hundred-year-old giant, feral rhodies had been pruned back to manageable sizes. Trimming the bottom boughs on several huge cedars opened the view up considerably. Hell, he had a view he didn't know he had. Blackberry vines no longer wound their way through the yard like coils of barbed wire on a battlefield.

He had to hand it to Kelsie. When she set her mind to something, she worked like a stubborn dynamo. Her willingness to get her hands dirty and jump right in with the rest of them earned his grudging respect.

Zach shook his head. *Women.* No man in his right mind could figure them out, and no man wanted to dig through the mysterious recesses of their minds, especially not a devious mind like Kelsie's.

He cringed as he recalled her last words this evening as he walked her out to her car. *Tomorrow we start on the house.*

No way in hell did he want anyone poking through his house. He guarded his privacy like vicious dogs guarded a junk yard. No one knew the real Zach, not even Tomcat. This house was his sanctuary. He didn't want Kelsie or anyone else sissifying it to make it acceptable to some hoity-toity group of millionaires. He didn't give a shit what they thought, but he did give a shit about staying on the team.

Well, crap. What the heck choice did he have but to tidy up one room and limit the party to that area? Yeah, right. He could see Harris now. The ass would conduct tours of the worst parts of Zach's house just to embarrass the hell out of him.

He couldn't win for losing.

CHAPTER 8

A Loss on Downs

Kelsie pulled up in front of the old house converted into one-room apartments, where she'd rented a room two weeks ago. While the place wasn't exactly the Ritz, it beat living in her car.

For three days she'd slogged through Zach's treasures, which consisted of garbage most thrift shops would reject. She'd never seen so much junk in her life. She collected enough pop cans to fund an entire school's extra-curricular activities for a year. The guy never threw anything away. She'd make him watch that television show on hoarders and hopefully scare him straight. His aversion to using a garbage can definitely required an intervention.

Picking up Scranton, she mounted the creaky front steps and opened the flimsy front door. Trudging to the top of the stairs, she turned right down a narrow hall to the one-room studio smaller than her closet back home and a lot less elegant.

She stopped dead. All of her worldly belongings were stacked in a heap outside the door. A clasp on the door was locked with a hefty padlock. A note taped to the door ruffled in the breeze from a nearby open window.

She tore the note from the door and read it. She'd been evicted for not paying the rent due a few days ago. It had to be a mistake. She'd paid for a month.

"You need to leave this building now. Tenants only." Her former landlady stood near the stairwell, huffing from the exertion of climbing the steep stairs. Sweat dripped off her double chin and settled in the cleavage of her enormous boobs.

"Mrs. Tremain, there's been some mistake. I paid a month's rent."

"You paid for two weeks." In between the wheezing and coughing, the large woman didn't seem impressed.

"I gave you four hundred dollars." Kelsie portrayed an air of confidence. She'd straighten this out. It was all a misunderstanding.

"That's two weeks rent at two hundred a week."

"No, you said—"

"To hell with what you think I said, here's the agreement you signed." She flashed it in front of Kelsie's face. Kelsie snatched it from her and scanned it, stopped, and read it more slowly.

"But, I, I thought—"

"I don't give a flying rat's ass what you thought. This is what you signed. Pay another two weeks or get your skinny behind out of here."

Anything short of an elephant's butt would be a skinny ass compared to the one Kelsie's now former landlady sported. The catty thought gave her a teensy measure of satisfaction.

"I'll get it to you in a few days."

"You don't have it now?" The woman glanced at her watch, probably missing one of those reality shows about rednecks with mullets running a moonshine operation out of the back of their pawn shop and hunting for Sasquatch in their spare time.

"No, but—"

"Sorry, missy, I don't do charity. If I fell for every sob story, I'd be broke." Mrs. Tremain glanced at her watch again and tapped her foot impatiently. "You have five minutes to get your crap and yourself out of here before I call the police." The woman waddled off, her heavy footsteps thudded on the stairs. A second later the door slammed to her first floor apartment.

Well, at least in jail she'd be warm and get three meals a day. Kelsie shuddered. Perish the thought. She'd never survive in jail, not with the sheltered life she'd led. Those women would chew her up and spit her out.

Kelsie sank to the floor and buried her face in her hands. Her tears fell like Seattle rain. Scranton placed his little paws on her shoulder and licked her face. She held him tight as her tears wet his wiry poodle coat, badly in need of a clip. Even her dog looked like a mutt, just like Kelsie must.

She'd no one to blame but herself. She'd spent too much money on stupid stuff. Not to mention, using the last of her dollars to pay for a second dumpster load. Funny how quickly one thousand dollars drained from her bank account like a wound that wouldn't stop bleeding.

Until Zach's gala, she'd not see another penny from the Jacks. She'd be back to living in her car with the nights getting colder and danger lurking in the darkness. Not that she'd seen any evidence of being followed lately, but then again, maybe she'd been too busy to notice.

Tucking Scranton under her arm, she started stuffing her clothes into suitcases. After a dozen or more trips, she'd loaded everything in her car. The entire time, Mrs. Tremain watched, hands on her ample hips and a scowl on her face. The woman stood on the sagging front porch as Kelsie struggled down the stairs with her last load and watched as she drove away.

The late September sun gave way to angry gray clouds and a heavy mist of rain, pretty much matching her mood. Her first inclination was to run to Zach. Despite their past, he'd take her in because that was the kind of man he was. Only she didn't want his pity, nor did she want to be under his thumb, to let him realize how he held all the cards, while she played with an empty deck. Despite being financially and emotionally wrecked, Kelsie had her pride and her hard-won independence. Going to Zach would surrender both.

When she'd finally left Mark, she'd made a promise to never put herself in a situation where she depended on a man for her very existence. She wouldn't do it now. She'd rather live in her car. Only where to park said car?

As she rounded a street corner on a virtually deserted side street, headlights shone in her rearview mirror, momentarily blinding her. Frowning and feeling a bit paranoid, she turned down another street. The black sedan followed a few blocks back. Another turn. Still, it was there. Kelsie slipped down an alley. The car followed. Heart pounding in her chest, she gunned it out of the alley, through a yellow light, and around another corner. She caught a glance at the sedan stuck behind cars at the lights.

Patting herself on the back for getting away did nothing to alleviate the fears. Her hands shook on the steering wheel and her insides churned like an angry ocean. It'd been a few weeks since she'd been followed. She'd all but convinced herself the guy had been a figment of her wild imagination.

Only he wasn't. He was all too real. And he was back.

She recalled Mark's final words to her: *I'm not done with you. I'll make your life a living hell. Keep looking over your shoulder. You'll never know when I'll show up.* At the time, she convinced herself they were idle threats spoken by a man accustomed to having things his way, except for a divorce he hadn't wanted.

Kelsie drove around for several minutes, chewed on her already trashed fingernails, and found herself on Zach's street, despite her best intentions. Somehow being near the big lug gave her security. The type of security she'd not felt in quite a few years.

No lights shone in the windows of his big house. Good. She inched into his driveway and squeezed her little car between his garage and a hedge of holly in a spot she knew was not visible from the house and couldn't be seen from the street.

It took several minutes for her heart to stop thumping, and her pulse to return to near normal. She gnawed on a piece of beef jerky she'd grabbed earlier from Zach's house and drank some bottled water. Hopefully she wouldn't need to pee until morning. Being homeless sucked big time. When she started making money, she'd never again callously disregard a person holding a sign on the street corner.

Angling her seat back, Kelsie huddled under a couple coats and a blanket. Scranton burrowed under the layers with her and curled up in a ball on her chest. Pretty soon his snoring echoed through the quiet evening.

Sure, she could ask Rachel or Lavender for help. They'd take her in, but she didn't want to be in their way or cramp their love lives. Besides, Zach, so far, didn't have any social life to cramp. In fact, her job included helping the loner build a healthy social life, even if she died trying. Except for her sleeping accommodations, this was perfect. He'd never see her parked here. Plus, the guy left home before sun-up and came back after sundown.

So for now, she'd sleep in her car, spend all her spare time at Zach's. Maybe she could eat and shower there. Sleep inside during away games. She huddled deeper under the coats, wondering if she could sneak in and sleep on the couch if it got too cold.

Yeah, it could work. It wasn't the best plan, but it was a plan. Kelsie closed her eyes, comforted by knowing Zach slept a few yards away.

* * * * *

Zach dropped into the chair across the table from Kelsie. He hated fancy restaurants, hated dressing up, hated wasting the money. Besides, he wasn't in the best of moods anyway. The team lost another game, making their record two and two. He needed to be studying game film not wasting his time with this bullshit.

With a long-suffering sigh, he glanced up at Kelsie. She stood behind her chair, glaring at him. His brows drew together as he gazed up at her. She gave him one of those look-down-her-nose frowns. He'd messed up. Again. He racked his brain in an attempt to figure out what useless rule he'd violated this time.

"You're forgetting something."

"Uh." He glanced around, not that he'd find the answer anywhere but, damn, he couldn't remember all this crap. He had a brain for football plays not for etiquette. "You look like nice tonight."

She continued to stand. He jumped to his feet and stood, vaguely recalling he shouldn't sit until she did. Only she didn't sit. She shook her head as if he was the most clueless moron she'd ever been saddled with, which was just about right, he figured.

Zach sighed, feeling like an idiot without a clue. "I take it that's not it."

"Zach, are you honestly this oblivious?"

"Yeah, probably." He raked a hand through his hair, smoothing it out, yet the action made her frown all the more. "I don't know what you want."

"A gentleman pulls out a lady's chair for her."

"Ah, hell." With an annoyed sigh, he lumbered to her side and yanked out her chair. She sat down with exaggerated daintiness. He shoved the chair up to the table, dropping back into his own seat.

"Try it again."

"Are you fu—" Zach paused. "Flipping kidding me?"

"Keep your voice down. People are staring." Kelsie glanced around the room. Zach noted the various people looking down their royal noses at him, just like Kelsie did. "We'll keep practicing it until you get it right, understand? This is your test. We've gone over fine dining for the past week."

Zach tugged on the collar of his shirt. "I hate ties."

"I know, you've told me a thousand times over." Kelsie moved to stand beside the chair. "Do it just like we practiced it."

Zach glowered at one old lady in particular who wouldn't stop staring. She quickly looked away and whispered something to her equally wrinkled companion.

Kelsie shot him an impressive evil eye as she sat down. He didn't know the beauty queen had it in her.

"That was inexcusably rude." Kelsie folded her hands in her lap.

Zach imitated the gesture. "So what? She was rude."

Kelsie was doing a lot of sighing. "You just don't get it. Even though I dress you up, make you comb your hair and shave, you still look like a feral man posing in a suit, more at home in your bare skin than clothes of any kind."

He shrugged, not doubting the truth.

"Next week we're getting you a civilized haircut and a decent suit."

"Not on your life. All this fancy-assed crap is bad enough without you turning me into some pansy like Harris."

"I hadn't noticed Harris was a pansy. He seems quite masculine to me."

Irritation flowed through him. He hated being compared to Harris and found lacking. "You seemed to like a real man when I kissed you."

She didn't rise to the bait. "Zach, I need you to put some effort into retaining this information."

"Listen, every minute I spend on this useless garbage is one less minute I spend watching game film."

"Haven't you watched enough game film over the years?"

Zach didn't expect her to understand. Nobody understood but his teammates. It was about the game. It was always about the game. Nothing mattered but the game. Football was all he'd ever had, and all he ever would have. He'd fight heaven and hell to keep it in his life until he drew his dying breath. Kelsie wouldn't get that, not at all. She'd never played the game. How could anyone who'd never felt the sting as pads smacked against pads, swallowed the gritty taste of dirt in their mouth, or smelled the freshly mown grass understand the brotherhood each player felt with his teammates—well, expect for Harris.

"I want a ring. In order to get one, I have to be able to dissect everything the opposing offense is capable of doing, every week. I'm the one who calls the defensive formations. I'm the defensive captain. The guys look up to me and expect nothing less. I can't let them down, but this damn manners crap is interfering with my ability to be a good defensive captain and teammate."

Kelsie sighed. "I'm not doing this because I get a perverse pleasure out of it. I'm doing it because it's my job, and Lumberjacks' management is paying me to teach you some social graces. If you'd cooperate, we'd spend less time going over the same information."

"You sure you don't get a perverse pleasure out of making me jump through hoops?" He frowned at her, certain she did just that. After all, it was all about what Kelsie wanted, always had been.

"Believe what you want. I have a job to do. So do you. Your job is to learn some basic manners so you don't embarrass the team in social situations." She snapped her napkin at him then folded it neatly in her lap.

Zach imitated her actions, down to the napkin snap. "Happy?"

"Ecstatic. You could turn down the charm a little. It's blinding me."

In spite of himself, Zach laughed. Hell, he didn't possess a charming bone in his big body, and they both knew it.

"Now order a bottle of wine and go through everything like we practiced it."

"You mean sniffing the cork and all that bullshit?"

"Yes, all that bullshit."

Zach grinned. "Keep it up, and you'll be sounding like me."

"Not a chance in thousand lifetimes." She graced him with one of her dazzling smiles, the same smile she used on him in high school when she needed a lackey to do some kind of dirty work for her. In a way she still did. She needed him to mind his manners so she could get a hefty contract with the Jacks and torture more unsuspecting players with her lethal charm.

Despite all she'd done to him, he'd cooperate because he didn't have an option, and somewhere deep inside, he wanted to please her.

CHAPTER 9

Illegal Use of the Hands

Zach froze and listened. A sound, just a slight sound. There, he heard it again. Snoring? Someone, somewhere snored in his house—and it wasn't him.

He pulled back the covers and stood, wading through the clothes littering the floor. He grabbed the Alex Rodriguez autographed Louisville Slugger on the dresser and hefted it in his hands. He'd locked up his hunting rifles downstairs in the gun safe. The bat would have to do.

A sliver of a moon shone through the open blinds. Zach slept with the window open, liking fresh air and a frigid bedroom. He wasn't scared exactly, but adrenaline ran hard and strong through his veins.

Wielding the bat, he crept through the house toward the noise. A floorboard creaked under his feet. He froze and listened. Again, the snoring. From his den, the room Kelsie called his man cave. He peeked around the corner of the doorway and spotted a figure huddled under a blanket on his couch.

Damn.

He could almost understand an intruder sleeping in his house back when the yard made the place look abandoned. But now? As a matter of course, he sympathized with the homeless. Heck, he'd been homeless himself a time or two in high school. He'd dedicated every Tuesday night for the past twelve years toward working with homeless kids, but he didn't appreciate one sleeping on his couch uninvited.

He paused. A heavenly fragrance floated toward him and nudged his memory. At least this person didn't smell. In fact, he smelled damn good. Maybe some cross-dressing guy or something.

A little black nose poked out of the edge of the blanket. A pair of dark, beady eyes glared at him and a small threatening growl sounded from the little rat. Only it wasn't a rat, it was Kelsie's despicable little foo-foo dog, Scranton. Which meant the body under the covers happened to be Kelsie's.

What the hell was she doing sleeping on his couch?

His dick immediately rose to the occasion, always up for a pretty woman lying on his furniture. Damn, the thing needed to learn some discretion. Kelsie was a man-eater, not a woman to be toyed with if a man planned on keeping his balls intact and his heart whole. Not that she hadn't already bitten off several pieces from both.

Crawling out from under the blanket, Scranton stood on top of Kelsie's chest. He growled again and showed his tiny yellow teeth. The hair stuck straight up on his back, which looked ludicrous and non-threatening on a scruffy poodle.

Kelsie moaned and rolled over, knocking the dog—if you could call it that—to the floor.

Picking himself up, the little shit launched himself at Zach's ankles, as if his ejection from bed was Zach's fault. His little teeth buried in Zach's skin like a thousand needles. He tried to shake off the vermin without really hurting it.

"Dammit, let go, you little shit."

Kelsie sat up, rubbing her eyes.

"Call this damn thing off, would you?"

Instantly awake, Kelsie leapt up and pulled Scranton into her arms. The little shit continued to growl and snarl at him. "You scared him."

"I scared *him*?"

"Yes, don't sneak up on us like that."

"Sneak up on you? You're in my house." Leave it to a woman to twist this around into being his fault. "I heard snoring."

"Scranton snores like a big dog." Confusion replaced her usual cool demeanor. She stared up at him all rumpled from sleep and sexy as hell. Her normally perfectly styled blond hair stuck up in places and was plastered to her head in others.

"No shit. He woke me up all the way upstairs." He found her messiness adorably appealing. Her vulnerability called to every protective male instinct he possessed.

"He has a bit of a respiratory problem."

"A bit? He sounds like my Uncle Wes after his billionth cigarette."

She shrugged. Scranton lifted one side of his lip, showing some teeth.

"What are you doing here? It's five a.m."

"Oh, it is? Sorry. I was working so hard I didn't want to quit."

"You weren't working. You were wrapped in a blanket sleeping on my couch."

"I was just taking a nap before I went back at it."

He didn't believe her, not one bit. Whatever her reason for staying here couldn't happen again. Not if he intended to keep her out of his bed and his heart. After that kiss a week ago, he'd be hard pressed to do so if she crashed on his couch again. Funny how life changed. He didn't have a clue what her deal was, but she'd definitely come down in the world. Perhaps she'd sniffed out a temporary sugar daddy and figured she'd move in and make herself comfortable.

Not going to happen.

This Zach didn't fall prey to conniving women. This Zach had been down that road a time or two too many. Especially with this woman.

If Zach didn't have money, she'd never give him a second look. That's how women like her operated.

Why she'd left her big-shot lawyer husband with his political aspirations, Zach didn't understand. Those two shallow people made a perfect pair. There was a story here, but he didn't give a damn what it was. Lord, just get him through the next several weeks with his heart intact and his dick zipped inside his jeans.

Kelsie sat on the edge of couch. Even with the weary lines around her eyes and her defeated gaze she still radiated a natural beauty which put other women to shame. She looked so lost and discouraged. He grabbed the back of a chair to stop his feet from carrying him across the room to her. His ankle stung like hell where the rat's teeth had left holes in his skin.

Squaring her shoulders, Kelsie gazed up at him, a new resolve in her sky-blue eyes. "Well, time to get back to work." She looked him up and down. Her gaze stalled out in the vicinity of his bare chest.

Zach's balls tightened and his cock ached to have her. "Hey, I'm going back to bed. Don't make noise."

"Yes, sir." She shot to her feet, stood at attention, and sketched a salute.

A chuckle caught in Zach's throat when he caught sight of her nipples through the thin material of her t-shirt. She wasn't wearing a bra, and he wished she wasn't wearing anything. Their gazes met. Her eyes turned a dark, smoky blue, looking a lot like desire. At least he wanted to believe it was desire.

Zach's feet carried him across the room in a few long strides before he could jumpstart his common sense with a kick to the ass. So much for all his bullshit declarations regarding staying away from women like her.

He reached out, drew her in and crushed her tall, slender body to his big burly one.

She stared up at him, as her hands dangled limply at her sides. Her eyes fluttered shut as his mouth descended on hers. He couldn't stop himself, and she made no move to stop him. He tasted her lips, sweet as his grandma's homemade vanilla caramels. He'd loved those caramels, but not as much as he loved Kelsie's lips.

She hesitated for a moment, then wrapped her arms around his neck. Her soft lips moved against his, promising to make all his fantasies come true. His head denied it all. But his head wasn't in charge right now. He angled his mouth, deepened the kiss. His tongue engaged in a sensual dance with her tongue and the rest of his body wanted some of that action.

Kelsie let his lips have their way. In fact, she encouraged him. Her body relaxed against his. Her hips leaned into his hips. Filling his big palms with her fine butt, he pulled her midsection against his dick, rubbing her up and down against him. She hooked one of her legs around his waist, angled her hips to grind her crotch against his.

Sweet and wild, prim and proper Kelsie had hidden an erotic streak that would challenge even a jaded man like him. He nibbled on her lower lip before plunging his tongue back into her mouth.

"Zach. Oh, Zach." Her throaty whimper almost brought him to his knees, while her tongue tangled with his.

Something in her voice struck him as odd and penetrated into his fuzzy brain. She was using him for his money, for what he could do for her business. She didn't care about him. Sex was just another way to control a man. She knew all the tricks and most likely had learned quite a few more since she'd been in high school.

Don't trust her.

Once he slept with her, it'd be all over. He'd be her slave, do anything she wanted. Then she'd dump his ass for the next pretty boy who came along and offered more than Zach. She was the beauty to his beast. It'd never work. She never meant for it to. The sooner he got that in his thick skull, the better. He was a means to an end, not the final goal.

Calling on every ounce of willpower he possessed, Zach let go and jerked away from her. Rapidly backing up, he put several feet between them and extended his arms, palms out, to keep her away.

Kelsie looked up at him through heavy-lidded eyes and confusion flitted across her features. Worrying on her lower lip with her teeth, she smoothed her hair back from her face. Her breasts rose and fell, and her nipples poked against the cotton fabric. He couldn't drag his gaze away from her chest until Kelsie wrapped her arms around herself as if protecting her body from his ogling. He really was an uncouth beast and an idiot to boot.

Unable to face her or himself, Zach fled the room like a cowardly kicker as the opposing team bore down on him.

* * * * *

Shivering in the cold room, Kelsie waited until minutes later when she heard Zach's old truck rumble out of the driveway and down the street. She ran to her car and stuffed a bag with clean clothes, makeup, and shampoo.

Entering his bathroom, she touched a finger to her lips where Zach's rough mouth teased hers only moments earlier. Dazed, she shook off the aftereffects of an erotic journey with an untamed man. If Zach hadn't ended it, she'd be vertical on the couch right now with his big body on top of hers, moving over her, inside her.

Such thoughts should've horrified her. Instead, the wetness between her legs increased, and the rest of her body echoed a resounding "yes."

The man exuded sex appeal albeit in a primitive way. Perhaps primitive appealed to her. Perhaps she'd had her fill of deceptively cultured men, men who knew how to dress and act while they lied and led double lives. Maybe she'd traded in that false dream for one of a man who said what he thought and didn't fret the consequences. An honest man. A rare breed in her world. Or at least her former world.

Turning on the water for the jetted tub, Kelsie stripped off her clothes. Glancing around and not finding any bubble bath, she poured a generous amount of Zach's cheap shampoo into the water and climbed into a warm, soapy heaven. She pressed the button for the jets, and sank down into the water. The pulsing jets didn't cure what ailed her. She needed a man's hands on her body, a man's penis inside her, and a man's lips on her breasts. But the man she wanted had just rejected her.

But she had the jets and her imagination.

As if she'd done this before—which she hadn't—she spread her legs wide, bracing her feet against the side of the tub and positioned herself so one of the jets hit just the right spot. She pulled her nether lips apart and adjusted her hips until the needle-tight, pulsing spray of warm water caressed the folds of her sex. She turned up the jets and slipped a finger deep inside her. Letting the water stroke her aroused clit, she thrust her finger in and out. Her orgasm built inside her, compounded by the water assaulting her clit and her finger creating its own brand of sexual pleasure. She imagined Zach's big hands on her body, running up her sides, cupping her breasts, tweaking the nipples, finally sliding between her legs. He'd part her thighs and plunge two fingers to the knuckles inside her, moving them in and out in a rhythm. Then he'd replace those fingers with his large body. His penis would slide inside her, filling her, his sweaty, hot body rubbing against hers.

Oh, mercy. Saints in heaven, save her from this man.

Kelsie pumped her fingers harder. Harder. Harder. She came in a rush, crying out into the large, empty bathroom. "Zach. Oh, Zach. Yes. Yes. Yes."

She closed her eyes and let her orgasm carry her away until her slamming heart slowed in her chest and the blood stopped pounding in her ears. Far off in the distance, she heard a noise, like heavy footsteps. She blinked several times, trying to process her thoughts. A sound much like a man's gasp penetrated the haze. She craned her neck toward the door.

"I forgot my wallet." Zach stood a few feet away, staring down at her. His brown eyes dilated and his nostrils flared, he looked every bit the wild, untamed male ready to claim his mate.

And she felt every bit like the female wanting to be claimed.

* * * * *

Zach couldn't move, not even to blink.

Kelsie started to scramble out of the tub, must have realized he'd see her in all her naked glory, then sank back into the water. Oh, God, he should've kept walking when he'd peeked in the bathroom to see what all the groaning and splashing was about.

He'd almost expected to see her getting it on with one of his teammates, maybe a rookie with a big contract. Instead, he'd caught her getting it on with his jetted tub.

He couldn't leave. Not now. He'd die first, and his randy body would never forgive him. Despite every warning bell jangling in his head, his body ruled this moment. She looked so hot and sexy in his tub, her eyes half-lidded from coming. Soap subs concealed part of her body but not those perfect nipples he'd dreamed about from adolescence to adulthood. He had to sample her. Just this once. He had to know if the fantasy came anywhere close to the reality, had to touch the creamy skin, had to sink his hands under the water and find her sweet spots.

She started to lift her body out of the tub. He put a restraining hand on her shoulder. The hot, wet contact traveled through his fingers, up his arm, and straight into his bloodstream, immediately disengaging his brain and engaging other parts. "Don't move. You look like a woman who could use a man's touch instead of her own." His voice sounded foreign to his own ears, deep and gravelly and barely in control.

Zach hesitated briefly, giving her a moment to protest. She didn't. He shucked out of his jeans, briefs, and T-shirt in record time. Kelsie swallowed and licked her lips, her eyes on his erection.

Oh, God, thank you for this gift from heaven.

He sank to his knees next to the tub. She met him halfway. Her warm, plump lips welcomed his. The next thing he knew, she thrust her tongue into his mouth, taking the lead. He let her have it. Gladly. She sucked his tongue into her mouth, circled it with her own tongue, breathed life into him like no woman ever had. Her soapy breasts rubbed against his hairy chest. A groan was ripped from his throat, as she kissed him with reckless enthusiasm.

Out of breath, she pulled back, a smile on her face, and a wicked twinkle in those blue eyes. "There's room for two in here."

"Oh, yeah." He grinned and started to get into the tub. She splayed a hand across his chest to halt him.

"Condom?"

"Oh. Yeah. Condom." She wanted him to get a condom? That meant they were doing it. Really doing it. He scrambled to his feet and ripped open drawers in the bathroom vanity. Stuff went flying as he frantically look for a condom. Oh, crap. Where the hell was one? It wasn't like he brought women here or even had women during the season.

Damn. Damn. Damn.

Faster than he hustled onto a football field, he hustled into the bedroom and rummaged through drawers, desperate to find one condom. Nothing. He ran down the stairs, taking them three at a time, out to his truck. Checked the glove box. There had to be a condom somewhere.

Only there wasn't. Not one. Not a damn one.

His dick shriveled in disappointment.

He trudged back upstairs, back to the bathroom. Kelsie was out of the tub and in his bathrobe, staring at him with shuttered eyes. He'd taken too long. His shoulders slumped, and he leaned against the door jamb, attempting to look casual.

"I thought you'd changed your mind." She shot him a tentative smile as she pulled on a pair of very small panties. Her gaze flicked to his dick, and it immediately rose to attention.

"I couldn't find a damn condom." Frustration seeped into his voice, he couldn't help it.

She shrugged and stared at the floor. "Call it divine intervention. So not a good idea. You and me, that is."

Hell, he'd known that, but he hadn't cared when he'd seen her masturbating in his tub. The blood returned to his brain as it escaped his penis, like troops retreating from a losing battle.

Without a word, he quickly pulled on his clothes and left the house for the second time this morning, before they both changed their minds and decided to go with unprotected sex.

Someone up there was looking out for him.

Damn it.

CHAPTER 10

Blitzed

A few nights later, Zach cradled the urn he'd carried around with him for sixteen years. He ran a hand across his eyes to wipe off a combination of rain and tears. He swallowed around the big lump in his throat, then he carefully placed his baby brother's ashes in the small hole he'd dug in his backyard.

Wade, his younger brother by two years, stood next to him and hiccupped, drawing his sleeve across his face. Zach bowed his head and slid a glance at Wade. His brother's brows scrunched together then he bent his own dark head.

Clasping his hands in front of him, Zach pushed the words past the boulder-sized lump in his throat. "I don't know if you're really out there, God, but I hope you are. I hope life doesn't end after we die because our little brother deserves a better life than the short one he got on earth."

"Amen." Wade's voice cracked from the pain of their shared loss.

"Amen." Zach raised his head and picked up the shovel. Grief shot sharp arrows of agony through his heart. He tossed the first shovel full of dirt into the hole. Wade took the shovel from him and followed his lead. The only sound was the thud, thud, thud of the dirt landing in the hole and the patter of raindrops on the ground.

Dropping the shovel, Zach raised his face to the skies. Big drops of rain pelted his forehead, ran down his cheeks, into his eyes, plastering his hair to his head. He didn't care. Not one bit.

Neither did Wade. Their clothes stuck to them like they'd fallen overboard on stormy seas. In some ways they had.

Zach picked up a cool marble slab the size of a coffee-table book. Kneeling down, he placed it on top of the exposed earth. He ran a finger over the indentations on the marble, squinting in the light of dusk to read aloud the words he'd committed to heart.

Gary Joseph Murphy
Beloved brother and best friend
Finally home at last
Rest in peace

Looking skyward again, the rain mixed with his tears. "I promised you a big Victorian home with a view one day, little brother. I hope you like it." His last couple of words hung in the air with no other sound than the patter of a steady rainfall.

Finally, Wade cleared his throat. "He loves it." His brother pushed at loose dirt with his toe and shoved his hands in the pockets of his raincoat.

The rain stopped as if the hand of God moved across the skies. A few rays of the setting sun poked through the clouds, spreading diamonds of light across the waters of Puget Sound below. A ferry chugged toward Elliot Bay, delivering residents to downtown Seattle. Large fir trees stood on guard around the yard as a slight breeze rustled their limbs. The stately old mansion embraced them like a grandmother welcoming her grandchild home from war.

It was the type of view he and Gary dreamed of having one day.

Zach's mind transported him back to the trailers he'd lived in, the cars, the back alleys. His family never lived anywhere more than a few months before their dad started drinking again and lost whatever current job he'd managed to finagle. Then they'd be booted out on their asses and sent on their way. Each place was worse than the one before it or not a place at all but a car or a tent.

Until that night.

That fateful night exactly seventeen years to the day was burned into Zach's memory like a wildfire ravaging the landscape of the forest, leaving ugly black scars. Wade and Zach were big enough their father couldn't overpower them anymore. Not so Gary, who'd always been more sickly and slight then his older brothers, and they'd become his protector.

That weekend their father had been languishing in jail again. Zach didn't even remember for what. Their mother was having an affair with a bottle and had passed out on the living room couch. Life as normal in the Murphy household. Wade slipped out for a hot date.

Despite the possibility that the asshole who fathered them could be released at any time, Zach couldn't resist attending a local beauty pageant to lust over the unattainable Kelsie. She'd actually mentioned the pageant to him that morning in biology class, which was as good as an invitation in Zach's book. He'd snuck into the back row of the auditorium, clutching pink grocery-store roses in his big hand.

Kelsie had strutted her stuff in a skimpy evening gown, while he'd fantasized about touching her creamy skin and kissing those plump, pink lips. Afterward, he'd paced back and forth at the backstage door, rehearsing his words, and working himself into a lather.

Kelsie waltzed out the door on the arm of Mark Richmond, the team's star quarterback. She glanced Zach's way. Her blue eyes flicked to the flowers in his hand, and so did her date's.

"Give it up, Murphy. She's too good for you." Richmond laughed and ushered Kelsie toward his car. She glanced over her shoulder, her expression full of pity, shame, or disgust. He'd never been sure which.

Defeated, Zach walked the three miles home, head down, tail between his legs. A block from his house, flashing lights had illuminated the usually dreary neighborhood. A crowd gathered on the pot-hole filled street to gape at the house with yellow, crime scene tape wrapped around it.

The very shack his dysfunctional family called home.

Wade stood alone near the crime scene tape. When he caught sight of his big brother, he threw his arms around Zach and sobbed a few coherent words. "He did it."

"Did what?" Even then he knew the worst had happened.

"Shot Mom and beat Gary with a baseball bat. They don't think Gary will make it through the night." The anguish in Wade's voice almost destroyed Zach, but he had to be strong for Wade and Gary.

The Cactus Prairie police had already hauled their father off to jail. Zach swore if he ever set eyes on that man again, he'd kill him. At fifteen Wade got sent to a great-aunt's in Ontario. Zach's coach took him in, not out of any burning desire to help him, but because his senior year of football was underway and the team needed him.

Gary hung on surrounded by tubes and machines. Zach spent every spare second holding vigil over his brother's hospital bed.

Zach turned away from the view of Pudget Sound and glanced up at the bathroom window, recalling Kelsie's soapy wet skin in his bathtub. She'd been his weakness then, and she still was. Several months later Gary succumbed to his injuries. That very night Zach went to the country club dance still reeling from Gary's death hours earlier and hoping a night with Kelsie would help ease his pain. It hadn't. She'd ripped his heart out that night in more ways than one. He'd never forgiven her. How did a person forgive that depth of cruelty?

Some of the most traumatic events in his teenage life were linked to Kelsie, as if she were his bad luck charm or something.

Damn, he'd almost slept with her a few mornings ago. He'd known from the moment he'd first spotted her in his freshman home room class that if he ever did it with her, there'd be no turning back. His heart would be lost to her forever.

All these years later, that bald fact still echoed the raw truth. He could not sleep with Kelsie. He'd never recover. She'd use him and leave him and his irreparably broken heart in her wake as she jetted off after a better catch.

Kelsie had to be down on her luck, living in some dump that she didn't want to go home to at night. Why else was she in his bathtub? Why did she avoid telling him where she lived? Maybe she was living in a homeless shelter. Zach shook his head, finding it hard to believe her life had sunk that low. Not Kelsie. She'd find some way to manipulate some poor fool into parting with his money just for pleasure of gazing on her beauty every day.

Some poor fool like him.

"Hey," Wade spoke softly.

Zach gave a guilt start and blinked rapidly. He'd forgotten his brother was even there. "I have to be getting back to the airport. I've got a game tomorrow." Wade played damn good hockey on an NHL team that was currently a Stanley Cup contender.

"I'll drive you."

"Nah, don't worry about it. I'll get a taxi."

"You sure?"

"Positive." To prove his point, Wade used his fancy smartphone to call for a ride. Sticking it back in his pocket, he turned to Zach. "How about a quick beer before I go?"

"Yeah, sure." They walked inside. Zach snagged a couple brews from the fridge, popped the tops, and handed one to his brother, the only person left on this earth that he cared about other than his teammates.

Wade's eagle eyes dissected him like they'd dissect an opposing team's goalie. "How's everything going?"

"We're two and two, but we'll get it together. Lots of young players on this team."

"You and I've been stuck on some shitty teams over the years." Wade held up his bottle. "Here's to winning the Cup and a ring before we retire."

Zach clinked his bottle against his brother's. "We will."

"Yeah, we will. I hear rumors Seattle might be getting an NHL team."

"Sounds like it."

"Who knows? Maybe I'll end up here." A car horn honked from the front of the house. "That's my ride, Zach. Take care, okay." He held his hand out to Zach. In a rare display of affection, Zach pulled Wade into a bear hug. Being men's men, they didn't linger.

"Have a safe trip."

"I will."

Zach followed him to the front porch and watched the taxi drive away. Just like that, Wade walked back to his own life and left Zach alone with his memories and his guilt.

A few roses grew on the once wild but now trimmed bush near the walkway. Hell, he hadn't even realized he had roses until the team descended upon his yard. Stepping off the porch, Zach tore a deep orange rose from its stem, ignoring the thorns biting into his fingers. Roses reminded him of Kelsie, beautiful but with the ability to inflict pain.

Zach squatted next to his brother's final resting place. He laid the rose on top of the marble. Gary liked orange. Orange and blue had been his junior high team's colors. He'd strutted around in his jersey on Zach and Wade's game days, proud as their pit bull after he'd chased off the neighbor's cat—the same pit bull his father shot in the head while the kids watched because the animal dug in the backyard. Like anyone noticed with all the weeds and garbage. Bottom line: Zach knew the old man did the dog in because the kids loved their pet.

Gary had to be in a better place, smiling down on him right now from his seat on a fluffy cloud surrounded by junk food. Gary had loved junk food, the greasier the better. Surely in heaven, a guy didn't need to worry about clogging his arteries, if angels even had arteries.

Zach buried his head in his hands as a sob welled up in his throat. He didn't fight it. The tears he'd never shed all those years ago slipped down his cheeks. No one would see him. Harris might love to probe for weaknesses, but the guy had better things to do than hide in the bushes waiting to revoke Zach's man card.

He couldn't even work up the energy to give a shit about Harris right now. The harsh reality of things put a jerk like that in perspective. Zach would tolerate an entire team of Harrises just to see his little brother's smile one last time.

Shaking off the bittersweet memories, Zach swiped viciously at the tears and rubbed his eyes. He stood and almost fell on his ass. His right leg tingled all the way up to his hip from lack of circulation. He stomped it on the ground, ignoring the spikes of pain.

The rain started again.

"Good night for now, little brother. I love you."

Zach tried the back door and found it locked. Walking around the house to the porch, he dropped into the creaky porch swing, not wanting to go inside just yet. He must have fallen asleep because when he woke he was cold and stiff. He stood and stretched, his hand on the doorknob when a flash of light pulled his attention to the street. Ever since the team cleared his property, Zach's view of the street had opened up. A dark sedan extinguished its headlights and drove slowly up the block.

Keeping to the shadows he stepped off the porch and behind a sturdy old cedar and peered around a trunk bigger than a fifty-gallon drum. The car, similar to the one he'd seen at Jacks headquarters a few weeks ago stopped directly in front of his house. A few seconds later, it crept forward and down the block. Zach listened. The car engine didn't fade away. Instead it got louder. The guy must have turned around.

He stepped out from behind the tree and sprinted toward the car. He caught the startled expression on the driver's face, the same guy from a few weeks ago. Zach lunged for the passenger door handle, but the jerk gunned it, leaving him grasping nothing but air. A second later his forward momentum took him down and he hit the concrete with a thud and rolled to his side.

"Damn." Zach pushed to his knees, ignoring his skinned palms and stared after the car as it careened down the block and out of sight. Getting up, Zach wiped off his hands, flinching slightly as his knees protested the abuse. If he got his hands on that jerk, he'd make him sorry.

A glint of silver tucked back in the corner behind his garage caught his eye. If it hadn't been for his chase after the stalker, he'd have never seen it. He walked toward the small compact, stepping as quietly as a six-foot-three, two-hundred-fifty-pound guy could while wearing cowboy boots. As he crept closer, the motion-sensor light on his garage flipped on and illuminated the surrounding area. Tucked next to the garage in what used to be an RV parking spot, was a small car.

Zach stopped in his tracks.

Kelsie's car.

Puzzled, he moved closer and peered through the steamed-up windows. Alarm skittered through him, his heart beat faster. Finding a clear section of the window, he pressed his face against it. Inside the car, Kelsie huddled under a small mountain of blankets. She'd reclined the front seat and slept curled up in a tight ball. Two beady eyes belonging to Kelsie's eagle-bait dog peeked from beneath the covers and watched him.

He held his breath waiting for the yapper to let loose. Scranton wrinkled his nose and dismissed him as insignificant. The little rat turned his back and burrowed beneath the patchwork quilt.

Zach raised his hand to knock on the window and ask why the hell she was sleeping in his driveway. He squinted into the darkness. His frown deepened. Boxes were stacked in the backseat, along with a makeup bag. Clothes hung on the hooks on either side of the back doors.

It looked like she was living in her car. Zach updated his assessment. No, actually she *was* living in her car. No doubt about it. No wonder he'd caught her sleeping on his couch.

Zach straightened, torn between taunting her and leaving her alone. He knew how it felt to be reduced to being homeless. He'd hit some pretty low times in his younger days. Yet, Kelsie didn't have the poor background he did. He couldn't believe she didn't get money in the divorce settlement or that her wealthy parents allowed her to live like this. Something didn't add up. Something that was none of his damn business. She'd made her bed now she'd need to lay in it, even if that bed happened to be the front seat of a car. Karma's a bitch. She deserved this. Even as the words formed in his mind, he didn't feel vindicated or even satisfied. He felt pity and sadness she'd been reduced to this.

The vengeful side of him tried to goad the nice guy into waking Kelsie up and kicking her out of his driveway. The nice guy side refused to do so.

The nice guy won.

The least he could do was let her keep her pride. And keep her safe. From what he wasn't sure. Hell, he wasn't even certain who the guy was following: Kelsie or him? And why?

And who would keep him safe from Kelsie?

* * * * *

The sound of Zach's diesel 4x4 pickup woke Kelsie from a restless sleep. She inched the blankets down until just her eyes peeked above the covers. Zach's taillights faded in the distance as he pulled onto the slumbering street and disappeared from sight. A homeless girl had to love a man who left at the crack of dawn and didn't return home until late into the night, especially when she knew where he hid his key.

Of course, one slight problem when said man returned home unexpectedly. Her face flushed at the thought of him catching her masturbating. Thank God she'd managed to avoid him ever since by leaving before he arrived home, parking down the street, and returning once the last light went off in his house. Last night, he had company. She'd seen the taxi pull up and drive by with a man in the back.

Interesting. Zach never had company, let alone the kind that arrived and left in a taxi rather than in their own over-sized vehicle. She'd heard once that a man compensated for the size of his penis with the size of the truck he drove. Not so Zach. They were both huge. She'd seen firsthand. Her face went from hot to flaming at the thought.

Scranton snored in her ear, his little body curled up on her shoulder. She moved him off her and placed him on the passenger seat. He grunted, turned a few times, and curled back into a little ball. He was so not a morning dog. Sitting up, Kelsie squeezed her legs together. She had to go pee. Bad. She gazed at the house, dark in the early morning light, then opened the car door and made a run for the front door. Fishing the key out of its hiding spot in the dead begonia on the front porch, she let herself in and made a dash for the powder room in the grand entryway.

After doing her business and splashing water on her face, she walked back outside to get Scranton and the necessary toiletries for a shower. She'd wash a load of clothes today, too. A twinge of guilt tweaked her conscience. She was using Zach, and she knew it, but desperate times skewed her newly discovered ethics. Despite his house's messy condition—and she was making a dent in it—getting ready for the day in Zach's house beat the leering men in the homeless shelter or the questionable cleanliness of her previous apartment. Besides Zach would never know. The guy lived and breathed football twenty-four seven. It wasn't like her activities cost him money, and she'd been putting a lot of her own personal sweat into making his house presentable.

She cringed and held her hands to her mouth. That sounded like the old Kelsie, the one who could justify any selfish act. Taught from a young age to indulge in the luxuries that came with a sense of entitlement, Kelsie had taken her life for granted. The hurtful things she had done never made her feel better inside, they made her feel worse.

Maybe Mark had been her punishment. Beautiful, spoiled, privileged Kelsie had learned the hard facts of life after her wedding. Abuse didn't have an economic barrier or an educational barrier. It hid behind false smiles and guilt-laden apologies.

The night she'd asked for a divorce his emotional abuse had turned physical. He pummeled her face with his fists. Once the blows knocked her to the ground, his vicious kicks to her ribcage broke two ribs and cracked a few more. Eventually, she passed out. She'd woken up in a hospital bed, her *doting* husband sat near her bed and chastised her for her clumsiness one moment and then ignored her as he discussed a case with one of the senior partners in his law firm.

She'd faked sleep, hoping he'd leave. He did. She'd thrown on her bloodied and torn clothes, hoofed it out of the hospital, and straight to a ruthless female divorce attorney. But Mark gathered the wagons. Within twenty-four hours, not one member of his family or hers spoke to her, ostracizing her as sure as the Amish shunned those whom they deemed evil. She left town as soon as the divorce was final.

Now the man she'd hurt the most in high school held the power to destroy her.

Oh, Zach. She sighed. If only life could have been kinder to both of them.

Kelsie went back to her car and gathered up her things. She dumped her dirty clothes on top of the dryer to sort and glanced out the window in the back door. Something was different. Out of the corner of her eye, she noticed the square of dirt where there'd been lawn yesterday. Some kind of flat marble stone sat on top of it. Wondering what Zach brought home this time, she scooped up Scranton and went to investigate.

As she read the inscription on the marble slab, a cold knife edge of sadness sliced into her gut. The knife twisted with such wrenching pain that she dropped to her knees in the wet grass and dirt. Scranton wriggled out of her arms, shook himself off. After casting an accusing look in her direction, he trotted off to take care of business.

Kelsie barely paid him any attention. The date on the slab struck her like her ex-husband's blow to her cheek.

Back in high school, Mark and Kelsie had been in one of their frequent break-up phases. At Marcela's insistence, she'd invited Zach to the country club ball. Shimmering decorations and a mirror ball couldn't hide the ugliness of that night. Her friends bullied Zach, using the information she'd gladly given them to cement her place in their circle. Mark had been the one to break Zach, making sure everyone knew all the sordid details of why Zach's father was in jail for murder. One vicious right hook from Zach and Mark dropped face first into the pasta salad like a duck shot out of the sky with a hunting rifle.

The last time she'd seen Zach, he'd been handcuffed and sitting in the back of a patrol car. They'd locked gazes. His misery caused by her betrayal was etched in the strong lines of his face. She'd never forgotten that look, carried it with her all these years as her cross to bear. She owed him, and she came to Seattle to repay the debt.

The cold fingers of regret wrapped themselves around her throat, as Kelsie traced the date of his brother's death with an index finger. The date swam before her eyes.

The cruelty of what they'd done to Zach that night strangled her. She couldn't breathe, couldn't get her lungs to function. She gasped and swayed as the world spun like an out-of-control merry-go-round ride. She struggled to stand, but her knees buckled. She crawled to the bushes and threw up last night's dinner then collapsed in a heap in the wet grass and dirt, her chest heaving. Tears ran down her face, while sobs wracked her body. The taste of mud mingled with the salt from her tears.

Kelsie Carrington-Richmond was a bitch of the worst kind. She didn't deserve to be in the same company of a man as kind as Zach Murphy.

The date of his brother's death had been the very day she'd taken him to the country club ball. She remembered because earlier that afternoon her family had celebrated her daddy's birthday.

CHAPTER 11

Scrambling for a Few Yards

Kelsie sat silent and motionless in the midst of sixty-five thousand screaming fans. She'd been a fool to allow Lavender and Rachel to drag her to this game. She couldn't keep her eyes off Zach, and the more she watched, the more she wanted him, only she didn't deserve him.

Two days ago, she'd seen direct evidence of what a bitch she'd been to Zach. She couldn't come to terms with the depth of her cruelty. Just thinking of that cold, hard slab with his brother's name on it caused her throat to constrict and her eyes to fill with tears. She'd been such a bitch, such a ruthless, opportunistic bitch. So much guilt weighed her down, she might as well have been carting around a seventy-five-pound backpack.

The crowd around her collectively groaned, jerking Kelsie back to reality. Rachel stared at her. "Are you okay?"

"Yes, I'm fine. Just fine."

Rachel shrugged and went back to watching the game. Kelsie blinked and focused her gaze on the field below her. Zach stood a few feet behind the defensive line shouting signals for a change in defensive scheme to his teammates.

Kelsie hadn't grown up in Texas for nothing. She knew enough about football to recognize missed tackles. Zach had his share in the first three quarters. According to Rachel, he'd messed up a few defensive audibles, too, meaning he didn't read the offense correctly and called for the wrong defensive formation. The Packers exploited every one of his mistakes.

Kelsie leaned forward, elbows on her thighs, knuckles pressed against her mouth. Her sole focus was the football field several rows below. Darn, but she wanted to bite a fingernail, not that they weren't already gnawed down to the quick due to the trauma of her life the past several years. She'd always been a nail biter, an unfortunate habit that drove her mother bat-shit crazy. After all, a beauty queen must have perfect nails and perfect every-fricking-thing else.

At the end of the second quarter, Zach lined up in the defensive backfield. She watched him survey the offense. He cupped his hands to his mouth and shouted to his defensive teammates over the din in Jacks' stadium. Getting down in his stance, he reminded Kelsie of a panther watching a delectable baby zebra wandering too close to his kill area. As soon as the ball was snapped, Zach sprang into action, his big body catlike with fluid, athletic grace. He might be rough around all his edges, but the man boasted some mighty fine edges.

The tight end suckered Zach into following him only to have their running back dart past him untouched for a fifteen-yard gain. Kelsie covered her mouth with her hands and groaned. She felt the quick looks of her friends but stared straight ahead, pretending to be oblivious. Only she wasn't and neither were they. They didn't say a word, so Kelsie hoped she'd dodged a bullet.

"Zach's a sweet guy." Rachel pushed her long hair behind one ear. A diamond earring worth enough to finance a small town's fire department sparkled in her ear. Kelsie loved diamonds, especially ones big enough to choke a Texas Longhorn. Or at least she used to love them. Now they didn't seem to be such a big deal.

"I adore Zach." Lavender bounced to her feet, waving wildly at a hot dog vendor, bought three, and gave one to Rachel and Kelsie. Kelsie never ate hot dogs. Her mother hadn't allowed junk food in her diet. In fact, she barely allowed food in her daughter's diet. *Hot dogs added unnecessary pounds besides not being good for the complexion.* God, she was thinking just like her mother. She took a big bite of the hot dog and savored the juicy dog slathered with mustard.

"You know, Kel, you might want to watch one of the other ten players on the defense once in a while, or you'll give the impression you've got a thing for our defensive captain." Lavender wiped a bit of mustard from the corner of her mouth.

"Or watch the offense when it has the ball instead of the bench." Rachel patted her arm.

"It's that obvious?" No sense denying it.

"You two circle each other like sparring partners, yet the chemistry's so intense it's like being zapped by static electricity. You guys remind me of Tyler and me when we first met."

"And Derek and I. So why don't you fill us in with all the sordid details?" Rachel said.

"Yeah, are you sleeping with him?"

"Are you guys a couple?"

"Or fighting like we did?"

Kelsie looked from one to the other as they gazed expectantly at her. She didn't like to talk about her past, yet something told her she could trust these two women, unlike most of the female friends in her life and all of the males. "I was a bitch to him in high school. More than a bitch, I was a mean, cruel bitch. Zach doesn't forgive and he doesn't forget." *And I can't blame him.*

"Ty knows that story." Lavender closed her eyes, rolled her head back, and chewed on her hot dog like a woman having a food orgasm. Another drop of mustard dribbled down the corner of her mouth, and she dabbed it with a napkin.

"Life's too short to hold grudges. Maybe you can help him work on that?"

"I'm the last person to give him advice on that subject. He hates me."

"He might hate being attracted to you, but he doesn't *hate* you."

"I almost destroyed him in high school. When he was at his lowest point and just needed a friend, I offered friendship just to help my friends bully and ridicule him."

"You don't seem like that type of person."

"I was. If one good thing has come of my circumstances the past ten years, it's that I've developed empathy for people other than myself. I've put the mean girl to rest for good."

"After the game, you can tell us the entire story while we're waiting for the guys." Lavender licked her lips and wadded up the napkin.

"Starting with high school and ending with why you're here."

"I don't know if that's a good idea."

"Maybe not, but you could use a few friends, and we're here."

"Then we'll come up with a plan to get those two hard-headed men to cooperate with each other instead of butting heads."

Kelsie looked from one to the other, seeing nothing but earnest sincerity on their faces. She nodded, knowing that once she let that proverbial cat out of its crate, it'd never go back in again.

* * * * *

Zach stalked the sidelines, shouting encouragement to the Jacks' offense and berating the opposing team's defense. The O-line kept caving, allowing Harris to be sacked three times, yet they were still ahead by three points no thanks to Zach with a few minutes left to play.

He hadn't been his usual single-minded self. As soon as he'd spotted Kelsie sitting a few rows behind the bench with Rachel and Lavender, he'd been distracted. No matter how hard he tried to concentrate on the game, her gaze burned into his back like a hot summer sun. As a result, he played one of his worst games in years. He made too many mistakes, misread the offense and fucked up his defensive audibles, resulting in too many big gains for the offense. His tackling was sloppy and a step off. Stupid fucking rookie mistakes, and Zach was no rookie.

Three and out, the offense came back to the bench. After the punt, Zach strapped on his helmet and went back to the trenches. He checked the offense and called a change in formation for the defense to blitz. He got down in his set formation and waited for the snap of the ball. The ball snapped, and he anticipated a run. He stepped sideways, assuming the running back would be coming his way. As a result, he left the middle of the field open. A second later, the Packers tight end caught a ball in the middle of the field and galloped twenty-five yards for a touchdown and the win.

Game over. The Jacks dropped to two wins, three losses. Not a pretty picture.

Zach stood under the showers for several minutes, but he couldn't wash off the stench of defeat. His teammates avoided him, giving him a wide berth. Zach toweled off, wrapped the towel around his waist and walked into an unusually quiet locker room.

Harris stood at the locker next to him, talking quietly to a few reporters. They glanced Zach's way but his murderous glower stopped them as sure as a prison wall separated the innocent from the guilty. And Zach was guilty as hell of a piss-poor game.

Several minutes later, the reporters left, the locker room cleared out except for a few stragglers. But Zach made no move to leave. He slumped on the bench, propped his elbows on his thighs, cupped his chin in his hands, staring at his locker, but not seeing it. He'd lost the game for them, not just on that last play, but on overall crappy play throughout the whole, frigging game.

"Tough game, but we're still in a good position to win the division. The season is young." Tomcat slapped him on the back and moved on to his locker, not expecting an answer.

Bruiser strutted by in wrinkle-free slacks and a blazer with a polo shirt. The blond surfer boy dressed like he'd walked off the pages of a fucking Nordstrom catalog. Zach didn't care much for Bruiser's stylin' and profilin' as the kid liked to call it, but he appreciated how hard the back played. Despite his pretty boy appearance, Bruiser deserved his nickname and reputation as one of the toughest backs in the league.

Bruiser paused next to Zach's locker. "Hey, man, you played a hard game."

"I played a piss-poor game."

Bruiser shrugged one shoulder and wandered off, probably had a hot date with his mirror.

Behind Zach, Harris cleared his throat. The quarterback was in as foul of a mood as Zach. In fact, the heat of his gaze scorched the back of Zach's skull like a desert sun burns a bald head. Zach glanced at Harris, but the guy now had his back to him and was digging through his locker as if he'd lost something. Maybe his guts? His fighting instinct? His no-quit attitude? Oh, yeah, he'd lost that last year. This year the QB managed to fake interest in the game.

Zach ran a hand through his thick hair. As if he should talk. He played like a rookie today. At least Harris hadn't made any glaring mistakes, even if his play was uninspired. Zach hated losing, and for once it was on him as much as Harris.

Irritated, Zach itched for a fight. "So, go ahead. Say it."

Harris turned around, his face a perfect mask of indifference. He'd make a killing on the Vegas poker circuit. "Say what?"

"That I lost the game for us."

"Last I counted, there were at least twenty-two other guys on that field today, not counting special teams and substitutes." Tyler slipped on a pair of expensive sunglasses, effectively blocking out Zach's ability to read his eyes, not that he'd been able to read much anyway.

"Yeah, but I played like crap."

"So did I. What the hell? Instead of wallowing in pity for the next twenty-four hours, let's figure out how to do it better next week."

Zach's mouth dropped open, good thing it wasn't fly season. He'd be ingesting an entire belly-full of them. "I called the wrong defensive plays. Got suckered into going after the running back and left the tight end wide open."

"You sure as hell did. You're a better player than that." Harris paused and rubbed his temple. "So the fuck am I. I got caught in the pocket with my pants down and got sacked three times. I'm a better player than that. My pussy-whipped cousin didn't get open and fell down in the end zone and missed a perfect pass from me. He's a better player than that. We all fucking sucked."

Derek's head snapped up from the next locker over. "Hey, wait one damn minute. That wasn't a perfect pass. And I fell down diving for the overthrown ball."

Tyler snorted and turned his gaze on their star running back. "And Bruiser here couldn't have found a hole in a donut let alone in the Packer's defense."

Bruiser's head snapped up from his locker. "Bullshit, if there'd been holes, I'd have found them."

"My point is blame isn't going to get us anywhere. We're in this together regardless of which side of the ball we're on."

A couple defensive guys stood around, shuffling their feet. Some glanced at Zach, as if expecting a response.

Zach didn't disappoint. "I'll take care of my guys, you handle yours." The minute he said the words, he regretted them. He never missed an opportunity to stuff his big foot in his mouth. He couldn't let it go, couldn't cut Harris any slack. The guy played hard today, despite the screw-ups for which the entire team shared the blame. Yet Zach knew how the fans and the press operated, win or lose, it was all on the quarterback. Not a job he'd want.

Tyler's eyes narrowed, and he leaned forward, getting into Zach's face. His menacing expression telegraphed a challenge not wasted on Zach. "Then see to it the offense doesn't have to carry the defense, and we're all good."

Zach leaned forward himself until their faces were inches apart. He could smell Harris's fancy aftershave and see the small scar above his lip. "Yeah, we're good. More than good."

Tyler dismissed him, shrugged into his leather coat, and strolled from the locker room.

"You don't ever learn, do ya?" Tomcat shook his head as if Zach might be missing a few marbles.

"Don't like the guy," Zach mumbled and dropped to the bench to pull on his shoes.

"You don't have to, but we're all teammates. The way you behave you'd think the offense and defense played for two different teams."

"Sometimes I wish we did."

"You're an idiot."

Zach didn't have an answer for that. Tact for him was an art form in which he'd never graduated above crayons. In fact, he couldn't even color between the lines.

"He cut you some slack today. Could've chewed your ass but he didn't. Could've thrown some of the blame your way. He didn't. That's leadership, buddy. You might try practicing it yourself." Turning on his heel, Tomcat stalked from the room.

Heat slid up Zach's neck and settled on his cheeks. He'd failed again and didn't have a fucking clue how to succeed. He couldn't get past his resentment of Harris, just like he couldn't get past his bad history with Kelsie or how good she'd looked all soapy in his tub.

He needed to get past it. He didn't need to trust either person, just forgive and move on.

For the team. For himself. For his future. And most of all, for that elusive, fucking ring.

CHAPTER 12

Faked Handoff

Rachel and Lavender swept Kelsie along after the game like a tidal wave of girl power, insisting she join them for drinks and dinner. Her stomach growled at the thought of a thick prime rib when she couldn't even afford a cracker.

At halftime, the two women had been persuasive and didn't take no for an answer, before Kelsie knew what hit her she'd poured her heart out to them in an abbreviated history of her life, minus her current living situation, or lack of. She didn't want their pity, and she didn't get it. She got their understanding and acceptance, and that meant a hell of a lot more.

They flashed passes at the bored security guard as they pushed their way past hoards of fans into the sanctuary of the wide hallway near the locker room. Kelsie knew she should leave, but she had nothing better to do. Sitting in a warm bar beat shivering in her car, and deep down she hoped Zach would join them.

Poor Zach. And maybe poor her. He was going to kill her if and when the scheme they hatched during halftime came to fruition. He'd see her stamp all over it. Next week, Rachel planned to present Operation Team Unity to the coach. If HughJack jumped on board, he'd call the men into his office and pronounce their sentence, which was exactly how Zach and Tyler would see it. Zach would be furious at her meddling and rightfully so, but it was for his own stubborn good and the good of the team. For now, Kelsie buried her worries deeper than the Titanic was buried at sea.

Derek and Tyler walked out of the locker room together. Their hair was wet from recent showers. They weren't exactly the picture of happiness, more like pent-up frustration.

Bruiser in his slacks with the knife-blade crease and crisp black shirt strutted behind them, glancing around as if looking for his adoring fans. A lady's man to rival all ladies' men, Bruiser was almost too pretty for words with his deep tan and streaked blond hair. He reminded Kelsie a little too much of her ex-husband. She slid behind Rachel and Lavender, hoping to stay out of Bruiser's well-honed, womanizing sights. Only five-foot-ten former beauty queens didn't exactly blend in with a crowd. His eyes lit up when he spotted her, and the running back barged to her side like a bargain shopper when the doors opened on Nordstrom sale day.

"Ah, I knew you wouldn't play the coy one for long. I see you're waiting for me, honey." The sly devil slid right up to her and wrapped his arm around her waist. In her Jimmy Choo boots she towered over him by a few inches. Most guys would have a problem with that. Not Bruiser. A girl had to admire the guy's brash confidence, even if she didn't admire his cockiness. If she stepped on his foot with her lethal heels, the Jacks would lose their best running back. Still, it was damn tempting, as she'd long ago outgrown false flattery.

Zach stalked out next and tramped down the hall toward them, all dark and brooding like some gothic romance hero. Kelsie's heart stepped it up a notch, and she trembled slightly. Licking her lips, she forced herself to breathe. Bruiser grinned, obviously assuming she was reacting to him.

Zach's posse of defensive teammates straggled out behind him. Spotting Tyler, he made a show of looking the other way until he caught Kelsie out the corner of his eye. His mouth turned down into an even larger frown. Bruiser grinned at Zach, obviously knowing he was pissing off his teammate.

"So where's dinner tonight, guys?" Bruiser squeezed her closer. She elbowed him in the ribs, hard, and he grunted in pain but didn't loosen his hold.

"We got a private room at The Steakhouse." Tyler grabbed Lavender's hand and pulled her against him, turning the full power of his intense blue eyes on her. "Unless, you'd like to forget dinner and dine on some wine and chocolate at home."

Lavender giggled. "We're going to dinner." She leaned in close to her boyfriend, but Kelsie stood only a foot away and heard her. "You can have your way later."

"You can count on it." One smile from her, and Tyler's foul mood seemed to lift like the sun breaking through the clouds after a spring storm on Puget Sound.

"Count me and pretty lady here in. I plan to wine and dine her," Bruiser flashed his thousand-watt smile.

Despite the thought of a full meal, this Kelsie didn't use people. She opened her mouth to protest, but the wind rushed from her lungs as Zach hauled her to his side. Bruiser's arm hung out in space as if it surrounded an invisible woman's waist. He took one look at Zach's murderous glare and swallowed.

Backing up a few steps, Bruiser held his hands up in surrender. "Hey, man, sorry. Didn't know you two were an item."

"Keep your hands off," Zach grumbled, his menacing gaze took in every man there, daring them to cross that line. Tyler raised one eyebrow but kept his thoughts to himself. The other guys looked everywhere but at Kelsie.

"Don't worry. I don't play on another man's playground." Bruiser regained a portion of his swagger for the guys' benefit.

Tyler inserted himself into the conversation with a loud snort. "Bullshit, Bruiser. You play any chance you get." He turned to Lavender and tucked a lock of her red hair behind her ear with a loving smile that seemed so out of place on his bad boy face. "If you're in, let's go. I'm starving. Dinner's on the team captains tonight. Next game, the rookies pay."

A collective cheer went up from the group of players, except the rookies. Zach groaned. Mr. Tightwad hated to part with even a portion of his wad of dough. The crowd swept Kelsie along and out the double doors into the dark night. She fully intended to beg off, despite her state of hunger, only Zach wasn't letting go of her. She needed to keep her distance despite how nice it felt to be claimed. Theirs was a business relationship, and it needed to stay that way.

The team members and significant others headed to their respective modes of transportation. Her so-called friends dispersed faster than a flock of geese after a gunshot. They knew exactly what they were doing—leaving her at Zach's mercy. Even worse, leaving her sex-deprived body at the mercy of his hard, hot body.

She'd get even the next chance she got.

Zach yanked her against him just as Mountain Morris, their huge right tackle, astride his even larger Harley roared out the parking lot, sending water flying from several mud puddles.

He pulled her out of the way just in time. Kelsie found herself wrapped in his arms and staring up at him. The palms of her hands spread across his chest. His heart thudded erratically under her palms, mirroring hers. She gazed up at him. Big mistake. Bigger mistake than mixing navy blue socks with a black slacks. Usually full of disdain, his expression softened, easing the hard planes of his face. The big hands grasping her shoulders slipped behind her back and pulled her closer. His hot breath teased her lips. She tilted her head. Her lips parted. Waiting. Wanting. Needing.

A car horn honked, and they jumped apart. Tyler sped by, waving at them through his open window. Lavender and Tyler's laughter filtered back to them as he sped down the street.

"Bastard," Zach muttered and backed up a few steps, shoving his hands in his pockets.

Kelsie ran a shaking hand through her hair. "I'd better be going. Home that is."

Zach squinted at her, studying her intently in the light of a street lamp. "And where is that exactly?"

Kelsie opened her mouth then clamped it shut. The lies that once flowed so easily from her lips, didn't come so easily anymore. She'd learned the hard way that each lie came with a price. "Oh, I had a little studio in Fremont."

"Do you now?" He didn't seem convinced.

She ignored the question and started walking. "Have a good dinner."

He jogged to catch up then easily matched strides with her, his hands still shoved deep in his pockets and his gaze avoiding hers. "You aren't joining us?"

"I'd better not." She stared straight ahead, wishing he'd go away and wishing he'd stay.

"It's a social situation. Aren't you gonna hang out and coach me?" They walked together across the lot.

"You'll do okay with that crowd."

"Ah, because those are my people?"

"Something like that."

"Fine, I'll give you a ride to your car. It's dark and rainy."

Kelsie slapped down the panic. He couldn't see her car. Couldn't see all the stuff stacked in it. One glance, and he'd know the truth. "No, really. That's fine."

Then she saw it. She stopped dead in her tracks as a cold blade of fear knifed through her. Her life tilted crazily. The black sedan with dark windows idled in a parking space across from the stadium. She hadn't seen it in a few weeks, and hoped her stalker had given up. She should've known better. Zach followed her gaze. He stiffened but didn't comment.

"You're right. I'd be derelict in my duties if I didn't help you out tonight."

"Yeah, I thought so." With a shrug, Zach motioned toward his truck. Kelsie quickly followed. He unlocked it and opened the passenger door for her.

"Thank you, Zach." She took the hand he offered and allowed him to help her step up into his large beast of a vehicle, which so fit the man. Once she was seated inside, he shut the door.

Instead of getting into the truck, he broke into a run across the street. The driver of the car saw him coming and gunned it out of there. Zach stood in the middle of the deserted street until the car disappeared from sight. Fists clenched and his body tense with frustration, Zach turned back to the truck. Getting in, he gripped the steering wheel for a moment. Kelsie said nothing because she didn't know what to say. A few seconds later, they pulled out of the lot onto the street. She shivered and hugged herself.

Zach glanced at her as he tailgated Bruiser's sports car down the street. "Who the hell is that guy?"

"You've seen him before?"

"A few times." He chewed on his lower lip and stared straight ahead.

Kelsie went cold inside. "Where?"

"Lately?"

"Yes, lately?"

"In front of my house and at Jacks headquarters."

Kelsie dug her fingernails into the cloth seat and swallowed the bile rising in her throat. "Your house?"

He nodded. "Is he following you?"

Did that mean he'd been there while she'd been sleeping in her car? Had he seen her? Taken pictures of her homeless and alone? Stared in the window at her? She shivered at the thought, felt like she'd been violated, and hugged her body.

Did her ex know her circumstances? After all, how would it look if his ex-wife would rather live on the streets than be married to him? Especially with his political aspirations.

She'd either have to tell Zach the truth or weasel a way into his home somehow. If she slept with him... No. Kelsie gripped her hands tight in her lap. Old Kelsie would be that manipulative. She refused to consider it, though the picture of them, tangled up in his sheets, made her tingle all the way to her toes. If she slept with him, it would be because she cared for him, not because she was using him.

Zach glanced at Kelsie. The street lamp lit up her face as she chewed on a fingernail. She looked over her shoulder to see if the sedan followed. Zach flicked his gaze to the rear-view mirror.

"So, level with me. Do you know anything about that guy?"

She sucked her lower lip into her mouth, as her brain worked overtime. The truth wouldn't work, not without telling him the entire story and revealing the source of her private shame. Just a few minutes ago, she'd sworn off lying. Now she'd concoct a lie. One in many to cover up her past.

"I'm not sure. I've never talked to him." Okay so that was the truth.

"I did. Once. When I saw him at Jacks headquarters. Claimed he was reporter trying to get some dirt on me. Thought you were my girlfriend. Something tells me that it's not me he's following."

Kelsie shrugged and studied him in the dashboard light. He stared straight ahead, his jaw clenched, his dark eyes narrowed and determined. She resisted the urge to touch him, to let his strength flow from him to her, to give up her hard-won control to him and let him take care of her. Because Zach would protect her, he was that type of guy.

"Why would he be following you? Are you in some sort of trouble?" He glanced at her, and she instantly looked away.

This happened to be where the truth parted ways with fiction. "I think my parents hired him. They're worried about me out in the world by myself. It's a nuisance, nothing more."

He frowned. His dark brows drew together. "You don't act like it's nothing."

"I just don't want him to report back to them. They might insist I come back, and I don't want to."

"Why don't you want to go back there?"

Kelsie squirmed. "My divorce was pretty ugly. I needed to get out of town for a while."

"It's more than that."

She turned to him. "Maybe. But it's really not any of your concern."

His jaw tightened, and he didn't look at her. "No, it's not."

Sleeping in her car was becoming a less viable option. Sure, the guy hadn't done a thing yet other than stalk her and threaten what small measure of safety she'd had over the past few weeks. She needed a plan. "What we need to worry about is getting your house in order before this party."

He rolled his eyes. "I don't give a damn about Veronica's party."

"It's your party."

"Somehow I suspect it was your idea, and you sold her on it."

Somewhat glad to have Zach's stubbornness as a distraction from her stalker, Kelsie jumped on it. "Quit wasting energy fighting it. We're having a gala at your house. You will behave and be a gracious host if I have to squeeze your balls in a vise to get you to cooperate."

He raised one dark eyebrow and chuckled at her out-of-character rank language. "You've been hanging around me too long. I'm rubbing off on you. Next thing you know, you'll be throwing darts with the good ole boys down at the Crossroads Tavern."

Kelsie smiled. "I could probably set aside my social indoctrination long enough to whoop your ass at darts."

"You're on, lady." A smile split his face. Funny, when he smiled he looked really handsome. Not drop-dead gorgeous like Tyler or suave and smooth like Bruiser, but ruggedly handsome like a young John Wayne. Kelsie loved old movies, especially Westerns.

She'd always been attracted to the strong, brooding type. Zach fit that bill. And he fit way too much else she desired in her new life, but he could never know. Couldn't know because there was so much about them that would never work. For starters he still saw her as the same girl who used people and crushed them under a stiletto when they'd outlived their usefulness.

Only she wasn't. Not that he'd ever believe it because the man held his grudges closer to his heart than most people held their loved ones.

The type of loved ones that neither Zach nor Kelsie had ever had in their lives.

* * * * *

Zach tolerated the rest of the evening, watching his good money go down the guts of guys who ate more than an entire platoon of Army Rangers after a night-long march. Even worse, Kelsie sat next to him, not giving his cock a moment of rest. The damn thing rose to the occasion and stayed there despite his attempts to forget about her luscious body, her incredible scent, and her stunning thousand-watt smile.

Even worse, his gut clenched with worry every time he recalled the fear on her face when she'd spotted the dark sedan.

Didn't she get it? Someone was stalking her. He didn't feel good about scaring the shit out of her, but he'd hoped she'd come clean about her reasons for sleeping in her car. She didn't.

While he might buy the story that her controlling parents—especially her bitch of a mother—might hire someone, he doubted that would be more than an annoyance to her. She hadn't been annoyed, she'd been terrified, like a hunted animal about to get cornered with no way out.

He hated feeling responsible for her well-being, yet for some unfathomable reason, he did. If something happened to her outside his home, he'd never forgive himself. On the other hand, he understood pride all too well. To invite her to stay in his spare bedroom compromised that pride. Despite all she'd done to him, he couldn't do that to her.

He'd come up with another solution.

Yeah, right buddy. Like screwing up her future plans by refusing to cooperate on this stupid-assed gala? He blew out a breath and shoved his hair out of his eyes.

Kelsie nudged him. Her disapproving glare indicated he'd committed another social blunder. "What now?"

"Don't comb your hair at the table."

"I'm not."

"You are and with your fingers. That's even worse." She hissed at him. "Go wash your hands."

"My hair is clean. I just took a shower. What's the big deal?"

She gave him one of those *how can you be so stupid* glares, the kind he'd seen his entire life. Zach rose from the table and stalked to the bathroom. Maybe he didn't give a shit if black-sedan guy whisked this annoying woman off to parts unknown. Hell, at least she'd be out of his hair. *Literally.*

Only he did care. He just didn't want to.

A few hours later with his credit card drained by tons of hungry football players, he left the restaurant and drove home alone. Kelsie had bummed a ride with Derek and Rachel, which really frosted his nuts. He tried not to take it personally because he suspected the reason had to do with her entire life's possessions being stacked in the backseat of her car.

The problem was his dick really wanted to take her home and to end this bullshit denial between them. Zach never believed in beating around the bush. If you wanted something you went after it. He wanted Kelsie, but did he dare go after her?

Every part of his body down to his big toe answered with a resounding yes while his heart squeaked out a pansy-assed no. The rest of him wasn't listening as he pulled up to the garage, parked his truck, and mounted his front steps. Grabbing a brew from the fridge and a blanket, he returned to the porch. Turning off the outside lights, he settled onto the porch swing and waited.

At some point during the evening, he dozed off. He woke up a few hours later, stiff and cold. Kelsie never showed up.

CHAPTER 13

Slammed to the Turf

Kelsie folded her hands in front of her and waited for Zach. Today's lesson would be on making small talk, as in intelligent, polite conversation. She opened Mabel Fay's book and re-read the first paragraph, taking some comfort from the familiar words:

Refined and proper manners will be negated if one hasn't mastered the gift of polite conversation. Many a time a slip in manners, such as a gentleman who slurps his soup or chooses an improper wine to pair with a meal, can be overlooked if said gentleman masks minor improprieties with witty, charming conversation.

So not Zach.

Kelsie giggled at the thought. She glanced at her watch. The man was late.

A few seconds later, he stormed into the room and glanced around. When he saw her, relief washed across the angular masculinity of his face, though his irritation still shone through, along with something almost resembling fear.

"Where the hell have you been?" He stared down at her like a man feasting his eyes on his last meal.

Oh, boy.

"Right here waiting for you." She kept her voice calm, even though his appearance caused a major earthquake inside her.

"I mean for the last week and a half."

"HughJack cancelled last Tuesday's lesson citing a special team meeting." He'd noticed? She tamped down her pleasure.

"I know that, but you didn't reschedule."

She blinked at him. He wanted her to reschedule? "I'm not following you."

He opened his mouth then shut it, as if he'd already said too much. He dropped into the chair and clasped his hands on the table in front of him.

"Zach? What's going on?" He looked so distraught, she reached for his hands, but he jerked them away.

"Nothing."

Like nothing, hell. "You barged in here like a man in a panic."

"Just hadn't seen you around. I was concerned. You know, what with the trench-coat guy and all that." He met her gaze, and she saw the worry reflected there. A warm, fuzzy feeling like when Scranton licked her cheek ran through her. Only this man licking her body would be cataclysmic on the affection scale.

"As you can see, I'm fine." Sometimes she wondered if anyone would report her missing if she disappeared. Maybe Zach would.

"Where have you been?" He leveled her with a direct gaze.

She'd asked Rachel and Derek not to mention where she was to Zach, and she had to admit she was a little surprised they hadn't. It had been such a relief to have a place to stay and she didn't want Zach to find out she was dependant on them for her housing.

"It's not really any of your affair, but when Rachel and Derek gave me a ride after the last home game, Rachel got a call from her barn help. The woman had a family illness and needed to be away for a week. I volunteered to fill in. I've been staying in their caretaker's cottage so I wouldn't have to drive back and forth twice a day." Not that she had a home to drive back and forth to. She'd gone straight to the cottage that night and stayed there ever since. The caretaker would return in a few days so she'd be back to her car after that.

"Oh." He looked down, but not before she caught the deep red coloring his face. Finally, he glanced upward. "You know how to care for horses?"

"Seriously? I rode hunters as a teenager. Mother insisted on it. All well-bred girls took riding lessons, so she said." Kelsie's stomach knotted at the memory. She'd loved riding those gentle beasts, but her mother demanded her daughter take home only blue ribbons at horse shows until Kelsie hated everything to do with horses. She'd purposely started losing at horse shows just so she could quit riding.

"Zach, let's get down to business. Did you read your homework?"

He rolled his eyes and sighed. "This is total bullshit. The team's lost as many as they've won, and you're asking me if I've read Mary Kay's worthless advice."

"Mable Fay, and it's not worthless." Kelsie bristled, defending the woman she'd considered her guiding light over the years.

"Whatever." He waved her off. "Let's get this over with."

"You're not taking this seriously. Veronica and Coach Jackson expect your full cooperation." Kelsie tried for the stern teacher voice, but it came out as bitchy whine. "Do you have your copy with you?" She'd found him a dog-eared copy at a used bookstore.

He looked down at his hands and shook his head.

"Do you know where your copy is?"

He lifted one shoulder, still not meeting her gaze.

Busted.

She pushed the book across the table to him. "Please read this over. I'll give you a few minutes."

Zach hunched over the book but not before casting an irritated glance in her direction.

This man was the most exasperating, frustrating man she'd ever known. When he bent his dark, shaggy head, she itched to comb his hair into some semblance of order. She swallowed, imagined taming that unruly mop. She'd run her fingers through it and feel its texture as she added product for control, brush it out of his eyes so she could take in every feature of his ruggedly handsome face. Tracing those uncompromising lips with her index finger, she'd tease them into relaxing. And if they didn't, she'd be forced to use her lips. His lips would tighten, but she'd persevere until he softened them, opened for her tongue. Next thing, she'd be draped over his arm as he feasted on her mouth.

The book slammed shut, and Kelsie jumped a foot out of her chair. Flustered, she fumbled for her notes, and they slid off the table. Zach knelt down at the same time she did to pick them up. Her forehead bumped his forehead. She raised her gaze and so did he. A few inches separated her mouth from his, that very mouth she'd been fantasizing about a few seconds ago. If she just leaned forward a little, pretended to lose her balance and conveniently forgot that touching and kissing was so not a good idea she could be kissing him.

Zach beat her to it.

His mouth touched hers and set off a series of explosive chain reactions in the rest of her body. He tasted her like a wine expert with a rare bottle of chardonnay. She applied pressure to his lips, parting her own. He accepted the invitation with his tongue and deepened the kiss. Burying his fingers in her hair, he pulled her closer.

"So, how are the lessons going?" Tyler Harris's taunting voice hit her like a wrong-way driver on I-5. She shot to her feet and so did Zach, knowing both their faces were redder than a tourist who'd fallen asleep in the hot sun on a beach.

"Go to hell," Zach growled.

"If I do, I'm taking you with me." Chuckling, Tyler winked at Kelsie and left the room.

Stricken, Kelsie looked at Zach. "What do you think he'll do?"

"I'll take care of him." The grim resolve on Zach's face didn't bode well for Tyler's health or throwing arm.

She wrapped her fingers around Zach's biceps to keep him from going after the quarterback. "That's what I'm afraid of." Kelsie could still hear Tyler's laughter as it faded in the distance.

She didn't have a good feeling about this. Not at all.

* * * * *

Three and four.

They were fucking three and four. Three sorry-assed wins, four fucking losses.

A record like that didn't get a guy into the playoffs, let alone the Super Bowl. Frustration welled up inside Zach to the point of exploding. It didn't help that worry and guilt over Kelsie distracted him to the point where he couldn't concentrate. To add insult to insult, his old team—the perpetual league doormats that he'd given the best twelve years of his career—had just whipped the Jacks' asses on Thursday Night Football. After years of mediocrity, the Detroit Devils were six and one and leading their division. The team's owner hinted that cutting Zach in the off-season might be one of the reasons for their success.

What if it was? Zach slumped onto the bench in front of his locker and toweled off his wet hair. He felt sick to his stomach. Nothing had gone right tonight. Nothing. And not just for Zach.

Harris's QB rating was at its all-time worst. His receivers dropped balls left and right. Zach's defense left holes big enough for an elephant to lumber through at slow speed. Zach himself didn't play a stellar game and he laid the loss right where it belonged, at his own big feet.

Harris stopped in front of his locker, hands on hips, murder in his laser-blue eyes. Zach glanced up in the middle of lacing his shoes.

"Get your fucking mind off your beauty queen and on the field."

Obviously, Harris was looking for a fight, and Zach didn't mind giving it to him. He was sick and tired of the quarterback's criticism from the sidelines, as if the jerk had ever played a down of defense in his pussy-assed life. Zach shot to his feet, unmindful of Harris's extra inch of height. He had forty pounds of muscle over the QB.

"Are you accusing me of putting a woman over football?"

"Not accusing. Stating a fact." Harris stepped forward into Zach's space. Their faces only inches apart. Fury radiated off Zach in waves. He itched to plant his fist in Harris's smug face. The asshole had been begging for it for months.

All noise in the room ceased, even the endless rap music from Dante Reed's corner of the locker room stopped. The players shuffled their feet. Some kept their backs to their battling team captains, others openly gaped like bystanders at the scene of a bloody crime.

"Well, how's this for a fact? You aren't playing any better. Maybe you should practice what you preach." Out of the corner of Zach's eye, he noticed Derek and the backup quarterback, Brett Gunnels, inching toward them. Brett was a quiet guy and not big enough at five foot ten to be better than a career backup in the NFL, but the guy had guts. Zach would rather see him starting than Harris when Harris's head wasn't in the game. Yet, if Harris's head was elsewhere, where the hell was Zach's? Down south?

"Hey, now." Derek, the team peacemaker, attempted to step between them, but neither Zach nor Harris budged.

"Stay out of this," Tyler snarled. Derek didn't retreat but didn't make another move to interfere. Brett stood his ground, too, ready to break up a fight, while Zach's defensive line moved behind him, like his own personal posse of defenders.

Shit, any minute they'd have a brawl in the locker room.

"Kelsie isn't my problem. You are." Zach flexed his fingers, walking a thin line between strangling Harris and decking him. He had no doubt he could lay the guy out in one or two punches. "My grandma could play better football than you and with a lot more desire."

"Fuck you. I'm giving it everything I've got. You shouldn't shit in someone's backyard until you clean up the crap in your own."

"You're scaring me, Harris." Zach's booming laugh echoed across the silent locker room. Only then did he notice a small group of local reporters inside the locker room door, witnessing the team dysfunction for themselves, complete with high-def cameras.

HughJack pushed past the reporters breathing fire. "Get the fuck out of here," he spat at the reporters and booted their asses from the room with one homicidal glare. They scurried out the door, a couple of them getting stuck as they did so. HughJack slammed the door after them so hard Zach felt the vibration through the soles of his shoes.

Oh, crap.

Zach's anger deflated along with his chances for a Super Bowl ring. Even Harris backed up a step and plastered a friendly smile on his face. "Hey, Coach. Murphy and I were just having a little fun with the reporters. Nothing serious."

HughJack looked from one to the other with a scowl that struck fear in Zach's heart.

"Tomorrow morning. My office. Six thirty a.m. Don't be late."

"Six-thirty?" Harris's whining faded off into the sunset when HughJack swung around at him.

"You got a problem with that?"

"No, sir. I'll be there." Tyler stood up straight as if at attention. Zach half expected the suck-ass to salute or lick the coach's feet.

HughJack pinned Zach with his penetrating gaze. "And you?"

Zach nodded with a sinking feeling in the pit of his stomach that his days with this team were numbered. Even Kelsie's charm and manners couldn't get him out of this mess.

* * * * *

Rachel, Lavender, and Kelsie sat in a private booth in a pub near Jacks Stadium. Kelsie had survived a couple tense days waiting for the fallout from Tyler's discovery of Zach and her. So far nothing happened. Maybe Tyler would keep his mouth shut. After all, he did seem to like Kelsie, despite what he felt about Zach.

"Oh, I forgot to pay you. Thanks for taking care of our horses." Rachel opened a checkbook and scribbled out a check, handing it to her.

Kelsie glanced at it, surprised by the amount. "It was my pleasure. I love horses, but I can't take this. It's too much." The old Kelsie would've pocketed the check and been annoyed it hadn't been more money. The new Kelsie handed it back. She'd had a wonderful place to live for over a week in exchange for a few hours of work.

Rachel stared at the check and tried to hand it back. "Please, take it."

Kelsie shook her head, doing a friend a favor without expecting something in return felt liberating. And Rachel had become a friend. Despite how desperate Kelsie might be for the cash, she wouldn't ruin that feel-good feeling by accepting payment.

When Kelsie didn't take the check, Rachel pushed it into her hands.

Sighing, Kelsie tore the check into small pieces. "Consider this a favor from a friend."

Rachel shrugged and smiled. "If that's how you want it."

"Hey, ladies, shhhh. Listen." Lavender pointed to one the many televisions hanging around the room.

Kelsie's head snapped upward just as she heard Zach's name mentioned on the post-game show. Two sportscasters sat at a large table. A large still picture of Zach and Tyler in uniform was displayed behind them.

Kelsie brought her hands up to her face. "Oh, no." Her heart sank to the basement.

Rumors of team unrest on the Lumberjacks came to a head today after the Jacks' fourth loss. A locker room altercation between offensive team captain Tyler Harris and defensive team captain Zach Murphy had to be broken up by coaches and teammates.

Clips of Tyler and Zach in each other's faces and about to come to blows followed the news reports full of speculation and some facts. The short clip ended when HughJack stormed into the locker room and booted the press from the room.

Unnamed sources close to the team indicate the friction between Murphy and Harris has been escalating since training camp. This recent altercation was set off by Harris's comment regarding Murphy's dedication and lack of focus since he's been dating a former beauty queen. The sportscasters went on to cite statistics to prove their point along with how well Zach's former team was doing without him.

Dread welled up inside Kelsie. Dread for Zach, knowing his status with the team had just shifted from a comfortable lead to a twenty-one-point deficit in the fourth quarter.

She knew, too, that if Mark saw this, he might very well figure out who the "former beauty queen" was. Her fingers curled around her drink as she decided that her problems would have to wait. Right now, Zach was going to need her.

The three women looked at each other.

"I wonder if HughJack is reconsidering our plan now?" Last week Rachel approached Veronica and the coach with the women's plan to force Zach and Tyler to get along. HughJack hated the idea and said thanks but no thanks.

Lavender shook her head and sighed. "Who knows. Ty's gonna be unbearable to live with tonight. I'd better head home so I can be ready to diffuse the bomb."

Rachel stood at the same time as Lavender. "Me, too. You okay here by yourself?" Rachel tossed a hundred on the table. Most likely, her way of compensating for Kelsie not accepting her check.

Kelsie nodded. "I'm fine." Only she wasn't fine. She was sick to her stomach.

What would HughJack do now that the feud hit a very public forum?

Kelsie watched the clips on the sports channels unable to draw her eyes away from the train wreck.

Her cell rang, and she answered it without checking caller id, hoping it was Zach.

"Kelsie?" A crisp, businesslike female voice left no doubt in Kelsie's mind who was on the other end of the phone.

"Yes?"

"You've certainly done a fine job with Zach." Veronica's displeasure reached through the phone and grabbed her by the throat. "Was this your intention all along? Did you create your finishing school just to snag an athlete?"

"I—I—It's not like that."

"What is it like?"

"There's nothing going on." She didn't have anything to say for herself.

"That's not why I hear."

Damn Tyler Harris.

"Do you expect the Lumberjacks organization to throw good money away so you can seduce one of our players?"

"I'm not seducing anyone." Kelsie hated the panic in her voice but couldn't keep it out.

"Well, you're certainly not teaching him manners and tact either. You're fired."

"Excuse me?"

"You're fired, and I expect you to return the deposit you received from the team."

Kelsie went cold inside. She'd just been doused with a bucket of Gatorade without the high of winning the game. Raising her hand to her head, she bumped her drink and the cold, sticky liquid spilled into her lap. Grabbing napkins, she frantically worked to clean up the mess, hold the phone, and keep herself together, all at the same time.

She couldn't pay back the money. She'd cut off all her other financial options, and this business was her only future. She needed her finishing school to be successful. "But—"

"No buts. The team no longer needs your services. After this incident tonight and Zach's sloppy play, I can only surmise your influence has had a negative effect, rather than positive, your business is a sham, and you are nothing but a desperate woman."

True on all counts, but damn it, Kelsie wasn't giving up. "It's too late to move the gala elsewhere. The preparations are well underway."

Silence for a long moment then Veronica sighed heavily. "I'll figure out something."

"Zach will still host it, and he'll be the polished man I promised he'd be."

Veronica snorted. "Why? What do you get out of this?"

"If it's successful, and we raise more money than last year, you'll use my business and recommend it to others."

"And if not?"

"I pay back the money and match it with a donation to your charity of choice."

Veronica waited so long to answer that Kelsie thought the call might have dropped. "Fine. I'll agree to that."

Kelsie let go of the breath she'd been holding then sucked it back in again when she glanced out the window of the pub. Across the street stood trench-coat man, leaning up against his black sedan and smoking a cigarette.

Things just went from bad to worse.

CHAPTER 14

Goal-Line Stand

Zach's house was dark when Kelsie doused her headlights and coasted into her usual parking area. Scranton peeked out of his hiding spot sequestered under mounds of warm blankets. He opened one eye, blinked a few times, and slipped back under the covers. Kelsie sighed. She wished she was small enough to curl up under those blankets, but doing so in the cramped car seat didn't quite work. Glancing around, she hit the door lock and hoped she didn't need to go pee in the middle of the night. Not with her stalker making an appearance less than an hour ago. She didn't believe he followed her here, but he knew about this place so it'd only be a matter of time before he checked it out.

So why the hell did she come here then?

Because she felt safer knowing Zach was a hundred feet away? Because deep down she trusted him? Or was it more complicated than that? Maybe she had more than a high school crush on the big, tough football jock?

Kelsie rubbed her empty tummy and sighed. Brushing her teeth in the pub's bathroom, she missed the comfort of Rachel and Derek's little cottage. Funny how those things she took for granted such as running water, a toilet, and electricity became so valuable when she didn't have them. Rain spattered against the window and distorted the trees outside into an ominous scene from a horror movie. A clap of thunder sounded, and Kelsie jumped. Her teeth chattered and not because of the cold. Scranton whimpered and dug deeper, reminding her of a gopher she'd witnessed digging a tunnel through her grandmother's flower garden. It hadn't ended well for the gopher. She hoped it ended better for Scranton and her.

Lightning lit up the car followed by another crash of thunder. Kelsie dove under the blankets and threw them over her, huddling beneath them. Scranton scrambled back underneath and plastered his shaking body against her ribs.

Her heart slammed in her chest as if it, too, wanted to escape the confines of the car. Her breath came in short gasps. Her hands shook with fear. Somewhere out there was a man who made it his business to mind her business at the least and wished her harm at the worst.

She couldn't do this anymore. Couldn't live in this car never knowing what lurked outside ready to do unspeakable things to her. There had to be another way. Maybe a live-in nanny or caretaker or something. Anything but this.

The wind picked up and flung buckets of water against the windows louder than an angry ocean surf. She shivered as the gloom and damp moist air waterlogged every cell in her body, frightened and thinking about what she'd give right now to feel safe and have a warm bed.

Tap. Tap. Tap.

Kelsie froze, certain she didn't hear what she thought she'd heard. She held her breath and didn't move. Her heart pounded harder than a drummer in a heavy metal band.

Tap. Tap. Tap. A little louder this time.

Oh, God. Oh, God. Oh, God.

What if it was the stalker? What if he had a gun? She didn't want to die. She wanted to live and prove she could be a better person. Shouldn't a person be allowed time to show they'd learned from their mistakes? Yet, what did a predator care about redemption?

"Kelsie." The gruff, muffled voice sounded concerned not predatory. Still she didn't move. "Kelsie." Now the voice sounded impatient and a lot like—

With trembling hands, she pulled down the blanket, wiped some moisture from the car window, and looked out.

Oh, crap. She'd been outed.

Zach's face was pressed up against the window, his wet hair plastered to his head. Rivulets of water ran off his nose and clung to his eyelashes. Her wildly beating heart didn't stop its runaway pounding. It pounded even harder now, the fear gradually being replaced with other emotions.

Kelsie almost preferred the fear.

Humiliation surged through her. Worse humiliation than being turned down for job after job or being belittled by her ex for some minor transgression. She never wanted Zach to see her reduced to this—homeless and living in her car. She ducked her head under the blankets and sent up a silent prayer that the man would just go away.

"Come in the house," his deep, husky voice carried through the glass and over the sounds of the storm.

His tone didn't allow any discussion, but when did that ever stop her? Peeking out from under the mound of blankets, Kelsie shook her head.

Zach yanked on the door and found it locked.

She turned her back to him and gathered the blankets around her like protective armor.

Pound. Pound! POUND. He'd break the window if he kept that up.

She turned to glare at him and mouthed *go away.*

He shook his shaggy head, sending droplets of water flying.

They stared each other down for what seemed like an eternity. He didn't flinch despite the rain pouring down his face and dripping off his nose and chin. He'd be sick if he stayed out there much longer.

Kelsie caved first and ended the standoff.

With a sigh, she unlocked the door and decided to put on airs—a bad habit she'd picked up from her mother—and act as if he were disturbing her in her house late at night.

Zach wrenched open the door, and she almost fell out. Righting herself on the seat, she clutched the blankets to her chest while smiling her lil-ol-me smile as if he were a pageant judge. She faked a nonchalant yawn and rubbed her eyes.

Zach didn't smile back or even react. "Let's talk in the house. I'm drenched."

She raised one eyebrow in her best imitation of a snobby English blue blood. "Please."

"Please." He didn't say it like he meant it. He said it like he'd love to strangle some sense into her, but she ignored that small detail. She didn't need a second invitation. Her stalker was out there somewhere, watching her every move and possibly plotting all sorts of evil deeds.

Gathering Scranton, Kelsie sprinted barefoot through the rain into the house and didn't stop until she was huddled on the edge of the leather couch near the blazing fire crackling in the massive stone fireplace. Zach sank onto the couch next to her and dangled his hands between his knees, water still dripping off him and forming a small puddle on the hardwood floor. She stared at the dancing flames, not certain if the heat on her face was caused by the warm fire or her own mortification.

"You're sleeping in your car."

Well, duh. "Obviously. Can't get anything past you, can I?" She hated the sarcasm in her voice, but it just slipped out.

He almost smiled. "You haven't. You've been sleeping out there off and on for several days now with the exception of the week you took care of Ramsey's horses."

Okay, so, so much for assuming he was oblivious to anything that didn't involve football and sex. "You knew?"

"Yeah, I figured you had your reasons, and they were none of my business."

"I'm trespassing."

He shrugged. "It's supposed to get down to 29 degrees tonight."

Scranton crawled off her lap and onto Zach's. The traitor licked Zach's impressive bicep, as if to thank him for the rescue. Tentatively at first, Zach petted the tiny dog. With a contented sigh, the little poodle curled up on Zach's lap, barely bigger than the large hand stroking Scranton's back. A second later he was snoring like a three-hundred-pound lineman after a tough Monday Night Football game.

"We were doing just fine in the car."

He glanced down at the dog. "Tell that to Scranton. Besides, I thought you might want to sleep somewhere warmer."

"I'm just between places to live. I apologize for not asking your permission, it's just a bit of an embarrassing situation to be in." Embarrassment didn't begin to cover how she felt about her circumstances. Try demeaning. Demoralizing. Humiliating. Hopeless. Desperate. Yet, given the chance, she'd live in her car over going back to the stifling, domestic cell in which she'd been imprisoned for ten years.

"It's not safe for you out there, Kel." His kind brown eyes met hers. She so did not deserve his kindness. She'd come here to apologize to him, not be rescued by him—well, okay, maybe that wasn't entirely true.

"I'm fine." *Like hell.* She flashed back to trench-coat guy standing outside the pub tonight. So far, he'd never approached her. What if that changed? What if he wasn't a PI, but some nutcase stalking her until the moment he decided to attack or worse?

"You can have one of the spare rooms. Take your pick. The blue room has the best bed." Zach's voice buzzed in her head as if far away.

"It has the only bed."

"True."

Did he expect her to share his bed? "Zach, thank you so much for the offer, but I can't stay here for free." She couldn't take advantage of him any more than she already had. This new, improved Kelsie didn't use people. Especially not someone like Zach.

"Then pay me to rent a room, whatever you think is reasonable." His chin jutted out with his usual stubborn resistance to any opposition.

"I'll be out of my present situation soon." *Liar. Liar. Liar.*

"Oh, did the Jacks sentence more players to your tutoring?" He tried to smile but didn't quite succeed.

She hugged herself tighter as the futility of her situation settled like a dead weight in her stomach. "No, actually the opposite." There now, honesty might hurt but it also made her feel as if a weight lifted off her chest. Incredibly liberating, even though temporary denial might feel a hell of a lot better in the short term.

The stark truth hidden in her words didn't go over Zach's head. "Veronica fired you?"

Kelsie nodded and gnawed on her last good fingernail, willing herself not to cry. God, she hated the helplessness, but she would not let this situation defeat her. She raised her head and looked him squarely in the eyes. He, on the other hand, appeared torn.

"It's because of me, isn't it?" Guilt flashed across his face like a neon sign.

She would not let him own the blame. "I didn't do my job. Actually, I failed miserably." Kelsie forced a smile and tapped his broad chest. "But don't think you're getting out of your classes, buster. I told Veronica I was committed to my task and to the gala." Her finishing school wasn't finished yet.

He captured her hand and held it in his big one. She lifted her face and met his troubled gaze. "You can't stay in your car. It's not safe, and the weather is nasty."

"Staying in your house is not an option for me. I have nothing to offer in exchange."

A flare of desire crossed his face, and he looked away as if ashamed.

"Is that what you want?" Maybe an obvious question, but she needed to hear the answer.

He shrugged, his gaze focused on the fire.

Kelsie chewed on her lower lip and stared into the fire, too. The flames danced wildly, mimicking the flames inside her. It wasn't like she was an innocent virgin or even an innocent. She'd used her body to win a beauty pageant and a spot on the college cheerleading team. Could she bargain her body for a safe, warm place to stay?

After entertaining the possibility for a brief moment, she kicked that idea out on its ass. She'd risen above her past, never again would she sink that low. Not even for her own personal safety and comfort. Which didn't mean she didn't want to sleep with Zach. Oh, Lord, she wanted to be wrapped in his strong arms more than she wanted to take a shower with soap and hot water or sleep in an actual bed. This independence thing could be exhausting. It'd be so easy to let someone else take charge for a while.

No. No. No.

"I want you, too, Zach, but not in exchange for rent. Not like that." She needed to make him understand that she wanted him for him—no other reason. She scooted closer until their thighs touched.

He flinched and rose to his feet, backing away from her. "I would never ask you to prostitute yourself like that." He stared down at her. His handsome face a kaleidoscope of conflicted emotions.

"I know you wouldn't." He held her in higher regard than she held herself.

He shoved his hands in his pockets, his jaw working as if he was trying to spit out unspoken words.

Oh, Lord, she really did want him, not just physically, but emotionally. She wanted to wipe the sadness and confusion from his face and replace it with desire and pleasure. She wanted to be the one to make him forget the pain of his past, if only for a little while. It was the least she could do for him, especially after what happened to his brother and her cruel role in his agony.

She'd give herself to make him happy, then she'd go back to sleeping in her car with her pride a bit tattered, but still intact. She hadn't been with a man except Mark in over a decade, and her ex had been a selfish lover, putting his needs and desires above hers. Instincts told her what kind of lover Zach would be—kind, tender, caring, yet passionate. He'd take her to heights she'd never reached, teach her what sex was really about. She wanted that. Wanted his comfort, his kindness, his athlete's body. She needed to feel desired again, needed to feel the touch of a man who cared about more than himself.

She needed to heal. And she needed to forget about the stark reality of her present situation. Just for one night.

Kelsie made her decision in the time it takes to snap a finger. "That doesn't mean I don't want you because I do. I really do. Right here. Right now. No expectations. No strings."

Zach's nostrils flared, and he worked his jaw. His heavy-lidded gaze told her all she needed to know. Even if she *was* making a huge mistake. At least she was doing it for all the right reasons.

* * * * *

When Kelsie stood and started walking toward him, Zach stood stock still, as if the slightest movement might drive him to his knees. Maybe it would. With his elbows locked and his hands fisted inside his pockets, he didn't pull her into his arms.

His head pounded over the tug of war going on inside it. Use her like she'd used him? Send her away with a few hundred dollars? Be sucked into the vortex that was loving Kelsie? Or run like hell while he still had a measure of sanity?

Fuck, what the hell was he doing? About to jump in bed with the woman who'd caused shitloads of grief in his life. Gary would be disgusted with him for being so weak. Neither brother had ever liked Kelsie. They thought she played Zach, which she did. Only this Kelsie seemed—different. Way different.

"I want you, Zach. Let me ease some of your pain. Just you and me. No past. No future. Just here and now." She whispered in his ear, her voice all soft and breathless.

If he got any stiffer, he'd shatter. Putting his hands on her shoulders, he pushed her away and held her at arm's length. "I'm not in pain." At least not the emotional pain she was hinting at.

She took a small step back. "I think you are, and I'm the cause of a lot of it. Let me help you." With trembling fingers, she fumbled with the buttons on her flannel nightshirt.

Zach, being a normal healthy guy, stared at her breasts, like a kid anticipating the unwrapping of a Christmas present. After the last button, Kelsie slipped out of the shirt and let it fall to the floor.

He licked his lips and swallowed. Not once, but twice. He sucked in a labored breath, and his loyalty to Gary warred with his attraction to Kelsie. She was so beautiful it actually hurt to look at her.

"Kelsie. Please." His voice came out hoarse and rough. He was surprised he'd managed to croak out the words. He forced his eyes away from her luscious body, but within seconds he was looking again as she kicked off her shoes, unzipped her jeans, and pushed them down her long legs, stepping out of them. She stood before him, naked except for a purple lace bra and a pair of black lace panties.

He blinked and nearly laughed. He'd totally expected her bra and underpants to match perfectly. Didn't matter, she'd look fucking incredible in anything. Or nothing.

Her gorgeous breasts rose and fell with each breath she took, hypnotizing him, pulling him deeper to the point of no fucking return. A lock of her blond hair tickled the edge of her bra cup. He wanted to wrap that golden strand around his fingers and brush his hand against the creamy white skin.

"What's wrong? Am I still wearing too many clothes for you?"

Too many clothes?

Ah, hell, she was wearing far too little. At least too little for his shaky control. So why the hell was he resisting? This was Kelsie, the woman he'd lusted after since ninth grade. Unattainable

Kelsie, with the incomparable beauty and charm. Kelsie, offering her body to him. *To him.*

He'd never had a problem taking from women in the past, not that he did it often, but on occasion. Why the hell did it bother him this time?

Pride? Fear? Or—

Gary.

Outside the house in the raging storm were Gary's ashes. Inside stood the woman he'd picked over Gary. Not once. But twice.

Scranton barked, causing them both to turn in his direction. Kelsie's little foo-foo dog sat on his couch and watched their every move as if recording it for all time in his miniscule little pervert brain. Zach turned his back on the dog.

"Now for you." Kelsie looked him up and down, her eyes clearly telling him she was ready to give him what he'd dreamed of for almost two decades.

His turn? Like he could even get his fingers to work if he wanted. He must have telegraphed the indecision. She moved forward, all fluid grace with creamy skin that smelled of flowers.

Her fingers touched the skin at his collar, and he bit the inside of his cheek to stop the groan. She slid her hand down and unbuttoned his shirt with excruciating slowness. He held his breath until he thought he'd pass out from lack of oxygen. She pushed the shirt off his shoulders, and he shrugged out of it.

God help me, and Gary, please forgive me. He was a weak, weak man, but he wasn't the only warrior throughout history who'd sold his very soul for a woman.

Their eyes met, and there was so much more there than lust. Or at least that's how he wanted to see it, poor lovesick sap that he was. Her vulnerability called to his protective male instincts, and her sweet body called to everything else.

She slid her fingers down his chest, with a soft and delicate touch, and he trembled. His lungs emptied of air and his heart fluttered like a fucking cherub's. She bent down and those dream-a-thousand-dream lips of hers closed around his nipple.

Damn. Damn him to hell.

She licked the painfully tight nub then sucked. Licked then sucked. He groaned and buried his fingers in her hair. She sucked on his other nipple then sank to the floor on her haunches. Unzipping his jeans, she hooked her fingers in the waistband and lowered them—briefs and all—down his hips and freed his erection—one very happy-to-see-her erection.

One gentle shove and he sank to the couch, as if he were a ninety-pound weakling not a two-hundred-fifty-five-pound NFL linebacker known for his toughness.

She cradled him in her hands, ran her fingers across the velvety tip of his penis, then slid her fingers underneath to cup his balls. The blood in his brain rushed to his dick, robbing him of rational thought. He sucked in a breath and gripped the couch cushions, leaving finger impressions.

Heaven clashed with earth as her luscious mouth touched the tip of his cock. It jerked, as if it had a mind of its own. He'd always been firmly convinced it did.

Kelsie Carrington, his dream girl, had her mouth on his cock. He had to be hallucinating. Hell, whatever it was he didn't want to wake up. He wanted her any way he could get her. Because right now he couldn't resist.

He doubted he'd resist tomorrow night or the next either. He just hoped like hell it didn't ruin his game. Maybe it'd improve it.

Maybe…

Crazy thoughts rattled through his sex-muddled brain, but one fact blasted through the fog like a ferry horn sounding across Puget Sound during a storm.

His fantasy girl was offering herself to him and claimed not to want anything in return. This time he'd be the taker. He'd earned this.

She'd been his fantasy his entire teenage life and some of his adult life. But in his fantasy she'd come to him because she loved him and wanted to be with him forever. Together they became the family he'd never had. It hadn't been just a quick fuck. It had been special to both of them. Something that bound them together for all eternity.

He couldn't do it. Not like this. He couldn't destroy the last remnants of his dream for one night of satisfaction. The Kelsie who dwelled in his fantasies didn't do one-night stands. She held to a rigid morality and insisted on commitment. Totally fiction, he knew, but his imagination wrote this story, and he wasn't deviating from the plot it'd written. This old-fashioned novel required old-fashioned morals. There needed to be more, at least for him, even if the more only lived in an outdated fantasy. He couldn't control her feelings and her actions, but he could his.

Zach was fucking going to hate himself, but he did the noble thing—the dumb-assed noble thing he might live to regret for the rest of his days. He put his hands on her shoulders and pushed her back on her haunches. Ignoring her shocked expression, he shot to his feet, pulled up his boxers and jeans and zipped them before he changed his mind. She stared up at him with lust-clouded, confused, blue eyes.

"I can't do this. It's not right." His body, still numb with lust, couldn't believe its bad luck, while what little of his brain still functioning applauded his morality. He wanted her but on his terms, and an outrageous plan started to take form in his usually practical brain. He wanted his cake and to eat it, too, even if that cake was a mirage that disappeared the closer he got to it. For a brief moment in time, his dream would be a reality—his reality.

"It's not right?" Kelsie blinked several times and regarded him through hazy eyes. Her clenched hands were still held out in front of her as if she'd been praying. To his cock. A cock that once again twitched with need. A cock he'd denied the pleasure of a lifetime.

"No, this isn't how I imagined our first time together." Zach paced the floor. Once. Twice. Three times. He ran his hand through his thick hair. Then paced some more.

"How did you imagine us, Zach?" Kelsie rose to her feet and pulled on her jeans and shirt and hugged herself.

"I—I just thought it'd be special. Different." He tried not to look at her, tried to make sense of this entire screwed-up evening when a flash of something metallic caught his eye. Halting his pacing, he stared out the window at the storm just as a dark sedan crept by on the street, with its lights out. It stopped near his driveway for several seconds then continued its slow crawl down the street. He turned to Kelsie who'd moved to stand next to him.

"What is it? Is it him?" Her face, flushed with the promise of sex a second ago, turned whiter than the chalk lines on a football field. She shoved her knuckles in her mouth and bit back a heart-wrenching hiccup of a sob.

Then he knew. For sure. She *was* in danger and scared shitless. Every protective instinct he possessed went on red alert. He'd get a hold of that prick following her and show him a thing or two. Without thinking, Zach sprinted from the room and out the front door, slamming it behind him. He ran into the street just as the asshole made his second pass. He caught the man's startled expression. The driver accelerated with a squeal of tires leaving Zach in the dust. The car disappeared around a corner.

Chest heaving, adrenaline still rushing through his veins, he turned back to the house.

Kelsie stood in the doorway, hugging herself again.

"It's him." She spoke with quiet dread and bone-chilling fear. She continued to study Zach as if trying to read his expression. Her lower lip trembled and there was a small band of sweat on her forehead. Zach reached for her hand. It was cold and clammy. He led her back inside, back to the warmth and coziness of the fireplace. She pulled away from him and stood with her back to him next to the fire.

"Who is that guy, Kelsie? I don't believe for a moment your parents hired him."

"I don't know."

"He has you scared shitless. Is he dangerous?"

She shrugged. Zach stepped up behind her and wrapped his arms around her, pulling her backside against his front. Her body was as stiff as a corpse in a morgue. Even so, as her fine ass pressed against his crotch, he immediately developed another boner.

"How long has he been following you?" Zach fought to keep his voice level, hard to do with only a thin layer of clothes separating them and his mind flashing to her kneeling in front of him.

"A while. It started right—right—after—the gala where I first saw you." Her voice rose to an almost shriek.

He rubbed his hands up and down her arms, trying to soothe her. "You must have some idea why he's following you."

"I think my ex hired him to keep tabs on me."

Her smug, self-righteous asshole ex-husband. Yeah, Zach knew Mark Richmond well. Scaring the crap out of Kelsie would be just the thing he'd do to get his rocks off. "Are you concerned about Richmond? Do you think he could be dangerous?"

She wrenched out of his arms and turned to face him, chewing on her lower lip. Her eyes, filled with unshed tears, met his. "I think he could be."

"Did he abuse you, Kelsie?" He clenched his fists, wishing he could slam a fist into Richmond's smug face.

"He did emotionally, yes, from the very beginning. He's controlling."

"Did he ever strike you?"

"Not until the end when I asked for a divorce."

"What do you mean not until the end? What did he do to you?"

"I don't want to talk about it." She swept her hand across her forehead.

"You can't stay in your car anymore. It's not safe, and he knows you're here." As if she was any safer with Zach, but for very different reasons.

"I have to. I don't have any money." She closed her eyes and hiccupped again.

Zach struggled with his rigid morality and his baser instincts. "Move in until things get straightened out." He'd never lived with a woman before. Hell, he'd never even invited a woman into his house. Yet, he couldn't let her go back to living in her car, no matter what it cost him. He'd abandoned his baby brother when he'd needed him most. He wouldn't abandon Kelsie, couldn't live with the guilt if anything happened to her.

"I can't." Even as she uttered the brave words, he caught her nervous glance out the window. Her hand trembled as she reached down to stroke Scranton. "I've been a taker all my life, but no more."

"I'm not asking you to take anything. I have room. It's not a problem."

"It is taking. Using you. I won't do that. Especially not to you. I have to do this on my own. My own way. I can't move in with you."

"Why not?"

"Because I know you. You're not the type of guy who lives with a woman. I won't have you compromise your beliefs for me. Am I right? Have you ever lived with a woman?"

She had him there. In a rare moment of baring his heart to her in high school, he'd told her than he'd never live with a woman who didn't have his ring on her finger. Marriage meant something to him even though it had never meant a damn thing to his parents. She'd laughed and called him a hopeless romantic. He didn't consider himself romantic. He just wanted a life like a fifties sitcom—a woman who loved him and a real family with 2.5 kids and a dog. He glanced at Scranton—a *real* dog.

Kelsie seemed to read his mind. She touched his cheek and he suppressed a shudder. "See? I can't move in here. I can't take your charity either."

"Okay, then, marry me." He blurted out the words that'd been forming in his mind for the past hour. They just tumbled from his mouth and shocked him as much as it did her.

Yet the second he said them, he knew he meant what he said. As stupid as it might be, Zach wanted to marry her, and he wouldn't take the words back.

Not tonight. Not ever.

CHAPTER 15

Throwing out the Playbook

Zach watched Kelsie stagger back a step or two. Her mouth fell open, and her hand flew to her chest. Her lips moved and nothing came out, like the guppy in the fish bowl he kept on the counter. He'd rendered her speechless.

The second Zach uttered those two words, he made his decision, and he'd stick with it to the crazy, bitter end. Marriage to Kelsie might be a dumb-assed idea, but it made perfect sense in a skewed logical sort of way. Now if he could only convince her of that. He wanted her so bad the desire sat hot and heavy on his tongue, sent sharp pains to his heart, and kept his cock in a perpetual state of horniness. But he wanted her as his, even if for a short while and as stupid as it might be for a man who prided himself on practicality. He'd dreamed of this moment for most of his life, now he threw common sense over the goalposts.

She kept shaking her head and making these unintelligible noises, as if she'd forgotten the English language. Meanwhile, Zach's mind and body were all-in, rushing to concoct reasons his insane proposal made perfect sense.

Finally she managed to squeak out a few words. "You don't mean that." Then she laughed, a nervous, I-must-be-dreaming-this laugh. Her gaze bounced around the room, as if she were looking for an escape or something solid to hang onto.

Zach's jaw moved in a circle as he weighed his words because saying the right thing had never been one of his strong points. He lifted his head, his gaze meeting hers. The second he looked into her blue eyes, he knew the answer as clearly as a Seattle summer day in August.

Gary, forgive me. I hope you'll understand.

"I do. I mean it." He pinned her with the same intensity he used on the opposing team's quarterback. He saw past all her walls and into the scared, insecure little girl cowering underneath all the selfish bitchiness. Maybe it was the hint of vulnerability that attracted him in the first place, those few times she'd let down her guard with him.

He'd wanted her since their teenage years, wanted to be with her bad, so bad he'd deserted his brother, left him alone to deal with an abusive father. Now he was making another stupid-assed decision by letting her into his life in the most intimate way possible, not just as a lover but a wife. But it was his decision and he'd own it.

With jerky motions, Kelsie clutched her shirt to her chest. "This is so not a good idea."

Like he didn't know that? Every time he got involved with Kelsie a disaster happened. Now he'd invited disaster into his calm, private life. Yet, he wouldn't take back the offer because he didn't *want* to retract it. He ran his hands through his hair and pushed it off his face. Along with a haircut, he also needed a shot of his usual practicality. Yet practicality also told him she was in grave danger with no one to protect her but him. She was alone, and she needed him. He liked being needed. He liked being her knight in shining armor. He liked the idea of putting his ring on her finger even if it didn't mean the same thing to her as it did to him. He'd change her mind just like he changed an opposing offense's game plan when they couldn't run the ball against him.

First, he struck at her doubts with a dose of common sense and a pinch of well-placed guilt. "I won't be able to live with myself if something happens to you."

"You're proposing marriage to keep me safe?" She didn't look nearly as convinced as he felt.

"Among other reasons. I'll admit, it's extreme, but I'm not asking for permanence. Just through the end of the season." He shoved his own doubts and guilt into his no-regrets closet and slammed the door. Besides, she'd be a definite help to him when it came to landing that college coaching job after he retired. With her skills, Kelsie could teach him enough to be able to navigate the political waters populated by the university's athletic fund donors.

"How is this any different than me living here for nothing?"

"Because being my wife doesn't come without a cost."

"And what is that cost?" If her trembling smile was any indication, she was actually softening to the idea.

"Living with me for one."

She snorted, a damned unladylike snort.

"And you'd be my built-in buffer in social situations." Zach was on a roll now. The justifications rolled off his tongue. "I'll be the doting husband following your lead, nodding sagely, hanging on your every word. No one will expect me to talk when you're around. Hell, the men won't even notice. After I win my ring this year and retire, it legitimizes me as a contender for a coaching job I have my eye on."

"How does it do that?"

"College coaches have to be good at fundraising and recruiting, which requires a certain level of class. You're a classy woman. The guy you pick has to be at least somewhat classy."

"You would think." She tried not to smile. So did Zach.

"Look at Tomcat and LaShonna. She dresses him every time they go out, and he looks like a million bucks. He just follows her around carrying a glass of wine and smiling. Doesn't have to do a thing. He's already received offers to do college play-by-play once he retires."

"What if you don't win a ring this year? Are *you* retiring?"

"I'm winning that ring." He'd win or die trying.

"So what is this important job?" She was stalling, grasping at something other than the real subject of this conversation, he could tell.

He'd humor her for a while. "One of the defensive assistant coaches for the University of Washington is retiring this year. I want his job. I spoke to my agent, and he gave me the same line HughJack did. Get out there, tuxedo and all, and start schmoozing folks."

"You think my presence will help you get that job?"

"Yeah, your ability to say the right thing at the right time, and you always know how to dress or act in any situation."

"Maybe you need to learn how to behave in social situations instead of relying on someone else? Make small talk. Charm your co-workers, team owners, university donors. That type of thing."

He shrugged one shoulder. "I guess." It was a huge concession from a proud man with a stubborn streak larger than the state of Texas.

"Maybe you should start with Tyler."

Zach rocked back on his heels and shook his head. "No way. Not that ass."

"You don't think you'll need to deal with bigger asses than him in your future career? Maybe it's time you learned to cope with people you don't necessarily like."

"I don't think there are bigger asses than Harris out there." He tempered his opinion with a half smile.

"Of course there are. What about the brash young freshman who hasn't proven a thing but still has that cocky, disrespectful attitude? How are you going to handle him?"

"The way you teach me to handle him."

"Good answer." She almost smiled.

"So will you do it? Short-term. Until the season is over and I get the job." The more he said the words the easier it became to convince himself it was a solution for both of them.

"Teach you some manners? I've been trying."

"No, marry me."

"Zach, really. This is a crazy idea."

"It's a practical idea." Okay, so maybe it really wasn't so practical. In fact, it was pretty darned crazy, stupid, and irresponsible. Even more, it was like making a pact with his own personal devil, the woman who'd been his obsession when he should've been concentrating on keeping his baby brother safe. Maybe in some weird, twisted way this *was* his payback. God was forcing him to keep Kelsie safe as penance for not being there for Gary.

But who would keep his heart safe from Kelsie?

* * * * *

Marry him?

Kelsie's head buzzed, as conflicting thoughts battled for supremacy inside her muddled brain.

Zach's idea was nuts, crazy, absolutely insane.

She absolutely could not consider it.

Yet, she was.

Desperate women did desperate things. Right now, she wasn't sure what made her more desperate: homelessness, fear, or being in need of a hot night with a hotter man?

Good or bad, Zach Murphy attracted Kelsie on a physical level, always had, even though she'd masked her interest behind friendship and then ridicule. This would not be an unconsummated marriage of convenience, and it wouldn't be one either of them would escape unscathed. But could she keep it just physical? What if her heart entered into it? Maybe it already had, or she wouldn't even be considering this, would she?

Kelsie glanced toward the window. She could go back to living in her car, but only a too-stupid-to-live woman would do that. Yet, how stupid would marrying Zach be? She'd just gotten out of one bad marriage that almost destroyed her. She'd crawled her way back slowly, and she never wanted to be under another man's control, especially a man who had a score to settle.

What if his marriage proposal was a way to get even? How well did she really know Zach anymore?

She didn't have a lot of confidence in her judgment. She'd thought she'd known Mark. When it came down to it, she hadn't known him at all, from his first pointed criticism of her yellow sun dress the day after their wedding to the time she asked for a divorce, and he beat her almost to death, and she awakened in a hospital a day later. Then, to add insult to injury, her own parents had believed every word Mark said, devastating her.

Kelsie had stood on the outside looking in. She'd filed for a divorce and asked for nothing because Mark would maintain control if she'd gotten alimony. Terrified he'd punish her for leaving him, she'd run away. Only he had tracked her down. It was only a matter of time before he struck, and this time she might not be so lucky as to survive.

But…

She stared at Zach's kind face. She wanted to trust him, but she didn't—couldn't—trust any man. Zach's pure size and strength combined with his career in a violent sport forced her to be cautious.

Sure, there'd been warning signs with Mark, but she'd ignored them. A nearly fatal mistake. Once that ring circled her finger, she'd become his possession, walking, talking, and dressing exactly as he decreed. She might as well have been locked in a cell for ten years.

What about Zach? A marriage would mean more to him than it would to her, despite all his practical justifications. Would that be fair to him?

Her gaze slipped downward, past his wonderful lips drawn in a firm, straight line, his strong, square chin, those broad shoulders and wide chest, to his flat stomach. Lower still. His cock, the very one she'd been worshipping minutes ago, strained against the fabric of his jeans, and begged for mercy. Or was it retribution? She licked her lips, her eyes still down south. Her brain turned fuzzy, as she imagined all that glorious muscle and brawn on top of her, moving inside her, making her come in a rush of passion.

Oh, God, help me.

Zach cleared his throat, shifting from one foot to another. "Well?"

"Zach, I can't." She croaked out the words, betraying the raw need behind the refusal.

He ran a large hand over his face then stared her down with determination in his eyes. "I need you to do this for me. It's the quickest way for me to achieve my goal while the window of opportunity is open." Then he played the one card that trumped her ability to say no. "You owe me one."

"I—Zach, I don't think this is a good idea." Suddenly, her knees gave out, and she sank down in a chair.

"It makes sense on a lot of levels. The most important of which is it would keep you safe." He gained confidence, his voice clipped and strong, as if he wouldn't be denied. His naked chest dotted with dark, wiry hair swam in front of her face.

Kelsie shook her head to clear it. "I can't think with you standing there half-naked."

"I could be totally naked if that would help." He chuckled.

Her gaze slammed back to his crotch, and Kelsie's face heated up like a spaceship rocketing to the sun. "You're not helping."

He grinned, as if he assumed he was in control of the situation. "Take a half hour, I'll be in the kitchen making a snack."

Kelsie closed her eyes and bit her lower lip. He was right. Her life couldn't get any more screwed up unless Zach turned out to be as controlling as her ex.

Deep down her instincts had warned her about Mark. Her instincts didn't say the same thing about Zach. Not at all.

Lord, she wanted him. Like she'd never wanted another man.

She buried her head in her hands. Scranton crawled into her lap and pushed his wet nose against her cheek. His little tongue licked her chin. Kelsie hugged him to her, finding a small measure of comfort in his warm little body.

The push-and-pull in her head ping-ponged from yes to, *Are you freaking nuts?*

Zach offered stability she hadn't had in a while, but he was a strong personality who'd try to dominate her. He attracted her. She wanted to sleep with Zach with or without a marriage, yet something in his eyes warned her that he cared too much. She could break his heart again, and then she'd be back to being the selfish opportunist she'd once been.

She needed her independence, but she could set boundaries with him. On the plus side if he didn't comply, she'd leave. And she'd be able to get her business on track. Not only could she help legitimize Zach as a contender for the coaching position, but he'd legitimize her business. After all, if a woman could give a man like Zach a little culture and social graces, she could do that for anyone.

Kelsie rubbed her cheek against Scranton's soft fur while the battle raged in her head with more controversy than a presidential debate. She'd done worse to get where she needed to get, but she was a better person now. A far better person.

A deal with a brawny, brown-eyed devil might be the worst or best deal she ever made.

She lifted her head and glanced out the window again. Somewhere out there was a faceless man who followed her relentlessly. He might have stood near her car countless times and stared in the windows, his face pressed against the glass as she slept. He might have taken pictures of her or followed her into the public park bathroom in the dead of night when she needed to pee. Even worse, what might he do in the future? What might he be capable of? She couldn't stay in her car at Zach's, not now. She'd be back to a deserted parking lot or a city park. All alone. At the stranger's mercy.

No one would hear her scream. They'd find her bruised, naked body in a dumpster.

Kelsie shuddered.

She had few options and fewer choices, but one thing she knew for certain, Zach would keep her safe, and she owed him. It was the reason she'd come to Seattle. She could pay her penance and be an asset to him. She could help him land that coaching job by schmoozing those touchdown club donors, the coaches, and their wives.

Wouldn't that be a win-win in a bizarre sort of way?

Kelsie stood, still holding Scranton. "What do you think, little guy? Does living here beat living in a car?" Scranton wagged his tail and yapped. Staying here apparently had his vote.

Sometimes given to rash, split-second decisions, Kelsie made one. Squaring her shoulders, she walked into the kitchen before she changed her mind.

Zach glanced up when she entered, his brow furrowed with worry, as he clenched and unclenched his hands. Finally he shoved them in his pockets and leaned against the counter in a casual pose that was anything but.

She cleared her throat. "Can I tell you a story?"

"I guess so." His brows knitted together in the cutest way, as confusion crossed his rugged features. She found his vulnerability endearing. It sealed the deal in her mind.

"I was in Starbucks a few days ago, and a woman came in on the arm of man. She wore Ann Taylor, and he wore Fremont thrift shop."

Zach frowned and squinted at her, as if he was certain he was missing something.

Kelsie rambled on. "They didn't seem to fit. A woman needs a man who complements her in appearance but doesn't steal the limelight."

"Okay." Zach frowned, obviously clueless as to where her babbling was headed.

"The man's stubble and his long shaggy hair made him look like a homeless person. He needed a stylish haircut. He needed a shave. She needed to take him shopping for well-fitting clothes at a store that did tailoring. He was a big man and off-the-rack stuff wouldn't fit him properly."

He frowned. "Custom-made stuff is expensive."

"But quality lasts and men aspiring to certain positions need to wear clothes befitting of the position."

"How do you know he was aspiring for any position other than the missionary one?" Zach's mouth twitched into a half smile.

"Because I listened to their conversation. He'd been trying to find a job and couldn't." She did something very old-style Kelsie and snorted her snobby little snort. "A guy won't be hired for certain types of jobs dressed in redneck casual."

He raised one eyebrow. "So you would've dressed him for success?"

"Yes, and I would have made sure he looked the part every time he went out in public. No more holey jeans or ratty T-shirts."

Zach's dress of choice. He shifted his weight, still resting his butt against the counter. "Maybe that's what makes him most comfortable."

"If that's the case, then he wasn't the right man for that woman."

"He may have been the perfect man behind closed doors. Maybe she likes the challenge of a project."

"She does, but the project needs to cooperate to get what he wants, and spend his money to fund the project."

He started to smile, as if he'd finally figured out the method to her madness. "The project will cooperate but under protest."

"Good. Then I believe things will work out to be mutually acceptable to both parties."

"So that's a yes?" He stared at her earnestly, like a little boy pleading for a second piece of double-chocolate birthday cake. Only she was the cake. She couldn't disappoint him. Not this time, even though a small sane part of her screamed at her to run like hell.

She wouldn't run. She wouldn't hide. She'd face the music and give him her answer.

"Yes."

Zach blew out a long breath, relief replaced the tension in his body. He looked as if he didn't know whether to hug her or shake her hand. Finally, he patted her on the shoulder.

"I suppose you'll want a big ring?" His long-suffering sigh said it all, behind a glimmer of a smile.

Her racing heart, sweaty palms, and wet panties said more. A whole heck of a lot more. She nodded and walked out of the room, needing distance and wondering if she'd lost her mind.

CHAPTER 16

Offsides

As a kid, Zach avoided the principal's office as much as he tried to avoid his father's belt. Rarely did he have to sit in that stiff wooden chair while the fat, old principal wheezed like a guy in need of a good shot of oxygen. Zach became adept at flying under the radar and not catching anyone's attention, especially his father's. This talent served him well in his NFL career. He preferred to prove himself in the trenches rather than in television ads or Sports Illustrated.

Yet, here he was, called into the coach's office at six-fucking-thirty a.m., the adult equivalent of the principal's office. Even worse, Harris sat in a chair across from the coach, chatting with the man as if they were lifelong buddies. HughJack never chatted. The man's endless energy didn't allow for meaningless chatter. Derek sat in another chair, looking pissed that they'd dragged him into this mess.

True to form, HughJack wasted no time. Zach's butt barely hit the chair before he squelched the niceties and launched into the reason he'd called this meeting.

"Your dislike of each other is affecting this team's performance. Your very public argument in the locker went viral. It's trending on Twitter, whatever the hell that is, but the front office tells me it's not a good thing."

Tyler cringed and Derek studied the desktop. Zach wrung his hands and said nothing, even as a healthy dose of guilt clenched his gut.

"I tried to stay out of it. Let you work these problems through yourself." Coach skewered them both with an accusing glare.

Tyler leaned forward, avoiding Zach's gaze. "We're working on it. Zach and I won't sacrifice the team because of our differences."

HughJack looked skeptical. "How are you working on it?"

Both men looked at each other. Obviously, silver-tongued Tyler was at a total loss for an answer as much as Zach was.

"I, uh, advertised Zach's gala on my website." It sounded lame, and by the way HughJack puckered up his brow, he knew it.

Zach snorted. "Beware of quarterbacks with websites."

"Fuck you. Just because I don't do things the way you do them, doesn't mean I'm any less dedicated."

"You ever heard the saying that if you're good at something, you don't have to tell anyone about it, because they already know?"

"Hell, yeah, they know, but I'm making sure they don't forget. They'll remember me long after you're old, fat, and too feeble to toss a football around your backyard. There is a life after football, Murphy. You'd better figure out what that is because you're getting to the end of your shelf life."

"That's enough." HughJack pounded his fist on the table so hard his coach of the year trophy fell over. With a frown, he picked it up and examined it then set it upright. "I gave you two selfish clowns a couple months to work out your differences. You weren't mature enough to do it so the women in your lives and I have done it for you."

"Women? What women?" Zach couldn't imagine Kelsie getting involved in team affairs. Kelsie, his fiancée, just thinking the words made him forget where he was.

"*Your* women. The ones in your lives. All three of them: Rachel, Lavender, and Kelsie."

"Oh. Uh, yeah, my woman. We're engaged." Zach blurted it out just like he'd blurted out the proposal, feeling more than a little pride in saying it.

Tyler and Derek both gaped at him, but HughJack didn't miss a beat. "Congratulations, maybe she'll pound some sense into your thick skull." HughJack's eyebrows slammed together with that don't-mess-with-my-game-plan glower. "Rachel, Lavender, and Kelsie devised a plan to teach you two knuckleheads to work together regardless of your personal opinions of each other. I didn't like it at first but, hell, after last night's display, I'm willing to try anything."

Oh, crap. This did not sound good. The terrible trio and the coach conspiring together?

Tyler shot him a quick worried glance, and for once they agreed on something. They were screwed, really screwed. Even worse, she'd betrayed his trust, and there engagement wasn't even twenty-four hours old.

Harris sat back in the chair and rubbed his face. He blew out a ragged breath. "What kind of plan?"

"Every Tuesday, you'll meet and work on the gala. Together. No competition against each other. Just you and Zach. If the gala fails, you both fail as a team of two."

"But, we—"

HughJack cut Tyler off. "You're the team captains. Don't disappoint me. I expect you to put as much effort in this as you would any must-win game because this is a must-win for both of you."

"In what way?" Zach braced himself for an answer he might not want to hear.

"Do I really need to answer that, Murphy?"

Zach shook his head, feeling like a kid who'd been chastised for giving the wrong answer in class.

"Working together, you'll beat the amount of money we raised last year for the Seattle Hearts for Homeless charity."

"But last year was a record-breaker because that timber baron heiress died and left her estate to the charity." Tyler's face paled. He looked as if he was going to throw up.

"Then you've got a lot of work to do. Seattle is crawling with software CEOs and ancestors of timber barons." He looked pointedly at Tyler. "Like you."

Zach stared at Harris, his mouth dropping open in surprise. "You have that kind of history?" His nemesis having ancestors like that somehow didn't fit with the guy's image.

"How do you think Twin Cedars got built?"

Zach shrugged, feeling stupid that he'd forgotten that simple fact. "I thought it was rum-runners."

"That too." Tyler didn't take the least bit of offense.

"Regardless. Find new sources of donations." HughJack pulled the conversation back to the issue at hand.

"They aren't that easy to find," Tyler hedged. Zach noticed he dug his fingernails into the palm of his hand. "Not in this economy."

"What if we don't achieve it?"

"You'll be benched. Both of you for the first half of the first playoff game of the season or if we're on the verge of not making the playoffs then the last game of the season."

"You wouldn't do that."

"I wouldn't? Try me? Call it tough love. I've had enough of your bullshit ripping the team apart. Keep your differences to yourselves. On the surface you'd better be so enamored with each other that your teammates will think you're suffering man crushes."

"They'll never buy it. We can't do this." Harris clenched his jaw so hard Zach expected it to shatter any second.

"I trust you boys to rise to the challenge."

"You're nuts." Harris's angry look would've incinerated a lesser man.

"You won't be the first to claim that." HughJack shrugged, glowering at the two angry jocks.

Derek finally spoke up. "Coach, why am I here? I get along with everybody."

"You are the mediator, the final word in any dispute, what you decide is law. Keep these idiots out of trouble." He turned back to Zach and Tyler. "Your hatred of each other is killing this team. I thought about benching you both without this scheme, but now I have a way to do it and put it on both of you. Remember, this charity is very important to Veronica. Don't screw this up."

"But coach, we can't—" The look on HughJack's face caused Zach to swallow the rest of the sentence.

"One more word from either of you, and you'll be riding the bench for the rest of the season. I'm not so sure I shouldn't do that anyway." Coach looked down at his computer, dismissing them.

Zach had no intention of letting this team down by warming wood during the season. Harris stood and looked at Zach, his expression unreadable. Zach looked right back.

Harris leaned close. "Thanks, asshole." Heaving an exasperated sigh, the jerk walked out of the office.

Zach shot a hopeful glance at the coach. HughJack shook his head without ever hearing the question. Shoulders slumped, Zach left the room.

His life was being jettisoned right into the cold waters of Elliot Bay without a life jacket. The coach was forcing him to be best buddies with Harris, and Kelsie—his future wife—had had a hand in this. She'd gone behind his back just when he'd convinced himself maybe she'd truly changed, and he could trust her.

Yet, for a Super Bowl ring, Zach would sell his nuts to science. He wasn't so sure how he felt about his bride-to-be, except for the sex part. He definitely knew how he felt about that.

* * * * *

A few hours later Zach walked in the door as Kelsie stood on a six-foot ladder and cleaned cobwebs from the ten-foot ceilings in the parlor. She felt his powerful presence before she saw or heard him. Belatedly, Scranton lifted his head and yipped a half-hearted hello and went back to sleep.

Zach's heavy footsteps echoed across the hardwood floors. Kelsie didn't turn around. She stretched as far as she could to reach one large cobweb in the corner. The ladder teetered precariously then tipped. A scream ripped from her throat as she grabbed the air for something to break her fall. That something happened to be Zach. He caught her in his strong, muscular arms and pulled her to his solid chest. Gasping, she clutched his shoulders and buried her face in his sweatshirt. She clung to him, breathing in his clean, woodsy scent, and waited for her wildly beating heart to slow to an idle, while Zach held her stiffly to him.

Only it didn't slow, it sped up, pounding in her chest like the bass on a teenage boy's car. She nuzzled his neck, while his scent permeated every cell in her body right down to her wet panties. Lord, but she wanted this man. Now. She nibbled at his neck. He groaned but rather than responding in kind with those hot lips, his body tightened.

Realizing he was angry, Kelsie wriggled out of his arms, uncertain what she'd done to upset him. Straightening her clothes, she wiped the cobwebs and dust from her shirt. If her mother could see her now, she'd collapse in a dead faint. Carringtons did not do manual labor, especially dirty manual labor, and she'd done plenty lately, but the place was looking pretty damn good. In fact, it looked like a place that even Kelsie's snooty mother would be proud to call home.

She lifted her gaze to meet his. Desire and anger merged together. His nostrils flared as if he'd caught a whiff of her own need. It had to be rolling off her in waves.

He looked around the room and his gaze fixed on something. He looked more pissed than Scranton had the time she'd informed him they'd run out of dog food. He continued to stare as if she'd sold his prized possessions and spent his last dime. Kelsie followed his gaze to the pile of shopping bags still sitting in the entryway.

"I made an appointment with a tailor recommended by Lavender. He does all of Tyler's suits. You'll need at least one tux and a nice suit for less formal occasions. We'll start with the tux for the wedding and—" Her voice dropped off. "Zach? What's wrong?"

"Did you leave anything in the stores?"

She knew what he was thinking—that she'd jumped at the first opportunity to spend his money. Instead, she'd been quite frugal and was proud of it. "I bought you a few things."

"I don't need any more clothes. I have plenty."

"I thought I made things clear last night. Not the right kind. We need to make a good impression, and that has a cost."

"*We* do?" He swung his gaze back to her, disappointment melded with irritation in those chocolate depths.

"Yes. Us. If you want out, now's the time." Let him think the worst of her, it'd keep him from getting attached down the road.

"I already gave you my word." He set his jaw in that so-familiar stubborn way of his.

"You look miserable."

"Maybe it's the thought of having the same tailor as Harris."

She laughed in spite of herself. "Don't worry. And I didn't max out your credit card."

He grunted.

"You're home early for you." She glanced at her watch to verify. It was only seven thirty. "Hoping to find me in the tub again?" She teased him with a wide smile.

His eyes darkened at the memory, and his lips actually turned up at the corners. "Not a bad thought, but actually the power's out at the facility so we couldn't watch film. Some idiot backhoe operator digging nearby broke the underground power line." Zach walked over to a framed painting and fingered it as if to straighten it, only he made it more crooked. She expected him to comment on his missing football posters, but he didn't.

"Tell me what's wrong?"

He met her gaze, and she braced herself at the look he gave her.

"You sold me out to Coach."

"What?" She didn't understand. She hadn't talked to HughJack in over a week.

Uh oh. She broke out in a cold sweat and wrung her hands together. She really wanted to bite a hunk out of her thumbnail. "HughJack decided to implement our plan?"

"He sure did. Why didn't you warn me?"

"Because your coach said he thought our idea was stupid. I guess he changed his mind. Besides, it's for your own good."

"Forcing me to work with Harris is for my own good?" He stalked toward her.

Irrational fear clawed at her insides, and Kelsie backpedalled a few steps and hugged herself.

He frowned and moved closer to her. "I might be upset, but I'm not going to hurt you."

"I know." She hated that she'd reacted like that to him, but she couldn't help herself.

"Have you seen any more of the stalker?"

At the mention of trench-coat man, Kelsie glanced toward the window and the street beyond. "Nothing. Not a thing." She'd been looking over her shoulder, but so far no stalker.

"Good. I've got the security guys coming tomorrow to install a complete system."

"Thank you."

"I want you to feel safe here."

"I do."

Motioning to her, Zach turned and headed for the door. When she didn't follow, he stopped in the doorway and motioned to her. "Let's go get something to eat. I'm starved."

"Dressed like this?"

"Where we're going, you'll look just fine." He didn't wait for her response, just headed out the door.

Grabbing her purse, Kelsie ran after him, a little annoyed at his high-handedness. He helped her step up into his huge truck, and she patted herself on the back for teaching him a smidgeon of manners.

"Where are we going?" she asked, as they drove out of the city and headed east.

"To my kind of place. I've had enough of fancy dinners to last a while." Zach stared straight ahead and didn't say another word.

"Is this payback?"

"Damn right. Let's see how you blend in with the common folk."

Kelsie had never been much of a blender, more like an attention-grabber, but she'd do her best to fit in and demonstrate to him that good manners made friends in any social circle.

She stared out the window as the rain pelted it and ran down the glass in a steady stream of water, acutely aware of the virile, somewhat angry man a few feet from her. Her hand moved to the console, but she stopped it there. He wouldn't welcome her advances, not when he'd sworn celibacy until they said "I do."

The freeway gave way to a four-lane highway which gave way to a two-lane country road. Streetlights became few and far between until they drove down the main street of a small town. A sign proclaimed it to be Millville. Millville consisted of a half dozen blocks of mostly boarded-up buildings and ancient houses. Zach pulled into a parking spot in front of the most happening place in town. At least it was the only place with a sign of habitation.

She eyed the dump with skepticism. "What is this?"

"The Squatch. Best home-cooked meals west of the Columbia River."

"The Swatch?" The log structure looked old enough to have been constructed by the first loggers in the area. She didn't care for the looks of the place or for the group of rough-looking men and women standing near the doorway smoking cigarettes.

"The Squatch. You'll see." Zach hopped out and greeted the group as if they were old friends. Kelsie's stomach rumbled and she stepped out into a mud puddle, drenching her new shoes. She swore she'd been dumped into the middle of that country western song about the city girl who married the country boy.

Skirting past a couple Harley-Davidson motorcycles parked on the sidewalk and under the building's eaves, she nodded politely to the group near the door. They stared back at her. The woman frowned. The men looked her up and down like hunters sizing up a doe.

Following Zach in the door, she stopped in her tracks. A life-sized, stuffed Sasquatch, looking eerily real, stood near the old stone fireplace. The mangy thing had seen better days just like everything else in this hovel. Its huge yellow teeth must have been donated from a poor, hapless bear. All in all, the hideous thing probably gave small children nightmares. Good thing the state of Washington didn't allow children in bars.

"Cool, huh?"

Kelsie turned to Zach and shook her head. He guided her toward the bar with a chuckle. At least the place put him in a better mood.

He looked around the room. "These are my people, Kelsie. Get used to it." He motioned her to an empty bar stool next to him.

Kelsie slid onto the stool, careful not to touch anything. On the other side of her sat a wiry little man arguing with an equally wiry woman about the merits of catching moles with traps versus a good mole-hunting dog

The waitress wandered to the counter, gave Kelsie the once-over, and raised a-who's-this-chick eyebrow at Zach, who just shrugged. "What'll ya' have?"

"How about a glass of merlot."

"Don't have none of that fancy French wine, but we got a box of Mer-lot." She phonetically pronounced the two words.

"That'll be fine." She folded her hands primly in front of her and ignored the man next to her who was now eying her boobs.

"Enjoying yourself?" Zach grinned at her. Oh, yeah, payback was a bitch, and he'd likely only begun.

"Immensely." A bit of the old Kelsie's scathing sarcasm leaked into her voice.

"Now you know how I feel when I'm with your people." He took a long pull off his cheap beer and sighed with satisfaction.

Kelsie's *people* didn't use chewing tobacco or smell like cigarette factories. They rarely drank beer, and if they did, it was a microbrew. And forget wine in a box. She shifted uneasily, feeling their eyes upon her and knowing she didn't fit in.

The waitress came back, flashing her disgust and disapproval like the mega electronic casino billboard bordering I-5. She stopped next to Zach and placed a possessive, bony hand on his muscular thigh. Kelsie stared at the hand with its red-tipped nails as it caressed Zach's leg. He shifted uneasily and cleared his throat. Answering the bellow of the big, fat customer lounging in the back near the pool table, the woman cast one last threatening glance at Kelsie and sauntered off.

"Old girlfriend?" Kelsie kept her tone light even as she fought off the urge to mud wrestle this woman for Zach. God, this place was rubbing off on her.

"Wannabe girlfriend." He stared at the college football game on the television hanging above the bar.

"That's what I thought." She laid a possessive hand on his thigh.

"What's it to you anyway?" He stared at her hand and swallowed.

He had her there but she'd done enough beauty pageant interviews to think quickly on her feet. "I am going to be your wife. If there are other women in your past and present, I deserve to know."

"I'm surprised you care."

She dug her fingernails into his leg, but he didn't flinch. "Despite the circumstances, I won't cheat on my husband."

"And I won't cheat on my wife—despite the circumstances." Their eyes locked. The sexual tension arced between them, sizzling and smoking like a short in the wiring. Her wiring definitely shorted out when he was near.

"Good. Keep it that way. You wouldn't want to see what a former mean girl can do when she's pissed off."

He faked a shudder. "Nope, I'll keep my privates intact, thank you. Never know when I might need to use them."

Kelsie gazed into his warm brown eyes. She liked this Zach, liked when he softened his edges a little and relaxed. She liked how he smiled with his whole face, especially his eyes, and those rare dimples came out. Yes, if Kelsie Carrington-Richmond didn't watch herself she might do something inexcusably dumb and fall hard for a guy like Zach, which wouldn't be fair to him.

She looked down at her Mer-lot and swirled the red liquid around in her glass. She needed to keep her freedom and her emotional distance because if she dropped her guard she might end up right where she was last year.

She hadn't gained those hard-won inches of freedom just to lose them to another man.

CHAPTER 17

Charged a Time Out

Zach, having pre-wedding jitters, needed a little normalcy in his life so he spent Tuesday night the way he'd spent every Tuesday night since he joined the NFL, volunteering for a homeless family organization, Family Ties, which worked to keep families together even though they didn't have a roof over their head.

Zach did what he could, giving of his time along with a generous anonymous donation every month. Sometimes, Zach almost caved under the futility of it all, but he soldiered on, taking care of his little piece of the world as best he could.

Dedication to helping the homeless happened to be the one thing he had in common with Veronica. At times his resistance to the gala twisted his gut with guilt, not just because of Kelsie, but because each year it raised a significant amount of money for Seattle's homeless charities. And here he was being a shit about hosting it. He supposed if he dug deeper, it wasn't because he didn't want to support the cause. Obviously. But more because these fancy things had a way of bringing out the bumbling idiot in him. Without exception, he did something stupid and ended up looking like an uncouth moron.

Only this year he'd have Kelsie, not just as a mentor, but as a wife. He'd left her planning a wedding with the girls at his dining room table earlier this evening. She'd looked damn good, smiling and laughing, her eyes sparkling and her lips parting to show those white teeth. He ached for her and walked around in a perpetual state of horniness. It seemed like he'd sported a boner for days.

Thank God HughJack gave Harris and him a reprieve until after the wedding. Zach couldn't handle all this stress at one time: playing nice with Harris, keeping his hands off Kelsie, and getting hitched.

Shaking off his worries, Zach slogged through a large puddle, and down the sidewalk. He tipped an imaginary hat to the old vet known only as Danny. As usual the man sat on a bench under an awning next to the homeless shelter. Danny smiled a toothless grin and touched the bill of his new Lumberjacks ball cap in response, the very cap Zach had given him last week.

"How's it goin', Dan?" Zach paused and dug in his wallet.

"Good, man. My bones are aching, means it's gonna be a rainy fall and a cold winter."

"You would know better than me. Why don't you let me put you up in a room for the winter?"

"Nah, I'm fine right here. Walls give me claustrophobia." Danny took a puff on a cigarette stub he'd most likely found on the sidewalk. Zach tried not to think about it.

"I understand." At least, he understood as well as anyone could who'd never been in Danny's situation. The man served in Vietnam and was a POW for a year. Dan hated to be penned either in jail or behind the confining walls of an apartment. Still, it didn't seem right that someone who'd given so much to his country should live on the streets. Despite Zach's best efforts that's where Danny stayed. In fact, he seemed to resent any interference from Zach except his friendship. Pride was a powerful thing. As was the bottle. Danny held tightly to both.

Zach tucked a twenty in Danny's shirt, even though he knew the man would spend it on cheap whiskey. Pushing his way through the heavy door, he walked past the reception area where a large black woman sat with a pile of knitting. She made hats, gloves, and scarves to give to the people who came into the shelter.

Anitra nodded, smiled, and never missed a stitch, or whatever it was called in knitting.

A couple dozen kids of varying sizes and ages waited for him in an adjacent room, empty except for a few scratched tables and rickety folding chairs. They leapt to their feet with excitement, remembering he'd promised them a special surprise for this week's visit.

These kids shared a common bond. They were part of an alarmingly fast-growing homeless family population. He gave a high five to Ricky, an enthusiastic twelve-year-old who wanted to be a fireman. The kid had grown up in a middle-class neighborhood until his father lost his job and unemployment ran out. Now they lived in a tent in the mayor's tent city. Next he greeted Caleb, a quiet ten-year-old, who came to life when Zach talked sports. He lived with his two sisters and single mother in their car. She lost her job and her boyfriend on the same day, finding herself on the street.

Tonight, Zach had chartered a bus, and they were making the half-hour trip to Seattle's Museum of Flight, where he'd arranged for a special private evening. Afterward, they'd dine on pizza and juice at a local pizza joint.

"The bus leaves in five, guys. Load up." Zach motioned toward the door. The kids ran for it, yelling and screaming with pure joy. A half dozen chaperones followed at a more adult pace. The kids' enthusiasm never ceased to amaze him. God, he wanted to take every one of those kids home with him to his big, rambling empty house.

He'd done that once or twice before he'd come to Seattle, and it'd ended in disaster. Now he tried to give his time without getting personally involved. Doing as much as he could without having these kids' situations drag him down.

Just like with Kelsie. Sorta. Actually he'd tried to not get involved but he *was* involved, about as involved with a woman as a man could be, which was not the same thing. In fact, it was much worse than involved, yet he didn't see another option, no matter how stupid his solution was. He worried about her stalker. He worried about her being homeless. He worried he might not stop the next time he found her naked in his house. He groaned just thinking about the soap sliding off her shoulders to nestle between those creamy white breasts. Shit, his penis was rising to the task again. *Down, boy.*

Zach refocused his attention on the sweet little boy still sitting in a chair and clutching a child-sized football. The kid looked up at him with sad brown eyes, and Zach's heart melted like a wax on a stovetop. He reminded Zach of his brother.

Andy was new to his little group, about eight years old, and stick thin. His family was newly homeless. His sister had been in and out of Children's Hospital with cancer. Their family spent every penny on her treatment, the mother and father worked when they could. They'd recently lost their home. It was a sad situation all around.

Zach slid onto the chair next to him. "Aren't you going?"

Andy rolled the ball around in his hands.

"Hey, buddy, don't you want to see all those planes?"

Andy stared at his hands and nodded.

"They've got a space shuttle flight simulator."

The little boy twisted the sleeve of the tattered coat draped across his lap.

"Do you like space? I do. I wish I could go there someday. Don't you?"

Andy shrugged.

Zach dug in his pocket and found the individually wrapped Frango mint chocolates—the best chocolate on earth—he carried with him every Tuesday. He held one out to Andy. Andy grabbed it from his palm like a hungry dog diving into a bowl of food. He tore off the wrapper and stuffed it in his mouth. The look on his face was pure heaven.

"Good chocolates, aren't they?"

"The best. My grandma used to buy them every year at Christmas time, but she's gone now." His face fell at the memory.

This was the most Zach had ever heard him speak. "Is she gone to heaven?"

"Yeah. She gave us a home. Then she died. My uncle kicked us out of the house and sold it." The sadness in his tone almost undid Zach. "That's why we don't have a place to live."

"Hey, I'm sorry about that. You'll get another house. Soon. I'm sure." Zach clapped a hand on his bony shoulder.

"Before Christmas? If we don't get one before Christmas, Santa won't be able to find us."

"Santa will find you wherever you are. He doesn't need a house." Zach stood and picked up the child, standing him on his feet.

"Let's get a move on. Everyone's waiting for us."

Andy wrapped his tiny cold hand around Zach's. "Do you have any more chocolate?"

Zach laughed, causing the boy to smile. He gave him another. "Here you go, but don't tell the other kids. They'll be jealous."

The boy nodded. "It'll be our secret."

"Absolutely."

Zach walked to the bus with the little boy holding his hand, warmed by the fact that he could bring joy to a small boy, even if only for a moment.

He wished he could share such simple joys with Kelsie, the kind money could never buy, wished they could be like other couples and work side by side to help these families. He needed to be careful of expectations that would not happen.

They weren't going to be a normal, loving couple.

But the sex would be damn good.

* * * * *

The next week flew by with all the wedding preparations. Kelsie worked night and day until she fell into bed exhausted at night, which was a good thing or Zach's self-imposed celibacy might not have made it to their wedding day.

They'd planned the wedding for the bye week, a week and a half away. Rachel had volunteered their ranch house in the country, and Kelsie gratefully agreed. Zach wanted it to be an intimate affair, if you could call a wedding with every member of the Lumberjacks team and front office intimate.

Zach mostly kept to himself, working even longer hours than usual and sleeping on the couch while Kelsie took over the master suite. He avoided her as much as she avoided him, while the sexual tension in the house grew to unbearable proportions. Kelsie spent some lonely nights in that tub, but nothing relieved the need building inside her.

There'd been no trench-coat man sightings since the night of the proposal, and the newly installed security system gave Kelsie a measure of comfort. Even so, she never went anywhere alone, always inviting the girls to join her.

Zach still hadn't gotten over what he saw as her betrayal by forcing him to work with Tyler. At least Kelsie managed to convince the coach to wait until after the wedding before Tyler and Zach served their sentence together.

Kelsie spun in front of the mirror at the bridal shop, oddly excited about her upcoming nuptials. Regardless of the circumstances, she wanted to make this wedding a memorable occasion for Zach. In a few short months all that would be left of their short union would be the memories. She wanted him to remember her fondly.

"Are you sure you want to do this?" Lavender frowned at her, her carefully plucked brows in a grim, straight line. The woman was going to be a hard sell. In the corner, Rachel madly texted someone—had to be Derek—probably their version of phone sex, especially considering the look of rapture on her face. A twinge of envy slid through Kelsie. Even back in their honeymoon stage, Mark never enjoyed that kind of closeness or bantering. Ever serious and critical, he paraded her around like a soulless Barbie doll whose only purpose was to serve him. But Zach, now there was a man who would practice fifty shades of phone sex. She didn't know how she knew that but she did.

Kelsie stared at herself in the mirror. The classy off-white dress off the sales rack was the perfect dress for a woman's second marriage—especially when the marriage happened to be a sham. Well, except for the physical part. She wanted to drop her panties and feel Zach sliding inside her and—

Lavender snapped her fingers in front of Kelsie's face. "Hey? You sure you want to do this?"

Kelsie blinked a few times and met Lavender's concerned gaze. After considering her words, she chose the truth. "I don't deserve Zach, but he thinks I do."

"I love that dress." Rachel joined them and slipped the cell phone in her purse. Kelsie expected to see smoke curling out of the purse any moment.

"It works for the circumstances."

"And what are the circumstances?" Lavender pushed, not the type to give up easily. How could she be if she was with Tyler?

Kelsie didn't respond. Rachel and Lavender exchanged a glance, and Kelsie braced herself for a lecture.

The lecture didn't come. Well, not exactly.

"Zach's a nice guy. He's had a tough time of it. He needs a woman in his life for all the right reasons."

Kelsie bristled and fought the defensiveness bubbling inside her. They were concerned about Zach. Nothing wrong with that. In fact, it was admirable. Kelsie couldn't pin that trait on herself. How admirable was it of her to marry a man because she'd reached rock bottom, and he offered to bail her out?

Self-loathing curled inside her, but she pushed it away. She was a survivor. Survivors did what they had to do to survive.

"Zach will love you in this dress. You look like a princess." Rachel walked around the dress, examining it at all angles. Kelsie had already figured out Derek's wife was the queen of denial. She liked everything in her life neat and tidy, and all her friends to be happy and content.

"Thank you." Her gracious southern charm kicked in. She could do southern charm ad nauseam with the best of them.

"Just treat him well. He's a good guy."

"I know." And how would that work? Zach had worshipped her for so long, how would he deal with the real Kelsie, warts and all. Kelsie would break the poor man's heart once again, not by choice but because she wasn't any good for anyone. Her talents consisted of setting a gorgeous table and smiling for the judges while walking her walk. Not much to set her future on. Not much to start a marriage on. But then this wasn't a real marriage. Well, except for the sex part, and she couldn't wait for the sex part.

Lavender interrupted her thoughts. "So the Tuesday after the wedding the boys will be working together on this fundraiser."

Rachel nodded. "Derek wasn't exactly happy that he'd been enlisted as referee."

"Tyler was beyond pissed, but he loves a good fight because he lives for the making up."

They both looked to Kelsie. She couldn't quite say the same. In fact, she suspected Zach had briefly entertained booting her out on her ass and ending their entire farce of a marriage.

But he didn't. He needed her party planning expertise as much as she needed a place to live. And maybe just maybe, they actually needed each other.

If only—

CHAPTER 18

Threading the Needle

Zach stared at himself in the mirror hanging on the wall in one of the Ramseys' spare bedrooms. He didn't recognize the pussy-whipped guy who stared back at him. Was this what marriage did to a guy? Made him look like a sissy boy. Zach hated looking like a sissy boy. Hell, he hadn't even put a ring on her finger yet. That came in less than an hour. Damn. He was nuts to be doing this if she'd changed him this much already.

Other than their weekly Tuesday lesson, Zach barely saw Kelsie. She was busy running up his credit card balance with wedding preparations. He'd quit checking the account online after it hit five figures.

Yet, he'd been the one who'd insisted on a real wedding for his fake marriage. He couldn't see marrying Kelsie at the courthouse, despite the circumstances. He should've known she'd take the opportunity and run with it, including tuxes, bridesmaids, and the entire team as guests. Even Kelsie admitted she'd gotten caught up in the moment and gone a little overboard. Not that he'd deny her anything. His penis was making all the decisions right now.

Zach ran his hand through his now short hair. It'd been cut and styled this morning and girlie smelling stuff had been massaged into it. He'd never live it down if his defensive line got a whiff of him. They'd brand him a wimp, and that'd be the end as he knew it. Oddly enough, he didn't really give a shit as long as Kelsie liked it.

"Don't muss up your hair. It looks wonderful." Horatio, the flamboyant little guy Kelsie hired to dress him and do last-minute preparations, assessed him, needle in hand. Zach considered him a man-sitter, an insurance policy that Zach would conform to her idea of how a groom should look.

Zach rubbed his clean-shaven skin. He'd drawn the line at a manicure and pedicure. Next thing he knew Horatio would be trying to paint his nails or pierce parts of his anatomy. *Good luck with that, buddy.*

Horatio flitted around him, pinning the suit in places, sewing up a storm, then standing back and saying "tut-tut" every few minutes. Finally the little pest stood back and grinned. "You look gorgeous."

Zach clenched his jaw. "Uh, thanks."

"You two make a handsome couple." The guy tugged on Zach's suit pants getting a little too close to Zach's package for his comfort. He shot Horatio a warning glance threatening enough to send the man scurrying back.

"That'll do. You look fabulous. Your bride will be falling at your feet." Zach groaned at the mental image conjured by that statement. By the look on Horatio's face, Zach's bride wasn't the only one falling. Zach crossed his arms over his chest and glared down at the guy.

Tyler sauntered in looking like Mr. Spit-and-Polish to Zach's spit. It didn't matter how much you dressed Zach up, he still felt like what he was, a poor boy from the wrong side of the tracks. He tugged on his bow tie and refused to acknowledge the quarterback.

"Damn. Is that you, Murphy?" Harris walked a circle around him, chuckling the entire time.

Zach grunted and swiped sweat off his forehead. You'd think this was a real marriage with love and all that crap, as nervous as he was. Even Harris wasn't getting to him.

"Wow. You clean up pretty good." Tyler stopped in front of him and sniffed. "Whoa. You smell better than Lavender. Maybe you two can share perfume tips."

Zach said nothing, too nervous to give Harris's needling much credence. "Hey, Horatio, help Mr. Harris out here. He's a little disheveled." Zach mentally slapped himself on the back for his use of a word like "disheveled" and for the horrified look on Harris's face.

"Oh. Oh. Oh." Horatio gestured wildly with his manicured hands, just about peeing his pants as he feasted his eyes on the quarterback. The little guy rushed to Tyler's side and fussed over him. To Harris's credit, he didn't preen like a peacock or kick the little guy to the curb. Instead, his eyes bugged out, and he backed up a step as the pesky Horatio straightened Harris's tie.

When Horatio raised his hands toward Harris's face, Harris shook his head and fended the guy off. "Do. Not. Touch. My. Face. Or. My. Hair. Comprende?"

Horatio's shoulders slumped and he stepped back. Zach almost felt sorry for him. Harris didn't. Zach frowned, feeling a little protective of good ol' Horatio.

Lavender poked her head in the door. "Zach. You look incredible."

Zach shuffled his feet and felt like saying "Ah, shucks," as the heat rose to his face. Lavender crossed the room and kissed his cheek. She wore a sexy black dress showing a lot of skin in the back and cleavage in the front, yet still managed to look classy, not tacky. Harris swallowed and gripped the back of a chair as he stared at her. The man had it bad. Really bad.

"Ty, we need you in the living room to help move some chairs around." With a final wink at Zach, she left the room. Harris just about fell all over himself following her. Pathetic to see an alpha male reduced to a mega wuss.

Zach couldn't stop himself. "Harris."

Tyler turned, his hand on the doorknob, even as he cast a longing look in the direction Lavender went.

"Man, she has you whipped. I'd never let a woman tell me what to do."

Harris chuckled. "Just wait asshole, I used to say that. You day is here, and I've got a front-row seat."

"Never happen."

"Yeah, right. Bullshit. That's why you smell so good." Harris shook his head. "All a guy needs is the right woman. The one that makes you see that there's nothing else in your life that compares to her."

Zach frowned, not expecting the baldly honest answer from his arch enemy. "Is that how it is with you?"

Harris nodded and bolted out the door. Zach shook his head. He'd never be that stupid over a woman. He'd done that more than once with Kelsie, and she'd been in total control and almost ruined him. Now he had the control, and he intended on keeping it.

The little guy flitted around him like an annoying fly on a hot summer's day. Zach waved him off. "Hey, I think Harris might need some more help."

Horatio didn't even bother to ask if Zach needed anything else, he ran for the door and toward his latest man crush.

Zach drew in deep, calming breaths. The same routine he went through before a big game, attempting to calm his frayed nerves and squash the butterflies pounding against his stomach like a prize fighter about to win the bout.

Stay calm. Stay focused. Stay relaxed. This is just a business arrangement. Mutual to both of us.

Only he didn't believe it, not totally. He'd been in love with Kelsie for years and part of him still was despite all the things she'd done to him and all the time that'd passed. Tonight they'd consummate this marriage. She'd open her creamy thighs, and take him inside her. He'd never be the same. Never. And he didn't give a fuck what it cost him as long as he had her now. He adjusted his package, hoping for some relief but no such luck.

Harris stuck his head back in the door, Horatio hot on his heels with a brush in hand. "Hey, we're ready. Get your ass out here."

Zach shook off his nerves and strode out the door like he got married every day. He took his place at the makeshift altar in front of the large stone fireplace. The house was crammed to overflowing with his teammates and the team's staff. Even his brother Wade had flown in for the ceremony and would rejoin his team tomorrow in Vancouver.

Wade studied Zach as he took his place next to him. "Didn't recognize you for a moment."

"Yeah, she cleaned me up."

Wade chuckled. "And here I'm supposed to be the pretty one."

Wade had always been the handsome, suave brother, figuring out early what Zach never quite grasped: You get a lot more girls with bullshit sweet talk than with blunt honesty.

"You're sweating like a pig about to be loaded up for market."

"I feel like one."

"You and Kelsie Carrington. Who'd have believed it?" Wade shook his head and grinned. "Beauty and the beast."

"Hey, now, Kelsie's still a good-looking woman." Zach attempted a joke to lighten the mood.

His brother looked him up and down, from the tips of his shiny black dress shoes, his perfectly tailored tux, and his neatly styled hair. "You're a pretty man yourself. If I weren't your brother, I'd—"

"Enough. You've been spending too much time with only a stick and puck for company."

The rowdy crowd hushed and called Zach's attention to the back of the room. Rachel and Lavender stepped forward down the short aisle and stood in their places. Then Kelsie appeared, and Zach's heart crashed head-on into his ribcage. The damn thing must have stopped beating because he couldn't breathe anymore.

Kelsie looked straight into his eyes with a sparkling smile aimed straight at him and his mortally wounded heart. Her smile buried itself deep inside his soul. At that moment, he knew he'd do all this wussy stuff again and more for this woman.

He also knew he'd never fallen out of love with her.

Nor did he give a shit that he'd forgotten all about a prenup.

* * * * *

Kelsie gripped the pink roses tighter until the stems dug into her palms. This was Zach? Zach, the guy with the shaggy hair, perpetual stubble, and clothes a homeless person wouldn't wear. She couldn't believe her eyes until he smiled a nervous smile that was all Zach.

Her Zach was gorgeous, a man as handsome as any man she'd ever laid eyes on, a man who exuded pure maleness from his every pore, but he also was the epitome of kindness. The very kindness that shone in his soft brown eyes.

She stepped forward on Tomcat's arm, walking slow, taking her time. The big man at her side measured his steps with hers. She may never have another wedding again, so she'd savor every moment. Besides, she basked in the limelight. Her smile was genuine and for the first time in years, true happiness and contentment filled her, as if all was right with her world. Glancing left and right, she made eye contact with each and every guest. They smiled back, enjoying her happiness. Until one scowling woman sitting on the far side of the room caught her eye. Veronica. And she was not pleased. Not in the least. Kelsie turned away from her, not about to let the witch rain on her parade. Even if it was Seattle.

Kelsie took her place at Zach's side. He leaned toward her and mouthed the words *You're beautiful*. She mouthed back, *So are you*. He blushed, actually blushed.

Her heart full of joy, Kelsie stood beside Zach and listened to the preacher's words and spoke her vows with sincerity, as if part of her believed them, even more than during her first marriage.

Zach took her hand in his. His big hand completely engulfed her smaller one. His palms were sweaty. So were hers. The ring he placed on her finger was modest, so like Zach, nothing like the rock Mark had branded his possession with—the very rock that became a symbol of slavery not partnership.

"You may kiss the bride."

A collective cheer rose from Zach's rowdy teammates. He turned to her, almost apologetically. Screw the apologies and regrets. She wrapped her arms around his neck, stood on tiptoes, and planted a wet kiss on his lips. For a moment, he stood absolutely still as if in shock, his hands to his sides. A second later, he regained his wits and dipped her over his arm into a deep kiss worthy of a scene from a classic movie. Kelsie lost herself. All the other people in the room faded away. All she wanted to do was kiss her Prince Charming.

Zach lifted her upright and pulled back first, obviously rattled by the crowd gathered around hooting like a bunch of drunken sailors. She clung to him, her hands gripping his biceps. Their eyes met and he grinned at her, dimples and all. She smiled right back.

"Congratulations, Mrs. Murphy." His grin stretched wider than a football field.

"Thank you, Mr. Murphy." Kelsie Murphy? She'd never considered a last name change, but she'd rather have Zach's last name than Mark's. On the other hand, why go to the bother of changing your last name when you'd just be changing it back in a few months?

The next hour or two passed in a whirlwind of champagne, laughter, outrageous stories, and good-natured ribbing. As she gazed into Zach's kind brown eyes, she said her own silent vows. The last thing she wanted to do was hurt this man.

A realization slammed into her with the force of a Mercedes speeding on I-5. Zach, Mr. Tightwad himself, never asked her, the shopping queen, to sign a prenup.

What did that mean? Could it be possible that Zach Murphy actually trusted her?

She hoped so with all her heart because gaining his trust mattered to her. A lot.

CHAPTER 19

Running it Back for a Touchdown

Fake marriages required fake honeymoons. Zach hadn't planned on a honeymoon even though the bye week allowed a little latitude for time off. Instead, he figured he'd head home and get up at five a.m. to start his workout and game study. Same as usual. Just because he'd signed a piece of paper didn't mean his routine had to change.

Yet Tyler Harris, in a rare moment of generosity, whisked them into a limo, which took them to a floatplane on Lake Union and flew them to Washington's San Juan Islands. A few hours later, around midnight, Zach and Kelsie stood in the grand entry of the Harris family's century-old mansion, Twin Cedars, near Friday Harbor.

"Wow, this is incredible." Kelsie stared around the two-story room with a look of utter amazement. Zach had visited the run-down mansion in the spring with his new teammates as an uninvited guest. Grudgingly, he gave Harris credit for diving into the restorations on his ancestors' home. Zach had figured the guy would sell the priceless waterfront estate the first chance he got. Only he didn't. Instead, he'd poured tens of thousands of dollars into restoration, going against everything Zach thought he knew and believed about the guy.

Zach hated it when people didn't fit in the boxes he crafted for them.

Kinda like Kelsie. That beautiful, untouchable mean girl from his high school days refused to stay in her box, which left Zach off balance and uncomfortable. He liked people to meet the expectations he'd formed for them, not blow them all to hell. Not that either Harris or Kelsie were in danger of that, but Kelsie had punched a few holes in her box.

Homer, the old man who'd opened the door for them, tottered toward the grand staircase. "This way." He crooked a bony finger in their direction. Zach grabbed both their bags and started to follow the senior citizen up the stairs. At the last minute, he remembered his manners and stood back to allow his new bride to walk up the stairs ahead of him.

His new bride.

Homer swept open the door of a large master suite, which had been recently remodeled and reminded Zach of some English king's room—leave it to Harris. The large canopy bed dominated one corner of the room, complete with this drapery-like material allowing the large four-poster bed to be shut off from the world. The soft, rich carpet sank under his shoes. The traditional paintings on the walls encouraged romantic thoughts. Who'd have figured Harris to be a romantic?

"Here you go. There's a bathroom in there. The house is empty. The workers won't be in tomorrow so enjoy yourselves. I'll let myself out." The man winked at Zach and tottered out of the room. Kelsie stood in the doorway, looking around the room.

Zach stared at her like the lovesick fool he was. He couldn't believe she was here, and she was his wife.

His wife.

She turned to him, and his knees almost gave way. He grabbed the door jamb just to hold himself upright. She smiled at him, a tentative smile that touched his heart. Swallowing back the raw emotion clogging his throat, he entered the room, battling anxiety and nerves. This night had to be perfect.

She stood in the doorway as if waiting for something.

"Oh, crap. I forgot." Zach hoisted Kelsie into his arms and carried her across the threshold. She laughed, as he swung her to her feet, and the soft, happy sound nestled in his heart and burned in his memory.

Kelsie wandered around the huge room with the large bay window and French doors opening onto a balcony. Zach tagged along after her, feeling like a stray mutt panting after a purebred poodle. In the bathroom, a large jetted tub sat in an alcove with a bank of windows giving a spectacular view of the waterways and the islands. His deprived libido flashed images of Kelsie in another tub, naked, soapy, and pleasuring herself. Damn, but he wanted that job, wanted to replace her fingers with his fingers, or even better, his cock.

Zach crossed to the wine bottle sitting in an ice bucket near the tub. He opened the bottle and poured two glasses, handing Kelsie one. She gave him a stiff, tight smile and took a sip then turned toward the French doors.

Zach frowned, not sure what he'd done wrong. She'd been fine a minute ago. He followed her onto the balcony into the cool night air. No city lights glared off the water below them or blocked out the brilliance of the stars in the night sky. Kelsie leaned on the balcony railing and sipped her wine. Zach stood behind her, the wine glass gripped in his hand while he wiped his other sweaty palm on his jeans.

"It's really pretty." Okay, stupid thing to say but what else was a guy to say to his new bride?

"It's beautiful. I can see why Lavender raves about this place." She angled her body toward his, a million unspoken questions shining in her bright blue eyes. Zach was pretty damn sure he didn't have one answer to any of those questions. He was operating blind, just as she was. He doubted *Mabel Fay Buchanan's Book of Southern Charm and Etiquette* covered honeymoon night etiquette.

Uncertainty flickered in her eyes and poked a hole in his resolve to keep his distance. Zach took the wine glass from her hands and set both glasses on the railing. He stepped into her, hands on either side of the railing, and effectively blocked her escape. She stared up at him. He leaned into her, filled his nostrils with her sweet scent like wildflowers in a mountain meadow. Zach bent down, wanting, needing to kiss her. To make this marriage more than just a piece of paper and a mutual agreement between two people who each had something the other needed.

He hoped like hell he didn't screw this up.

* * * * *

As soon as Zach's large body and strong arms penned her in, waves of claustrophobia slammed through Kelsie, as if she'd been locked in a car trunk with no way out. She squeezed her eyes shut and fought the panic rising inside her. It wasn't Zach's face, but Mark's face that swam in front of her, his eyes dark with an obsession to dominate her, show her his strength.

That had been the first step. Then came the subtle jabs to her fragile confidence, the tearing down of everything she'd worked to build. The criticism turned to ridicule and belittlement. Then the emotional abuse escalated into total isolation and control and finally a physical beating. She couldn't let another man do what Mark had done to her.

Only Zach wasn't Mark.

He never would be Mark. Zach was one of the few good guys. Her heart told her so even as her brain battled her instincts, but the instincts won. She had to get free, get away, reestablish her control.

In an almost blind panic, she put her palms on his solid chest and pushed. Hard. Confusion clouded his features. He staggered back a few steps and stared at her with soulful brown eyes, like a golden retriever who'd been dumped off in a strange neighborhood—lost, alone, and abandoned.

"I didn't mean to assume." He shuffled his feet, hands at his side, and stared at his big feet. He felt like the awkward oaf he'd always been. Probably always would be. Obviously, Kelsie saw him that way. She took advantage of his retreat, slipped past him, and into the bedroom.

Looking drained and beaten, Zach hoisted his duffle bag. "I'll sleep in another room tonight."

She clutched her coat to her chest and nodded. "That would be best." Disgust rose inside her like the rapidly rising waters of a river in a flash flood. In his mind, she'd rejected him. In hers, she didn't deserve him. Didn't deserve a good man. Not a user like her. "Zach?"

He stopped in the doorway, hand on the doorknob.

"It's not you, it's me."

His crushed expression said he didn't believe her. A second later the door shut behind him.

Self-loathing clawed at her gut, a wild beast ripping away all the bullshit to the despicable person underneath. Running to the balcony, she gripped the railing and heaved huge gulps of air into her lungs. Kelsie squeezed her eyes shut and willed herself to get a handle on her emotions. Slowly her breathing returned to normal. She slumped onto a patio chair.

She'd changed. She swore she'd changed. If one good thing came of those hellish years with Mark, it had to be her compassion for others because without that she had nothing.

And for the immediate future, she had Zach, sweet, kind, rough-edged Zach. Instead of mounting his own attack, he'd backed off, like a true gentleman, more than Mark would ever be regardless of his polished manners and supposed good breeding.

Oh, God, she was so confused. She should go to him now. Talk to him. Make him understand what was going on in her head.

If this were a real marriage, she'd lay it all out for him because only with complete honesty could they survive. Only this wasn't a real marriage and they didn't need trust or respect to get through the next few months. They just needed to cooperate with each other and tolerate each other.

Yet, something inside Kelsie wanted more. Needed more. Zach might be the only man who could heal her. Only at what price to him?

She crawled into bed and tried to sleep.

A few hours later, Kelsie gave up on sleep. She'd tossed and turned and played the entire night over and over in her head. She'd overreacted. Panicked. And she felt stupid. Really stupid. And weak. And she despised weakness, especially in herself. Just because she didn't want to be under another man's control didn't mean she couldn't sleep with a man. She so wanted to sleep with Zach Murphy. She wanted to feel those bulging muscles ripple under her fingers. She wanted to rake her fingernails across his broad back. She wanted to wrap her legs around his waist and urge them both onto something incredible.

Because despite all her misgivings and excuses, sex with Zach would be incredible. She just knew it. The same instincts that had told her to run when she'd stood at the altar that first time, told her to stay put and make of it what she could. Zach wouldn't hurt her. She needed to believe that. Needed to trust her own instincts and to trust him. The only way to take a step forward instead of backward was to jump into the deep end with both feet and pray she could swim. It didn't matter if she dog-paddled or treaded water as long as she didn't drown.

Picking up her phone, she texted a message to Zach: *I'm sorry and lonely.* Slipping out of her jeans and shirt, she left on the lacy bra and panties—matching— and pulled on a silk robe courtesy of Rachel and Lavender. She quickly doused the lights and lit a few candles then stood near the French doors and waited.

A few seconds later, the hall door opened and Zach's large body filled the doorway. The light from the hallway spilled into the room and cast shadows on his handsome face. He'd yanked on a pair of faded Levis and left the fly unzipped. No underwear. His bare chest sprinkled with dark chest hair rose and fell. His dark hair, still full of product, stuck up in several places with one wayward lock plastered against his forehead. He glanced around the room until he spotted her.

Kelsie sucked in a breath, managed a tentative, yet encouraging smile. His eyes flashed with fire, though hooded with wariness. He ran his hands up and down his thighs, the action flexed his biceps. She cleared her throat, as one hand lifted of its own accord, wanting to stroke those football-honed muscles.

"What took you so long?" Despite the tremor in her voice, she kept it low and sultry, playing a seductress as best she could. As best as her fragile confidence would allow. Obviously, it was good enough for Zach.

"I, uh, uh." Despite his size, he didn't look intimidating. He looked as uncertain and insecure as she felt.

"Zach, come here." She smiled at him, a welcoming, apologetic smile. "I'm sorry."

"Nothing to be sorry for. This was a business arrangement. I thought it might be more." He shrugged one shoulder. "My mistake." Tentatively, he walked across the room until he stopped a few feet from her. His dark eyes traveled up and down her body until their gazes met and held like a magnet to a magnet. The raw hunger in his eyes sent a thrill of fear and pleasure up and down her spine.

"I was scared, Zach."

"I shouldn't have come onto you when you don't find me, uh, well, attractive."

Kelsie had to laugh. He looked so earnest, so sad. She reached up and cupped his face in her hands. "Zach, I do find you attractive. Maybe too attractive. Perhaps, that's part of my fear. I just got out of a bad, long-term marriage. A really bad one. I'm gun-shy."

"What happened? You can tell me."

"I will. I promise. Sometime soon. For tonight, let's see where this goes. No preconceived expectations."

"Well, except you'll run interference for me at parties, and I'll pad your bank account." His lopsided smile did more for her than a day at the spa.

She inhaled the scent of this man and rubbed the pads of her thumbs across his stubble. "About that. You didn't have me sign a prenup."

"Should I have, Kelsie? Are you going to rip me off? You told me you're not a mean girl anymore, not a user. So I guess I'll find out, won't I?" His dark eyes dilated and his breathing sounded harsh.

"You trust me not to take you for all I can?" Something warm and fuzzy took root in her heart. No one had ever trusted her to do the right thing before. Never. But Zach did. He put his trust in her. Maybe she didn't deserve it, but she'd find a way to earn his trust.

"I'm going to try."

"And I'm going to prove to you that I'm not the selfish bitch I once was."

"I'm counting on it."

Another smile tickled the corners of his mouth. Kelsie loved making him smile. She stared at those lips like a woman seeing paradise after a long drought in hell, which was essentially pretty close to accurate. She wanted him, and common sense be damned.

By the fire smoldering in his deep brown eyes, they just happened to be on the same page for once.

Standing on tiptoes, she pressed her lips against his. His mouth softened, his arms circled her waist, and he pulled her close. His erection rubbed against the thin material of her robe and rubbed something even deeper and long buried inside her. Her earlier panic stayed in its box, replaced by an undeniable truth whispering in her ears. This felt so right. So very right.

They kissed and her passion ignited like a match thrown on a field of dry grass consuming all her senses. Zach tugged on the belt of her robe until it fell open. His hard chest pressed against her softer skin, singeing her with a heat hotter than a Texas summer sun.

She'd known all along, even back in ninth grade, that they would be a combustible match. The danger to her heart loomed so real and frightening, she sought to keep it from overwhelming her. She wouldn't turn him down twice. She'd already bruised his ego one too many times. Tonight was payback for all she owed this man. And pay him back she would. Handsomely. Passionately. And without regrets. Tonight she'd give him her body and possibly something more. Much more.

Zach groaned and pushed the robe off her shoulders. He stepped back to stare at her with a sharp intake of breath. Kelsie let the robe slip to the floor and stood in the doorway with the moonlight bathing both of their bodies.

"You're beautiful."

"Thank you." She looked him up and down. "So are you, in a very male way." There was nothing remotely feminine about this man. Every square inch of his body was pure testosterone. Just the way she liked him. She lowered the straps on her lacy bra, reached behind and unfastened it, letting it join her robe in a heap of silk and lace on the floor. Zach growled, a pure male sound from a man barely tamed by civilization. He reached out a large hand and tentatively cupped her breast, running his fingers over it, as if memorizing every inch of skin. Bending his head, he sucked her nipple, so gentle and sweet the sensations almost undid her. She wasn't used to gentle.

Her sexy linebacker lifted her in his arms and carried her to the romantic four-poster. Placing her on top of the down comforter, he lay next to her. His big hands stroked her body, naked except for an immodest g-string. She closed her eyes and willed herself to relax—not hard to do considering the magic web Zach wove around her.

Kelsie sighed and slammed the suitcase shut on her misgivings over being controlled, along with her other dysfunctional hang-ups. She closed her eyes and enjoyed his rough hands roaming gently over her body, as if she was the orchestra and he, the conductor. She wanted to make beautiful music with him all night long.

After all, it was their honeymoon, such as it was, and she'd already wasted valuable hours because of her baggage.

Zach's tongue and mouth lavished more attention on her nipples than he did over the television during Monday Night Football. Oh, dear, now she was even thinking like him. He slid his free hand down her ribs, across her belly, and under the miniscule crotch of her g-string. He cupped her mound and lifted his head. "You shaved."

She nodded, unable to form one coherent word.

"I like that. I like a woman bared to me in all ways including her body. Are you bared to me, Kelsie? All of you?" His husky voice reverberated through her body, sending pulsing waves of passion to the center of her sex.

"I'm trying," she gasped.

"That's good enough for now." Zach eased his large index finger past the folds of her opening. She tensed slightly, expecting pain out of habit. Zach hesitated. His eyes met hers with a thousand unspoken questions lingering in his dark gaze. She turned her head away, not wanting him to read how far she'd sank with Mark, how much she'd tolerated, how little she'd thought of herself.

"Relax," he whispered, his husky voice soft and gentle. He touched his finger to her clit, rubbing back and forth in a gentle motion until she begged him with her body to go deeper. He slid his finger inside her with deliberate slowness, taking his time, waiting for her to push him deeper with her hips. She did. Once he'd gone as far as was possible, he pumped his finger in and out, all the while rubbing her clit with his thumb. The clouds opened up, and she saw heaven, pure heaven. Only the streets weren't paved with gold, they were paved with Zach's kind eyes and crooked smile, much better than rooms full of gold and designer clothes.

Kelsie tossed her head back and forth on the pillows, so very near to coming. To going to that heaven she'd only glimpsed. Chewing on her lower lip, the explosion built inside her. One more circular rub of his thumb launched her straight to that heaven at the speed of light—or was that lust. Zach held his finger inside her, waiting until she floated back to earth.

Lost in the haze of an incredible orgasm, Kelsie lay boneless and spent. She'd never experienced such an incredible high and only with a man's finger. But not just any man. Zach. Proud, stubborn, sexy Zach. And for now, her Zach.

Zach shifted off the bed and shucked off his jeans. He fished a condom out of his pocket, ripped it open with his teeth, and rolled it down over his cock. Turning to her, he pulled down her underwear and discarded it.

"You came prepared?" She smiled up at him, and he smiled back.

His grin spread from cheek to cheek, revealing dimples she'd never seen before. He crawled back on the bed, between her legs. He ran his naked body up hers until his chest hair tickled her nipples and his breath fanned her hot cheeks. "I need you, Kelsie." He spoke as if asking permission. His voice betrayed the strain of holding back.

He needed her. Her? He needed *her?* The poor man had no idea what he was getting into.

The lid on her baggage opened a crack, and claustrophobia and panic threatened to escape. *No. No. No.* She wouldn't hurt Zach like that again. Kelsie tucked her insecurities back inside, slammed the lid shut, and latched the suitcase. She locked it and threw away the key. With a welcoming smile, she gazed up at Zach, as a woman who'd battled her demons and won. Set free and ready to tackle the next chapter in her life.

"I'm yours," she said, and she meant it. She touched Zach's face with her finger, ran it down his stubble, even though he'd shaved several hours ago, it still darkened his jaw. This was a man. All man. And for now, her man.

Zach pushed her legs apart and guided his cock into the slick, wet opening recently occupied by his clever and talented index finger. He shuddered, closed his eyes for a moment, as if savoring it and filing it away for the future.

She'd bet her beauty queen crowns the man's cock was even more clever than his finger. He took it slow, giving her time to adjust to him physically and emotionally. Sure, she'd been with other men before her marriage to Mark, including some older, experienced men, but Zach was different. She didn't know why, but sometimes words didn't do feelings justice, even the words in her head.

When Zach's penis rested inside her fully, the head rubbed against her deepest spaces. She'd never had a man this large or this gentle and caring. Even sweet. He filled her body and he filled her mind and soul. She wrapped her legs around his waist and held him to her, pushing him deeper by adjusting the angle of her hips. He stared down at her, holding himself up by his arms so he didn't crush her with his large, muscular body. His face reflected deep concern even as she read the tension of holding back emblazoned on the creases around his lips and eyes.

"Make love to me, Zach."

He nodded, his lips tightened, his eyes hooded. He withdrew then thrust back inside, with an easy, steady rhythm obviously designed to maintain control over his body. Kelsie didn't want control. She wanted Zach, the man. She wanted the passion he showed for football directed at her, given to her. She wanted to be more desirable to him than a coveted Super Bowl ring.

Kelsie buried her fingers in his hair and kissed him as if he held the key to eternal youth. Maybe he did. He kissed her back and the wilder their mouths mated the wilder their bodies followed until his controlled thrusts exploded into a wild frenzy of thrusting hips and sweaty bodies punctuated by groans from him and whimpers from her.

Kelsie's body swept her mind into another wild ride, only this time Zach traveled with her. Higher and higher they climbed, like bungee jumpers riding a tram to the top of the cliff, and then they jumped off together, clinging to each other in a moment so intense neither was certain they'd survive, so they held on, determined to make a few seconds last a lifetime. When they hit the end of the cord, they didn't die but bounded along, drawing out the pleasure, until only a gentle swaying remained.

Zach rolled onto his side, taking her with him, his partially-hard cock still inside her. She lay on top of him. Her cheek pressed against his chest, wet from his sweat. She filled her nostrils with the sweet scent of sex, so uniquely theirs. It mingled with the scented vanilla candles burning about the room.

Somewhere inside her, he'd permanently branded his name on her heart.

CHAPTER 20

Naked Bootleg

They must have fallen asleep because Kelsie woke to the sound of rain hitting the windows of the old house. Zach stirred next to her. His crooked smile warmed her heart. She reached out to him, kissed his warm mouth, and smiled back.

Drunk with hazy feelings she couldn't decipher, she needed to explain her earlier behavior.

"Zach, I'm sorry I overreacted. It had nothing to do with you."

"You said that." He nibbled on her collarbone.

"I know. I need to explain more."

"Okay."

"Zach, this thing between us isn't just about sex."

"Really? What's it about?" His tone was playful, hers was serious.

"You. I love being with you because of who you are." She needed him to understand that the former selfish girl wasn't using sex to manipulate him or draw him into her web. "Maybe in my younger years I might have used my body to get what I wanted, like winning pageants, but this isn't like that."

He pushed her off his body and sat up against the headboard. The frown on his face cut a trench down both sides of his jaw. "You used your body? Did you sleep with the judges?" He looked like a husband who'd just discovered his church-going wife moonlighted as a stripper.

Kelsie sat up and gathered the sheets around her. "I'm not proud of what I did, Zach." She couldn't bear to look him in the eyes. Maybe she'd been too honest this early in their relationship.

"You slept with the judges?" He repeated and scrubbed his hands over his face. When he looked up again, their gazes clashed. Confusion warred with denial on his ruggedly handsome face.

"I did what I thought I had to do." She searched his eyes for understanding, desperately needing someone in her life to forgive her and help heal some of the overwhelming guilt nesting inside her like squirrels running amok in the attic.

"But you didn't really sleep with the judges?"

Kelsie stared at her hands, tried to find the words to explain her actions. "There was a lot of pressure on me to win by my family."

"But you slept with the judges?" His brain seemed to be stuck on that one horrible fact from her past. His expression closed off, shutting her out.

"Zach, I had to win." She tried to touch him, but he jerked away, as if she might soil him.

"I have to win, too, but I have my boundaries, my ethics." He combed a hand through his close-cropped hair.

"I had to win to survive at home."

He shook his head. "I don't understand."

"You think my childhood was wonderful because we had money, don't you?"

He nodded.

"Well, let me tell you. It was hell. Pure hell." Kelsie needed to make him understand. She didn't want him to think the worst of her.

"I can't imagine it was worse than mine."

"Not worse, but it wasn't good either."

"Tell me why it wasn't good. What did the poor little rich girl ever have to worry about?"

Kelsie took a deep breath and dredged up a past she'd attempted to bury in her backyard of bad memories and mistakes.

"As far back as I can remember, my mother paraded me on stage before judges, made up like an unnatural doll and looking way older than I should have. The consummate beauty pageant mother, she didn't allow me to play with other kids—I might get dirty—or to ever appear out of costume down to the heavy makeup which transformed my face into the face of a hooker. My life was constant practice, countless hours of dance lessons, baton-twirling lessons, and beauty makeovers. My weekends were beauty pageant after beauty pageant."

"What about your father? Where was he in all this?" Zach still held his body away from her, but his accusing gaze softened slightly.

"My father stayed out of it, obviously grateful we weren't in his hair. Besides, he had his own high expectations. Carringtons do not get bad grades. Carringtons always present themselves with class and dignity. Carringtons aren't allowed to have human failings. The first pageant I remember losing was at the ripe old age of five years. My mother locked me in my room without dinner, access to a bathroom, or water for twelve hours."

"No bathroom?" Zach frowned, not looking quite so judgmental anymore.

Kelsie stumbled on before she lost her nerve. She'd never told this to anyone. "When I turned thirteen, Mom declared me too flat and made an appointment for breast implants. Terrified, I ran to my father. It was the first and only time he put his foot down when it came to me. My parents almost divorced over what I secretly called Operation Big Boobs. Instead my mother resorted to buying push up bras, custom-made. So, yes, I guess I was programmed from diapers to win at all costs, no matter the price."

"So you slept with the judges?"

"Once. Not an old guy. A younger one from a washed-up boy band."

Zach shook his head and rubbed his eyes, as if he couldn't quite figure out what to do with this information. When he glanced up, he looked so sweet and so confused that Kelsie couldn't help herself. She ran a finger along his jaw line, over his pursed lips. He pulled away, got dressed, and left her alone with her turbulent thoughts and a bucket full of regrets.

* * * * *

Zach stared out the window at the rain falling on the bay beyond. His thoughts scrambled with conflicting realities or at least his reality as he'd known it.

When he'd woken in bed with Kelsie after an amazing night of sex, he'd been afraid to open his eyes, to find out it'd all been a dream, an erotic figment of his usually boring imagination. Yet her soft body was sprawled on top of his harder one melding their sweat-slicked skin together. Soul-deep satisfaction had settled in his bones. No man could imagine this, especially a practical man who rarely left reality behind.

He'd left it behind last night. Not only left it behind but jettisoned it right out of his comfortable galaxy into uncharted territory. He'd always known that one night with Kelsie, the girl of his fantasies, would ruin him for any other woman, and now he was sure it damn well had.

Then she'd dropped the bombshell. She'd traded her body for a Miss Whatever sash. She'd prostituted herself to get what she wanted. How the hell did he know she wasn't doing that now? Did it even fucking matter since they were both using each other in this crazy-assed marriage of theirs? A stupid idea from the beginning, it seemed even more ridiculous in the morning light. Especially considering how tarnished his princess was.

Funny thing was, knowing what he knew, he'd still make the same decision. He wanted her, no matter the price, no matter how temporary, no matter how damaged he'd be at the end of the relationship. He'd make a deal with the devil to keep her for as long as possible. Perhaps, he already had.

Kelsie ran a delicate hand along the bump in his right collarbone, and he stiffened. He'd been so deep in thought he hadn't heard her approach. "What happened?"

"Broke it in college." Her hair brushed against his shoulder, and he breathed in the heady scent of her shampoo and expensive perfume blending with the smell of sex and sweat.

"Have you broken a lot of bones over the years?"

"A few." Some playing football, some caused by an abusive father, but Kelsie didn't need to know about Zach's upbringing.

She planted a kiss on the bump and laid her cheek against his shoulder. "You're so invincible."

"Hardly. I wish it were true." He was a pansy everywhere but the football field and especially when it came to her.

She lifted up and gazed into his eyes, her brows furrowed in the cutest way. He was so screwed. "Zach?"

"Yeah?" He stroked her hair, marveling at how the strands slipped through his fingers.

"I saw the memorial to your brother in the yard." She stared into his eyes, as if plumbing for his deepest secrets.

He grunted in response, not wanting to pile his personal pain on top of her painful admission.

"I'm sorry, Zach. You were with me at the country club the day he died. I didn't know. I really didn't know."

"I don't want to talk about it. Not now." *Not ever.*

She looked crushed, as if he'd just told her an eagle had swooped down and carted off Scranton. "Sorry. I know some things are best left alone."

"This is one of those things. Okay?" He softened his voice, knowing he'd sounded too harsh.

"Okay." She wrapped her arms around him, laid her head against his chest and closed her eyes. Her small hands clutched his back. Actually, it felt good to be needed like this. He shut his eyes, put his arms around her, and tried to live in the moment, not the past.

When it came to Kelsie, he'd been the one to trail after her like a puppy begging for a pat on the head. She'd tossed a few crumbs his way during their high school years just to keep him on the line, to use him when the need arose, to carry her books or stroke her ego or make her latest boyfriend jealous. He'd been nothing to her but a means to an end. Just like that pageant judge.

Zach shuddered. What made him believe things had changed one little bit when it came to him and her? Except one big thing had changed. This time he held the cards and the money, and she held nothing.

Except his fragile heart.

* * * * *

That afternoon they left and as soon as the float plane landed on Lake Union, Zach dropped Kelsie off at home and headed to HQ to watch game film. It was after midnight when Zach dragged his tired body into the bedroom he would share with Kelsie.

Trying to concentrate on film had been next to impossible. His concentration broke several times as his mind drifted to Kelsie's face and the look in her eyes when he drove her over the edge during sex. Nothing could stand in the way of his quest to win a ring. Nothing. Not even his dream girl wife and fantasy-come-true in bed.

Zach stripped off his clothes and hesitated beside their bed. Kelsie's arms were wrapped around his pillow. Her little dog snored at the foot of their bed. This was his life now. With a sigh, he crawled into bed next to her. Immediately, she wrapped her arms and legs around him and clung to him. Zach held her tight, his resolve evaporating like steam from a whirlpool tub.

"Where were you?" The worry in her sleepy voice caused a twinge of guilt.

"Working." He rose up on one elbow, fear rolled through him. "Are you okay? Is something wrong? Have you seen that guy?"

"No. Not at all. Not since that night you proposed. It's as if he's disappeared into the mist."

"Let's hope he stays that way." He'd done all he could, installed a state-of-the-art security system, and paid a company to make a pass by their house every hour. Maybe the jerk found an easier victim.

Kelsie bit her lower lip, her gaze slipping to the window and back to him. "I was just lonely. It was so late, and I hadn't heard from you."

"Sorry, I'm not used to updating someone else on my plans. I was watching game film. It was damn hard though." He ran his hand up and down her spine.

"Because of me?" She lifted her head.

"Yeah. The sex between us is fucking fantastic. I'm a man. How can I not be distracted?" He sat up and pulled away from her, unable to think clearly when she rubbed her body against him like that. "I've been thinking. We're halfway through the season. I can't afford to lose focus. Maybe I should sleep in a separate bedroom for the rest of the season."

He rolled to a sitting position and swung his feet to the floor.

Kelsie grabbed his arm with amazing strength and surprising desperation. "No, that is so not going to happen, buster."

A warm feeling settled in his gut. She wanted him here with her. Zach couldn't deny her. Once the season was over, she'd leave him, and he'd never know the feel of her silky skin sliding across his rougher skin. Or hear her whimper when he touched just the right spot. Or see her brilliant smile when he made her laugh.

He hated his weakness for her, hated that she only had to say a few words, and he panted at her feet, lovesick fool that he was.

Love?

Yeah, dumbshit, love. He'd loved her from the minute he'd laid eyes on her in ninth grade, and despite what she'd done to him, he still loved her. No one would dispute his stupidity or his insanity. Especially considering how cruel she'd been to him, yet he kept coming back for more.

But right now, the object of his high school obsession wanted more nights with him and he couldn't deny her. He might be a strong guy, but he sure as hell wasn't that strong.

Fumbling for a condom and putting it on, he rolled back onto the bed and pulled her into his arms. She came willingly, placing one of her longer-than-heaven legs across his body to straddle him. She might be a she-devil in disguise, but he'd gladly burn in damnation for the rest of his life for one more moment with her.

After flipping on the bedside lamp, Kelsie placed her palms on his chest, pushed him back down on the bed and leveraged her hips over his large dick. "I want to see you." Her throaty whisper sent a shiver running along his thighs.

He closed his eyes and waited for flesh to meld with pleasure. She lowered herself onto him, sheathing him inside her like an expensive glove made just for him.

Him, and no one else.

When she'd taken him inside fully, he opened his eyes and met her starkly blue ones. Something lingered behind her attempts at bravado, something he couldn't put a finger on. Could it be regret that she'd sold her soul to this particular devil? Or was something else putting those wrinkles above her pretty brow. He didn't want to be the one who made her unhappy. He wanted to make her happy, find a way to keep her in his life, regardless of the circumstances.

Not a good situation for a man who prided himself on not needing anyone. The sooner he faced facts and admitted he meant nothing to her but a means to an end, the sooner he could accept this false marriage as nothing but a farce and quit trying to read more into it.

Using her arms for support, she lifted herself up and then lowered herself back down, one excruciating inch at a time. And there were a lot of inches, if he did say so himself. She threw back her head, her blond hair a tangle of tawny curls. Then she lowered her head with a feral growl of female satisfaction as she fully seated herself on top of him. Her hair danced across his chest in silken waves, and he groaned the groan of a dying man. What a helluva way to die.

Over and over again.

If he could, he'd convict her of homicide and lock her up in this bedroom to serve out her sentence.

A few more times she tortured him with sensual slowness. Unable to take it anymore, he grabbed two handfuls of her incredible ass and drove her home. A wild woman smile dominated her beautiful face. He raised her up and drove her back down. She added her own power to their combined thrusts. She lifted him to ecstasy and took the trip with him, as his orgasm came in wave after incredible wave.

Definitely murder in the first degree.

She collapsed on top of him and soon fell asleep. Zach stared at the ceiling, his mind whirling with how he'd keep himself focused on his goal of winning a Super Bowl.

Somehow that goal seemed to pale in comparison to the woman cuddled against his chest.

He loved her.

Now what the hell was he going to do about that?

CHAPTER 21

Running the Option

Tyler's high-rise condo was so silent you could hear the tension crackling through the room like rain on high-tension electrical wires. Kelsie wrung her hands and racked her brain for something witty and ice-breaking to say. Nothing came to mind. She glanced at her girlfriends. Rachel raised one eyebrow while Lavender just shrugged.

Tyler sat on one side of the table, his handsome face as hard as granite. Zach sat on the other. His chin jutted out at that stubborn angle Kelsie recognized meant trouble to anyone crossing him. Derek sat at the head of the table, looking every bit like a man being led to the gallows. Tyler's cat, Coug, jumped onto Ty's lap and purred so loud he could have been heard on the street several stories below. Ty stroked the cat and acted as if the rest of the room didn't exist.

Standing behind Zach, Kelsie took a chance and stepped close enough to rub his knotted shoulders. He didn't move or react. In fact, his shoulders tightened all the more.

Careful not to disturb the cat on his lap, Tyler propped his booted feet on an empty chair. He pasted a surly grin on his face. Zach glared right back, not budging an inch.

"You need a cat, Murphy." Tyler finally broke the silence.

"A cat? Her little rat dog is bad enough."

Kelsie glanced around at the mention of said rat dog. She should've left him home but he hated being alone. As soon as she'd put him down on the floor, Tyler's evil cat started stalked him until Scranton cowered under the couch and refused to come out. Meanwhile, the cat appeared insufferably pleased with his furry little self.

"Yeah, a cat." Tyler turned to Lavender. "Hey, Vin, find a grouchy tomcat for Murphy next time you volunteer at the animal shelter."

"I don't want a cat. I hate cats."

For some reason Lavender and Tyler found that statement hilariously funny.

"I know just the cat." Lavender winked at Tyler.

"Good. Cats are humbling experiences. You could use one." Tyler grinned with smug satisfaction while Zach's scowl turned downright stormy.

"You get me a cat, and I'll—" Zach came halfway out of his chair. One hand on each shoulder, Kelsie pushed him back down in his chair. He was fuming to the point that steam should've come out of his nostrils.

"So guys, we've got a lot of work to do." Kelsie leaned over Zach's shoulder and smiled at him, but her smile wasn't working. Not tonight. He looked as if he'd rather do wind sprints than give an inch.

Tyler slammed his feet to the floor with a bang that sent all three women jumping and catapulted Coug onto the carpet. Shaking himself off, Coug glanced over his shoulder with one of those death looks only cats could administer. "We do not have a lot of work to do. You three do. You set us up. You fix it. I'm getting drunk." On that note, Tyler rose to his feet, stomped to the refrigerator, grabbed three beers and an opener and popped the caps. Returning to the table, he plunked down in the chair and passed out the beers to the men. Then he held up his bottle. They clinked bottles and effectively ignored the women.

Well, at least they were *getting along.*

Sorta.

Zach took a long pull on his beer and leaned the chair back on two legs. He stared at the ceiling and said nothing. Tyler whipped out his cell phone and started pressing buttons. Derek yawned and glanced at Rachel. Clearly, none of them wanted to be here.

Kelsie couldn't blame them. She didn't either, but she felt responsible for this mess. Taking a deep breath, she pulled up a chair and sat down beside Zach, notepad in hand. "So gentlemen, how are we going to raise enough money to beat last year's donations? Let's brainstorm some ideas."

Pen poised, she waited.

And waited.

And waited.

"Brainstorming means you just throw out ideas. No idea is too stupid or too outrageous," Kelsie suggested.

Nothing.

"No one criticizes ideas. Just throw them out."

Nothing.

"Throw them out."

Nothing.

"Uh, now."

Kelsie looked to Derek, Rachel, and Lavender for help.

Lavender sat down next to Tyler. "We need to start calling the wealthiest people in the area."

"Yeah, and we offer free tickets to a playoff game for each donation over a certain amount," Rachel added.

"I can hit up some of the software companies in the area," Derek suggested.

Tyler rolled his eyes, and Zach snorted.

"Do you two have better ideas?"

Tyler blew out a long-suffering breath, or at least it sounded like one. "We need to go after the heavy hitters, and they already have season tickets."

"Then how do we suck them in?" Zach flicked his gaze to Kelsie for a brief moment. The heat in his dark eyes sent a tingle of desire to her sex. Dang, she'd never been so crazed when it came to sex as she was with this guy. They'd both discovered sleep was highly overrated.

"We offer them a night out with a jock." Kelsie threw it out there. "Dine with the team captains at the Space Needle. All proceeds to charity."

"Oh, no, I'm doing this stupid-assed gala because I don't have a choice, but I'm not doing one more high-brow affair. No way."

"Sounds stupid to me." Tyler actually agreed with Zach.

"Fine, then you two come up with something and don't leave the room until you do."

Zach frowned, his mouth turned down so far at the corners it almost reached his chin. Tyler threaded his fingers behind his head and stared at the ceiling. Neither of the stubborn children were budging.

Nodding at her friends, the three girls left the room and slammed the door after them.

* * * * *

Zach stared at the closed door. Nothing worse than one pissed-off woman unless it was several pissed-off women. He knew women. If he didn't comply with Kelsie's demands, she'd withhold sex from him. Even Harris and this fucking gala weren't worth losing one night in bed with Kelsie. The scary-assed thing was that it wasn't just the sex. Oh, he'd wanted it to be just about sex, but it wasn't. His crush had turned into something worse, something more fatal to his emotional health.

Love. It had to be the most frightening four-letter word known to man.

If only she felt the same. But she didn't. He was a means to an end. A way to get what she wanted, and also, he now believed, a way to give back to him. *She wanted to give to him.* Imagine that. He'd be a fool to read more into her affections. She didn't love him, but she did feel guilty, and she was fond of him. At one time, that would've been good enough, but now he wanted more.

Tyler snapped his fingers in front of Zach's face, causing him to startle. "Hey, dumbshit, come back to earth." Tyler blew out a long sigh. "Lavender's going to make my life a living hell if we don't come up with a viable plan."

Derek shot them both a murderous glare. "Hey, how do you think I feel? You two assholes are the reason I'm stuck here instead of in bed with my lovely wife. Let's make a list of possible donors and start calling them. Nothing new or exciting, just plain, old-fashioned fundraising."

"Where do we get a list like that?" Zach rubbed his forehead. He had the mother-of-all headaches. The cat climbed off Tyler's lap and onto Zach's. Lying down, the little shit dug his claws into Zach's jeans. "Dammit. That hurts." Zach glared at the cat.

"Jacks headquarters. They have all that kind of crap. And Veronica. She keeps track of who's who in Seattle," Tyler smirked at the cat, as if telling it to dig deeper. "I'll take HQ."

"Then who's talking to Veronica?" Zach feared he already knew the answer.

Both Tyler and Derek's heads swung in Zach's direction. He threw up his hands. "Oh, no, not me. She hates me, thinks I'm a Neanderthal."

Tyler snickered. Derek ran his hands over his face and groaned.

"You're just the person to talk to her. Show her how far you've come, what a great job Kelsie's done smoothing those jagged edges in just a few days or marriage." Derek seemed way too fucking pleased with himself. And Zach used to like the guy.

"Yeah, that's true. Show her how our pageant queen soothed an angry beast."

"I'm not an angry beast." He'd never been a fighter or a troublemaker off the field. He left it all out on the field. Just because he didn't subscribe to Mabel Fay's Manners Magazine or see the value in bullshit social niceties, didn't mean he was a jerk.

"Take Kelsie with you so she can run interference."

"I don't need to take Kelsie. I'm not a total moron."

Derek and Tyler exchanged looks. "You'd better take Kelsie," Derek decided.

They were right, yet it pissed Zach off that he had to depend on someone else. Still, the owner's ball-busting daughter did instill a bit a fear in every man who ventured near her. She emasculated any guy who wandered within her sphere of influence and turned him into a wuss who lived with his mother.

Yeah, he'd take Kelsie with him and keep his privates intact.

* * * *

Zach wiped his sweaty palms on his black slacks. Kelsie had picked out the damn things at Nordstrom's, and they cost more than the rest of the clothes hanging in the closet, minus the suits she'd also purchased. Crap, maybe he was a moron, a cheap-assed moron. Meanwhile, Kelsie sat next to him playing her part as the dutiful, yet strong-willed wife, dressed to the hilt in a sexy, soft pink suit she'd bought on that same shopping spree. Zach had converted a spare bedroom into a closet for her expanding clothes and shoe collection.

It took them a week to get an appointment with Veronica, and she made them come to her house in the evening instead of meeting with them at Jacks HQ. Zach figured it was intentional.

At least the team won their last game, which should put her in a reasonably good mood. Plus, he'd played nice with Harris, complimenting him in front of the press. Thank God the man had deserved his praise.

Zach's after hours activities should've left him exhausted. Instead, he'd been all over that field, stuffed the running back behind the line of scrimmage countless times, and sacked the quarterback twice. He'd been awarded defensive player of the week.

Yet his on-the-field accomplishments paled compared to the elegant, sexy woman who'd been his partner these past couple weeks. Damn, just looking at her now puffed him up with pride, while desire infiltrated his tight control. Zach forced his thoughts away from his gorgeous wife. This definitely wasn't the time for a hard-on.

Veronica breezed into the room, a glass of wine in hand. The woman liked her wine and could be a mean drunk. He hoped to God it was too early in the evening for her to be beyond her first glass.

Veronica ran her disapproving gaze over Zach and graced Kelsie with a tense smile. His wife—it still seemed weird to think that—stood and they did that air kiss thing women often did. At Kelsie's prodding look, Zach lumbered to his feet. Veronica took a seat across from them, and Zach sat once the ladies sat, like a well-trained dog. He hated this bullshit manners crap. What the hell difference did being pompous make?

Zach hated phonies. So why was he married to one? Even temporarily? The obvious answer was sex and keeping her safe, not that he'd seen a sign of her stalker in a few weeks. The not-so-obvious might be in part because Zach believed—or wanted to believe—she'd changed. Yet, the cynical side of him laughed at the ludicrous thought that anyone could change that much. Zach sighed. Maybe a person could. Maybe Kelsie's first marriage truly did change her.

Veronica snapped her fingers and a servant magically appeared. The tall thin man stood in the background. "Yes ma'am?"

Zach almost snorted out a laugh. The guy had an English accent. Who the hell employed an English butler anymore?

"Wine for my guests please. And some appetizers."

Zach stiffened. Oh, crap, he didn't want to eat or drink in front of this woman. Whenever he did, disaster happened, not just the time he'd spilt wine on her dress. At a pre-season party welcoming new teammates, Zach bumped her from behind, causing her to dump an entire plate of spaghetti on her expensive white suit. Then he'd insulted her prissy boyfriend-of-the-week by asking if he was gay because he was a hairdresser. Not exactly politically correct and just the beginning in a long line of bad situations with the owner's daughter. Thank God Mr. Simms's sons weren't nearly as uptight. They were good guys.

The butler poured a miniscule amount of wine in a glass and handed it to Zach then the guy stood nearby as if waiting for something. Zach glanced at Kelsie. She nudged him with a knee. Zach tried to remember all the dumbass rules for drinking wine that they'd gone over. He held it up to his mouth and took a sip. The stuff tasted like crap. Swallowing, he plastered a smile on his face and nodded. "That'll be fine."

Kelsie smiled encouragingly at him and squeezed his thigh in a show of support, an action which went straight to his sex-crazed cock and brain. Veronica frowned, cluing him in to the fact that he'd screwed up again. Somehow.

The butler smiled sympathetically at him and filled his glass about a quarter full then filled the ladies'. Next, he positioned a tray of appetizers so small they were barely bigger than Zach's pinkie. He stared at the miniscule bites and his stomach growled.

"Damn, those are small. What are you guys going to eat?"

Veronica glared at him, not finding his remark the least bit amusing. Kelsie smiled demurely, as if he'd commented about the weather.

Zach reached for a handful and stopped himself. He drew his hand back, stuffed his hands in his lap and waited for Kelsie and Veronica to take one first. Shit, he just said another stupid thing. It came out of his mouth before he could contain it like a defensive line of all rookies trying to stop an all-pro running back.

Veronica's face puckered into an expression of absolute disapproval. She sighed and picked up a tiny piece of something and placed it on her tongue. She savored it as if she were eating a huge, juicy steak. "So I understand you're looking for a donation list for the Christmas gala?"

Kelsie deferred to Zach. He sat up straight and tried his nicest smile. "Yes, we'll be calling the potential donors in an attempt to get a commitment from them for dinner and the silent auction, which will also be offered online."

"Let's hope you start winning games. It'll help your case." Veronica glared pointedly at Zach.

"We won last week." Zach defended not just himself but his team.

"Barely, and to a mediocre team."

Zach caught the warning in Kelsie's eyes. She turned to Veronica. "The arrangements are coming along nicely. Zach's old mansion is perfect for this."

"As you know, this gala has been hosted by my family in our home for years. So it's definitely associated with our name and the team. I'm expecting this year's to be as spectacular as past galas."

"We'll do you proud." Zach forced a smile.

She didn't appear to believe him. "You don't have a choice. Either of you."

Zach scooped up a couple tidbits and popped them in his mouth. Good thing he could barely taste them because what he could taste, tasted like crap.

A short time later, Zach left with a bruised and humiliated ego, but he had the coveted list. Kelsie managed to get a commitment from Veronica to call some of the billionaires personally. Zach pulled out of the long, winding driveway and onto the street.

"You did fine." Kelsie leaned over and kissed his cheek.

Zach squared his shoulders and puffed up his chest. "You really think so?"

"Yes, better than a few months ago." She rubbed his knee. Her touch went straight to his dick.

"Veronica didn't appear to think so."

"Veronica expects perfection. I don't."

"Good then, I don't need to do any more of this manners crap."

"Yes, you do. We'll continue the Tuesday lessons before you meet with Tyler."

"Yeah, but we're married now. I don't need to worry about this shit. You'll take care of it for me."

"What about at parties?"

"I'll follow your lead just like Tomcat does with LaShonna."

"It'd take an elephant to lead you in the right direction."

Zach frowned. "You just said I did okay."

"You did. And I'm proud of you and your progress, but there's still a long way to go."

Zach sighed and kept his eyes on the road. "I'm trying. Really I am."

"In your own weird way I believe you are."

She had no idea how hard he was trying.

Trying not to fall so deeply for her that he'd never recover.

* * * * *

Kelsie sat in the passenger seat and chewed on her lower lip. Zach's aftershave teased her nostrils, making her hyperaware of the big man next to her, not that he needed aftershave to catch her attention. His pure physical presence did that. She studied his face in the dashboard light and loved what she saw.

Over the past few weeks, she'd explored every inch of his muscular body, run her fingers through his thick dark hair, and kissed his very sexy mouth. She marveled at how such a big powerful man could be so gentle and caring.

A lock of his dark hair fell across his creased forehead. She pushed it aside, while he gripped the steering wheel, as if attempting to concentrate on the road. She placed her hand on his knee.

"Zach?"

"Yeah?" He stared straight ahead, but his hands tightened on the steering wheel as he maneuvered his too big truck around cars parked on too narrow streets.

"I want you." Her voice sounded oddly breathless. She always wanted him. In fact, wanting occupied way too much of her time. Sure, she'd enjoyed sex before, but not like this. Never like this. This melding of two minds and two bodies went beyond normal sex.

"Right now?"

Kelsie smiled and slid her hand higher until she stroked his crotch. His erection strained against the expensive fabric of his trousers. She took mercy on him by unzipping his pants, if you could call it mercy. She wanted her hands on him.

"Kelsie. Stop." His hoarse growl didn't have anything to do with stopping. In fact reading between those lines, his voice screamed go, go, go.

"You're so sexy in such an incredibly male way." She slid her hand under the waistband of his boxers and stroked him.

A tortured groan was ripped from his chest. His eyes rolled back in his head until he almost hit a parked car and swerved to miss. "Damn. Woman. You're going to make me crash."

"Then pull over. We're still several minutes from home, and I can't wait. I want you now." He'd reduced her to this, so sex-crazed she'd do it in a car on a residential city street.

"You're evil." By his tone of voice, he loved her brand of evil.

"Always have been. Always will be."

For a moment his expression faded to confusion. She knew why. Bad choice of words. She'd reminded him of what a manipulative bitch she'd been, but this wasn't about manipulation. This was about lust, pure animal lust and a lot more.

Kelsie glanced around the street, looking for a likely spot, a dark, secluded spot. A small city park with a small lot for a few cars was only a block away. She pointed at it, and Zach read her mind. He sped toward it while Kelsie milked his cock with her hand. Just as he turned into the parking lot, she lowered her head and took him in her mouth.

"Oh, damn." He braked to a stop, rammed the truck in the park, and switched off the ignition in a series of frenzied moves. Kelsie opened her mouth wide and took him inside. He arched his hips and pressed deeper into her mouth. Burying his fingers in her hair, he pushed her down further. When the head of his penis touched the back of her throat, she pulled back. He let her, even though his fingers tangled in her hair.

She licked the bulbous tip, sliding her tongue along the velvety skin and savoring the salty taste.

"Kelsie, I don't recall this in your manners book. What's the proper protocol?" He groaned and shook his head back and forth, eyes squeezed tight.

"Protocol?" She glanced up at him, keeping her fingers wrapped under his hard shaft.

"Yeah, for giving your husband a blow job in a truck in a public park. Is there a proper way to have public sex?"

"We're not having public sex. Yet. We're only in the foreplay stage. But no, there's not a proper way. This is all very improper."

Zach glanced around the dark lot. Kelsie followed his gaze. Old cedars towered over the truck and cast ominous shadows. Kelsie shook off the creepy feeling someone might be watching them, like her currently absent stalker.

"Maybe we should go home." His voice sounded strangled and not entirely convinced as she rubbed his erection to make him forget who and where he was.

"You're a conservative guy, aren't you?" The throaty whisper didn't sound like her.

"You just figured that out?" He ground his teeth together while she moved her hand up and down.

"Your idea of sex is missionary or doggie style." Which was true, sorta. But did the man ever make good use of those two positions.

"I've never heard you complain."

"You won't, but we could start by being a little more adventurous." Why she was pushing this, she didn't know. Other than she'd always harbored a bit of a dangerous streak, like the time nineteen-year-old Kelsie had seduced the twenty-something pageant judge who was a former member of a defunct boy band. She got him so hot and bothered, they did it up against the wall in his private backstage dressing room after rehearsal.

And Zach put *her* on a pedestal? She wasn't just a mean girl, she was an opportunist. Actually, had been, but no more. This thing with Zach had nothing to do with opportunity and everything to do with overwhelming need.

"Does sex with me bore you?"

"Not on your life. Missionary sex with you is more exciting than kinky sex with any other man."

At first he puffed out his chest a little, then the full effect of what she'd said seemed to sink in. "You've had kinky sex?"

Well, yes. But fake husband or not, Zach didn't need to know. "It's just a statement. Doesn't mean anything." She bent down and took him in her mouth again. He pushed her down further onto his erection. Kelsie took him deep, fought off the gag reflex, and let him slide inside until her nose pressed against his pubic hair. He held her there for a moment, and she let him. She pulled back and took a gulp of air then went after him again.

"I'm gonna cum, baby, if you keep that up."

"That's the idea, but I'd rather have you inside me."

"I'm all in, honey. Lead the way."

"Good thing. You need to be all in. Get in the back seat."

He hesitated for moment, seeming to balk at her authoritative tone then climbed into the back seat, falling in a heap with his pants tangled around his ankles. Kelsie would've laughed, but she was too horny. She crawled after him.

"Condom?" She asked as he leveraged his big body onto the seat. He pointed toward the pants. She fished out his wallet and found a condom. "You're prepared." Zach carrying a condom around in his wallet didn't sit well with her. Did he think he might meet some anonymous woman somewhere that he'd need a condom? Maybe that waitress? Surely he hadn't planned on them hooking up in the truck? Then again, maybe he had.

She tore off the wrapper and rolled it over his shaft. He watched her. His thighs splayed, his head back against the headrest, and looking every bit a man who'd surrendered his body to her carnal pleasures.

Kelsie hiked up her skirt to her waist and yanked off her panties. "Are you ready for me, big boy?"

"My big boy's ready, and I'm ready." His brown eyes sparkled like hot fudge simmering on the stove. Only this had nothing to do with Grandma's house. She looked down, past his thick neck and broad shoulders. His biceps bulged from all the working out. Her gaze came to rest on his shaft, the condom glistening with moisture. She smiled the smile of a woman who knew what she wanted and what her man wanted and also knew they were both getting lucky tonight.

Kelsie straddled Zach's thighs and lowered herself down until the tip of his penis just grazed her sex. Gripping her shoulders to balance herself, she slid down onto his thick cock.

"Oh, yeah, baby, that's the way to do it." He grasped her waist in his hands, which almost spanned her waist.

"See, out of the ordinary sex isn't so bad, is it?"

"Would you call this kinky sex?"

"If that's what you want to call it, that's what we can call it."

"I haven't done this since high school."

She wriggled on top of him and pressed her crotch into his. "You need to get out of your conservative box."

"Why do I think you'll be helping me with that?"

"As long as I don't distract you from your mission of a ring." Kelsie rose up until only an inch of him was inside her and moved her hips in a slow, circular motion.

"Didn't seem to hurt my game."

"That's because best thing to do is it get me out of your system on a regular basis." She panted as she moved up and down on him.

"Hell, yeah. That's the only way." He sought her mouth, and she gladly accepted his lips and tongue. Their mating became a wild frenzy of slamming hips, panting, wet mouths, and tangled hair. She could tell by how his cock twitched inside her that he was close to coming. He knew it, too, and reached between her legs to thumb her clit taking her over the abyss with him.

Kelsie didn't want to be anywhere else.

Not ever.

CHAPTER 22

Losing Field Position

Over two weeks later, the Jacks' record was five and five. They weren't burning up the league, not like Zach and Kelsie were burning up the sheets every night and every morning.

For the majority of his life, Zach's world revolved around football, but now Kelsie had entered that orbit and sometimes he couldn't say whether Kelsie or football occupied the majority of his thoughts. But his game wasn't suffering, and that was what mattered the most.

Or it should have been.

Funny how a guy didn't realize how much he'd been missing until he found it, which had a lot to do with why he'd caved to her latest request just to see her smile. Zach never cared much for family gatherings, so attending Thanksgiving dinner at Derek's house wasn't his idea of fun. The place was packed, not only with teammates who had no family in the area, but with various family members complete with all the dysfunctional family crap that happens on holidays. Not nearly as dysfunctional as Zach's family had been, rather a normal state of dysfunction.

Obviously, Derek's brother-in-law Mitch didn't care much for Derek. Rachel and Lavender's respective fathers and brothers zoned out in front of football games. Derek's dad, stepmother, and sister were like a dream family for Zach.

Then there was Harris's family. Now they were interesting. All strong-willed women, and Tyler alternated between ignoring them and kowtowing to them. Neither approach saved him from their constant badgering. No wonder the guy had such a healthy ego. A guy would either learn to be impervious to their attempts to control his life or be turned into a sniveling coward. Harris might be a lot of things, but he wasn't a coward.

Actually, Zach almost felt sorry for Harris after he met his two ball-busting, man-eating sisters. Freddie and Estie, and damned if he knew which was which. They weren't twins but they might as well be. Close to six feet tall with long dark hair and faces models would die for, they most likely turned heads wherever they went. Zach noticed they didn't bring husbands or boyfriends, probably scared them all off. One was an attorney, the other a financial advisor. If Zach knew which one did the financial stuff, he'd hit her up for some advice, but he might get the wrong one, and one of his personal rules was to avoid attorneys at all costs.

Kelsie fit right in with the classy women, plus, her girl buddies Rachel and Lavender. Left to fend for himself, Zach started to skirt around Harris, who was getting an ass-chewing by his sisters over something when one of them snaked out a hand and yanked him into their little circle. Damn, that hurt. The woman must lift small men for a hobby. Good thing he didn't qualify.

"Freddie, drop it. Murphy and I are working on our differences."

The one Harris called Freddie turned a pair of blue eyes the same color and intensity as her brother's on Zach and pinned him. "You're prone to telling us what we want to hear. I want to hear it from him." She jabbed a lethal red nail into Zach's chest.

Zach backed up a step and cleared his throat. He just wanted away from these women with his balls intact. "Ty and I are buddies." He lied and refused to make eye contact with the sister.

"See?" Harris wrapped an arm around Zach's shoulders and grinned at him. The guy had missed his true calling. He should've been a con-artist.

Freddie narrowed her eyes. Her sister did the same.

"So, buddy, whadaya say we grab a brew and join the men in the family room? From the noise, I'd say the game's a good one."

"Sounds good." Together they bolted for the door, leaving the she-lions standing behind them, claws still extended and teeth bared.

They paused in the doorway, both glancing back. Blowing out mutual breaths of relief, Zach followed Harris to Derek's well-stocked bar and hitched a hip onto the barstool.

Zach took a good, long swallow of the beer Harris handed him. "Are they older or younger?"

"Older." The quarterback downed his beer in one long guzzle and opened another. Zach didn't blame him. He'd be in rehab with sisters like that.

"How did you live to puberty with them around?"

Harris chuckled. "What doesn't kill you makes you stronger. Between Derek and me, there were three older sisters. We lived on neighboring ranches. We did a lot of riding and hiking, anything to get away. Lots of guy trips with our dads."

Zach glanced around. He didn't see Tyler's father anywhere, and his mother was here by herself. "Where's your dad?"

For a brief moment, Harris's guard slipped on black ice and fell on its ass for all to see, but only Zach noticed. "He's not here." The words came out choked, as if someone were strangling the life out of the quarterback.

Harris's answer should've been Zach's clue, but a rare moment of curiosity drove him to ask more questions. "Where is he?"

"Dead."

"Oh. I'm sorry." Now Zach felt like the insensitive ass he always was.

Harris shrugged one shoulder and fingered the label on his beer. "Yeah, he died of a heart attack the summer before my freshman year of college. Just like that. One moment he was large as life, the next he was lying on the floor in the den. Gone. It was pretty devastating. Lavender's dad was my college coach. Without him and my family, I'd have never made it." Harris met Zach's gaze with true interest. "Where's your family?"

Zach started to evade the answer, but Harris had been honest with him and given him a little glimpse into what made him tick. "My brother plays NHL hockey. The rest are dead, in prison, or on the streets."

Harris's brow furrowed. He seemed to be working through how to respond to that. Finally, he shrugged and offered Zach a wry smile. "Family. Can't pick 'em." He held up his bottle in a salute.

"Yeah." Zach let the cold beer run down his throat, relaxing a little. This wasn't a high-society bash. He could deal with these people, even though the women in Harris's family struck fear in his heart. At least the rest of the guests seemed like average people. No pretenses. They were who they were.

With a jerk of his head, Tyler wandered over to watch the game. Zach followed him and squeezed onto the couch between Derek and a rookie safety from Florida. Tyler settled into an easy chair that one of Rachel's brothers just vacated. Obviously, it was every man for himself. You move, you lose.

He glanced around the room at the raucous group, oddly comfortable with them. No one here judged him—not even Harris. None of them cared if he used the proper fork or even if he used a fork. He caught glimpses of Kelsie bustling around the kitchen with the other women, all laughing and talking at once—pure female chaos. He hoped they didn't let her make the gravy. Her gravy tasted like cardboard and chicken broth. Regardless, the food smelled fucking fantastic. Kelsie wasn't the world's best cook so Zach appreciated a good home-cooked meal.

He ran a hand through his hair and stared at the game on television, not really seeing it. A million things raced through his head. First and foremost should be his goal of winning a Super Bowl. Yet, it wasn't. It was Kelsie who occupied his thoughts.

This past week, instead of concentrating while watching game film he'd been scheming how to get her to forget their agreement and stay with him after the season ended, however short or long that season might prove to be.

At five and five, they were still hanging on by a thread in the wild card hunt. Zach pushed Kelsie's luscious body into a compartment in his brain and concentrated on the game on television—or tried to. After all, they'd be playing this team in a few weeks. A very short few weeks.

He needed to be ready. Filter out all the distractions and focus single-mindedly on football, like he used to be able to do. Before Harris. Before this stupid gala. And before Kelsie in her current incarnation as a nice girl.

And before he fell head over heels in love.

* * * * *

Kelsie cuddled next to Zach and flattened her palms against his broad chest. The hitch in his intake of breath gave him away. He was awake. Scranton lay on the pillow next to her head. She rolled up onto his chest and stared at him.

"Admit it. You enjoyed today."

"Like I enjoy a tight end powering past me to score a touchdown." He squinted at her, his brown eyes hazy with sleep.

"You did. When I looked in, you and Tyler were debating some obscure football fact."

"He's a football trivia machine. Who'd have guessed? I couldn't stump him."

"I'm sure there are facets to him that'll surprise you, just like there are with you. Neither of you show your true colors."

"That's not true. I'm an open book."

"Your book is padlocked and stowed in a trunk."

"You think?"

"Zach, you are the most private man I've ever met. You're a loner, but I don't think you are by choice."

"Then why am I?"

"Because you don't want people to see the sensitive guy hiding under all that masculine posturing. Just like Tyler."

"Tyler's as shallow as that puddle outside the back door."

"That puddle is deceptive. Puddles are murky. You can't see bottom. You never know what secrets are concealed under the surface. Step in it and you'll see. After last week's rain, you could drown in that puddle."

"Once the sun comes out, it'll dry up again."

"Probably, but the sun never stays out for long, does it?"

Zach stared at her in the dim light. "Why are we talking about puddles?"

"We weren't really talking about puddles."

"I was. I don't know what the hell you were talking about."

Kelsie laughed. Zach liked to play the part of the dumb country boy, but he was sharp as they came. "Why would a guy who graduated with honors keep it a secret?"

"Are we still talking about Harris or puddles? Cuz I don't think Harris ever came close to a degree, and the puddle hasn't gone to college."

Kelsie chuckled. "I might be referring to a certain linebacker and what his nosy wife discovered."

"Maybe that linebacker's nosy wife shouldn't spend her spare time sticking her nose into her husband's business."

"Cold day in hell that'll happen."

She wanted to ask him about his brother again, about the etched marble stone in the yard, but she couldn't bring herself to do it. Not yet. Not with the season winding down and the Jacks hanging on by a thread, but the team had Tyler and Zach. By sheer force of will, both guys would carry the team on their backs if they had to. She believed in Zach. He'd get the job done. He'd get his Super Bowl ring. Thank God the stalker remained absent. Neither of them needed that added worry.

Kelsie ran her hands down Zach's pecs to his rock-hard abs, letting her fingers feel the ridges of muscles and the valley between.

"There's one thing that'll happen, cold day in hell or not." He seemed fully awake now. His dark eyes glittered with the now familiar fires of desire.

"And that is?"

"I'm hard for you." Hands on her waist, he pulled her up his body until his mouth was even with one of her nipples.

"You're hard for me in your sleep."

"Uh, yeah." He sucked her nipple into his mouth, lavished it with attention from his tongue, and had her squirming in under five seconds, which had to be his best record. Next thing she knew, he'd flipped her onto her back without letting go of her nipple, a true talent in her book.

He straddled her—the man did like his missionary position—and turned his attention to her shoulders and neck. She writhed under him, wanting the release only Zach could give. His erection rubbed against her inner thigh. She wanted it to rub a little higher and a lot deeper.

"God, woman, what you do to me." He spoke against her skin as his mouth burned a path across her collarbone and up her neck to her earlobe. Meanwhile a little further south, his talented fingers pinched and tweaked her nipples into hard little nubs. She wanted to feel him a lot further south. A certain spot between her legs begged for attention or at least the attention of a certain long, hard part of him.

"What do I do to you?"

He stared down at her, silent for a long while. "A lot. A helluva lot."

"Same here." She felt his smile in the darkness, could just make out his white teeth. Then his mouth covered hers, hungry and demanding. Giving and taking. Needing and wanting.

Kelsie wrapped her legs around his waist and showed him how much she needed and wanted, too. He got the message loud and clear. A moment later, his erection sent another message, this one to her very core, as he positioned himself and slipped inside her slick walls.

Her hips rose to meet his, and they found their rhythm together like ballroom dancers who'd been partners for years. Everything seemed so right, so natural, so hot with Zach. So damn hot. Hotter than a Texas sidewalk in August.

He thrust in and out making it last, carrying the passion to the very end, not letting her slip over the edge until he was ready. She'd start to fall, and he'd slow his pace or almost withdraw, pulling her back from the ledge, torturing her, and making her want him all the more. Time after time, he'd tease her like that until her body couldn't take anymore more and shuddered with her release. A scream erupted from her throat, and his name bounced off the walls of the dark room.

Zach thrust a few more times and came with his own shouted declaration, one which sounded like, "I love you, Kelsie."

Certainly, she'd fabricated those words due to her own euphoria-distorted state of mind.

Or had she?

As they slipped back to reality, he pulled her into his arms and held her close. She cuddled against him, feeling, safe, protected, and cherished. And loved? Yes, she suspected this was what love truly felt like.

CHAPTER 23

Wine and Football

Veronica paced back and forth, wearing a path in the plush carpet in her office at Jacks Headquarters, her devious brain racing faster than a punt returner with a clear shot to the end zone. The PI stood by the door, waiting, and not exactly patiently, which pissed her off. She had a right to be impatient, he didn't. He was an employee, nothing else, and didn't have a personal or professional stake in the outcome of this situation. No, he didn't bleed navy and gold like she did.

She fingered the piece of paper in her hand. "So, nothing more on her ex? Mark Richmond? Or the divorce?" She knew there had to be more information that would be useful.

"No, ma'am." The way he said ma'am made her skin crawl. She needed to find another PI, but most wouldn't do the stuff she paid this guy to do.

"How are the newlyweds doing?"

"Like newlyweds as far as I can tell. You told me to back off, and I have, unless you'd like me to get up close and personal, maybe get some pics?" He sounded way too eager.

She shook her head, highly annoyed he didn't see the situation clearly. "I'm not in the sex scandal business, and they're married. No dirt there."

"So is that all? What's next? Business as usual?" He tapped his foot on the floor.

Veronica considered her next move. She shuffled through some papers and handed him a folder. "I need to you check out this kid Dad's pressuring the GM to draft. I think he has drug issues and abuses women. Find out what you can."

The man thumbed through the papers. "Will do. I'll be in touch." He slipped out the door just as her father walked in.

"Who the hell was that guy?" He shut the door and entered her office.

"Just some salesman hawking an idea for a new kind of helmet." Veronica sat down in her chair and regarded her father.

"I understand Murphy and Harris are getting along quite well."

She snorted. "By whose definition?"

"I'm talking with Murphy's agent this week. I'm offering him a contract extension."

Furious, Veronica leapt to her feet and smacked the flat of her hand on the desk. "You can't do that."

"I can. There's a shortage of good linebackers in the draft and nothing out there in the free agent market. Murphy is playing well enough to merit an extension. He's brilliant when it comes to reading defenses, and he's barely lost a step in speed or power. By my estimation and HughJack's he's still one of the best out there."

"We need to groom a young guy."

"We are. We have a few on the roster, and who better to train them than a future Hall-of-Famer."

"Dad, you can't do this." Veronica hated the begging tone in her voice.

"Of course I can. It's my team. Don't you forget that." He turned back to the door. "Knowing how unreasonable you are about the linebacker, I wanted to give you forewarning. Live with it."

On that note, he left.

Veronica slumped in her chair and swiveled it around to stare out the window. Two more years with Murphy on the team could not happen. He was washed up, not worth the money, and his ineptness in social situations coupled with his public feud with Tyler did irreparable damage to an already damaged team. And to Veronica it was all about the team.

No, her father could not re-sign Murphy.

Not if she could figure out a way to prevent it. For the good of the team, of course.

She picked up the business card and dialed Mark Richmond's phone number.

* * * *

After winning their last game on Thanksgiving weekend, the Jacks were on the verge of another crushing loss. Zach once again sat on the bench and ground his teeth in frustration, as the offense blew the game. Bruiser fumbled a handoff. The Bears ran it back for a touchdown, putting the game out of reach with only fifteen seconds on the clock. Even so, Harris gave it the college try, throwing a couple Hail Marys into coverage, but none of the passes connected. If Zach didn't know better, he'd swear his great-aunt Gertrude had put a hex on his team. She'd been known to do that in the past, even from her grave in the Louisiana Bayou, though her football hexes were usually on the opposing team. Maybe he'd pissed her off somehow.

In a nasty slap of fate, his old team was leading their division and sure to clinch their first playoff spot in years—the same years he'd spent giving them all he had—while the Jacks, once a sure thing for the playoffs, might need a miracle to make it as a wildcard.

The clock ticked off the final seconds with agonizing slowness. Zach grabbed his helmet and trudged toward the tunnel to the locker room. Ahead of him, Harris sprinted into the tunnel, avoiding the press and the fans. In his situation, Zach would've done the same.

Once in the sanctuary of the locker room, Zach yanked off his sweat-soaked jersey and shoulder pads, then took a long drink of water. Harris sat on the bench next to their lockers and stared straight ahead, a man in a trance. Don't-even-mess-with-me was written across every hard line of his face, but warnings like that never stopped Zach. He needed to speak to Harris to show the team that they'd put their differences to rest—even if they hadn't.

"Your receivers were dropping perfect balls left and right. You did the best you could."

"My best wasn't good enough. I'm the quarterback. I'm responsible." Harris swung his murderous gaze toward Zach. He would've pinned a lesser man to lockers with that look, it didn't faze Zach.

Well, not too much.

Zach pulled off his shoes. "Hey, if you want to be a martyr, not my problem."

"I don't want to be anything but a winner."

"Yeah, well at least you have two rings."

"And I'm trying like hell to get you yours."

Zach glanced up and an honest response rolled off his tongue. "I know." He did know. He'd seen it with his own eyes.

"Yeah?" Harris met Zach's gaze.

"Yeah." Zach was shocked to realize he meant it. The Tyler Harris from last year had slowly returned to the fiery, reckless quarterback of prior years. It happened so subtly, Zach didn't see the changes until today. The guy hadn't quit on the team once, no matter how tough it got or how far down they got in a game, he kept trying. The young team surrounding them saw it. They also saw Zach and Harris's mutual dislike fading away to be replaced by grudging respect. Yet, they weren't winning like they should be. They might be one year off, but Zach didn't think he had a year left.

Which sucked the big one.

At least he had Kelsie waiting at home after a long flight, which was more than he'd had in the past. A lot more. Even if it was only for a few more weeks.

The team had to go all the way to the Super Bowl. Not just because he wanted that ring but because it kept Kelsie in his life that much longer. He sank down on the bench and buried his head in his hands as the truth broke over him like a rogue wave and pulled him into a strong undertow. It tore the oxygen from his lungs and dragged him deeper. He didn't think he'd ever be able to fight his way back to the surface because he didn't want to.

His priorities had shifted like the sands on a beach, so subtly, yet so permanently.

He wanted Kelsie even more than he wanted a ring.

* * * * *

For the next few weeks, Kelsie rarely saw Zach. Her husband spent every waking hour at the practice facility with a couple exceptions.

She did insist he spend an hour or two on Tuesday mornings continuing their etiquette lessons before he did his time with Tyler. He might not understand the importance of these non-football activities, but she did.

Not only did she stake her floundering business on the success of this gala, but more important Zach's future with the Lumberjacks and his consideration as an assistant college coach depended on his behavior.

And she saw him in bed. She saw a *lot* of him in bed, or at least felt him, every square inch of him, including her favorite nine to ten inches, not that she'd measured it. Oh, Lord, she didn't need to.

Still, she missed him horribly, wishing he were around more. Heck, she'd even spend evenings at The Squatch if she could spend them with him. She lay in bed every night, listening for the sound of his truck. The second she heard it, her heart jumped like a cheerleader after a touchdown and her body revved up and got ready to go. And go they did. All night long. How the man existed on a few hours of sleep a night, she didn't understand.

He'd hold her and make love, whisper to her in that gruff, straightforward way of his that had come to mean more to her than any poetry or flowery phrases ever could. Kelsie lived for those moments.

She crammed her days to overflowing with gala preparations, always carving out time for her new girlfriends, Lavender and Rachel, when they were available. Lavender was attending college to get a degree in gerontology and Rachel worked as a football scout for a couple small colleges. She'd been traveling quite a bit around the state until the high school football season ended a week ago.

At her request, Tyler had invited the UW's head coach and athletic director to the gala, along with some very powerful UW athletic club supporters. She was determined Zach would have the job he wanted when he retired from football.

Just this morning, Kelsie had drilled him on fine dining etiquette and the art of conversation one more time. He'd slumped in his chair, arms crossed over his chest, and scowled. When she'd finally asked him to sit up straight, he'd done so with a long-suffering sigh, and actually kept his elbows off the table. The man was picking up a few tips. Praise the stars above.

The gala was only a few weeks away. Workers bustled in and out of the house, putting up decorations and transforming it into a

Christmas scene right out of *Better Homes and Gardens*. Zach didn't say a word, but by his tense jaw, he wasn't thrilled wasting money on the one-time cost of decorating for this gala.

The stakes were getting higher as the season rolled on. Since Thanksgiving, the team had split their last two games, making their record six and six, as they dangled on the edge of making a wildcard playoff spot.

Later that evening after all the workers left for the day, Kelsie pulled into the practice facility. She'd cooked Zach his favorite and the one thing she could cook well, her mouth-watering fried chicken, as a small reward for his progress this morning, even if he'd been somewhat grumpy.

She poked her head in the film room and waited for her eyes to adjust. A few guys were sprawled in the chairs, but she couldn't make out Zach's dark head and broad shoulders.

Brett Gunnels walked toward her heading for the door. She smiled at him and he smiled back. His eyes opened wide, as if surprised she acknowledged him. Poor guy. As a backup, he was used to being ignored.

"Hey, Brett, have you seen Zach? I brought him dinner."

Brett opened his mouth, closed it, opened it again. He glanced around as if looking for a way out, like a man who knew a secret he wasn't going to reveal. "Uh, no, I haven't seen him for a while."

The cold knife blade of dread cut through her, though she couldn't explain why. "When did he leave?"

Brett shrugged and shifted his weight from one foot to another. He refused to make eye contact. This didn't look good.

"Have you seen him lately?"

"Uh, not for a few hours. He probably went with some of the guys to talk strategy." The man was a crappy liar.

A couple defensive backs skirted past them, but Kelsie was faster, she cut off their exit path. "Have you guys seen Zach?"

Bryson, a lanky corner grinned at her. "Zach's never here on Tuesday nights. Says he prefers to spend his Tuesday nights at home. Can't say I blame him."

"Thanks, I must have just missed him." *Never here on Tuesday nights.* Kelsie put on her best face and smiled at them, even as her world spun on its head and dumped her off the wild ride flat on her ass.

Zach wasn't spending his Tuesday nights at home, and he wasn't spending them here. She felt like she'd taken a physical blow by a heavyweight fighter right to her gut. She forced herself to stand up straight when all she wanted to do was double over in pain.

Despite how innocent his actions might be, he'd withheld the truth, which made him guilty in her book. She'd thought Mark had hurt her, but it was nothing compared to how this felt, Brett must have noticed the stricken look on her face. He patted her arm like a big brother would. "Hey, I'm sure he's home by now."

Right. She was sure he wasn't. "Are you hungry?" She'd be damned if Zach was getting one bite of this chicken.

"I'm always hungry." Brett chuckled. Kelsie briefly wondered why she couldn't have fallen for a nice guy like him.

She thrust the dinner in his hands. "I'd hate for this to go to waste." Because where she really wanted to put it was in Zach's sneaky, lying face.

Without another word, she turned and ran from the room and then the building. She didn't stop until she was safely ensconced in her car. She pressed her forehead against the steering wheel and gulped for oxygen, but her lungs froze and left her gasping for air.

Then the dam broke and the tears gushed like water from a broken water main. Yet the part of her who'd survived years of disappointment peeked out and insisted there had to be a logical explanation. Zach wasn't a cheater. He was one of the few good guys.

Bryson's words repeated in her head. Tuesday nights. Kelsie thought back. For the past several Tuesday nights, Zach hadn't come home until after ten. He'd seemed even more quiet and thoughtful than usual, and also a little more content. With his intensity, rarely did he come across as content or anything resembling relaxed, yet Tuesday nights came close.

Another woman stood out as the logical choice to keep an average man away from football for a few hours, yet the only thing Zach made time for besides football had been sex. With her. Until now. A little pinprick of jealousy stabbed Kelsie's heart at the thought of Zach with another woman.

But Zach wasn't an average man. Zach was loyal and honest and straightforward. In bed, he treated her like a princess. Considering the tender, affectionate, and passionate way he held her, how could he be seeing someone else?

He couldn't be. Just couldn't be. So where did he spend his time on Tuesday nights? Kelsie swiped at her tears and started the car. She aimed to find out.

* * * * *

Zach pushed open the door of the training facility's viewing room. Brett Gunnels, a good guy—for an offensive player—looked up as Zach sank into the plush, oversized chair.

"How's it going with Harris?"

"As good as expected." Brett and Zach shared a mutual dislike for Harris, though the quiet Brett rarely said a word about the man. Like most perpetual backups, he went about his business, did what he could to contribute to team wins, and kept his mouth shut about stuff he didn't like. Too short for an NFL starter, he'd been pegged as a backup from the first day he walked onto an NFL practice field. Traded from team to team, he'd never played more than a few games in the NFL, but decent games at that. The guy had an arm and was insanely accurate. He never complained, but Zach felt he'd gotten a bum rap because of size, and had the misfortune of playing behind the best QBs in the league. He'd only start if Harris had an injury. At twenty-nine, he'd been with the Jacks for two years and was now in the first year of a new two-year contract.

Zach knew him from a brief stint with Zach's old loser—now winner—team.

Brett looked at him kinda funny. "Did Kelsie find you?"

"When?"

"She came by a few hours ago looking for you. She looked pretty damn good if I say so myself. You're one lucky man."

"What did you tell her?"

"I told her you were probably headed home." He stared at Zach pointedly. "Obviously, you weren't. Man, if I had a woman as hot as her, I'd be home every chance I got."

Odd, she usually texted him when she couldn't find him. He checked his messages and found one from her. He texted back. *Be home in a few hours.*

It was more than a few hours later when he drove up the wet city streets of Queen Anne Hill. It was late, really late, and he was dog-assed tired. After Kelsie's manners lessons and meeting with Harris, he'd worked out for a few hours, and went to the see the kids at the shelter. After that he watched game film until his head swam and everything ran together in a jumble. He and Bret were the last ones to leave the practice facility.

Kelsie met him at the door, hands on hips, fire blazing in her eyes, and not the type of heat he normally liked to see, but an angry flame that'd nail any man's ass with one lick of its furious heat. Zach avoided angry females like he avoided Brussels sprouts and chopped liver. Only Kelsie wasn't chopped liver. Hell, he was the chopped liver, and she was prime rib. One-hundred-percent prime.

She seemed pissed, like a real wife would be because her husband wasn't where he said he'd be. Guilt tugged at his heart, even as her mistrust irritated him. In their current arrangement neither of them had the right to pass judgment or control the other's actions. Even if he did accept responsibility for not being straight with her. He couldn't quite say why he didn't tell her about his work with the kids, maybe because it was deeply personal to him, the last wall he erected around his fragile heart. If he told her, he'd be giving her a piece of himself that he'd never given anyone. He wasn't ready to do that yet.

He brushed past her, hoping she'd drop it after reading his stay-away body language.

She didn't. She followed him into the kitchen. "Hungry?"

"Uh, yeah, a little."

"I brought dinner by for you earlier. You weren't there. In fact, you're never there on Tuesday nights. According to your teammates, that's the one night a week you spend with me."

Ah, okay, that's what this was about. She thought he was screwing around on her. She should know him better than that, arranged marriage or not, he honored his promises until divorce do them part. And more and more he didn't want to part. He wanted to keep her so why the hell didn't he open up about his Tuesday night obligations?

"Yeah, seems I missed you."

For a moment her expression froze. "You were there?"

"An hour or so after you left."

"Where were you when I stopped by?"

"I thought this was a marriage in name only, a convenience for both of us. So why does it matter?" He pushed, needing to know the answer, needing to hear from her own sweet lips that it did matter. That he mattered. That *they* mattered.

She seemed to grapple with the answer and sucked her lower lip into her mouth. Zach wanted to take care of the chore for her, toss her on the kitchen counter among the canisters of flour and sugar and next to the basket of fruit. He sucked in a breath, his eyes glued to her lips, momentarily forgetting what they were arguing about.

"We promised we'd be faithful, marriage of convenience or not."

"I am faithful."

"That's not what the guys think. I could tell by the looks on their faces."

"Is that all there is to it, Kelsie? Is that all you care about? Just appearances?" Zach advanced on her, pushing her, wanting— hoping—to mean more to her than a method to advance her business, a man to mold into her idea of a man, a challenging project instead of a husband. Damn, he'd be happy to be both a project and a husband.

"This was a business arrangement." She swallowed and backed against the counter.

"With benefits." He hemmed her in with his bigger body and pressed his hips against hers, his hands on either side of the counter.

"Yes, with benefits, and we've both benefited every night. And while those benefits are still in force, I expect you to be faithful."

"I am faithful." He rubbed his crotch against hers, and her eyes rolled back in her head. Her pink tongue darted out of her mouth and circled her lips. He leaned in closer and inhaled the honey-sweet, sexual scent of her. His sweet Kelsie. He'd like to drown that verbal agreement of theirs in kisses, burn the fucking business arrangement in a fire of passion-stoked flames. Convince Kelsie of what he already knew. That she was his—and his alone—for today and all their tomorrows. Wishful thinking from a desperate man who'd never given up the dream of Kelsie loving him and him alone.

"Do you believe me?" He teased her with his mouth on her neck right below her ear, finding that spot which sent her to heaven. He liked driving her crazy because driving Kelsie crazy drove him crazy every minute of every hour of every day. He wanted her to be as nuts as he was.

"Yes," she spoke in a breathless gasp.

"Yes, what?" He slipped his hand under her shirt and slid it up to squeeze the mound of her breast.

"Yes, I believe you." Her breathy voice made his dick jerk. Kelsie stared at him with glazed eyes. She slid her hands under his T-shirt and along the sides of his rib cage, her caresses light and sensual, like a silk scarf fluttering against his skin.

Zach angled his head and lowered his face to her lips, ripe and slightly parted, as ready for him as he was for her. He touched his lips to hers, as soft and careful as his hands on her skin. Despite the lust surging through his body, he wanted more than just a hard, rowdy fuck, he wanted more than her body, and he wanted to show her that she was more than that to him.

He wanted her to trust him without needing proof of that trust but because she believed in him.

Holding her face between his hands, he kissed her and let all the feelings he'd kept bottled inside too long rise to the surface. She pressed against him, kissing him back, attempting to push the passion higher, but he didn't want wild passion tonight. He'd settle for nothing less than her soul. Her heart. Her love. Because he'd always loved her and always would—the former mean girl and the once socially inept jock. What a pair. But maybe they'd both changed enough that the thought wasn't so outrageous after all.

They had a chance if Kelsie wanted to play ball.

* * * * *

Kelsie melted like wax dripping down a candle. Zach's mouth tasted sweet and tender, all those things she didn't associate with sex, because in her experience sex with Zach was passion-ignited and hot, heavy breathing. This tender side of Zach left her off-kilter and more than a little turned on and wanting a lot more.

He'd distracted her by pulling her into his big strong arms. Those arms should've scared her, stifled her, made her run like hell for fear of being controlled and belittled, made to feel less of a person. But they didn't. Instead, she felt precious, safe, and content. She'd never felt those things with any other man, especially not Mark.

Zach made her feel like a person of value.

She pushed his T-shirt up his chest, and he complied by lifting it over his head and discarding it. Kelsie's body burned with need, but she followed the slow, gentle pace set by Zach. She took her time, perusing his body in the bright kitchen light which didn't conceal a thing. Zach's body was beautiful just as it was. Each scar told a story, and someday he'd tell her each one of those tales. She'd know him more intimately than she knew herself.

Someday?

She didn't know if they had a someday. For now she'd be satisfied with today.

He groaned into her mouth and unzipped her jeans. She shrugged them down her legs and kicked them aside. The panties followed. Wrapping his arms around her waist, Zach lifted her onto the counter.

"I think something's cooking in the kitchen." He grinned at her. His smile wrapped around her like a warm blanket just out of the dryer.

"I'm pretty sure I'm simmering."

"Hmmm. You smell like the best thing in here."

"Am I making you hungry?"

"Starved. But I think you're a ways from done."

"Perhaps a master chef might be able to bring me to a boil."

"I'm at your service, madam, using all the skills you've taught me to prepare an appropriate meal designed to impress the most jaded guest."

"Are you saying I'm jaded?"

"Not at all. I'm saying I need to work on presentation."

"Ah, you've been listening?"

"I wasn't just thinking about sex while you were teaching me about which wine glass to use for certain types of wine."

She opened her mouth to say something.

He held a finger to her lips. "Hold that thought."

Zipping out of the room, he returned with four bottles of wine, the necks gripped in his long fingers. Kelsie stared at him, wondering what the heck he had planned now.

"I think it's time to impress you with my knowledge."

Her eyes grew big, and she stared at the bottles grasped in his big hands.

"Before we start, we need to make sure we're both properly dressed."

She nodded mutely, as he left the room one more time. Kelsie craned her neck in the direction he'd gone. He returned a few minutes later with nothing on but a burgundy condom and bow tie around his impressive erection, and a crookedly tied one at that. He handed her a pair of stilettos and bowed deeply. "Your ensemble, madam."

Kelsie giggled and clapped her hands. Zach never kidded, never played around. Intrigued and more than a little turned on, she slipped off the counter, yanked off her shirt and bra, and slipped on the shoes.

"Now if madam would take her place."

"And my place would be?"

"Ah, let me help you with that, he gently laid her on the counter, leaving her legs dangling off the edge. Zach rolled up a towel and placed it under her head.

"Comfortable?"

"Yes, but it's going to be difficult to taste wines in this position."

"Not for me."

Now that sounded like fun. The bow tie bobbed in agreement. Scranton sat in the doorway, ready for an exhibition.

Kelsie lifted her head and pointed at Scranton. "Get the kid out of here."

Zach nodded and shooed him away. He returned with a corkscrew and opened the first bottle of wine, a rich, red cab she'd purchased at a little wine store down the street. Uncorking it, she expected him to give her a sip. He didn't. Instead, he dribbled the red liquid on her naked body from her breasts, down her stomach, into her navel, over her thighs. It ran down her crotch and mingled with the wetness of her sex. Kelsie gripped the countertop and watched him, waiting for whatever Zach came up with next.

"First, to examine the wine by sight." He bent down. His hot breath on her skin as he studied her body from different angles. "Ah, clear, sparkling, showing depth of color."

He *had* been listening.

"Now to swirl it." He circled his finger between her breasts where some of the wine had pooled. Then moved lower, teasing her with that circular motion over her midsection. Kelsie's legs fell open, and she wished he'd swirl between her legs. She groaned as his fingers teased but never quite hit the mark.

"Now to smell." Without touching, but close enough she felt his hot breath on her wine-slickened skin, he sniffed the length of her body. Straightening, he closed his eyes for a moment, as if savoring it to the hilt.

"And what did you find?" She managed a strangled croak.

"Fruity with just a pinch of saddle soap." He held his fingers about a half inch apart.

"Pinch of saddle soap?" Well, maybe he did need a little more instruction, but she gave him an A for effort.

"Yes, saddle soap."

She raised one eyebrow. "And what does that indicate?"

"The wine is full bodied and ready for consumption."

"Or ready to be ridden off into the sunset."

"We're a long way from sunset here, darlin'."

"Ah, consume away then."

The man took his job seriously. Starting at her neck, he licked his way down her body, paying special attention to her puckered nipples and leaving them tight with need. He sucked the small pool of wine from her belly button, and she drew in a sharp breath, tickled and aroused at the same time. He moved lower.

"A little more tasting is required." He poured more wine on her sex, grinning with enthusiasm far beyond most wine connoisseurs, but then most wine experts never tasted wine the way Zach did.

He spread her legs wide and placed them over his shoulders. Pulling her upward until his mouth met heaven. He lapped up the wine with long, slow strokes from the front to the back of her labia, pausing on each stroke to torture her clit. Kelsie arched her hips and bared herself to him as much as possible considering the position she was in.

He lifted his head, his dark eyes shining, his face wet from her juices and the wine. It was one of the sexiest sights she'd ever seen. "Ah, a balanced array of flavors, not too sweet or tart, but with a kick of spice and an abundance of class. Just the way I like it."

Right now she'd like it any way he wanted to give it. "Now that you've tasted it, perhaps you should partake of the entire bottle."

"Hmm. That seems rather tacky."

"Or adventurous, and I do adore an adventurous man."

"I do adore a woman who loves her wines." He dipped his head between her legs and partook some more. And more. And more. Until Kelsie panted and writhed on the counter, begging for mercy or release or both. He might be the one actually *drinking* the wine, but she was definitely drunk on him.

"I adore a man who takes his lessons so seriously." She gasped as he sucked her clit into his mouth. She hung on by a thread stretched to its breaking point. The next minute it broke, and her body shattered like a wine bottle on a tile floor, splintering her soul and her heart into a million pieces of extreme bliss that reunited with the beauty of a stained glass window.

Zach watched her with devotion on his face. An odd combination of pleasure and panic slid through her, as her heart picked its way among the leftover shards of glass and hoped it didn't get sliced in the process.

Lowering her, Zach pulled her to the edge of the counter and positioned his penis, bowtie still in place, at her opening. She smiled as he sank into her soft, slick opening with one long, easy thrust. He groaned the groan of a man in heaven and not ready to leave it for earth. He moved, retreating until the tip of his erection barely grazed her opening then thrusting back inside, deep inside, past all her defenses, past all her misgivings, to a place she kept secret from the rest of the world. Only Zach had snuck inside, and now that he had the key her life had just changed forever.

He maintained the slow, sexy torture, even though every vein stood out on his neck from the strain, while his biceps bulged and his eyes dilated.

With one final thrust, he held himself inside her, high and deep, his big hands spanning her butt cheeks, his balls between her legs. She tossed her head back and forth and begged him to take her home. Reaching underneath and between his legs, Kelsie cupped his balls, squeezing gently, while he reciprocated by rubbing her sensitized clit. They brought each other to climax at the very same time with hoarse shouts, lots of hot, slick skin, and panting.

Zach fell forward, his body heavy across hers and her heels pressed to the small of his back. Both of them too sated to move, their muscles turned to liquid and mellowed by their private wine tasting.

Finally Kelsie stirred beneath his crushing weight. He took the hint and sank to the floor, his back against the kitchen cabinets, chest heaving, breath coming in little, short pants, like he'd just intercepted a ball and run it back ninety yards for the score.

"What about the other wines?"

"We'll save them for another time. I liked this one just fine. We'll need to buy more bottles." He looked up at her. She sat on the counter gazing down at him, feeling inexplicably tender. "Did I pass the wine tasting test?"

"You scored an A in my book."

"I don't know about an A, but I did score."

She rolled her eyes and slid off the counter to cuddle with him on the floor. "The kitchen is a mess." Rivulets of wine ran across the counters and dripped down the cabinets to a puddle on the floor.

"Who gives a shit."

"I don't." She actually didn't.

He tilted his head and studied her. "Tell me about Mark."

She opened her mouth, then hesitated, torn between revealing how weak she'd been with Mark and wanting to give a bit of herself to Zach.

"Please." He looked so earnest, so sincere, she couldn't deny him.

She told him, every last sordid detail from "I do" to "I don't." She told him about how he'd beaten her down emotionally, stripped her of her confidence, belittled her into being nothing but a cardboard recreation of Mark's idea of the perfect wife, seen but not heard with no opinions of her own, her only purpose to make him happy, which was an impossibility. She told of the scene she walked in on in the bedroom and of him beating her almost to death when she asked for a divorce. Ending with him rallying the troops to his side with lies about her infidelities and how it'd been her boyfriend who beat her up.

Through it all, he held her tight. His brown eyes reflected sympathy for her and anger toward Mark, but never once did she see ridicule or censure or blame. Afterward, he whispered in her hair as she sobbed silently in his arms.

"I'm so sorry, baby. I'd break every bone in his body if it would take away your pain."

She raised her head and ran a finger over his chin. "You take away my pain, Zach. You, and you alone."

One lone tear ran down his cheek, and she kissed it away. They held each other for several more minutes before they climbed to their feet and cleaned up their mess.

Together. As a team. Just like a committed couple in love with each other.

If only it wasn't an illusion.

Maybe it wasn't.

CHAPTER 24

The Clock is Ticking Down

Another fucking loss. Six and seven with only three games left. When HughJack threw down the clipboard at least twelve times during the course of a game, it wasn't going well.

Thank God the plane ride from Arizona wouldn't be a long one.

Zach stood in the visiting team's shower and let the warm water run down his bruised body. It'd been too damn hot, something he wasn't used to, and he'd sweated a gallon or two. The subdued sounds of a losing team were muted by the running water. Today, there'd be none of the horseplay associated with a winner.

Next to him, Brett stood under a showerhead and stared blankly at the wall. The poor guy got into the games to hold the ball for the kicker and that was it. Zach guessed he was happy to play at all.

The defense had played like crap, like they'd been slogging through a deep, dark swamp for several hours. The offense limped along like a wheel missing several cogs. Five starters were out with injuries, including the majority of the receiver corp. Derek, Harris's favorite target, was nursing a sprained ankle. Even though he attempted to play a few downs, he couldn't beat his coverage or leap to catch the ball, resulting in an interception in the red zone. The young offensive line couldn't have held back a bevy of senior citizens on Bingo night. Harris spent more time scrambling for his life or flat on his back, ground into the turf by an ambitious rookie linebacker, than he did throwing the ball.

Zach felt every one of his thirty-four years. Damn, even his big toe ached. Turf toe or some stupid-assed term like that. He'd been invincible for so long that he'd considered himself impervious to pain or injury. Now he figured it was only a matter of time before he succumbed to the same fate as the majority of the team's wide receivers.

Last year, the team's implosion would've been the center of Zach's world, a tragedy of huge proportions. This year, while he hated it, he had Kelsie to go home to, which helped compensate for the team's losses. That simple fact scared the piss out of him more than never getting a ring. He could not lose his last chance at a ring *and* the women of his dreams, especially the woman of his dreams.

Then there was that stupid-assed gala, not to mention a Thursday Night Football game at home and only a few days to prepare, and he'd promised the kids he'd be there on Tuesday night for *their* big game against another group of kids. *Crap.*

Zach ran his fingers through his short hair. He hated messing with his hair, which was why he'd let it grow long. Kelsie saw to it that he kept it cut. Not that he gave a shit either way. He needed to win football games, and figure out how to keep Kelsie from walking out that door at the end of the season. Yeah, that's exactly what he needed to do. He needed a plan. A big one.

She'd pinned her hopes on this gala. If it was a success, her business would get an added boost. He'd do his part, be the guy that she wanted him to be, and prove to everyone how brilliant she was. He'd romance her, sweep her off her feet, impress her with how suave he'd become. As much as he hated the thought, he'd study Harris, pick up a few pointers on women. Speaking of Harris, the guy was a virtual donation grubbing machine. He charmed men and women alike, selling out the tickets to the gala and garnering some large auction items, along with donations. It looked like they'd surpass last year's total after all.

Grabbing a towel, Zach dried off and wrapped it around his waist. Back in the locker room, guys were dressing and talking in muted tones.

Harris sat on the bench and rubbed his throwing arm. Zach hesitated as he walked by. "You being a pussy again?"

"Screw you." Harris looked up and almost smiled. The quarterback looked haggard, beat-up, and exhausted. As much as he'd like to, Zach couldn't fault the guy's heart in the past few games, but even Harris couldn't stop this plane from going down.

Zach nodded. As long as Harris and he were needling each other, things were as they should be. He watched the man out of the corner of his eye, concerned one of those hits Harris took might have damaged his arm. Without the game-changing quarterback, they didn't have a rat's ass chance in hell of making the playoffs.

They might not be best of friends—and never would be—but Harris had earned a grudging respect from Zach lately as the two team captains presented a show of unity and attempted to keep the team together.

Only they were a platoon of soldiers with half their men down, while the wounded survivors fought on for honor and pride. Zach had spent the first twelve years of his life playing for nothing but pride. He sure as hell hadn't planned on doing so this year with this team.

He pulled on his slacks and buttoned his shirt.

"Now aren't you stylin'?" Harris looked him up and down. The QB shrugged into his shirt and winced when he moved his shoulder.

Zach studied him with concern, even though he wouldn't voice it. "Kelsie."

"I figured she'd been buying your clothes. That woman is good for you. You'd be wise to keep her around. You aren't such a single-minded jerk with her keeping you under control."

"Thanks. I'll be sure to pass that on to her."

"You do that."

Kelsie. The thought of her waiting for him at home this evening picked up his battered spirits. Sure, she'd been a little out of sorts about his Tuesday-night meanderings. He should just tell her the truth, but for some reason, he couldn't. Working with homeless kids was so deeply personal to him, and so private, he couldn't tell her, even though she'd spilled her guts about life with her ex.

He still didn't completely trust her, but he was getting there. They made a good pair in an opposites attract sort of way. For so long, he'd been a loner who hated parties and socializing and all those things she liked, yet parties weren't so bad with her at his side. She handled the small talk while he listened with interest and nodded in all the right places. He followed her lead on which utensils to use in what situations and how to properly sip wine. Oh, yeah, he'd definitely become a wine aficionado.

He smiled at the thought of Kelsie spread out on the counter with wine dribbling down all her hills and valleys. Damn, he loved those hills and valleys. They sure as hell were compatible when it came to their physical relationship.

"You must be thinking about sex."

Zach jerked his head in Tyler's direction. "None of your damn business."

"That's what I thought. Sex."

"Have you seen his wife? I'd be thinking about sex, too." Hoss Price, their big center, bellowed for all to hear. Several guys shouted their agreement and others chuckled. At least Harris's comment broke some of the tension in the room.

Instead of being pissed, Zach grinned with pride. She was his, and he planned on keeping it that way. For once, he didn't care as much about the taunting as he once would have. He just cared that Kelsie waited at home for him.

He'd show her how much she meant to him and convince her they belonged together.

How the hell did a guy who didn't have a way with words romance a woman? Zach didn't know the first damn thing about romance, but he bet Harris did. Or Mabel Fay. Hell, maybe there was a chapter in that book on romance etiquette.

An hour later, Zach settled into a seat on the team plane and opened Mabel Fay's book bent on gleaning some tips on romancing Kelsie. She worshipped Mabel Fay so any advice the old bitty might impart had to work on his beauty queen. First, he took a picture of himself reading the book and texted it to Kelsie, scoring some big brownie points. She texted back a picture which inspired him to get this romance thing down.

Zach went to work. Mable Fay was dry reading but he trudged through it. Four pages into the chapter, someone ripped the book out of his hands. Zach grabbed for it, but not before Harris read the heading at the top of the page.

"Chapter Twenty-Two—The Fine Art of Wooing Your Sweetheart." Harris threw back his head and laughed like a fucking hyena. Then the dickwad dropped into the empty seat next to Zach. A second later, Derek leaned over the seat in front of them.

Zach said nothing, just gritted his teeth and felt the heat rush to his now-exposed ears, wishing he'd kept his hair long.

Harris wiped his eyes with the sleeve of his shirt. "Damn, I needed a good laugh after today's game. Seriously, who calls it 'wooing' anymore?"

"Beats me." Derek shrugged, even the nice guy couldn't seem to stop the smile spreading across his face.

Zach yanked the book out of Harris's oversized hand and tucked it under his seat.

"You got problems in the romance department, Murphy?" Harris tapped his own chest. "You've come to the right place."

"I didn't come to you. You invaded my space."

"Whatever. I'm the king of romance. Aren't I?" He glanced at his cousin.

Derek rolled his eyes. "More like king of bullshit."

"Ladies love bullshit. For example, if they ask you if a dress makes them look fat, you don't say, 'Yeah, you look like a sow about to give birth to piglets.' No. No. No. That'll get you a night in the barn. Right, Dare?"

"That's what happened to our Uncle Arnold." Derek's smile grew wider.

Even Zach had to smile at Harris. Sometimes the guy was a pure nut.

Harris sat up straighter. "Uncle Arnold was lucky he survived with his dick intact. No guy wants to lose his dick. So you say, 'Honey, you're as sexy as hell in that dress, and I'd love to do you right up against the door of the dressing room.'"

"You call that romantic?"

"He does," Derek said. "Seriously, Zach, you two got married really fast. Did you ever do the flowers, chocolates, and the sappy words thing? Women love that crap."

"Uh…not really." Zach hesitated. He'd never been much for that stuff, a waste of money, but it was money he'd gladly spend on Kelsie.

"Oh, man." Derek slapped his forehead.

"He's not talking a grocery store chocolate bar and a handful of daisies. You need expensive chocolates from that gourmet chocolate place in downtown Bellevue. And roses."

"Red roses," Derek agreed. "The more the better."

"What do I say to her?" Zach couldn't believe he was asking for romance tips from these two clowns.

"Tell her that her hair's softer than silk, her smile lights up your life, and your world revolves around her," Harris suggested.

All true. Zach could say that because he felt that way.

"Make sure she knows you think about her night and day, and you'd rather die than live without her," Derek added.

"You guys aren't very original." Bruiser, the worst womanizer on the team, swaggered over. "You gotta be more poetic." Bruiser got down on one knee and clenched his hands to his heart. "Darlin', you are my warm fire at the end of long day, my sweet song when I need comfort, and my guiding light when all is lost."

The guys started laughing. Pretty soon other players were pushing and shoving to offer their own advice. Zach filed some away in his brain as possibilities. Most of it was pure garbage, but it brought the team together, showed them that the two captains could get along. He shook his head, realizing he hadn't thought of the game once since he'd boarded the plane. He'd been focused on how to romance Kelsie.

What had she done to him?

He could do this. He could tell Kelsie how much she meant to him without making a bumbling mess out of it. He could say what was in his heart without sounding like Bruiser delivering a line to his lover of the night. He'd make sure the words came from deep inside, and he hoped like hell Kelsie gave points for his sincerity, even if the words weren't perfect.

* * * * *

On Tuesday evening just before 5:30 p.m., Kelsie pulled into the practice facility's parking lot. It was dark, but she located Zach's big truck immediately, and she parked several spots away in an unlit corner, out of sight from anyone exiting the building.

She glanced around to make sure she wasn't being followed by trench-coat man, then realized it was the first she'd thought of him in a long while. Out of sight, out of mind. Hopefully, the guy had gone onto other prey. Maybe her ex had finally given up. She shook her head at her own thoughts. Fat chance of Mark becoming reasonable.

Popping a chocolate in her mouth, she chewed slowly. Zach had been behaving so strangely for the past few days, overwhelming her with roses and yummy chocolates, behaving like a doting husband, or far worse, a cheating one. Guilt often drove a man to shower his woman with material gifts when all the woman wanted was his affection and undying devotion. Kelsie popped another chocolate in her mouth. Is that what she wanted? Really wanted? And why did he continue to hide where he went on Tuesday nights?

She had to know and despite hating herself for reverting to past devious methods, she reverted anyway. Tamping down her guilt, Kelsie justified her actions every which way. After all, Zach had evaded her every attempt to quiz him on his Tuesday night activities, either because he didn't want her to know, or he wanted her to trust him and take his word for it.

Neither reason worked for a nosy woman.

Even though she did trust him. Deep in her heart, she knew he wasn't seeing another woman, but her inborn female curiosity couldn't let it go at that. When he came home on Tuesday nights, he seemed so different, even more quiet than usual. His change in behavior concerned her. If he wouldn't tell her what was going on, she'd find out for herself.

After an hour of hunching down in the car seat, her butt fell asleep, and she had a cramp in her calf. Maybe the joke was on her. Maybe he'd left hours ago in someone else's car. She'd give it until seven. If he didn't show by then, she'd go home. A slice of light spilled into the parking lot and caught her attention.

The side door opened and someone walked out. Even in the darkness, she recognized Zach's distinctive, determined stride. He got in his truck and barreled out of the lot. Keeping her distance, Kelsie followed. She had an insurance policy if she lost him. She'd grabbed his phone earlier that morning and programmed it so she could "stalk" him using her new iPhone's "Find Friends" feature. He'd be pissed as hell that she'd gone to such lengths, and there wasn't one part of her not nursing some deep-seated guilt over her deception. She'd come so far from her mean girl days, yet she'd reverted to the lying and manipulations when the going got tough.

She just needed to know. That was all. Once she found out, she'd head home, and he'd never be the wiser. Then first chance she got, she'd remove her permissions from his stalker app.

She lost him on the wet city streets when he gunned it through a yellow light, and she had to stop. The light took forever to change. By the time she got to the intersection a few blocks down from where he'd turned, his truck was nowhere in sight.

Kelsie pulled out her phone and opened the stalker app. She located him several blocks away and found his truck parked on a side street in a not-too-desirable section of Seattle. On one side of the street was a rundown hotel, on the other a homeless shelter of some kind. Her gut said he wasn't in the hotel having a liaison with a woman. Getting out, she stepped across the street to the shelter.

A man sat slumped on a bench near the door outside the entryway, a tattered blanket wrapped around his bony body. He wore a Vietnam veteran's hat, and he gazed up at her, his eyes haunted by horrors she couldn't come close to imagining and clouded with hopelessness. Her heart went out to him. Kelsie felt compassion for this man because she knew how desperate she'd felt not having a home. She dug in her purse and handed him a twenty. He took it in his scrawny hand, yellowed by some disease and nodded at her. A hoarse croak sounded from his parched lips. "Thank you."

"Sir, thank you. For your service."

For a moment he smiled a toothless smile. "You are welcome."

Swallowing back the choking tears and swiping a hand across her face, Kelsie pushed open the heavy old door, its glass smudged with a million fingerprints. She wandered down a long, narrow hall, her heels clicking on the old tile floor. At the end of the hall were double doors with small windows. She crept closer and peered through one window.

At the end of decrepit gymnasium stood Zach in sweats, surrounded by kids of varying sizes, ages, and ethnicities. He held a basketball in one hand. The kids sat in a half-circle around him and listened with rapt attention, laughing at times and smiling at others. Quiet, intense Zach was animated and enthusiastic. He picked out several of the smallest kids and directed them to one basket, throwing a ball to them. Then he placed a hand on a tall boy's shoulder, handed him another ball, and sent him and several others to the opposite basket.

The kids lined up, practicing jump shots and free throws, while Zach and the taller kid shouted encouragement and suggestions.

Kelsie sank away from the window. Why hadn't he told her he worked with homeless kids? Why had he thought she wouldn't want to know? Why didn't he trust her enough to tell her about something obviously so important to him?

But he hadn't told her. Just like he hadn't told her about his brother's ashes buried in the side yard. Why?

She knew the reason, and it trampled her like a mob of shoppers on Black Friday. He didn't trust her. Despite her opening up and telling him about Mark. They'd spent hours getting to know each other's bodies, but they didn't know each other's minds well at all.

Because they didn't have a future, and Zach didn't want one.

Even if Kelsie thought she did.

* * * * *

Zach tossed the ball to Billy. The kid caught it with the ease and grace of a natural athlete. "Make sure the little ones don't get run over by the big ones."

Billy nodded, taking his position as a squad leader seriously. The only praise the kid got all week was from Zach. His mother vacillated between running from an abusive husband and going back to him, certain he'd changed. Her kids were constantly pulled in one direction or the other. The only constant in Billy's life was this small band of kids Zach coached on Tuesdays.

Billy's mom was with a new boyfriend, and the kids had a roof over their heads, for now. Tomorrow could be a different story, one Zach knew all too well. He suspected the new guy would be as abusive as the old one because the cycle of abuse kept spinning slowly, over and over until a tragedy interrupted it, like it had in Zach's life.

He might play a violent sport for a living, but he avoided aggression off the field. He'd seen too much of it as a kid.

Catching movement, Zach glanced toward the doors, a face appeared in the window then it was gone. His eyes narrowed, and he frowned. He didn't like people snooping around here, and anyone who didn't identify themselves was a problem in his book. He signaled to Billy that he'd be right back and sprinted for the door. Slamming it open, he saw the outer doors close behind the interloper. If it was a reporter, he'd shove the asshole's camera down his throat. Zach didn't want anyone publicizing or profiting from his charity work.

He ran down the long hall and onto the street but didn't see anyone.

Zach turned to Danny huddled under a blanket near the doorway. "Dan, did you see someone just come out these doors?"

The guy nodded and pointed toward the end of the block where a car pulled away from the curb. Zach could just make out the blond head of the driver, and he knew the car.

Kelsie had followed him here. Or found him another way.

He fished his phone out his pocket and punched a few buttons. Disgust sliced through him when he saw it in full living color on his phone. The old Kelsie still lived and breathed.

She'd been stalking his every move via his phone.

She didn't trust him. Without trust, they had nothing, no matter how hot the sex.

Zach tossed the old veteran enough cash for a warm meal and a room for the night then trudged back into the building, devastated. He rested his forehead against the cool concrete block wall of the deserted hallway and braced his hands on either side of his head. Breathing in and out in a slow rhythm, he attempted to gain a semblance of normalcy before he rejoined the kids—which was damn tough to do when a trap door opened beneath his feet and catapulted him downward toward an unknown fate.

* * * * *

Kelsie lay in bed and waited for Zach to come home. Only he didn't come home. Feeling like a conniving bitch, she checked her phone. It showed him back at HQ. At midnight? Well, they did have a big game on Thursday night. But he could've at least called or texted her to let her know. Her heart filled with righteous anger. She didn't deserve this cold shoulder from him. She'd give him a piece of her mind when he got home. Mark used to pull this crap on her, and she'd let him.

No more.

Finally, around 1:30, she heard him come in the bedroom. He undressed and crawled into bed beside her. She kept her back to him, strung tight and ready to pummel her fists into the pillow in frustration. "You're late, where've you been?"

"You tell me." The hint of anger and disappointment in his voice put her on alert. He knew something. A little of her anger fizzled, but only a little.

"What's that supposed to mean?" She picked her words carefully, not sure she wanted to hear his answer but needing to hear it, yet still pissed in her own right.

"Don't play stupid, Kelsie. You haven't really changed a bit, have you?"

"Yes. Yes, I have." She sat and faced him, glaring at him. She went still inside, but the anger and disappointment simmered below the surface, even as she battled with her guilt. At least she was trying. What about him?

"Then tell me. Where was I tonight?" His cold voice chilled her and stalled her reaction.

"You weren't here with me. Seems you don't think enough of me to share your life with me, especially the important things." She tossed hurtful words back in his face and waited for his temper to detonate.

"Don't lie to me. I hate it." Zach switched on the light at the nightstand and sat on the side of the bed. He scrubbed his face with his hands and heaved a frustrated sigh.

"I hate it, too. Why didn't you tell me about your work with homeless kids? Why? Why?" Her voice climbed higher and higher until she was screeching.

"Because it's something private, something special, something I don't share with anyone."

"Not even your wife?"

"Especially not the wife who uses my phone to stalk me then follows me like I'm a cheating husband." He stood, hands on his hips and glared at her. She glared back, equally pissed off.

"If you'd been honest with me, I wouldn't have had any need to be dishonest with you." Damn him, damn him, for turning this back around on her. She'd done what she'd done because he kept a part of himself protected from her.

"I'll sleep in the other room. At the rate this team's going, you'll only be stuck with me for a few more weeks. Once this gala is over, you can waltz into your world of wealthy men and up-scale clients. You don't need an uncouth guy like me to drag you down."

"Do you think that's what I really want?" Kelsie grabbed her stomach, feeling as if someone had sliced her open and gutted her insides.

"Isn't it?" He looked so proud, yet she saw underneath his angry bluster a man who was lost and needing love. For a moment she wanted to pull him into her arms and tell him she was sorry and beg him to forgive her, but the stiff set of his body kept her away, reminding her of why she'd done what she'd done in the first place.

"You're so close-mouthed about everything. I had to know. I trusted you, but I had to know. You have to understand where I'm coming from."

"Do I? Do I really, Kelsie? Do you have any idea where I'm coming from?"

"A little. What I can wrench out of you. Your dad is in prison for killing your mom and beating your brother until he was brain dead. I know your brother's ashes are buried in the yard of this house. Why? Why of all the places you lived did you bury him here? Tell me, Zach, open to me. Be honest with me. I've been honest with you." She clenched her hands in to fists, digging her fingernails into her palms.

"You have? What about stalking me with your phone?"

The cold hands of guilt wrapped its fingers around her throat. "I'm sorry. I shouldn't have done that. If you'd only talked to me. Talk to me now, Zach. Why are your brother's ashes in the yard of this house of all the houses you've lived in? Why this place?"

He went white. "The only person who knows the answer to that is my brother, Wade."

"Trust me enough to tell me. Open up to someone, Zach. Take a chance on us."

"What about you, Kel, you gonna take a chance on me?"

"I am taking a chance on you."

"Only because it's to your advantage. How do you feel about me as a person? How do you feel about our life together? Do you want to end it in a few weeks?"

Kelsie swallowed. She didn't want to end it, but she didn't want to be the first person to say those words, only to have him laugh in her face and tell her "tough shit." She couldn't bear the rejection, the heartbreak of being without him, and she couldn't say the words she wanted to say without knowing where he stood.

When she didn't answer him, he turned on his heel and slammed the door behind him.

She reached out to him, but her plea died in her throat.

Kelsie Murphy did not want this marriage to end, and she had herself to blame.

CHAPTER 25

Loose Ball Foul

For the next few days, Kelsie drilled Zach on proper party behavior and casual conversation until his eyes glazed over and a hint of defensiveness and annoyance crept into his demeanor. They sniped at each other like the sex-deprived couple they were. Since The Fight, as she labeled it, he slept in the other bedroom and stayed clear of her.

The day of the gala she pushed him too far, harping on him about his clothes, his hair, his shoes. By the grim set of his lips, he wanted to stuff a sock in her mouth.

As soon as it was time for the guests to start arriving, Zach retreated to the deck, obviously preferring to stand outside in the clear, frigid night rather than act as a host. A twinge of sympathy tempered her anger. He hated social situations like this, and she knew it'd be difficult for him, but he wasn't getting out of his duties that easily. Not on her life. In a huff, she dragged him to the front door and lectured him on how to be a proper host. He ground his teeth and stared over her head. She reached a hand up to brush off a spot of lint on his lapel. At his warning glare, she snatched her hand away. He brushed the lint off himself.

She'd endured these last few days by pretending nothing mattered. That *they* didn't matter. That their future was no big deal, yet inside she was a mess. A huge, heartbroken mess. Meanwhile, Zach built prison walls around his heart, strung barbed wire along the top, and kept his distance.

As the first guests arrived, Kelsie lurked in the background, ready to jump in at the first sign of him floundering. Zach's jaw tightened and his brow creased, obviously perturbed by her hovering. She needed to stay close, make sure he was okay, be his lifeline, whether he appreciated her or not. She wouldn't let him free-fall. She'd figuratively hold his hand every step of the way.

Zach looked like a million dollars in his designer suit and carefully cropped hair. She loved how he filled out the shoulders of his tux and the easy athletic grace in his confident stride. She smiled with pride as women took second glances at him, looking him up and down. A few times Kelsie hooked her arm through his, just to stake her claim.

She tagged along as Zach led several teammates through the house. They all cleaned up so well that she barely recognized the men when they'd shown up in a group a few minutes prior, but their large, fit bodies gave them away as professional athletes.

They wandered through rooms transformed into a Victorian Christmas extravaganza and a testament to Kelsie's hard work and lack of sleep. The group halted in a room displaying the silent auction items to their best advantage with careful lighting and presentation of each expensive item. She almost smiled when she heard the pride in Zach's voice.

Hanging back as they moved on, Kelsie repositioned a helmet autographed by last year's championship team into a better spot under the makeshift spotlights illuminating the auction items. The rest of the room was bathed in Christmas lights nestled in sprigs of holly and cedar boughs.

"The house looks decent."

Kelsie jumped, not realizing she wasn't alone in the room. She turned to face Veronica. For once the woman looked sincere, as if she cared. Yet this was the woman who'd fired her without even one ounce of remorse and the same woman who wanted Zach off the team. "Thank you."

"I've been doing a little research. You came here from Texas, no money, and the only person you knew in Seattle was Zach. I'm thinking you planned all this, knowing he'd take care of you."

Kelsie measured her words carefully, even though she'd rather spit in Veronica's face. "I can take care of myself."

"My father wants to extend his contract for another two years. I'm dead-set against it. We both know you married Zach for reasons that have nothing to do with love. Take my advice. Get out while you can. Distance yourself. If you stay with him, I'll see that you never get another client in this town."

"Why do you hate Zach so much? He's never done a thing to you."

"Dad hired him to put some spark back in this team against my recommendations. He knew about his long-standing feud with Tyler but figured Zach's signing would put Tyler on notice that no one is sacred if they're not performing up to expectations."

"Zach has brought back the old Tyler, from what I understand."

"I wouldn't give him the credit. He's created a division in the team and too much strife."

Kelsie bit back a response, torn between defending Zach and bettering her business. "Zach and Tyler are working hard to settle their differences."

Veronica frowned. "All that matters to me is the team. I convinced Dad to put his trust in Tyler Harris, and I was right about him. He's the face of this franchise. We built a championship caliber team around him. Anyone who doesn't respect and appreciate all he's done for the Jacks is not welcome in my book."

So there it was. Zach's stubborn pride and public dislike of Tyler had earned him a powerful enemy. Of course, spilling a tray of drinks on the woman didn't help. "Zach wants what's best for the team. He has the same goals as you."

"Hardly. I want him off the team, at the least, benched. He's a deterrent. The sooner it happens, the better."

"Why are you telling me this?"

"Because you might want to run before tornado hits and save yourself."

"I'm not going anywhere and neither is Zach. Your father and the coaches are happy with his progress off the field and his performance on the field."

"Thanks to you. I was wrong about you. You do have a talent for smoothing those rough edges sported by most athletes. After all, good professional athletes are alpha, strong, aggressive, and bluntly honest. Tact doesn't win games. So of course they need help in that area. It's different than hiring an image consultant, but then, you know all this." Veronica looked her up and down then tapped her chin. "My father has interests in other sports teams, which would give your business quite the boost."

"But?" Kelsie definitely heard a but in there.

"Zach needs to be off the team first. You can help me with that."

Kelsie opened her mouth to chew Veronica's skinny butt then closed it, attempting to practice what she'd preached so often to Zach.

"Well?" Veronica tapped one toe of her Jimmy Choos on the hardwood floor. Tap. Tap. Tap.

Kelsie hesitated, momentarily torn between her old opportunistic self and the new Kelsie she'd worked so hard to reinvent. Taking a deep breath, she threw herself under Veronica's bus. "I'm with Zach, and he's on the team." Even as she sealed her fate she felt sick to her stomach and gloriously free at the same time. She'd never work in his town. She'd be living in her car and eating out of dumpsters. Yet, it felt damn good to stand up for Zach and do the right thing.

Veronica huffed. "We'll have to see about that." She leaned closer, a sly smile on her coldly beautiful face. "Did you ever wonder why your stalker went away after you married Zach?"

"What do you know about my stalker?"

"Enough to know that Zach hired him to scare you and force you into his arms for your own safety."

"Zach would never do such an underhanded, dishonest thing."

"Oh, wouldn't he? How well do you really know him?" Turning on a spiked heel, Veronica strode from the room.

Fanning her face, Kelsie headed for the powder room as she fought for composure. Veronica caught her off guard with that comment, but she did know one thing—she trusted Zach, and she didn't trust Veronica. Yet if Zach didn't hire the stalker, who did? And how the heck did Veronica know about him?

Unless…

Noises from the party filtered through the bathroom door. Kelsie put on her game face, straightened her shoulders, opened the door and strode into the room, pausing to chitchat with guests on her way to check on the bar and the food. Then she would find Zach and see how he was faring. She stepped into the kitchen. The caterers were busy working and everything seemed in order.

"Kelsie." The smooth, cultured voice behind her stopped her in her tracks. The night just went from bad to disastrous. A root of panic pushed up through the ground and attempted to take seed in her brain. She shook it off. Mark would *not* belittle her or scare her. She wouldn't allow it. This was her time. Her moment to prove how far she'd come.

She turned on him, all haughty and cold. "What are you doing here?" Each word steamed like dry ice. Funny, how much smaller and less threatening he seemed.

"I wanted to see what my wife was up to."

She raised her head higher. "I am not your wife."

"I told you when the divorce papers were signed that it would never be final. You'd come crawling back eventually." Mark's handsome face contorted into a cruel sneer. Kelsie wondered how she'd ever been fooled by him.

"But I didn't, did I?" She looked him in the eye, something she hadn't been able to do for years.

"You will. Soon. I understand your convenient marriage is about to become inconvenient."

For a moment, she hesitated, fearing he knew something she didn't. Judging by Mark's smirk, he caught her moment of indecision.

Any moment, he'd be moving in for the kill.

Only this time she'd be armed and dangerous with her newfound confidence and hard-won independence.

* * * * *

Zach tugged on his bow tie. Stupid-assed things. Tyler Harris stood across the room, smiling and talking with the billionaire geeks. Zach could barely manage to talk to his smart phone. In fact, when he talked to it, it talked back, and the phone had a major attitude. Meanwhile, Harris was cool and collected as if he were talking to buddies while bellied up to the bar.

Kelsie had been flitting nearby all night, spreading cheer among the guests. Zach caught the hungry looks of the men and envious looks of the women as she glided off in her pink sequined dress that dipped lower in the back than in the front. He shot murderous glares at any men who ogled her.

Sleeping in another room didn't work for him. Only he didn't know what to do about it. He'd worked his ass off trying to woo her with flowers and chocolates, and he hadn't a clue if his plan was effective or not. There had to be more. Between the sheets, on the counter, and in the backseat of the truck the two of them were beyond compatible. But relationships—uh, marriages—weren't built only on sex, they were built on love and trust.

He loved her, but could he trust her? Did it matter as long as they were sharing a bed? How much was he willing to compromise just to feel her silky skin on his? The answer seemed to be a lot, sorry sap that he was. Speaking of trust, Zach ground his teeth so hard his head hurt. Kelsie had followed him around all night as if she expected him to belch, fart, or spit any second and embarrass their guests' delicate sensibilities. Her hovering grated on his nerves and stretched his patience to the point of breaking. He hated this stuff, and Kelsie's lack of faith irritated and discouraged him. He couldn't do anything right. He never could. Not as a kid. Not as an adult.

Despite a few of Zach's minor mishaps, the gala was going off without a hitch. They were raising a record amount of money, and Zach had made sure some would be earmarked for the homeless shelter where he spent his Tuesday nights.

Brett walked up to him, beer in hand. "Boy, you are one lucky dumb shit."

"What do you mean?"

"Kelsie. She looks at you like you're the only man on earth."

"She does?"

"Yeah. You dickwad, don't you even notice?"

Zach shrugged, a little sheepish. "I thought I just saw what I wanted to see."

Brett rolled his eyes and wandered off, leaving Zach alone with his thoughts. He glanced around, glad Kelsie wasn't hovering anywhere near. His gaze darted around the room of milling people. Maybe he should ask her to dance, get her to thaw a little.

Only he couldn't find her. Finally he checked the last place he expected her to be—the kitchen. Staff bustled about the room with brisk efficiency, while the caterer organized and inspected. Zach's gaze swung around the room. He paused and blinked. Kelsie stood over by the breakfast table, hands fisted at her sides, shoulders thrown back, and a look of defiance on her face. He didn't like the threatening stance of the guy standing only a few feet from her.

Zach did a double-take.

It was Mark.

Even though his beauty queen appeared to be holding her own, Zach mounted his white stallion and rode to the rescue, only to rein himself in a few steps from her. One scathing glance from Kelsie broadcast loud and clear that she didn't need or want a white knight. Well, screw that. He'd rip the asshole's head off if he made one move toward Kelsie, gala be damned. In fact, if they were anywhere else but this damn gala, he'd already be mopping the floor with the guy's face.

The two continued their stilted conversation as if he weren't there. Mark looked like some model out of some fucking men's fashion magazine, but then he always had. Zach hated his type. Not only was the guy a pussy, but he had a way of making Zach feel like he didn't measure up. High school all over again. But not this time.

His protective instincts rushed to take over, but he cleared his throat and fought them off, bent on showing her how much he'd learned. "Mark, you're a long way from Houston."

"You're a long way from the trailer park," Mark sneered at him.

Zach bit back a retort and tried to remember Kelsie's lessons about tact and playing nice with others. He really wanted to plant his fist in the asshole's face. "I'm thinking about putting one in my backyard just so I'll feel at home." He kept his voice calm.

Kelsie stared at Zach as if he'd just donned a tutu and started dancing to *Swan Lake*. She blinked a few times. "Mark was just leaving."

"Actually, I'm not going anywhere."

Zach tensed up, ready to grab the guy by the scruff of the neck. *Never get defensive and don't make rash moves until you've considered all your options.* Kelsie's words bounced around in his brain. He took a deep breath. "I believe you may want to reconsider."

"I can handle this, Zach. I was doing just fine before you showed up." Kelsie pointed toward the door. "Good night, Mark."

"I paid good money to attend." Mark leaned against the kitchen table and crossed his arms over his chest.

"We'll refund your money. Leave. Now."

Zach clenched his fists then unclenched them. He let his arms hang loosely at his sides. *Think before you speak. Plan your words carefully. Diffuse a volatile situation with calming words.* "It would be best if you left. Let me escort you out."

"I'm taking Kelsie back with me." Mark stood his ground.

"You can't order me around anymore. You don't have the power to hurt me or control me."

"You'd pick this backwoods hick with no redeeming characteristics other than knowing how to tackle over me?"

"You abusive asshole. You aren't fit to breathe the same air as this man." Kelsie shrieked and lunged forward, but Zach was quicker. He wrapped his arm tightly around her waist and held her to his side. He would not be baited by this asshole, nor would Kelsie.

"I'm guessing Kelsie never told you the truth."

"The truth?" Zach's life teetered for a moment then righted itself. He noticed several of his teammates come into the kitchen. They must have heard Kelsie yelling.

"Come on, even you can't be that dumb and clueless. Did you honestly think it was a coincidence that Kelsie showed up at that charity event a few months ago?"

Zach didn't have an answer for that while Kelsie struggled to free herself.

"You're a pawn. I kicked her out when I caught her screwing around on me. She came to Seattle specifically because you were here, and she figured she could manipulate you into helping her out. You were her last resort. You always have been."

Zach shook his head, feeling oddly off-kilter. Kelsie jammed her elbow in his side, but he didn't let go. "You've been set up, buddy. You were always a sucker for her. She invited me here tonight to make me jealous. Sounds familiar?"

"You lying bastard," Kelsie tried to pry Zach's fingers from her waist.

Zach couldn't move, couldn't speak, could hardly breathe. Even his teammates who stood watching the whole sordid scene seemed to hold their collective breath.

He fought like hell to wrap his brain around Mark's comments, and one truth spoke louder than the rest. He stared Kelsie's ex square in the eyes and shook his head. "No, she wouldn't do that."

"What about the stalker? Did you really think I'd waste my bucks on a PI for her? She hired the guy herself to manipulate you into taking her in."

"I did not. You hired him." Kelsie craned her neck around to gaze at Zach with pleading eyes.

"No." Zach shook his head even as his world blew up like a planet being attacked on *Star Trek*. Mark was lying, he had to be, twisting things to his advantage.

"You don't think she married you because she loved you?" Mark snorted.

Actually, he knew she didn't. Her big blue eyes pleaded with him, yet he couldn't deny the guilt there. Mark was telling the truth, at least partially. She'd used him. Again. Made a fool of him. Again.

"Zach, it's not like that."

Kelsie seemed to have regained her composure. Zach let go of her. "Then what is it like, Kelsie?" His stomach rolled with nausea. His pride wouldn't let him throw up in front of his team.

"Not here. Not now. Let me handle this. This is my battle, not yours." Kelsie stepped away from Zach and turned to her ex. "I'm calling the police and having you removed from the premises."

"You know what?" Mark threw back his head and laughed, as if bent on goading Zach, but Zach would not be sucked into a physical altercation. He would not ruin Kelsie's gala.

"You're washed up. Without football, you're nothing, no better than your murderer father."

"You asshole. How dare you insult my husband like that?" Zach could feel every cell in Kelsie's body vibrating with uncontrolled fury. He realized he'd let go of her too soon and snaked his arm back around her. With one vicious stomp, she rammed her lethal heel down on his toe. He yelped and released his hold on her.

She grabbed a large metal mixing bowl off the counter by its handle and brandished it like a weapon. "Get the hell out of here. Now. Do you understand? You bastard. Get out." She advanced on Mark, swinging the bowl in front of her. Caramel sauce sloshed over the sides and drizzled across the floor. Mark's smile slid off his face. He backed up and regarded the armed woman warily.

Under different circumstances, Zach would've doubled over with laughter at the sight of Kelsie whipping the bowl back and forth within inches of this chickenshit's head. Zach's prim-and-proper lady was defending him like the fiercest of warriors with a stainless steel bowl—not exactly the warrior's weapon of choice.

"You've sunk to his level." Mark threw one last volley.

"I'll take that as a compliment, and you can take *this*."

Zach lunged for the bowl just as Kelsie attempted to heave it at Mark. They wrestled for it, Zach desperate to stop her from doing something so stupid as dumping it on Mark's head. She fought with him, finally stomping on Zach's other foot. He tried to hang on, but she jerked it out of his caramel-coated fingers with amazing strength.

Kelsie aimed the bowl at Mark's head, as Zach made a last-ditch grasp for it. Veronica hurried to Mark's side at the same moment the bowl hurtled toward Mark. The bowl hit its mark— literally—and Veronica got caught in the cross fire. Warm, sticky caramel sauce coated Mark and Veronica's hair and slid down their faces, necks, and torsos as slowly as slug moves across a sidewalk. Little bits of caramel stuck to Veronica's eyelashes and almost glued her eyes shut.

"Oh my God." Bruiser's words echoed Zach's sentiments exactly. Then the running back started laughing.

Mark didn't find any of it funny. "You fucking bitch." He looked ready to kill, sputtering and cursing and most likely seeing red along with gold from the caramel. Groping for another weapon, Mark grabbed a bowl of strawberry sauce and flung it. Zach and Kelsie ducked. The bowl flew between them, careening off Zach's shoulder and splattering Tyler Harris, who'd walked up behind them, squarely in the face. Red strawberries and sticky sauce coated him like a very pissed-off sundae. Zach wiped a glob off his own ear, part of the overspray. Kelsie sported a blob of strawberry on the tip of her nose.

Harris pushed past them. His blue eyes burned like a pilot light through a red strawberry haze. "You bastard." He shoved his hands in a bowl of liver pate, scooped up a ball and aimed at Mark. Mark dove for cover behind the kitchen island, and the pate ball hit HughJack squarely on his forehead as the coach entered the kitchen. Great aim. Deadly aim.

This was not good. Not good at all. HughJack's face turned redder than it did during a twenty-clipboard game.

As more guests crowded into the kitchen, the rookie running back shouted out a war whoop, grabbing another bowl.

The chef started screaming, "Not the caviar! Please, not the caviar!" The man sounded ready to cry.

A second later the caviar took flight, spraying across several guests and teammates, leaving globby messes of fish eggs clinging to elegant clothing.

Bruiser and LeDaniel took cover behind the island and peppered the growing crowd with olives and little hard pieces of bread. Shrimp was jettisoned from an undisclosed location. Bow-tie pasta flew across the room a line drive, headed for the team owner's crotch.

It all happened so fast. Within a minute participating teammates and guests had laid waste to the entire kitchen and the remainder of the food. Kelsie and Zach huddled in a corner out of the line of fire, at least most of it. Zach's stomach dive bombed to the bottom of his dress shoes and stayed there. They were both so screwed. So very, very screwed.

HughJack wiped pate off his lips and bellowed above the crowd. "STOP IT! NOW! What the fuck is going on here?"

One last piece of chicken smacked HughJack in the face before the mob quieted. Players glanced at each other and shuffled their feet. Guests picked bits of food from their hair. Zach and Kelsie rose from their safe place. Kelsie clutched Zach's hand so hard his circulation was almost cut off. Several of the wait staff swung into action and handed out towels.

Spitting out caramel and looking like a melted Snickers bar, Veronica turned on Zach. "You moron. You started this." A piece of shrimp was stuck to the caramel on her right cheek.

For a minute Zach blinked, then realized Veronica thought he'd flung the first bowl, not Kelsie. He jumped on her assumption, anxious to save Kelsie's reputation and her business, even as he knew he might very well be sinking his own career in the process. "I was giving that ass there what he deserved."

"You are never playing another down of football on my team." Veronica's sticky claws were out, as if she meant to draw blood.

Zach shook his head. "Even a layer of caramel can't make you sweet." Big mistake, but it came out of his mouth without him thinking. Somewhere nearby, he heard Bruiser laugh and Tomcat snort.

"I'll have your head." Veronica included them all in her scathing look. Perhaps it'd be a multiple beheading.

"Wait a minute. I threw that first bowl." Kelsie stepped forward, madder than he'd ever seen her. She turned on Zach. "I told you. I can fight my own battles." She swung back toward Veronica. "This jerk insulted my husband."

Mark, wiping his face with a wet rag, shook his head. "I'm done with you, bitch." He pointed at Kelsie.

"Don't you call my wife a bitch." Zach lost it. Too hell with manners. He pulled back his arm, hand fisted, ready to lay the guy out on the floor. Fingers like a steel vise and smelling of strawberries, closed around his biceps and pinned his arms behind his back.

Harris growled in his ear. "Don't make this worse for Kelsie."

Mark shook his head and little drops of caramel flew everywhere. "I'm fucking out of here." He shot a glance at Zach. "You're a dumb idiot, just like you always were. Enjoy her while it lasts." He stomped away, squishing with every step.

More guests had poured into the kitchen area. The caterer, recovering from shock, frantically yelled instructions to her staff to clean up the mess in a futile attempt to salvage the evening.

HughJack shouted at Harris. "Get him out of here for now." He looked pointedly at Zach. "We'll talk first thing Monday morning. You sure as hell better hope this doesn't make the papers or the Internet tomorrow."

Tyler and Derek grabbed his arms and pulled him away from the crazy-assed caramel woman, while her father and brothers rushed to comfort her.

"It's probably already on Twitter by now," Derek muttered as they shoved Zach toward the door and away from the scene of the crime and out of Veronica's sticky clutches. Dumbfounded with shock, Zach staggered across the room.

Kelsie stood away from the group of people, her knuckles in her mouth and said nothing.

While his future imploded around him, Zach blindly allowed Harris to usher him out of the room.

* * * * *

A food fight had obliterated Kelsie's world, and blew it into millions of tiny, unrecoverable pieces. And she, Kelsie Murphy of the impeccable manners, had started the entire thing. She didn't know whether to sob or laugh hysterically.

Veronica gripped her father's jacket lapel, leaving a caramel handprint. "You need to suspend Murphy for disciplinary purposes. Look at all the witnesses. You can't let him get away with this type of behavior. We had a deal with him."

Mr. Simms backed up a few steps, as if trying to get away from the candy fallout. "We'll talk in the morning. All of us."

HughJack nodded his agreement.

Kelsie couldn't stay quiet any longer. She ignored Veronica and pleaded her case with Mr. Simms and Coach Jackson. She already signed her finishing school's death sentence. Her next words might put her directly in the electric chair, but she couldn't let Zach take the fall for this.

"I threw the first bowl. Not Zach. He's taking the blame for me. Zach has come so far. He's worked hard not only on the field but off. He's the first one in the building in the morning and the last to leave. He would not jeopardize the most important thing in his life—his team—over something like this. He's done everything you've asked, buried the hatchet with Tyler, worked tirelessly on this gala, studied hard to improve his social skills. How can you punish a man who's made such an effort, especially for something he didn't do?" She looked from one to the other, hoping to see a glimmer of understanding and sympathy in their eyes.

The two men gave nothing away. Veronica, caramel dripping off her chin, shook her head. "Nice try. But Zach threw that bowl."

"No, he didn't. Zach passed the test. He learned his lessons better than his teacher did."

Veronica didn't budge. "You'll never convince me."

"We need to get you home." Her father ushered her from the room without another word.

The excitement over, the crowd dissipated, heading back to different parts of the house—or a shower—jabbering and laughing. Their lives hadn't been destroyed, like Zach's had and Kelsie's.

Kelsie swallowed past the giant-sized lump in her throat and went in search of Zach. She found him sitting in the upstairs tower bedroom on the curved window seat staring out the window. He looked as if he'd just been told he'd never win a ring or play another down. As far as she knew, that may well be true. She walked over to him, her heels clicking on the hardwood floors. He didn't as much as glance her way.

"Zach? Are you okay?"

He stared out the window, proud, yet sad. Kelsie sat next to him and took his big hands in hers. They were cold.

"Did your ex leave?" His voice sounded weird. He jerked his hands away from hers.

"Yes, I don't think he wanted to stick around since he was wearing most of the dessert and the rookies were eyeing him hungrily." Her attempt at humor was met with silence.

Long tense silence, except for the muted sounds of the band in another part of the house and occasional voices drifting up from the deck.

Zach looked up, attempted a wry smile. "I don't think the crowd will forget this gala."

"There is that." She cleared her throat. "Zach, I didn't invite Mark, and I didn't hire a PI to trick you into marrying me. You have to believe me."

"I do believe you, except for one thing." He looked up at her with the saddest eyes. "Why did you come to Seattle, Kel?"

He had her there. By the devastation on his face, he read the truth in her expression. "Zach, it wasn't like that, really. Yes, I knew you were here. I didn't have anywhere else to go, and I'd changed so much, learned so much. I had to apologize to you for everything before I could move on with my life."

He snorted as if he wasn't buying it. "You didn't think I could help your career?"

"I—well, yes, I hoped maybe you could at first. But now—"

"Now, what?" He stared out the window, his strong profile contorted with grief.

"There's more to it than that. I thought we might have the start of something good. Something lasting. Only you would never open up to me."

"About why Gary is buried here?"

"Among other things. That's only a symptom of a larger problem."

Zach swallowed and cleared his throat. "I buried Gary's ashes here because he'd always dreamed of owning a Victorian mansion. His forever-home. So I finally bought him one." He stared out the window and a lone tear ran down his face.

Kelsie's heart stalled, then exploded in her chest in a rapid series of frantic drum beats. Zach never cried. Never.

She fought for the right words, the words to make everything be okay. Only for once, she couldn't come up with anything.

"I never let anyone in, not even my brother, not since high school, but I was letting you in again, Kelsie. Learning to trust you. Believing in you." Zach met her gaze, lines of deep sorrow cut trenches into his rugged face.

"Zach, please, I should've told you why I came here, leveled with you."

"It's not just that. You followed me everywhere tonight, never once let me out of your sight. You didn't trust me not to screw this up, as if I didn't realize how important this was to you."

"Zach, I just wanted to be there for you. To support you."

"Support me! Hell, you wanted to control my every move, my every word."

Kelsie gasped. He made her sound like her mother. Oh, God, she was nothing like her mother, was she?

"You had to make sure this poor Texas boy didn't soil your perfect gala and ruin your ridiculous business."

She grabbed hold of his statement and attacked. "You think my business is ridiculous?"

"Well, yeah? Who does it help except you? Does it give a homeless man a coat for cold winter nights? Does it provide a warm meal for a disabled veteran on the streets? Does it cure a child of cancer?"

"No, but, it—"

"It what? Perpetuates a bunch of outdated, snooty rules that don't say a damn thing about the person underneath."

She couldn't argue with that logic. "Manners are part of civilized culture. Without them we'd be animals."

"Like tonight." His wry chuckle didn't reach his eyes. "What about compassion? Caring? Giving?"

Kelsie couldn't speak. Her mouth opened but nothing came out.

"You used me, Kelsie. Just like you used me in high school, just like you used the team, and those pageant judges because nothing gets in the way of what Kelsie wants. Nothing. Not even a man who was fool enough to believe he loved her."

"You loved me?" She grasped the words and held them to her heart, searching for the glue to put this mess back together.

"I've always loved you, worshipped you, carried an Olympic-sized torch for you. I got over it once. I'll get over it again."

"But—"

He held up a hand to stop her. "I'll sign any divorce papers you want. Hell, I don't even care if you ask for spousal support or whatever the hell they call it."

"Are you telling me it's over?" She locked her knees so she wouldn't collapse to the floor in a heap of blubbering female regret.

"It never even started. Not really. This was a stupid idea from the beginning."

She turned away from him and started throwing clothes onto the bed from the closet with shaking hands. The tears flowed freely down her cheeks and blurred her vision.

"You can stay here until we play our last game. That was our deal. I'll sleep elsewhere." Zach's harsh voice softened. "This is for the best, Kelsie. It would never work between us. We're too different."

"I know." She hiccupped.

"It's best we end it now before one of us gets their heart broken." He stood there for a moment, as if he wanted to say something else, but he didn't.

"It's too late for that."

"I know." Zach walked from the room. She started to run after him, stumbled and fell against the bed. She sank to her knees on the floor and sobbed into the soft fabric of the down comforter.

Her heart cracked apart and left a gaping hole no one could fill but Zach.

CHAPTER 26

Forward Progress

Zach stood near the window, the dreary day outside highlighted his obvious misery. In one corner sat Veronica, arms crossed over her chest, as she glared at Zach. Her father sighed and leaned forward in his executive chair, while HughJack paced the floor.

They were going to suspend him, possibly for the rest of the season, or cut him, and cut their losses. The Zach Experiment would be considered a major disaster. He'd torn the team in two with his blatant dislike of their popular quarterback—the man who'd legitimized the Seattle Lumberjacks as a contender.

Zach stared at the practice field and Lake Washington beyond. So not the way he'd planned to finish his NFL career. And definitely not the way he'd planned to finish his marriage to Kelsie. Out with a fizzle, no fireworks, no last-ditch effort to save his career or his marriage. They'd both just sputter out like a wick buried in candle wax until all light was extinguished.

Gone was his hope for a ring, his lifelong dream. And gone was the other lifelong dream—Kelsie. Somehow a ring paled in comparison to losing Kelsie. He'd never thought they'd click like they did, in bed and actually also out of bed. In fact, for her he'd dress in some stuffy suit for a night on the town just to see her in a sexy evening gown or bring home a bouquet of roses just to watch her face light up.

She used him and now she wouldn't want to align herself with the man who'd been labeled a major fuck-up by his NFL team— probably his last team. Which explained why she'd called in the cavalry—her ex. Yet, even as he thought the words he didn't completely believe them. She'd been truthful with him at last, and he believed what she'd told him.

The door slammed open. Zach yanked himself out of his pity party and looked up just as Tyler Harris bullied his way into the inner sanctum of the owner's office. He looked madder than a swarm of yellow jackets having their hive doused with water.

"Harris. Get out. I'll deal with you later." HughJack jabbed a finger toward the door. Tyler ignored it and stomped into the room, slamming the door behind him.

"Like hell, I will. Zach didn't throw the bowl. Kelsie did. I saw the whole damn fucking thing."

Veronica rose to her feet. "You're lying. You jocks stick together."

"Really? You think I'd defend him if it wasn't the truth? We've barely said a civil word to each other all season."

Mr. Simms looked at his daughter. "Is what he says true?"

Veronica wrapped her arms around her body and glared at Zach. "That's not how I saw it. He started the food fight."

Tyler rounded on Veronica. "You say you want what's best for the team, so prove it. Admit you had a hand in this."

All eyes in the room turned to Veronica. Silence reigned, except for Harris's heavy breathing. The guy must have run to get here. Veronica refused to look at Zach, or anyone else for that matter. She crossed the room to the small bar and poured a glass of ginger ale.

Harris waited, hands on hips, chest heaving, displaying a level of patience Zach would never master. But then his ability to stay in the pocket and wait for plays to develop and still not get sacked was legendary. A skill he sorely needed this year considering their offensive line.

Three months ago, Zach would've preferred suspension to allowing Harris to defend him. He'd come a long way. Now he stood back and gratefully let the quarterback present his case, knowing for once they were all on the same page.

"Daddy, this was a test for Zach. You wanted to re-sign him. I didn't. He failed the test miserably." Veronica turned and pleaded with her father.

HughJack jutted out his chin. "She's right, Zach. You're suspended. Your behavior might have been goaded by Mr. Richmond, but you didn't handle your reaction properly. You failed to meet the requirements we outlined for you a few months ago." He'd have been throwing a clipboard if he'd had one in his hands.

"You're suspending him for something like that? It's not even related to his performance on the field." Tyler fisted his hands and stepped in between HughJack and Zach, toe-to-toe with his coach.

"You're taking Murphy's side?" A smile tugged at the corners of HughJack's mouth.

"We need him." Harris's steely blue eyes narrowed with determination.

Zach stood behind Harris and kept his mouth shut as he watched the coach. Zach suspected both he and Harris were being played.

"He's a detriment to this team. He started that food fight, and ruined the gala. The sooner he's off the team, the better," Veronica recovered her stride and jumped back in the conversation.

Harris rounded on her. "He's not a detriment. Not to me. Not to you. And definitely not to the defense."

HughJack's eyes narrowed. Zach knew Harris was walking into a trap but had no way to warn him. "I never change my mind."

"There's a first time for everything. If you suspend him, you'll have to suspend me, too. I'm as guilty as he is, and I'm calling bullshit on this entire thing."

HughJack studied both of them, not bending an inch. "You're both team captains. You're responsible for the actions of your team. Half the team and all the rookies joined in that food fight." He turned to the owner and Veronica.

Tyler had the guts to grin. "Yeah, they had a helluva good time."

"I for one, did not have a good time. That incident reflects badly on the team and my family." Veronica lifted her head, getting that haughty rich-bitch look Zach used to see on a teenage Kelsie, the one that didn't fit her anymore.

Tyler turned to Veronica. "Who gives a shit about your reputation? We had a record-setting fundraiser."

Veronica ignored her favorite player and turned on Zach. "Zach deserves to be benched. He behaved like a moron at the gala. That was the deal. He broke the agreement." On that note, she cast one last threatening glance at Zach, brushed past Harris, and left the office.

HughJack almost looked sorry. Zach knew they'd put him between a rock and a hard place. Zach hadn't conformed to the terms of the agreement in HughJack's mind. "That was the deal, Zach."

HughJack turned toward Tyler who lifted his chin in defiance, as if daring the coach. "For unacceptable leadership behavior, I'm benching you both for the first half of the next game."

Zach nodded, and Tyler glared at each man before he strode out of the room. Turning, Zach followed him into the hall. Neither spoke as they walked down the stairs. Swallowing, Zach turned to Tyler. "Thanks, I—"

"No, thanks. We've got a football game to win from the sidelines, at least part of it. Let's get started."

Together, they headed for the film room. Maybe hours of film would burn out the image of Kelsie's stricken blue eyes when he had told her they were through.

* * * * *

Kelsie performed the physical motions of being a wife. She cooked, she cleaned, and she tried to wrap her head around what happened to destroy the fragile bonds they'd forged. She and Zach barely spoke. He went about his business, and she went about hers, what there was left of it.

Kelsie made it her mission to do as much of the gala cleanup as possible by herself, just to show Zach that she didn't need his money. She underestimated the sheer amount of lights and Christmas decorations and garbage littering the huge house. The kitchen looked like a war zone and the parlor didn't look much better. Regardless, she toiled away like Cinderella, only her Prince Charming had resigned from the job.

Day by day, she made a bigger dent in the mess, but it was nothing like the dent in her heart.

Mark had to be behind this entire disaster. He'd probably hired the PI to scare her and showed up at the gala to further ruin her life just because if he couldn't have her, no one could. That was the type of man he was. He hated that she'd moved on and found someone else.

Lavender told her Zach and Tyler had been suspended for the first half of the next game. She tried to talk to him about it, but he just walked away. She knew the Jacks' playoff dreams hung by a thin jockstrap, and one loss would pretty much dash all but the dimmest hopes.

If only she could do something to help. Sex helped, but Zach wouldn't let her within a mile of him or his fine body. Dang, she missed that body with all its hard, bulging muscles and the dark crinkly hair on his chest. Those strong thighs and big feet and even bigger—

Kelsie dropped the broom she'd been holding and sank onto the couch. She needed another jetted-tub therapy since Zach didn't seem to want the task, but with her luck he'd walk in on her again. Maybe her naked, soapy body would entice him to crawl in the tub with her.

Scranton interrupted her thoughts with a low guttural growl. Kelsie's head shot up. A car without headlights crept by on the street. As she watched, it parked across the street. A dark sedan. A very familiar dark sedan.

Instead of fear, fury built inside her. She grabbed Zach's Alex Rodriguez autographed bat and ran out the door. She'd never been a Yankees fan anyway.

Brandishing the bat, she ran for the car. Trench-coat man stood several feet away, taking a leak. He yanked up his pants and started toward his car. She blocked his escape, swinging the bat in front of her.

He held out his hands, palms up. "Hey, look, lady, I don't want any problems with you. Just let me get in my car, and I'll be on my way."

"Like hell you will. Not until you tell me who hired you." She threatened him with the bat.

"I can't do that."

"Really?" Kelsie swung that bat hard against one headlight. It shattered into millions of tiny pieces. "You don't seem to like using these things anyway."

"You're fucking crazy. Leave my car alone." The guy tried to skirt around her on the sidewalk to escape.

"Not so fast, buster. Tell me who hired you." She smashed his windshield and watched with smug satisfaction as a nice snowflake pattern formed in the glass.

"Damn it. You're a crazy-assed bitch."

"You'd better believe I am. Tell me what I want to know, or you'll be walking home tonight." She did in the other headlight.

"Stop. Please stop." He begged like a coward. Trench-coat man didn't seem so formidable now. She couldn't believe she'd ever been afraid of the idiot.

"Who hired you? Tell me now or I'll start on the hood."

"Okay, just stop, please." He backed up several steps and regarded her warily. "Veronica Simms."

"Really?" She held the bat poised over her head.

"Yeah, really. Said she needed to find a way to bring Zach down, and you were it."

"What else?"

"That's it."

Kelsie nodded as it all became crystal clear. Veronica. All Veronica. She tossed the bat at the guy. "Here, sell this on eBay, and you might have enough to fix this car." She ran into the house and dialed a phone number from memory. "Don't you dare hang up on me." For a moment her threat hung suspended in air like a jumper teetering on the ledge. Mark's breathing on the other end of the line indicated she'd interrupted something strenuous. He'd never been known to hire his legal assistants because they could use a computer. Their skills lay in other areas.

"What the hell do you want?"

"The truth. Why did you come to the gala?"

"Oh, fuck. You're not going to give me any peace until I tell you, are you?"

"Nope."

"Fine. That Simms woman called me. I thought her plan sounded interesting, and she was footing the bill."

"So you came out here to harass me and drive a wedge between Zach and me."

"Honey, I sure did. And it worked from what I understand. You got your answers, now good night."

The line went dead. Kelsie sat down at the breakfast nook and considered her options. She wasn't done with Veronica yet, and she definitely wasn't done with Zach Murphy.

* * * * *

A few days later, Zach slumped on the bench, miserable, cold, and frustrated. Harris sat next to him, hating the helplessness of being benched as much as Zach did.

Out on the field, the Lumberjacks floundered like coho salmon washed ashore and dying with their last breath.

Brett couldn't complete a pass to save his soul—or the team's. Bruiser ran like a ninety-year-old man. The defensive line crumpled under the 49ers constant bombardment, leaving big holes, while the secondary staggered and weaved worse than his grandma's knitting circle after a few shots of Amaretto.

Zach buried his head in his hands and groaned when the Niners' running back skipped into the end zone untouched from twenty-five yards out, while the bodies of fallen defenders littered the field. Thirty-eight to nothing. Holy crap. At this rate, they'd be breaking a league record, and not one they'd want to break.

Even worse, Kelsie had barely spoken to him since the gala. He slept alone, thanks to his stupidity. He couldn't concentrate without her, couldn't play the game he needed to play, couldn't think of much else but her, even as his team imploded around him. Fuck, he needed her. Big time. His quest for a ring faded in comparison to his grief over losing her. And he had lost her. He'd told her it'd never work between them. Yet it had been working until he'd been an idiot who couldn't get past his damn pride and humiliation.

Someone nudged his shoulder. Zach looked up to find Harris studying him with determined intensity.

"Two more minutes of this shit, and we'll be off the bench." Harris nodded at the scoreboard as it mercilessly ticked off the seconds to halftime.

"This is a fucking disaster." Zach sat up straighter.

"Hey, I'm always up for a challenge." The cocky Harris grinned at him, but Zach caught a glimmer of concern in the quarterback's blue eyes.

"Yeah, we'll come back."

"As long as your defense gets their ass in gear."

"As long as your offense puts some points on the board." Zach shot back, but not quite as indignant as he could have been. The final second ticked off the clock, ending the first half.

"You and I will find a way." Harris stood up, clapped Zach on the back, grabbed his helmet and jogged toward the tunnel.

Only they didn't—find a way.

Yeah, the defense held the Niners to a field goal in the second half, and the offense scored thirty-five points, but it wasn't enough, leaving them with one must-win game left in the regular season.

Zach's dream of a ring slipped further out of reach, not just a Super Bowl ring, but a wedding ring.

CHAPTER 27

Game on the Line

Kelsie gripped the steering wheel of her car. Zach Murphy wasn't getting out of this relationship so easily. Not without a fight. She believed in him, and he needed to quit sulking and get over himself.

It was Christmas Eve. Damn it. They were still husband and wife, and she was spending Christmas Eve with her husband. They'd agreed they'd stay together until the season ended. This Kelsie kept her promises, and she was going to fight for her man.

She'd cleared out the rest of the decorations over the past week. She couldn't leave the mess for Zach. Knowing him, he'd live in that big rambling house for years never bothering to take down anything. Plus, she knew just the place to put them to good use.

She'd boxed up everything and distributed it to various charities, while Zach avoided her, spending his days and nights at the complex. One game left and the Jacks' playoff hopes hung in the balance. Zach had one last chance to realize the one thing he'd worked for his entire life. If they lost this one, there'd be no playoffs for the team. And no ring for Zach. She needed to be there for him, win or lose.

More importantly, she missed her big, tactless guy, missed gazing into those kind brown eyes so full of devotion, missed falling asleep to his soft snore at night, missed his big body heating the bed, missed his quiet intensity. Sure, they were an odd couple, total opposites on the surface, but way too similar inside with all their insecurities and the lack of love in their childhoods. She'd grown up in privilege with everything money could buy, except love. He'd grown up in poverty surrounded by drugs and abuse and risen above it. Kelsie liked to think she'd risen above her upbringing, too, and become a much better person.

She had one stop before Zach's house. She was headed to the shelter, the very one Zach visited on Tuesdays. After she'd donated a decorated tree to them a week and a half ago, she'd struck up a conversation with the enthusiastic director. Next thing she knew, she'd been scheduled to teach classes twice a week on proper dress and hygiene, successful job interview skills, and tips for keeping the job once you're hired. It didn't pay a penny, but the satisfaction more than made up for the money.

Using her contacts from the gala, Kelsie had wrangled donations of work attire. She'd also contacted local businesses, encouraging them to hire from her pool of people. The interest was heartening. Her program was only a week old but already one disabled veteran was hired as a barista and a father of four had started work at the marina.

Kelsie knew she'd found the thing she was meant to do, and she'd find the means to raise the funds to do it. Her Finishing School for Real Men was branching off into a Finishing School for Real People.

Now that Kelsie had lived life on the other side, she had a better understanding of how close to homeless most people are. A divorce, loss of a job, a death, any of these could put a person out on the street in a matter of weeks. She knew personally what desperation and hopelessness felt like. Her business might be in shambles, but she was first and foremost a survivor. She didn't want a penny of Zach's money and wouldn't take it if he begged. What she wanted was something money couldn't buy.

Arriving at the shelter, she opened the door, while Scranton peeked out of the Coach purse Zach had bought her a month ago.

Inside, the sounds of Christmas carols rose above the soft patter of the rain.

She entered the big plain room and was welcomed by the families enjoying Christmas Eve. It was a warm dry place, but she wanted more for them. She wanted every family in their own home, with a tree and a fire crackling in a fireplace.

She made her way around the room, handing out small gifts, nothing expensive, but practical items like shaving cream and deodorant. Stuff most people never thought about.

A cheer went up in the room and caused her to turn around. Her heart thumped happily at the sight of her husband.

Zach paused in the doorway, balancing boxes of pizzas so high they hid his face. He wore dress slacks and a slightly wrinkled white shirt. Well, it was a start. She couldn't help but smile. He put the boxes on the table and stepped back. The kids dug in, not waiting for an invitation while the adults lined up for their Christmas pizza.

Zach faced her. For a minute they stared at each other. He ran his hand through his short hair. Kelsie wrung her hands, but she didn't look away.

"What are you doing here?" His voice sounded tentative yet suspicious.

"I stopped by with a few gifts." She stood up straighter, rolled her shoulders back, and projected an air of confidence she didn't feel. Please, don't let him reject her. Not before they'd had a chance to talk.

"Why would you do that?"

"I know what it's like to be homeless. I donated that tree to the shelter. I offered my services. I've been helping them with interview skills, among other things."

He glanced over at the tree. "Oh, I thought it looked familiar. It was at my house."

She nodded, unable to read his reaction. "Yes, it was at our house."

His expression softened. "You're the one? The one who helped Marv and Judd get jobs."

"I'd like to think I helped." She shifted her gaze to the people in the room and smiled.

An hour later they stood outside the shelter. Inside, the lights from the designer Christmas tree twinkled merrily and lit up the rain-soaked street and sidewalk. Something about those lights warmed Kelsie's heart. As long as people treated each other with kindness and generosity, there was always hope. She felt hope right now.

"Are you heading somewhere?" Uncertainty clouded Zach's handsome face. She wanted to throw her arms around him and tell him it'd all be okay.

"Actually, I was going back to the house."

"I made plans to join some of the guys for dinner at the marina." His expression gave nothing away. She couldn't tell if he was relieved to have an out or sad.

"Dinner? Again? Didn't you get enough pizza?" She teased him, striving for a light tone.

He smiled sheepishly, that same smile she found incredibly sexy and enduring. "Yeah. Hard to believe, huh?"

"I'll be going then. I don't want to keep you." Just like that, her plans for the evening splintered into broken pieces and littered the floor of her heart. Kelsie turned toward her car, her heart aching for what could be, yet not even sure what that was.

She heard Zach's heavy step behind her. A second later, he wrapped his long fingers around her arm and stopped her. "Come with me." He almost sounded as if he were pleading.

"I don't want to horn in on your guy time."

"You won't be. I'm the envy of all the guys when you're on my arm."

"Oh, so that's the only reason you want me around?" She linked her arm with his and gazed up at him as hope soared inside her.

He looked her up and down and grinned his trademark wolfish grin. "No, actually, I'm sure you'll want to stick around until Santa lowers himself down the chimney and delivers his gifts."

"I have milk and cookies ready."

"So you'll join me tonight for dinner? And we'll come back here in the morning and help serve Christmas dinner here, at the shelter?"

"A hundred stampeding defensive linemen couldn't keep me away."

A couple hours and a painfully full tummy later, Zach and Kelsie walked along the almost deserted walkway next to the large marina. Christmas lights twinkled on the masts of sailboats, while one large yacht was lit up like a cruise ship. Zach reached for her hand. She held his tightly. Never wanting to let go.

"I missed you, Zach." There, she'd said it. Bared her heart and soul for him to trample if he so chose.

"We've been living in the same house."

"Yes. But separate."

He nodded. "I missed you, too. Sleeping in the other room didn't improve my game." He shrugged. "I don't know if it could ever work between us, but the deal was until the end of the season. Let's try it until then."

"And after that?"

"I don't know. I wish I did."

"I appreciate you coming to my rescue at the gala, but I needed to confront Mark myself."

"Just like I needed to handle the social situation myself, even if your intentions were good ones."

She smiled. "Touché. I'm a work in progress. So are you. No one's perfect." She wasn't giving up on them. Not yet. "I caught the stalker at our house a few nights ago."

Stopping abruptly, his mouth dropped open in alarm. "You *caught* him? What do you mean? As in confronted?"

She smiled. "With the help of your Louisville Slugger."

He frowned as if he couldn't quite process what she was saying.

"It took a little persuasion, but he told me the truth."

"Which is?"

She turned to face Zach, straightening the collar of his coat. "Veronica hired him. To try and get dirt on me and you. She also flew my ex out here to cause a scene."

"She sabotaged her own gala to ruin me? Ruin us?" He scrubbed a hand over his face.

"Hard to believe, isn't it?"

"Yeah, but what he said about you coming here. Was that true?" He shoved his hands in his pockets and stared down at her.

"Yes, I came here because you were here. I didn't know where else to go. You'd always been there for me before I acted so horribly and broke your heart. I had to see you. To set things straight. To apologize. I was hoping—" The words lodged in her throat.

"Hoping what?"

"That you'd be willing to forgive me, and that I'd have at least one real friend."

He pulled her into his arms and held her with a desperation that came through loud and clear. Wrapping her arms around his neck, she stared up into his troubled eyes. She wanted to wash away all the hurt, all the sadness, and make him happy. But it took two, and she wasn't sure if he was in the game or on the bench.

Standing on tiptoes, she kissed him, a kiss full of hope and promise, a kiss of forgiveness. He kissed her back, soft and tender, yet hesitant. When he drew back, he stared over her shoulder instead of in her eyes. She stroked the rough stubble on his cheek, and he shuddered.

Like a fog blowing off Puget Sound and revealing the Olympic mountain range beyond, Kelsie saw everything with amazing clarity. The truth surrounded her, enveloped her, and left her wondering if she'd always known and refused to see it, even as a teenager.

Kelsie Murphy loved her husband Zach Murphy. Her heart was all-in. Her body was all-in. Even her head was all-in. She loved him, and she believed he loved her.

But did he love her enough to work through their differences, learn to trust her and believe in her, make a family with her—the family they'd both dreamed of and never had. Could he get beyond their pasts and accept her as the person she'd become, not the person she had been? A tough task for a man prone to holding his grudges close to his heart, but he'd managed to tolerate Harris, could he finally forgive her?

His clean, earthy scent, like pine needles and soap, plain manly soap, mingled with the smell and taste of salt water from nearby Puget Sound. A hundred years ago, Zach Murphy would've been a lumberjack, a man who worked hard and played hard. A man with a work ethic and integrity. Today, he was still that man. A man a girl like her could fall in love with and *had* fallen in love with. Now, if only she could drive the deal home. Convince him that she truly did love him and that the old Kelsie had been laid to rest forever. Convince him he could trust her.

If only.

As she stared into those deep brown eyes on the most magical night of the year, she believed they could make it happen. They could take this fragile trust poking itself up through the wet earth, nurture it and turn it into a beautiful rose.

* * * * *

Zach ignored the curious stares of his teammates as he sat down at the table with Kelsie. True to form, the guys pretty much accepted her appearance and turned their attention back to consuming mass quantities of prime rib, garlic mashed potatoes, and veggies.

Tyler and Derek weren't present as they had family in town, but the small group of teammates that were there, enjoyed themselves.

Bruiser entertained the group with outrageous stories of his exploits. If they were true, the guy would have done everything from surfing in a hurricane to ice fishing in Antarctica. He might be full of shit, but his storytelling abilities kept the group laughing through the meal.

At the opposite end of the spectrum, Brett, the backup quarterback, sat quietly and listened to the conversations. He laughed along with the guys, yet with an underlying sadness Zach recognized. He used to be that lonely guy until Kelsie came along.

Zach rarely saw Brett with a date and wondered more than once if the guy was gay. Not that he gave a shit, a guy's sex life was his business. Brett was more private than even Zach was, and in his role as perpetual backup, no one paid much attention to him. The ultimate team player, he never complained, always participated in team charity functions, visited schools and hospitals, and kept out of trouble. A local guy, Harris wondered why he didn't spend the evening with family and childhood friends, instead of hanging out with teammates. Zach guessed it beat spending Christmas Eve alone. No one should have to do that.

His thoughts slipped to his brother Wade. He imagined Wade would be spending tonight with some tall, buxom blonde, just the kind Wade liked.

In some unexplainable way, he missed trading barbs with Harris. Who'd have ever guessed?

As if sensing Brett's quiet depression, Kelsie engaged him in conversation, asking him questions with such interest and caring the guy slowly opened up. Zach burst with pride at the kindness she displayed to his lonely teammate and earlier tonight at the shelter. He'd had no idea she'd been the one they called their angel.

Mean, selfish Kelsie didn't exist anymore. She'd been replaced by sweet, strong, caring Kelsie, his wife, the woman he loved more than life itself, his rock in a storm, his kick in the butt when he needed it. And he planned to need it for a long time.

Now if he could find a way to convince her.

CHAPTER 28

Out of Timeouts

Almost a week later, Kelsie Carrington-Richmond-Murphy sat in the owner's box with Rachel and Lavender on one side and Veronica on the other.

This past week, she and Zach didn't talk out their feelings. Instead, they'd talked with their bodies. If Zach's body told the truth, he didn't want out of the marriage either. But not wanting out and believing he should get out were too different things. If he didn't trust her then they had no future to build upon.

She glanced over at Veronica, who was so focused on the field she didn't seem to realize the rest of them existed. For reasons Kelsie couldn't fathom the woman had invited her, along with Rachel and Lavender to watch the last game of the season in the warmth and luxury of the owner's suite. Kelsie had wanted to say no, but she didn't. She'd decided to be a bigger woman than that. Oh, yes, gracious to a fault.

On the field below, a miserable Monday Night Football game played out, the last game of the regular season. Win or go home for the Jacks. Extend the season or finish it tonight.

Freezing rain blew in vertical sheets across the field, sometimes making it impossible to see a thing. The players on the bench huddled in hooded parkas, though Kelsie doubted even the thick, waterproof material kept out all the rain.

The coach called a time out and Veronica bolted for the bar. Kelsie focused on the players huddled on the bench.

After the loss a week before, the Jacks needed this one desperately. A win coupled with a loss by the Rams, who were currently getting stomped with a minute to go, and the Jacks were in the playoffs. A Jacks loss and they were done for the season. Simple as that.

Well, not exactly simple from where she sat. If they lost, Kelsie's marriage agreement with Zach could be null and void. They'd be free to divorce and go their separate ways. She didn't want to be free.

She'd had every intention of having it out with him, laying it all on the line. Only life had a way of postponing even the most important things. Zach hadn't needed the added drama in his life with the team's playoff hopes hanging by a shoe lace. After all, Kelsie was a football player's wife. During the season, it was all about the game. Any NFL wife worth her salt understood that harsh reality. Kelsie prided herself on being the best NFL wife her current situation allowed her to be, even going as far as joining Veronica for the game.

Speaking of the devil, Veronica returned and plopped back into the plush chair next to her, glass of wine in hand. Kelsie could do with her own glass of wine to calm her jangling nerves and woozy stomach. Game days did that to her, especially one as important as this. Zach's last chance at a ring. She wanted this for him as badly as he wanted it.

"I bet you're curious why I invited you to join me?" Veronica studied her over the rim of her glass, her red lips pursed in a severe, uncompromising line.

"You could start by apologizing for having a PI stalk me." Kelsie lifted the binoculars and followed Zach off the field as he headed for the bench. His uniform had already soaked completely through, and when he pulled off his helmet, his hair was matted to his head. Yet the grim determination on his face defied the weather.

"Oh, that." Veronica's tone blew it off as if of no consequence.

"You scared me to death."

"I didn't realize the PI was so inept that you knew he was there." She snorted as if her deception was of no consequence. "I think maybe we're two of a kind."

Kelsie lowered the binoculars and frowned. "No, we're not. I was like you once. I'm not anymore."

Veronica scowled, but Kelsie didn't care. Instead, she drove home her point. "In case there's any question, that's not a compliment."

"You've been around that cave man too long. Now you're sounding like him."

Kelsie sat up straighter and smiled her beauty queen fake smile. "Thank you. I do take that as a compliment. You could learn a few lessons in kindness and humility from him."

"And I was going to offer you a second chance working with some of our more challenging players. Of course, none as challenging as Zach."

"I won't work for you."

Veronica sat back and shook her head as if she couldn't believe what she was hearing. "You'd pick Zach over a lucrative career opportunity?"

"Of course I would. Apparently you have no idea what it means to love someone." Kelsie rose to her feet, while Rachel and Lavender stared up at her open-mouthed and wide-eyed. They may not have heard any of the conversation, but they could see her face.

"I think it best if I sit elsewhere." Kelsie nodded at her friends and left the suite.

Not having a ticket for another seat in the sold-out stadium, she wandered to a bar area and sat at the only empty bar stool. Only then did she realize her hands were shaking as the enormity of what she'd done hit her. She'd set a torch to that last bridge and burned it until it sank with a pitiful sizzle into the river.

Kelsie had done the right thing but at a huge personal sacrifice. When given a lucrative opportunity to be an opportunistic bitch, she'd turned nice girl, and in effect, achieved the goal she'd set for herself when she'd moved to Seattle months ago. She'd wanted to change, and she had. She'd supported Zach. Even if they parted ways, and he left her with a broken heart, she'd survive.

Maybe her business working with high-end athletes was going nowhere fast and her work with homeless people didn't exactly rake in the bucks, but she wouldn't have it any other way.

She liked her life as it was. A lot.

There were other sports teams in town. Of course, as Veronica had pointed out a while ago, her father happened to own a share in every one of them. She was so screwed. No paying job. Possibly no husband. No home. No nothing. But the only part of that she really cared about was Zach.

She sipped on a glass of red wine poured from a box and realized she quite liked it. She smiled, then grinned, then threw her head back and laughed loud and long, not minding a bit that everyone in the bar stared at her.

"Are you okay, ma'am?" The bartender kept his distance and regarded her warily.

Kelsie dabbed at her eyes with a napkin. "I've never been better." She set her glass down on the bar. She had her pride and her integrity. Things money couldn't buy. That meant more than all the gold bars in her father's Swiss bank account. And she wanted to share her newfound self with Zach.

She stood up with a new sense of resolve. She was a fighter, and fighters didn't give up. She'd throw one last Hail Mary and hope he caught it.

* * * * *

Zach lay flat out on the field. He blinked the sweat from his
eyes. Or was it rain? A big hand extended into his line of vision.
He followed the hand up to the shoulders, neck, then the face.
Tyler Harris towered above him, holding his hand out. Zach took
it, and Tyler hauled him to his feet. After which the quarterback
turned and trotted off to the huddle. Zach still cradled the ball he'd
intercepted on the Jacks' twenty. He flipped it to a referee and
jogged to the sidelines.

The seconds ticked off the clock. They were down by six. A
field goal wouldn't do it. Harris marched them down the field until
only twenty yards stood between the Jacks and a spot as a wildcard
team in the playoffs, twenty long yards. It might as well been
twenty miles. Zach paced the sidelines, sick to his stomach,
shouting until he was hoarse, along with the rabid sold-out crowd.

These moments were what Harris was famous for. He'd come
through. He always had. They didn't call him Mr. Heroic for
nothing.

Zach stopped and waited. The crowd quieted, sensing this was
it. The final moment of truth in an up-and-down season Zach
accepted partial responsibility for creating. Fourth down. Three
seconds on the clock. No timeouts. The final play in a season
where Zach had learned more about himself than he had in all the
other years he'd played football combined.

Harris called the play. It should've been a bootleg to Bruiser.
Only Bruiser slipped and skidded on his ass across several yards of
water-logged artificial turf. Harris didn't get to be the best for
nothing. He looked for a receiver. Once. Twice. He stayed in the
pocket until the last possible moment. They were all covered. He
tucked the ball under his arm, put his head down, and forged
ahead. There was a hole, a small one. Zach watched him power
toward it, shoving defensive players off his body left and right.

Zach yelled encouragement from the sidelines, not caring that the offense couldn't hear over the fan noise. Cold, freezing rain dripped in Zach's eyes, but he didn't give a shit.

Harris's helmet popped off as he barreled into the stomach of a three-hundred pound lineman. He went down, buried under a couple tons of human muscle. Referees waved their arms and started pulling bodies off the pile. Zach stared at the big television and saw it.

Short by inches.

His heart stopped. His lungs constricted. His body slumped. This year was supposed to be his last shot at a Super Bowl. Now it was gone. Down the tubes. Over before it even started. No playoffs for this team.

Out on the field the last tackler stood, and only Harris still lay on the field. The quarterback didn't move. Not one toe or one finger. The crowd hushed as they realized their beloved quarterback wasn't getting up. Even the opposing team halted their celebration to gaze at the field with concern. Several players knelt down in a circle and bowed their heads. Zach ran onto the field in a panic. He'd only felt such overwhelming fear once in his life, when his brother was put in the hospital. Zach never put much stock into praying, but he sent up a silent plea to the man above.

God, please make him be okay.

Several seconds ticked by, though it seemed like hours. Finally Harris opened one eye then the other. He wriggled his fingers, rotated his ankles.

HughJack held up three fingers in front of Harris's face. "How many?"

"Is this a fucking trick question?" Harris managed a lopsided grin.

HughJack breathed a sigh of relief. So did the rest of the team and staff standing around. Harris was okay if he was being a smart ass. They did a few more tests and then helped him to his feet. Zach rushed forward and grabbed his arm and slung it over his shoulder. Hoss, the Jacks' mountain of a center, did the same on the other side as Harris limped off the field.

Zach kept an eye on Harris in the locker room. The team trainers and doctors had cleared him as good to go, despite how rough the guy looked. He was one tough cookie, Zach had to admit with a newfound respect.

Harris sat on the bench, holding an icepack on his knee.

"You let it all out on the field today."

Harris looked up and smiled. Blood trickled from his mouth and from a gash on his head from a cleat. Bruised and bloody, Tyler met Zach's gaze. "And it felt damn good to play like that. All out. Balls to the wall. We just didn't have it today. Too many young inexperienced guys. But next year."

"Yeah, losing those veterans last off-season was a blow."

"But we gained a very important veteran. You played a damn good game, too, not bad for an old guy."

"Thanks." Zach ducked his head, somewhat embarrassed by the rare compliment from the quarterback. Sometimes the simplest answer was best, per Kelsie.

"I think you might still have a few more years in you, old man." Harris studied him, and their eyes met. Harris's gaze was open and friendly. None of the animosity of the past showed on his face. "I was wrong about you. You were just what the team needed. I'm sorry for all the hell I put you through."

A million possible responses raced through Zach's head, but only one thing truly begged to be spoken. He sat down beside Tyler. "I'm not. I learned more than I'd ever bargained for. Like you can't judge a guy by the clothes he wears or the words he says, but by his actions."

"And what did those actions show you?"

"That I'd be proud to call that man a friend."

"And so would I." Tyler reached out his hand, and Zach shook it. "I heard the GM offered you a contract extension."

"Yeah." Yesterday, he'd been called into the league office, fearing the worst and actually finding out the best. Until just now, his answer had been no, but Zach wanted to come back. To hell with the opening for a college coach. There'd be others.

"Are you taking it?"

"My lifelong dream since I picked up my first football was to win a ring. I chased that goal with a single-minded purpose, convinced that without a ring, my career meant nothing and my life meant even less."

"And now?"

"And now I don't quite see it that way."

"A good woman will do that to you." Tyler nodded and smacked him on the back. "Come back. We'll move hell and high water to get you a ring next year."

"I'm thinking about it."

"In the meantime, join me in the San Juans. I could use your help getting my retreat for veterans off the ground. I've been toying with the idea of a summer camp for homeless kids. I understand you do some work in that area. You in?"

Zach nodded, smiling in spite of their loss. "I'm in."

CHAPTER 29

The Clock Ran Down

Zach limped out of the locker room and walked to his truck. His one goal was to find Kelsie. The rain slowed to a steady drizzle, but still better than earlier. Considering his team lost its chance for the playoffs, he felt okay. Life was looking up in all areas—but one. The most important one.

Kelsie.

As he got closer to the truck, the very object of his thoughts emerged from under a nearby awning and walked toward him. His breath caught in his throat. Even bundled in a raincoat with the hood pulled up, she was striking, every bit the beauty queen who'd imprisoned his heart for life all those years ago. He'd never gotten a pardon for his sentence, and he didn't want one. Ever.

Zach walked toward her, feeling a lot like that awkward teenager who'd panted after her. He stared down at his feet and swallowed. "Hi."

"Hi. How about a ride home?"

Home. He liked the sound of it, but did she really mean home in the truest sense of the word? Zach had never had a home before. He'd bought his Victorian monstrosity because it'd been a childhood dream of Gary's. Only lately had it felt like home, since Kelsie added her little touches, and her annoying dog scampered around yapping, and her girlie stuff littered his bathroom counter.

"Are you going to open the door or are we just going to stand in the rain and gawk at each other."

"Oh, sorry." Zach fumbled for the keys and dropped them on the pavement. He scooped them up and unlocked the door, whisking it open for Kelsie. She climbed into his big truck in her usual ladylike manner. Damn, but they were the beauty and beast, all right.

He got in on the other side and drove toward home. Something made him take a turn into a parking area overlooking the waterfront. Somehow, he felt they needed a neutral place to talk, because for once Zach Murphy was going to bare his heart and accept whatever consequences came along. She didn't question why he didn't take her home. Instead she dug in her purse and re-applied her lipstick.

"The team offered me a two-year contract with incentives." Zach ran a hand though his short hair, wet from a combination of a recent shower and the rain.

"Are you going to accept it?" Kelsie put the cap on her lipstick and stared straight ahead. Zach stared at her lips and licked his own.

"I've always wanted that ring more than anything." God, he'd give it all up for Kelsie. "Now, not so much."

"Why not?" She looked at him and blinked those big blue eyes.

"I want you more."

Her eyes opened wide and her gorgeous lips parted. "You do?"

"Yeah, I do." He grabbed her hand and held it. Tight.

"Zach. You should go for the ring."

"You think I should?"

"Yes, while you're at it, how about two rings." She flashed her diamond wedding ring at him.

A lump of happiness clogged his throat. "I think I could manage that."

"I'll kick your butt if you don't."

"Now that sounds like something I'd say."

"This girl learned a lesson or two from the nice boy and quite a few from life itself. Zach, I'm sorry I shadowed you at the gala and didn't trust you to handle yourself."

He nodded. "I have an apology of my own. I understand you defended me at the risk of your business and your future."

"It was the right thing to do."

"And you did it. For me."

"Do you know why?"

"I hope I do. Tell me."

"Could the nice man ever find it in his heart to love the selfish girl?"

"No, he couldn't. But the nice man finds his heart bursting with love for the nice girl."

She smiled, one of those smiles straight from her heart to his. "I love you, too. My big, warm, kind, well-mannered man."

"I wouldn't go that far." He snorted then turned serious. "I love you, Kel. With all of my heart and every cell in my body, including the dense ones in my head." He wrapped her in his arms and held on.

Forever.

CHAPTER 30

For the Love of the Game

Kelsie and Zach stood side by side, arms around each other in their manicured yard near Gary's memorial stone. Kelsie couldn't stop the smile spreading across her face. Spring flowers raised their colorful heads toward a sun that warmed the chilly salt air and promised warmer tomorrows.

So much had happened. Zach signed a two-year contract with the Jacks. They accepted an offer to work with Tyler and Lavender to create a unique vacation opportunity for veterans and a summer camp for children in need. Kelsie brimmed with ideas for the camp and veterans' retreat. In keeping with the when it rains, it pours adage, Kelsie had gotten a call from Veronica just that morning hiring her to do some work with a couple players the Jacks drafted, definite challenges both of them. Kelsie accepted, but on her terms not Veronica's. And a few days prior to that, she'd been contracted by a major league baseball team to offer some classes to their players.

Side by side, she worked with Zach at the homeless shelter. Kelsie's training program for the unemployed homeless was gaining national recognition, not that it mattered to her. What mattered was all the people who benefitted by finding gainful employment.

She glanced at Zach, and her heart filled with love. Giving was so much better than receiving, and she wouldn't have changed a thing in her past because it got her where she was today. She'd purged that former selfish bitch from her soul to find the true

Kelsie underneath. Being a good person was so much more fulfilling than being a bad one, except in bed.

They'd raise their children with love and discipline, better than they were raised. And if life threw them bumps along the way, she'd pull out a page from their pasts and remember that what doesn't kill you, makes you stronger.

And better.

And more loving.

With Zach all things were possible, and Kelsie knew there wasn't anything they couldn't face together because they'd already faced the worst life had to offer and become better citizens and partners for it. And someday, parents. Yes, someday soon.

They'd name their first son, Gary.

Kelsie leaned into Zach and stood on tiptoes. He lowered his head and captured her mouth with his. They kissed in a silent promise that they'd always have each other.

No matter what.

Love was the ultimate bond for the beauty and her beast.

About the Author

An advocate of happy endings, Jami Davenport writes sexy romantic comedies, sports hero romances, and equestrian fiction. Jami lives on a small farm near Puget Sound with her Green Beret-turned-plumber husband, a Newfoundland cross with a tennis ball fetish, a prince disguised as an orange tabby cat, and an opinionated Hanoverian mare.

Jami works in information technology for her day job and is a former high school business teacher and dressage rider. In her spare time, she maintains her small farm and socializes whenever the opportunity presents itself. An avid boater, Jami has spent countless hours in the San Juan Islands, a common setting in her books. In her opinion, it is the most beautiful place on earth.

Boroughs
Publishing Group

Did you enjoy this book? Drop us a line and say so! We love to hear from readers, and so do our authors. To connect, visit www.boroughspublishinggroup.com online, send comments directly to info@boroughspublishinggroup.com, or friend us on Facebook and Twitter. And be sure to check back regularly for contests and new releases in your favorite subgenres of romance!

Are you an aspiring writer? Check out www.boroughspublishinggroup.com/submit and see if we can help you make your dreams come true.

CPSIA information can be obtained at www.ICGtesting.com
Printed in the USA
LVOW07s1551201015

459020LV00016B/1091/P